T0363393

WESTERN

Rugged men looking for love...

A Fortune Thanksgiving
Michelle Lindo-Rice

The Rodeo Star's Reunion
Melinda Curtis

MILLS & BOON

Michelle Lindo-Rice is acknowledged as the author of this work
A FORTUNE THANKSGIVING
© 2024 by Harlequin Enterprises ULC
Philippine Copyright 2024
Australian Copyright 2024
New Zealand Copyright 2024

First Published 2024
First Australian Paperback Edition 2024
ISBN 978 1 038 93533 5

THE RODEO STAR'S REUNION
© 2024 by Melinda Wooten
Philippine Copyright 2024
Australian Copyright 2024
New Zealand Copyright 2024

First Published 2024
First Australian Paperback Edition 2024
ISBN 978 1 038 93533 5

MIX
Paper | Supporting
responsible forestry
FSC® C001695
www.fsc.org

Published by
Harlequin Mills & Boon
An imprint of Harlequin Enterprises (Australia) Pty Limited
(ABN 47 001 180 918), a subsidiary of HarperCollins
Publishers Australia Pty Limited
(ABN 36 009 913 517)
Level 19, 201 Elizabeth Street
SYDNEY NSW 2000 AUSTRALIA

Cover art used by arrangement with Harlequin Books S.A.. All rights reserved.

Printed and bound in Australia by McPherson's Printing Group

A Fortune Thanksgiving

Michelle Lindo-Rice

MILLS & BOON

Michelle Lindo-Rice is an Emma Award winner and a Vivian Award finalist. She enjoys reading and crafting fiction across genres. Originally from Jamaica, West Indies, she has earned degrees from New York University, SUNY at Stony Brook, Teachers College at Columbia University and Argosy University, and has been an educator for over twenty years.

She also writes inspirational stories as Zoey Marie Jackson. You can reach her online at www.michellelindorice.com or on Facebook.

Books by Michelle Lindo-Rice

The Fortunes of Texas: Fortune's Secret Children

A Fortune Thanksgiving

Harlequin Special Edition

The Valentine's Do-Over
A Beauty in the Beast

Seven Brides for Seven Brothers

Rivals at Love Creek
Cinderella's Last Stand
Twenty-Eight Dates

Visit the Author Profile page
at millsandboon.com.au for more titles.

Dear Reader,

Thank you for choosing *A Fortune Thanksgiving*, a story that centers around my favorite holiday. There is something about that Thanksgiving that goes beyond gathering for good food to warm the heart and bring people together.

Both Imani and Nash became first-time parents, and it was so much fun having them experience that milestone together, sharing and overcoming many familiar fears that new parents face. Though Nash was doubtful about his ability to be a father to Colt, in time he grew to welcome his son into his heart and into his life with help from Imani. Imani had that strong family support and that independence but knew when it came to motherhood, she would need Nash's involvement.

But the best part of this story for me was watching Imani's and Nash's love for each other rekindle, sizzle, then blossom into something deeper and wonderful. The chemistry between these two people was off the charts, and it was fun to participate in this continuity with one of the hunky Fortune men.

I really hope you enjoy reading these characters' journey to love as much as I did. I would love to hear from you. Please consider joining my mailing list at michellelindorice.com.

Best,

Michelle

For my husband, John, the man of my heart.

Thank you to my editor, Gail, who provided me with this opportunity to write for a continuity, and Susan for all your assistance along with the rest of the Harlequin team. Special thank you as well to my agent, Latoya, and my sister, Sobi.

CHAPTER ONE

IF ONLY SHE could stop shaking, Imani Porter could go through with this spontaneous wedding of convenience. She could recite the vows to a man she didn't love to give her son a father. A son scheduled to make his appearance really soon.

That's why as she stood under the awning of the justice of the peace in Stone Crest, Texas, clutching her bouquet of water lilies at the beginning of November, she reminded herself she was doing the right thing. Then, taking a deep, calming breath, Imani looked up into the face of her friend Simon Evans, who had proposed to her just seventy-two hours before.

The stand-in for a man who told her he didn't want to have children.

Imani had the best daddy in the world. Phillip Porter. Of course, she wanted the same for her son.

Her bridal ensemble included a designer wedding veil, a white one-shoulder jumpsuit with a cape and a wide skirt. And finally, she'd donned a pair of peau-de-soie pumps that pinched her toes. All because she knew Simon wanted them to look the part of a happy couple. For the pictures...*and* for her baby's sake. Even though they weren't actually a real couple, she suspected Simon very much desired that to be the case. She had met him during graduate school, when they were study partners, and they had remained loose acquaintances.

Until she learned she was pregnant a month after her relationship ended with the man of her dreams. During a bout of nausea at a nearby gas station, she had run into Simon, who had purchased her ginger ale and crackers. He had stayed with her until she felt well enough to drive. Simon became a shoulder, a sounding board, a support, which she appreciated. But he didn't make her heart race or her palms sweat like—

No. No. No. She couldn't allow herself to think about Nash Windham when she was about to promise a lifetime to another man. Squaring her shoulders, Imani slapped a wide smile on her face and tipped her head back to peer into Simon's blue-black eyes.

Her mother called them shifty eyes.

He reached over to take one of her brown hands in his fairer ones at the same time the judge entered the room. "Are you ready to become Mrs. Evans?" Simon asked, his voice smooth, like the bass guitar he strummed from time to time. Right as Simon asked the question, the baby kicked.

A sign that her child agreed?

She nodded, her lower lip trembling. The baby kicked again and she looked away. Wait...did her son disagree with her decision? Her heart began to pound and dread piled in her stomach. Maybe she was making a mistake by taking Simon up on his spontaneous proposal. Maybe she shouldn't have accepted his offer to be her baby's stepfather. Maybe she should have listened to her mother and grandmother when they advised her to have Simon sign a prenup.

After all, she had the means to be a single mom. At thirty-two, she was the proud owner of Lullababies, a high-end baby specialty store she had started with her cousin right after finishing design school. An accomplishment she was proud of.

Simon released her hand to greet the judge. She gripped the lilies she held and gave him a tight smile before drawing a few deep breaths. Seeing her purse on the desk, she battled the sudden urge to snatch it and flee. *You can't back out now.*

"Are you cold?" Simon asked, rubbing her shoulders, which made her teeth grit.

"N-no. I-I've just never been married before," she squeaked out, forcing herself to meet his eyes.

He chuckled and ran a hand over his goatee. "Neither have I."

The judge cleared his throat. "Are you ready to begin?"

With a jerky nod, Imani and Simon turned to face the magistrate. She shook so much that a couple of petals fell at her feet. The judge commenced using the traditional vows they had chosen. With a gulp, she slaked a glance at her groom, taking in his wide shoulders, powerful chin and smooth skin. Anywhere they went, Simon made the women take a second look, got them all hot and bothered, but she remained oddly...unaffected. Unmoved. Then, suddenly, another face, another body—tall and muscular with thick, dark hair and sultry amber eyes—popped into her mind, spiking her heart rate.

Clenching her jaw, she shook her head, shaking Nash out of her psyche. She didn't need the heart quivers. What she really needed was to think of the man she was about to marry today. This marriage would be a partnership.

Her mother, Abena, and paternal grandmother, Zuri, believed that Simon was marrying her because she was a Porter. He had his eye on a big payout—her grandfather's billion-dollar oil business in Cactus Grove. Hammond Porter, one of the only Black billionaires in Texas, had begun training her to lead his business from the time she was a child. Imani was his chosen heir and he planned to pitch her ascension to the executive board at Porter Oil. All of which Simon knew.

But Imani ignored her mother and grandmother's suspicions and their insinuations that he was a rebound. Because, in truth, she didn't view Simon through a romantic lens.

Then why are you marrying him? Zuri had asked her several times.

Because...

Imani allowed herself to get caught up, listening as Simon recited his vows with that warm baritone and surprising sincerity in his eyes.

They were going to be a happy family, with a happy life and an even happier baby. Weren't they?

"I promise to love, honor and obey..." he said.

Yep. She could do this.

Then Simon winked. A slow, suggestive wink.

That snapped her out of the fairy tale and back to reality. Panic weaved through her body at a rapid speed, tightening her chest. She took choppy breaths, fighting a sudden wave of nausea, of dizziness.

No. No. No. She couldn't do this. Her baby delivered two powerful kicks. Imani lifted a hand. "S-stop. We have to stop. Right now."

Imani dropped the flowers, then snagged Simon's attention.

"I feel like I'm about to pass out." Sweat drizzled down the side of her face. She could feel the curls wilting. Dang it. Her stylist had warned her against getting a blowout with the day so humid. She should have listened.

"Is it the baby?" Simon asked gruffly. He wrapped his arm about her, his eyebrows furrowing into a deep *V*. She heard the judge calling for someone to bring her a glass of water.

Imani lifted a hand. "I just need...a second." She didn't have the heart to tell him that the thought of marrying him made her feel weak-kneed and sweaty—and not in a good way.

Simon scooped her close and led her over to sit on the judge's chair. She could faintly hear the judge asking for a medic. Her fiancé picked up a manila folder and pumped it back and forth, causing her curls to bob against her cheek. Next thing she knew, someone shoved a glass of water in her hand and commanded her to drink. As soon as she was finished, the paramedic on duty stuffed a thermometer in her mouth and wrapped her arm with a blood-pressure cuff.

"Is she going to be alright?" Simon asked, concern in his voice. Was he worried about the woman that she was, or about losing the perks of marrying an heiress? The fact that she didn't know the answer made her stomach bubble.

Oh, goodness. All this fuss made her face go hot, and the tighter the cuff got, the more embarrassed she became.

Simon was beside himself. "I hope this baby isn't trying to come today, of all days."

Was he for real? "What did you say?" she asked, enunciating slowly.

He stuttered, seeming to catch his faux pas. "I—I meant it's too soon. You're not due yet."

Of course, that's what he meant.

"Her blood pressure is elevated," the paramedic interjected, her voice steady. "But that's to be expected. A lot of brides get nervous." Peering down to look at her, the young woman asked, "Are you feeling contractions?"

"N-no. I'm only eight months pregnant so I've still got a few weeks to go. But my baby has been kicking up a storm."

"That's perfectly normal," she replied with a laugh, then patted Imani's arm. "I think your bride is safe to proceed. It's probably her nerves." The room cleared, leaving her alone with Simon.

More like Imani didn't want to get married. *Kick.*

And her baby didn't want her to do it, either.

Kick. Kick. Kick. "Alright, little one, I get it," she mumbled.

"What was that?" Simon asked, patting his brow. She couldn't look him in the eyes as he helped her to her feet.

"I'm sorry. I—I have to use the bathroom," she said, grabbing her purse and scuttling toward the door. Simon came toward her but she sped up and rushed into the hall. Imani hurried into the restroom so fast, she had to stop to catch her breath first before going into the largest stall. Once she was finished and had washed her hands, she dug into her purse for her sandals and changed out of her shoes.

She closed her eyes. Ah. What a relief. *You know what else would be a relief? Getting out of here.* Along with that thought came a sense of peace. And another kick from her little guy.

Decision made.

"Mommy hears you," she said. Quickly, she gathered her hair in a bun using a scrunchie from her purse, then opened the bathroom door and peered outside. Simon was a foot from the door. Waiting. Like a vulture with her as the intended prey.

"Are you okay?" he asked.

"No, but I will be." Imani raced down the hallway toward the exit with Simon following.

"Don't do this!" he yelled.

Imani waved a hand but didn't look back. "It's already done."

"If you walk through those doors. I'm done," he called out. "Lose my number."

She shrugged, unmoved by his idle threat, and sailed through the automatic doors. They opened with a swoosh and she ran out, grateful for the mild autumn day.

Imani beelined toward her Jeep Wrangler—a baby shower gift from Daddy—so glad she and Simon had arrived in separate vehicles. Simon had spent the morning at a spa—on her dime—while she had been at the hairstylist. Panting, she tried to stuff herself into the vehicle but the skirt was a pain. Good thing it was detachable. After snapping it off her waist, she tossed the flimsy material on the ground of the parking lot before settling inside the SUV. Imani took a moment to shut down her phone. Then, she pressed the gas, and peeled out of the lot.

A couple miles down the road, she slowed as a thought occurred. She couldn't go home. Simon might show up at her penthouse suite...accompanied by her mother and grandmother. She had planned to sublease her place since she would have been moving in with Simon temporarily while they searched for their permanent home. At his insistence. Simon felt she should purchase a more grandiose compound—again, his words—suitable for her elevated status as the next CEO of Porter Oil.

Abena and Zuri lived in Cactus Grove and had traveled to Stone Crest for the celebratory wedding brunch following her nuptials. The two women had been furious that a Porter would get married in a courthouse. But Simon had pressed her so hard to elope that she had caved, mollifying her family with the brunch.

Thank goodness she had insisted that Nia Okafur, her cousin and business partner, not reschedule the meeting with a new artist and the textile vendor they used. Nia had flown to Paris to meet up with an artist who made one-of-a-kind baby blankets. Imani's cousin would be back in time for her delivery and would take over the helm of Lullababies while she was on maternity leave.

Her stomach growled. The little guy had gone quiet. Despite the pitiful situation of her own doing, she giggled and wiped her brow. Spotting a creamery, she veered into the long queue of the drive-thru lane.

So since her penthouse suite was out, where could she go? She had packed her weekender with comfy pjs and lounge-wear, intending to spend her first night as a new bride at Simon's place. That had put her on edge even though at eight months pregnant, they wouldn't have been consummating their union. They had agreed to a partnership. Or, as Simon called it, *a merger.*

Ugh. He really had been all about the dollar signs.

Jumping at the chance to marry the heiress of Porter Oil.

Maybe she could reach out to her brother, Jonathan… Naw. He was all the way in Dubai with her father. They had been building Porter Oil's legacy overseas for more than a decade. Imani didn't know how her mother tolerated such a long-distance relationship but whenever her parents reunited, they acted like randy teenagers.

Whatever. That wouldn't be her.

She supposed that was why she had run out on her own wedding. She wanted something more and she was at the place in her life where she went for what she wanted. And she'd start with a huge serving of ice cream—even though her stomach felt squirrelly all of a sudden—then she'd drive to one of the nearby towns and do some shopping.

Imani moved up a space in the queue.

She squirmed in her seat as guilt flowered in her chest. The magnitude of what she had done weighed on her shoulders. Oh my gosh. Even if he had ulterior motives, Simon hadn't deserved her running off like that. If only she had listened to Nia, who begged her not to take Simon up on his sudden offer of marriage. What had her cousin called it? *A pop-up proposal.*

The rocky road ice cream on display looked enticing, making her salivate. It also made her think of the first time she had met Nash Windham. The tears flowed easy—the result of guilt, missing Nash and pregnancy hormones. She struggled to speak clearly when it was finally her turn to order. By the time she got to the checkout window, Imani's body was shaking from her cry fest. She was the worst person in the world.

The young man at the window bent over to hand her the cone. She was sure her cheeks were red and puffy from crying. "Ma'am, are you okay?" he asked, his eyes widening with alarm when he saw her round tummy. He gave her a stack of napkins.

"Actually? No... I feel horrible," she sniffled, wiping her face and reaching out to take the ice-cream cone before handing him a crisp twenty-dollar bill. "Keep the ch-change. That's the least I can do." Before he could utter another word, she drove off.

A sharp pain sliced across her lower back—a sign she needed to calm down. Imani drew deep breaths, gripping the wheel with her free hand, and then began devouring her cone. Eating her feelings. Since being pregnant, food had become her go-to for every emotion she felt—joy, fear, loneliness and now guilt.

Feeling another cramp, Imani pulled over and finished her treat. Then she cleaned her mouth before blowing her nose. *Oh, no!* There was a huge chocolate stain across her bosom. She lifted the middle console to take out the small bottle of hand sanitizer. After squeezing out a tiny dollop, she rubbed her hands and then poured some on a napkin. She gently dabbed at the chocolate but her garment was probably ruined. Plus, she could feel a headache forming.

A fitting end to her disastrous non-nuptials.

Oh, well. She would change once she got to the strip mall. Imani shoved the image of her plush comforter atop her four-poster bed out of her mind and started up the vehicle, appreciating the gentle whir. Eyeing the phone in her bag, she bit her lower lip and decided to turn it on.

Sure enough, her phone pinged with multiple alerts. Two from her mom, one from her grandmother, five from Nia.

And one from Simon.

Ignoring the low-battery alert, she pulled up his text. We can still do this if you change your mind. Ugh. This man didn't know when to give up.

Their friendship had run its course.

She blocked him and deleted his contact information, then rubbed her lower back. Tossing her phone in her bag, Imani avoided her reflection in the rearview mirror. She couldn't face herself.

She couldn't face anyone.

OH, LORD, SHE wasn't going to make it to the hospital. It was no use trying.

Parked on the side of the road, with no idea of her exact location, Imani wished someone would drive by. Anyone. Her phone had long died and she hadn't brought her charger with her that morning. She could see the cord on her coffee table and bit her lower lip to keep the panic at bay. How many times had her mother and Simon told her to keep a spare in her car? If only she had listened...

After spending a few hours engaging in retail therapy, very much unaware that she was in labor, Imani had been on her way home late that evening when the first serious contraction hit. It only took a few minutes before she realized her multiple trips to the restroom could have been her water breaking. Somewhere on her journey back, her vehicle navigation system had lost signal and she had made a wrong turn. Now she was well and truly lost in these back roads. And now low on gas, with labor pains, she couldn't keep driving and put herself and her baby at risk. So here she was, in active labor with only the cows and a couple of goats for company.

Breathe, Imani. Breathe. In, out. In, out.

Oh, it was no use.

Her contractions were now coming so fast and furious, about a minute apart, that she struggled with remembering how to do anything she'd learned in Lamaze class.

I can't have this baby, out here in the middle of nowhere, alone.

But it looked like she might not have any choice in the matter. Her stomach muscles tensed, her body priming for another contraction. Holding on to the door handle and gripping her leather seat, Imani bunched her fists and screamed.

CHAPTER TWO

As LONG AS he lived, Nash Fortune would never forget the terror etched across Stanley Trotter's face after his new part-time employee had fallen off the horse at the Fortune Family Ranch. As foreman, Nash was responsible for the well-being of every single worker, and the fact that it had happened on his watch had left him shaken.

He headed out the front door of County General Hospital that Friday evening, having paid Stanley a visit. Thankfully, the other man had only suffered minor injuries and would be released in a couple of days before recuperating at home. He had been in good spirits, surrounded by his wife and baby girl.

Stanley had introduced Valentina and his six-month-old, Penelope, his voice filled with pride. Nash had felt a twist in his gut. One that felt oddly like jealousy. Nash had backed out of the room with haste, stating that he had to oversee the feed delivery for the cows, all the while grappling with that foreign yearning for family. Which was ridiculous. He had five siblings and they all lived in separate houses on the thirty-five-hundred-acre cattle ranch in Chatelaine Hills, purchased from a wealthy family who had relocated to Arizona. And since learning he was a Fortune a few months ago, Nash had inherited even more family.

Every time he thought about the entire Fortune clan welcoming him at his grandfather's bedside, his heart warmed.

The bond between the Fortunes had made his decision easier to change his name from Windham to Fortune, though he would do anything to please his mom.

But he didn't have a wife. And he could have had one if he had allowed himself to fall for the only woman who had kept his interest past three weeks. *Imani Porter.* Just thinking about her made his insides quiver. He had met her outside an ice-cream shop when he lived in Cactus Grove, not too long after his father's death.

Their chemistry had been instant. With her smooth sepia skin, her generous lips and those ridiculous curves, Nash had wanted a taste of that more than the butter pecan in his hand.

Before he knew it, Nash and Imani were talking nonstop for hours and he had spent every free minute he had with her soaking in her sharp wit, her feisty spirit, her spunk. Nash remembered moments in bed where he would just watch her sleep, or stare into those dark chocolate orbs while she talked about her day. Just as Imani and Nash had reached the three-month mark, Nash's mother, Wendy, mentioned maybe it was time to start wedding planning.

Those words, spoken in jest, had scared him like nobody's business, but then when he broached the topic with Imani, expecting her to laugh along, she had grown serious and pinned that gaze on him. Like she had...*expectations.* Expectations of being a wife, a mother—she wanted five children, had even picked out names, he had learned. Expectations he hadn't shared. Nash had called it quits, though his heart had protested. And while he still missed that woman something fierce, Imani *was* the kind of woman someone settled down and started a family with. And Nash was doing none of that.

Nope. Not him.

His own father had pretty much cut him off, like he was one of his employees at Windham Plastics, and Nash had that man's blood in his veins. He couldn't chance messing up an innocent child's life, like Casper Windham had done to him. His father had been cold and distant all because neither Nash nor his siblings had been interested in working at the family business. He would never forget the disdain on Casper's face when they had expressed an interest in ranching.

"Ranching," Casper had yelled, "is beneath a Windham."

Nash had no idea how his parents had remained married for thirty-three years. He ran a hand through his hair and expelled Imani from his mind. The only reason he was even thinking about Imani and all of this was because of Stanley and his family.

Liar.

The truth was, that woman intruded in his thoughts more than he cared to admit. He had peeped her Instagram a few times, but Imani hadn't posted in months. In fact, her last post had been her dinner plate from their last date.

It had been a dinner they had shared because he hadn't liked what he had ordered. So she had given him some of hers. He had taken one last glimpse of their joined hands—his white, hers brown, resting at the edge of the table—and vowed to stay away from her Insta page.

Nash's new cowboy boots—a gift from his twin sister, Jade— crunched on the gravel as he made his way to his truck. The Lucchese Baron boots, made of cherry alligator-skin leather, cost about ten thousand dollars, and even though he was a Fortune, with more money than he could ever spend over centuries, Nash would never have bought himself a pair. He had to admit, though, that they kept his feet comfortable, especially after a long day at the ranch.

He toyed with the idea of manufacturing his own high-end boots with cork leather or some other alternative—and add to the many businesses the Fortunes had in the town—but he would tackle one business at a time, or hand off the idea to one of his siblings. Speaking of which, he had scheduled a family meeting on the eighth to discuss several ventures they were going into—the dairy farm, the petting zoo and fiber arts— where he planned to share his three-year strategic plan. Thankfully, his younger brother, Arlo, aka the ranch whisperer, was helping him look over the plans.

After jumping into his silver Range Rover, Nash put on Taylor Swift's "Back to December"—all Jade's fault—and began his trek home. His sister had dedicated that song to him when she heard about his breakup with Imani. She had done it as a spoof but the stupid song stayed in his mind and he tended to play it when he thought about Imani.

So, yeah, this had to be the thousandth time. Pitiful.

So many times, Nash had picked up his cell phone to call or had thought about paying Imani a visit, but he would keep telling himself he had made the right decision. She was better off without him and his messed-up genes.

Since it was a beautiful autumn evening, he decided to take the scenic route on the back roads and enjoy the colorful hues along the skyline. He had just finished the second replay of that darn song when he shot past a Jeep Wrangler pulled over on the other side of the road. It was angled so that its rear end jutted into the street. Adjusting his rear window, he peeked behind him. The hazard lights weren't even on. With the sun dipping low, that person was asking to get hit by a speeding truck or another passerby. A car shot by and honked its horn.

Nash didn't remember seeing anyone sitting in the driver's seat. Maybe the owner had had car trouble and left the car there. Yes, that made sense. He began to accelerate. But what if the driver was sick or something and he could have helped?

On impulse, he executed a U-turn and parked behind the vehicle, making sure he was a good distance from the curb. Nash hopped out of the Range Rover, went to his trunk to retrieve his jumper cables and then walked up toward the Jeep on the passenger side. He could hear a woman howling in pain and quickened his steps.

Tapping on the window, he yelled, "Do you need help?" making sure to keep both hands in sight. Because of the shadow, he couldn't make out the woman's face but he could hear her cries. She was sprawled across the back of the car. One leg was on the back headrest and other was on the floor. He averted his gaze.

"Y-yes," she called out, in distress.

Nash stiffened. *There was something about that voice...*

But then she said something that made Nash panic. "I'm in l-labor and it's t-too early," she said, hiccupping. "I was tr-trying to get to a h-hospital, b-but the baby is comi-i-in-ng." She dissolved into fresh tears. "I d-don't know wh-what to d-do." She tilted her head back and wailed. "My ph-phone d-died."

Nash had delivered a calf for the first time about three weeks ago, but he was ill-equipped to assist with bringing this woman's baby into the world. He yanked his cell phone out of his pocket, then called 9-1-1 and gave them his name, and a quick rundown of what was happening, turning his back to give the lady privacy.

He heard the clacking of keys before the operator said, "My name is Anna. The ambulance is on its way."

A loud groan came from behind him. "Hurry," he said, tamping down the sudden fear that he might actually have to deliver this baby out here in these back roads.

"I'll stay on the phone with you until the EMTs arrive. Can you tell me how far apart her contractions are?" Anna asked.

Nash opened the door and hunched his lanky frame inside, making sure not to bump his head. "How far apart are—" He felt his eyes go wide when he saw the woman, whose face was wet with perspiration. *"Imani?"* His mind raced.

Imani was here.

Imani was pregnant.

Imani was...*in labor*?

She lifted her head, her mouth popping open. "Nash? What are y-you—" A fresh contraction hit, cutting off her words. She closed her eyes and leaned deeper into the back seat. "I—I can't do this," she sobbed. Imani's eyebrows bunched together, and her lips pinched tight.

His heart hammered while his mind tried to grapple with what he was witnessing. Imani was pregnant...about to deliver a baby by the side of the road. How was any of this *real*?

"Sir? Hello? Are you there?" the voice on the phone asked. But all Nash could do was shake his head, his feet shackled to the ground. He was too overwhelmed to formulate words. To process what was happening.

Nash began to do the actual math in his head. *Is it possible that...? No, no, it couldn't be.*

"Help me-e-e-ee," Imani wailed, interrupting his flow of thoughts. "The baby is coming."

"Oh, God. The baby isn't waiting," he boomed into the phone, cupping his head with his free hand. "What do I do?"

"Okay, I'll walk you through all the steps but I need you to stay calm."

"Stay calm? Stay calm when a child is coming?" he yelled out. Imani was now crying. Seeing her body convulse alarmed him.

"Mom is already scared. You don't want her panicking," the operator said, the voice of reason. How could she sound so blasé when the most scary, miraculous thing was about to happen before his eyes? She urged him to inhale, exhale. Inhale, exhale.

To his surprise, that even, steady tone relaxed him. Somewhat. He followed her lead, then drew in a long, deep breath and squared his shoulders. "Okay. Okay. I'll try."

"Good—now, do you have a blanket or anything?"

Blanket! "Y-yes, I've got one in the back of my truck."

"Great, go get it. Put the phone on Speaker so Mom can hear while you go get the blanket."

"I'll be right back," he said, doing as the operator asked.

"N-no, don't leave me again," Imani begged, eyes welling.

That face gutted his heart. "I'm not leaving you," he assured her quietly, "I'm just getting a blanket." She pierced him with a gaze before giving him a jerky nod. He dashed to get it, his heart thumping along the way.

He returned in time hear her scream. Oh, Lord, if she kept crying like that, he was going to fall apart. He couldn't stand her being in pain.

"Owww," Imani moaned, then panted, her eyes closed, her head moving back and forth. "I've got to push."

"I know you do," the operator said. "But I'll tell you when."

Nash swallowed and cleared his throat. He could hear the faint sounds of the ambulance but there was no telling how far away it was. Anna directed Nash to place the blanket under her legs—which was a monumental feat between contractions—and then he was holding one of her hands. Well, more like she was squeezing his hand like it was a sponge, while he was yelling at her to push.

The ambulance in the distance was getting louder and louder. Closer and closer.

"*Push, Imani!* That's it. That's it. You got this."

She released his hand and gripped the edge of the seat. Finally, after one final strong grunt, a baby boy entered the world.

In his hands.

Whoa.

Body shaking, this time with a mingling of laughter and tears, Imani stretched her hands toward Nash. He placed the precious package in her arms, through his own wall of tears, while she hugged and kissed her baby. Somehow, Nash remembered to record the moment and snapped a picture of Imani and the newborn.

He heard the operator asking if the newborn had cried, but then the EMTs arrived and worked on clamping the umbilical cord. Nash fought back more tears when they extended the offer to him to cut the cord. What an honor.

Moving quickly, they wrapped the baby in a blanket. Then Imani's son opened his mouth and let out a piercing bellow.

The EMT worker was about to hand Imani the baby, but she gestured for him to give her son to Nash and asked for his phone.

Squaring his shoulders, he scooped the infant that already had a hold on his heart close to his chest. The emotional weight of the moment was his undoing. He could hear Imani's sniffles as his gaze pinned on the tiny curious eyes looking back at him, as he took in the fingers, the toes, *the perfection.* He patted the small head filled with light brown curls.

The next thing Nash knew, the baby was being gently extricated out of his tight grasp by the EMT, who was telling him they needed to get mother and child to the hospital. He registered the other paramedic helping Imani out of the rear of the Jeep and rushed to assist. She tossed Nash his phone, then yelled for him to grab two bags out of her trunk and to get her keys out of the ignition. One was a baby bag, she said, and one was her "motherhood" satchel, which she had kept stowed there. There were also a couple shopping bags and a huge weekender that she said she didn't need.

Right before they placed her on the gurney, Imani gripped

his hand. He snatched her close, needing the connection. She snuggled into him as they embraced, rocking back and forth, crying tears of joy and relief.

"You did good," he whispered, then took a picture of Imani and the baby, even as he heard the EMTs saying once more that they had to get to the hospital.

Imani nodded, then cupped his head and whispered, "And, you just delivered your son."

CHAPTER THREE

RARELY WAS HE ever without words. But when Imani whispered that sentiment to him, confirming what he'd known in heart to be true, Nash lost his breath.

He had a son.

One whom he had helped find his way into this world.

And his life would never be the same.

That stunning revelation buzzed around his mind as he watched the ambulance depart. Without him. He kept his eyes peeled until the vehicle was out of sight. Nash ached to get over to the hospital, but he knew he couldn't leave without securing Imani's vehicle. Rushing into action, he called for a tow truck. He'd have them drop the Jeep at his place for now.

All throughout the call, he thought of Imani's face as the ambulance doors closed. She had those brown eyes trained on him, their child in her arms. She had waved, like she was saying goodbye, like she had no expectations she would see him again.

His gut twisted. Was that what Imani wanted? Why she had kept her pregnancy a secret from him? To raise her child alone? As soon as the thought occurred, he chastised himself. She was probably honoring his wishes. Imani was an independent, proud woman and his desire never to be a father had created the rift between them that had ended their relationship. Of course, she wouldn't reach out.

Though he understood her reasoning, his heart hurt and his conscience churned.

How could he have known that the few seconds of holding such precious cargo would cause such a life-altering shift?

Regret whipped at him. He had missed seeing Imani's tummy grow round with their child. Had missed hospital visits—seeing his son's development in the womb, hearing his heartbeat. He gripped the back of his head and bunched his lips as he faced the knowledge that he could never get those moments back.

What if he hadn't driven this path this evening? He released a guttural groan. Would he have ever known? Would she have ever told him?

He could have gone on with his life, unaware, while there would have been a child yearning for him. A child with a cavity in his heart because of an absentee father. Nash clenched his fists. He couldn't let that happen.

But did he have the skills? That fear gnawed at him. Casper Windham hadn't. It wasn't far-fetched to believe Nash didn't, either.

Maybe he should stay far away from Imani.

Then his thoughts flip-flopped. But his son's piercing eyes served as a siren for his soul. Nash couldn't keep his distance just yet. He would at least check on the baby and Imani at the hospital.

Nash placed another call, this time to his brother Arlo, who answered on the second ring. "Hey, bro. Something came up—" *Something came up?* How distinctly vague. It was more like a meteorite had crashed into his life, obliterating his status quo. But mentally, he wasn't at the place where he could share the truth just yet. Nash snaked a hand through his hair. "I won't make it back to the ranch in time for the feed delivery. Miss Phyllis said she would call the ranch office when it was on its way. Do you think you can cover for me?"

"Yeah, right." Arlo snorted. "You just don't want to deal with Miss Phyllis. Everybody knows she's sweet on you."

Picturing the older woman with poufy blond hair that they believed to be in her seventies, and who ran the register at the

Longhorn Feed Store, Nash gave a little laugh. "Stop it. She messes with everybody that goes in there. Not just me."

"Yeah, but you're the one she says has the—" his voice took on a high pitch "—movie star looks."

This was what he didn't like about having siblings. A little extra attention from an older, slightly eccentric woman was fodder for some good old-fashioned ribbing.

Nash rolled his eyes, then said, "No, this has nothing to do with Miss Phyllis" in a much more serious tone.

"Wait... Are you okay?"

The concern in his brother's voice threatened to snap the small thread of his control. "I hope to be," Nash answered, his tone grave.

The line was quiet for a second. Nash imagined his brother was telling himself not to pry. After a beat, Arlo cleared his throat and said, "I'll take care of the feed. Handle your business and I'm here if you need."

"Thank you." As soon as the call ended, the tow truck came. Once he had Imani's vehicle squared away, he jumped in his SUV to make his way back to the hospital. The trip had his heart pounding just like before, but this time the reason was much more palpable.

He was on his way to see his child.

Surreal.

That knowledge made him grip the wheel tightly. Nash used the voice-calling app and got his mother on the phone. Since she currently lived alone, he and his siblings made a point of calling or visiting with her once a week. But today wouldn't be just a random conversation. Today, he was reaching out because he had a dire need.

Wendy answered, sounding oddly cheerful, more than she had been in months. Normally, he would have questioned his mother about her uncharacteristically chipper behavior, but she didn't give him an opening to respond as she yammered on about some sewing or knitting something special. He wasn't processing all she was saying, but to be fair, but he had big news filling his brain.

"Mom." She kept talking.

A little louder. *"Mom."* She still didn't hear him. Nash interrupted Wendy in midsentence with a firmer tone, to drop his news bomb. "Mom, I just delivered my baby."

A harsh intake of breath. Then silence for a beat before she breathed out, "Say what?"

"You heard right. I have a son," he croaked out, grappling with the unbelievability of those words. As of less than an hour ago, Nash was living a new reality.

"Son, if you're pulling my leg right now, this isn't funny."

"I'm not joking."

"You mean I'm a grandmother again?" she boomed. Oh, she was definitely listening to him now. Nash used the button on his steering wheel to lower the volume. "This is one hot season for my kids falling in love, having babies or finding babies."

She sure was right. One of his younger sisters, Sabrina, was now five months pregnant with twins she called Peach and Plum, and Ridge had indeed found a three-month-old baby, Evie, in a haystack, right along with her mother, whom Ridge called Hope since she didn't remember who she was. Nash could hardly keep up.

"Nash, did you hear me?" Wendy asked.

"I'm sorry, Mom. Did you say something?"

"I asked if you'd fill in details for me, son. Like, who is this mystery woman? And did you know about the pregnancy?"

"It's Imani." He waited for that bit of news to settle.

"Imani?" she screeched a few seconds later. "As in Imani Porter? Man, you're just laying it on me, right now. You know how much I loved Imani. I thought she was perfect for you. Remember?" Her voice escalated as she rattled on. "Wait. She's here in Chatelaine? What's she doing all the way out here? Hang on—did she move here from Cactus Grove? What are the odds? But what about her company? Oh, my goodness. Imani!"

Nash lifted a hand even though his mother wouldn't be able to see his gesture. "Mom, you have to slow down so I can answer even one of your questions," he chuckled.

"Oh. Okay…good point. You caught me off guard. Whew, let me take a sip of this lemonade and then I'll let you talk."

"Sounds good." When Nash heard a refreshing sigh, he

smiled and began. "I was on my way back from the hospital after checking in on Stanley, when I decided to take the back roads. And I spotted this Jeep on the side of the road at an odd angle. I don't know why but something made me turn around, and I'm glad I did because there was this woman hollering that she was in labor. So I called 9-1-1 and when I stuck my head inside, I saw Imani. *Imani.*" Even talking about it aloud, Nash still couldn't believe it. "The funny thing is, she had been pressed on my mind and the next thing I knew, I was helping her deliver our child. My son."

"Wow... Just wow." She didn't say anything for several beats. "Imagine that." The fact that his mom appeared awed and at a loss for words was rare.

"Yeah, with everything going on, I didn't get a chance to ask her any questions, like what she was doing here." A thought struck. "Unless she was on her way to find me?" Hope sprung wide like a flower in bloom. Maybe Imani had intended to tell him that she was having his child, but had gone into labor along the way.

"Whatever the reason, you were meant to be there at that precise time," his mother said. "You were meant to see your child enter this world, and you're destined to be in his life. What's his name?"

The fact that he had no idea made Nash once again question his place in his offspring's life. "I don't know, Mom."

"Oh."

Inadequacy lashed his heart. What kind of father didn't ask the basic question, like his child's name?

"With everything going on, I didn't think to ask. I was just relieved that Imani was alright and that little man was crying— Man, do his lungs work..."

"Don't go reading anything into that," Wendy cautioned. Dang, his mother was a mind reader. As usual. She continued, "For all you know, Imani may not have picked out a name yet. I know Casper and I had no idea what to call baby number six. I still don't know how we came up with Ridge, but it fits."

When he remained quiet, she added, "Shake it off, son. It

sounds as if this baby made a surprise appearance. What matters is that he's healthy."

Trust his mom to defend his oversight and offer up a rational excuse. Nash swerved off the road and onto the curb. He cupped his head and admitted, "I don't know if I can do this, Mom. I don't know if I can be a father. It's not like I had an exemplary role model."

"Son, you can and you have to. You're too hard on yourself and I blame Casper for that. Nothing you did was good enough. You don't even see your awesome accomplishment today. Lots of new fathers pass out or lose control during childbirth. Your own father threw up in the delivery room when you and Jade were born. I applaud you for your courage and for being there when Imani needed you most."

His lips quirked as he pulled back onto the road. "This is the first I'm hearing that about my father." He refused to refer to Casper as *Dad* anymore.

"Well, Casper was a proud man and he was all about appearances. He felt showing weakness was unmanly. Which was plain dumb. No nicer way to say that." His mother released a long plume of air. He could imagine her pacing back and forth as she emphasized her point. "Look, I know your father did his share of damage but you are one-half me as well and I'd like to think I was a good mother."

"Not just *good*, Mom. You were—are—the best. You single-handedly raised six of us, practically on your own. We are all thriving because of you."

"Oh, thank you for that." Her voice hitched. "Someday in the future, your child will say the same about you. Trust me on that."

Wendy's quiet certainty pierced through his doubts, and he exhaled. "Okay, Mom. I'll start by establishing visitation with Imani and I'll put in an ad for a nanny—"

"No. No, nanny, son. You need to be hands-on," Wendy insisted. "How else are you going to know for sure if fatherhood is for you?"

"Okay, Mom. I will do my best."

That was the best response he could give without lying to

his mom. Nash wasn't as convinced as Wendy seemed to be in his potential parenting skills. The fact was that he was a product of Casper Windham as well—an absentee father—which couldn't be so easily discounted.

"Have you told your sisters and brothers yet?" Wendy asked, once again jutting into his thoughts.

"Not yet. I'm very much still trying to wrap my mind around all this."

"This is not the time to isolate yourself, son," his mother warned. "This is the time to embrace us, to allow us to be your strength and to celebrate with you."

Nash relaxed his shoulders and leaned back into the seat. "Once again, you're right, Mom. This is why I had to talk to you first. You help me get my head right. As soon as I've visited with Imani, I'll let everyone know."

"Alright. I'll await your call to come see my grandchild."

"You got it."

After hanging up, Nash turned into the parking lot of the hospital and scanned the lot for a spot. He found one near the entrance and pulled in. Somewhere in that building was the mother of his son and his child.

That knowledge humbled and grounded him. Nash opened the door and ventured out, then strolled across the lot. Snapping his fingers, he decided to make a stop at the gift shop. There was no way he was going to enter that hospital room with Imani and his future heir empty-handed. After all, he was a Fortune now, and so was his son—he hoped to give his progeny his last name—and what was the point in having money if he didn't splurge when it counted?

But as it turns out, his last name had drawn a small group of onlookers including the press. Well, *press* was too generous a word for the two reporters in their town. He had provided his name to the 9-1-1 operator and somehow, the staff at *The Chatelaine Daily News* must have learned that Nash Fortune had helped a pregnant woman and were labeling him a hero. Ever since Sabrina talked him into plastering his face on that billboard across from the GreatStore in town as the face of the Fortune Family Ranch, he couldn't do anything without being recognized.

It was a daggone nuisance.

The reporters peppered Nash with questions—this was definitely juicier than cattle ranching—but he declined to provide a statement and made his way to the gift shop. However, they got their money shot of him carrying an oversize teddy bear and a gift basket.

Great. That picture would be front-page news in Chatelaine Hills. Thank goodness, they didn't know it was his son. *Yet.* When the elevator doors closed, Nash knew he had to get ahead of the gossip mill. The last thing he wanted was for his siblings to learn about the newest addition to the family from anybody but him. Nash sent a text to the group chat.

Guess who became a father today?

Then he shut down his phone.

CHAPTER FOUR

SEEING NASH WINDHAM hold his son in those strong arms was branded in her brain for life. What a story to tell their baby boy one day.

Telling Nash about his becoming a father was something she should have, *would* have, done if she had to do it all over again. Regardless of how he felt about fatherhood. The look of wonder and confusion on his face tore at her conscience.

No man should learn of his parentage that way.

It had been a shock for her when she first discovered she was pregnant, but she had *months* to get used to the realization that her life would change. Nash didn't have that luxury.

Snuggled under the plush comforter—a baby-shower gift handknit by her grandma—in her hospital room at County General Hospital, holding her son against her, Imani inhaled. Enjoyed the newborn baby smell, the feel of his soft skin and his small sighs as he slept in her arms. She released a breath of air and smiled. Nash should be here with her, sharing in the miracle of their child, equally enamored by the act of him simply breathing.

Imani had been researching the birthing process when she stumbled upon the fact that Black mothers and infants had a higher mortality rate than other populations in the US. That knowledge had left her shaken. And scared. Plus, going into labor in a deserted area had drastically reduced her chances of survival. So to have Nash show up when he did was an act of divine providence.

And for her, proof that Nash was meant to be a parent, even if he didn't believe he should be. That had been the actual topic of their last conversation as a couple. His feeling ill-equipped to be a husband or a father. Imani had disagreed, having gotten to know the caring, thoughtful man who was Nash Windham. Though they had been together for just three months, they had developed strong feelings for each other—okay, might as well call it *love* on her part—but Nash's fear had superseded everything else. He had been so vehement in his objections that she hadn't fought their inevitable parting.

Hadn't wrangled for her child to have his rightful father in his life.

Instead, mere hours ago, she had been about to give her son a replacement father. Imani wiped the sudden tears in her eyes from the guilt of keeping silent.

She had embraced impending motherhood—the all-day morning sickness, the sonograms, the Lamaze class, the gag-inducing glucose test. All of it. In fact, she'd *welcomed* it. Even the labor had been worth it. She touched the baby's nose, unable to suppress her smile. Because look at the outcome. Her heart expanded.

But now, she knew how wrong she was.

And how right Abena had been, when her mother beseeched her to tell Nash the truth. Maybe it was time she started listening to her mother and grandmother. She could hear their voices, cautioning her not to spoil the baby by keeping him in her arms. With a sigh, Imani rested the sleeping infant in the nearby bassinet.

Immediately, she fought the urge to pick him up. At seven pounds, nineteen inches, he looked so tiny, so…alone, in that plastic container, squirming, trying to get comfortable. Plus, his little cap was coming off. There was a card taped to the exterior with his birth weight, height and name written in permanent black marker.

Imani blinked back tears. Her little pumpkin's lower lip was trembling. One little foot stuck out from under the blanket. The thin receiving blanket, lined in pink and blue, must not be warm enough. She rushed over to retrieve a thicker blanket out of her baby bag to drape across his body.

Just as she was finished, the nurse entered the room. Heading straight for the sink to wash her hands, she murmured, "I'm back to check on you and baby. How are we doing?"

"It's going good so far," Imani said. "Thank you for the use of your charger. I'll call my family soon." As soon as the phone juiced up—there had been countless pings and voicemail message alerts. She had placed her phone on Silent while she cared for her baby.

"Wonderful. And you're welcome. It's good to get folks to rally around you and share your good news." There was the unspoken question of where the boy's father was, but the woman was too polite to ask.

Imani was feeling lonely but she was waiting to see if Nash showed up. She wanted them to have private bonding time before notifying her family. But it had been over an hour and he wasn't here yet... Nevertheless, she kept her tone confident, as she could see the older woman was concerned about her.

The nurse removed the thick blanket and placed it on the side of the bassinet. "Let's not do a thicker blanket," she said in a cautioning, matter-of-fact tone. "We don't want the baby to get too warm. Overheating can increase the risk of SIDS."

Imani's eyes went wide and her heart thundered in her chest. "I didn't know that," she breathed out, wrapping her arms about her. Motherhood was scary, much scarier than she imagined. How was she going to raise her child alone?

"That's why we're here. To help you," the nurse offered, giving her a kind smile. She then rewrapped him tight, like a butterball, before grabbing the handlebar.

"Are you taking him again?" she asked, eyes pinned on her son. She didn't want to him out of her presence, especially after that warning. Upon arrival, they had whisked the infant away to the NICU to check his oxygen levels and his body temperature before bringing him back clean, swaddled and crying at the top of his lungs. Then they had placed the tag around her hand and his ankle.

The minute she held him, he had ceased. Wow. The wonder of being his favorite person had flooded her with joy. Imani cherished the skin-to-skin contact, falling in love with him even more with each passing minute.

"No. I'm here to check in on you to find out how the nursing is going," she said. "He's at a good weight at seven pounds, but we want to make sure he's getting the nutrients he needs. The lactation specialist told me you had a good session."

Imani relaxed. "I got him to latch on like you showed me, but I don't know how much he actually ate. But he burped." She couldn't hold her proud smile.

The nurse beamed. "Don't worry. He's getting something. The first few days you're producing colostrum, which is all he needs." She smiled. "Did he get a diaper change?"

"Oh, boy, did he." Imani chuckled. "I had to put on a new onesie."

"Great. It sounds like you're doing well. Remember, you can always hit the Call button if you need any help at all." Imani nodded but she was hoping not to have to do that. When she went home, she would be on her own. Might as well begin now. "Can I get you some yogurt and fruit?" the nurse asked.

"Yes, that would great. Thank you."

At that moment, Nash entered the room. Imani's heart leaped at the sight of him. She knew her face reflected how she felt. Nash gave her a hesitant smile. He was holding an oversize teddy bear and a gift basket with an assortment of chocolates. "Hello. I hope it's okay that I'm here."

"I'm glad to see you," she breathed out, dabbing at her eyes. He placed the gifts on the ledge near the window. He wiped his palms on his pants and stood waiting.

Awkward. She couldn't think of a single thing to say.

"Oh, is this Dad?" the nurse interjected, looking between them. Imani could see the relief in the other woman's eyes. She could also see the slight panic in Nash's, but he was waiting for her to respond.

"Y-yes, it is," Imani answered, licking her suddenly dry lips.

Nash squared his shoulders and slid his glance over to the baby. "You can hold him," she offered, "but you have to wash your hands first." She chided herself for being so nervous around Nash. After all, he had seen her at her most intimate state.

Nash cleansed his hands and then took a tentative step toward the bassinet, then another, before closing the distance. He held on to the sides, his chin dipped to his chest and he just stared down at his son.

"I'll be back in a minute to get you tagged so you can see the baby anytime," the nurse said, giving a wave before leaving the room.

Nash's eyebrows rose. "His name is Colt." He shot her a glance, his eyes wet, his voice filled with genuine astonishment. "You remembered."

"Y-yes. I remember everything about us." Imani sniffled. This reaction couldn't be blamed on her hormones. She had written in *Colt Windham* on the card, a bold move, but she hadn't known if Nash would get it. Would appreciate the significance.

"So do I." His look of tenderness made her stomach knot. The air thickened between them, unspoken feelings lurking under the depths of their gazes. But she held contact. She wouldn't back away from the memories.

One night wrapped in each other's arms, somehow, their conversation had veered toward favorite names. She believed the topic was, if you could name yourself, what would it be... or something like that. Imani shared how she loved the name Olivia. And that's when Nash told her about his love for horses. He'd had pictures all over the walls in his room when he was a boy. Nash had asked his parents for a male horse for his birthday, as well as a cowboy hat and boots. He had proudly declared that he planned to name his horse Colt. Casper had yelled at his six-year-old son that getting a horse was a dumb idea and spewed that the name he had chosen was even stupider, and snarled, "If you're going to name a horse, give it a strong, solid name."

Nash had admitted to her he'd cried and cried, and though his mother consoled him, telling him that it was a lovely name, he had been heartbroken. His father had refused to give him the one thing he desired most—to be around horses. Casper had bought him LEGOs instead—something plastic. Like the family's plastic business.

Imani's heart had hurt for that little boy. She had heard the anger in Nash's voice as he recollected that painful memory. So she hoped that Nash would see her gesture for what it was—an invitation for him to be in Colt's life. An acceptance of a name Nash had chosen.

"What do you think of my calling him Colt?" she whispered.

"I think it's a wonderful name," he choked out. Then he admitted in a low voice, "Do you know even though I own several horses—Midnight, Onyx and Leviathan—I have never used that name?" He shook his head. "Wow."

"It's a strong name." Blinded by her tears, Imani had to grab a few tissues to compose herself.

Nash bent over and picked up the baby in his arms. "Hello, Colt." He sat on the bed next to her and they both watched the sleeping child.

At that moment, Colt sighed. Like he was content. Then he smiled. Like all was right with his world because he was in his father's arms.

Imani was so overcome, her shoulders shook as she quietly wept.

Nash touched her face briefly. "You have given me a gift I didn't know I wanted. I promise I will do my best to be a good father for Colt." He cocked his head. "I know you have a business back in Cactus Grove, but I would love it if you considered staying here in Chatelaine Hills for a while? I have a two-bedroom guesthouse behind my house on the ranch and we could raise our son together. Well, it's actually an old carriage house that the previous owners converted." Before she could respond, he added, "You don't have to answer now, just please think about it." His expression was earnest, almost like he was pleading his case, as if she needed any convincing. She wasn't about to deny her son this opportunity to have his father in his life—and she hoped this experience changed Nash's mind about fatherhood. Plus, she needed a place to hide out from her nonwedding drama.

It was a win-win.

"I don't need to think about it. I know in my heart it's what Colt needs. How about I stay for about four months?"

His eyes brightened. "That's way more generous than I thought you would give."

She rested her head against Nash's chest. "I'm looking forward to this time with you." She wouldn't mind *forever*, but she would take what he could give. For now.

Nash placed Colt back in his bassinet, gently resting him on his back.

"There's one more thing you should know. Two, actually." He tapped his chin. "No, make that three."

"Okay." She squared her shoulders, bracing herself for what he was about to lay on her.

"First, I changed my surname. I'm Fortune now. Nash Fortune."

Her eyebrows rose. "Whoa. I'd love to hear the backstory."

"I'll catch you up," he said with a wave. "Just know, for me, this name change was a new beginning. A fresh start. So I'd love for our son to also carry this name."

"Yes." Her heart expanded. "It's an easy fix as I didn't complete the official birth-certificate papers yet." She peered at him from under her lashes. "I was hoping we both would sign."

He gave a jerky nod, stuffing his hands in his pockets.

Imani could see Nash still had some qualms, which was to be expected, but she was glad he was taking the right steps for his child. She cleared her throat. "So what's the other two?"

"Huh?"

"The other two things you had to say," she persisted.

"Oh." He raked a hand through his hair. "I think our baby announcement is going to be front-page news, and I wanted you to be prepared. We might have reporters waiting outside when we leave the hospital."

She pursed her lips and teased, "So you're a celebrity now."

Nash rolled his eyes. "It was Sabrina's idea to slap my face on a billboard in town and I regret it."

"I did tell you when we first met that I thought you were a model."

"Please. Don't remind me." He exhaled. "And number three is that I've alerted my family about the baby. And if I know them, they are going to invade this space. I don't know if you're up to all that but I've held them off until tomorrow."

"Bring it on," Imani said. "It feels great to know my son is going to have a huge extended family." That made her think of her loved ones. "Speaking of family, can you pass me my phone? I'm pretty sure my mother is worried sick about me, and she'll want to meet her grandson. Plus, I've got to let my dad know he's a grandpa."

"I'm going to go check out the guesthouse, make sure everything is in order," Nash said, after handing her the device. She sensed it was more to give her a private moment with her relatives, which she appreciated. "I'll be back in an hour. Do you need anything?"

She wanted to say she needed him. *Just him.*

But one step at a time.

"Sure. I'd love some—"

"Rocky road ice cream?" he interrupted. "Snowman's Creamery here makes some of the best ice cream you'll ever taste."

She gave him a thumbs-up and settled into the bed. Even though six months had passed since their relationship ended, this man still knew her so well. She should have never entertained the idea of marrying anybody else. There was no replacement for Nash Windham...well, Nash Fortune. None. And it was time for her to accept that. She didn't care what his name was. If she couldn't be with him, then she was better off alone.

CHAPTER FIVE

"I DON'T THINK I'll ever tire of becoming a grandmother," Wendy said, gushing, as she smoothed her black fitted pants and observed Colt in the bassinet.

Both baby and mom were now asleep in the aftermath of his family descending on the County General maternity ward to visit the newest Fortune. And reconnect with Imani. Nash had lost count of the pats on the back he had received, along with remarks like "you'd better keep her around this time."

He had snorted before reiterating that their breakup had been mutual. Not that anyone in his family listened or cared. They had been too enamored with his son. Right along with Nash. He kept looking at the perfect specimen he and Imani had produced.

A heady combination of awe, wonder and fear nearly brought him to his knees. His siblings had only been there for an hour but when they left, the room was filled with flowers, fruit, helium balloons and cute stuffed animals.

Colt yawned and rubbed his eyes before smiling.

Nash snapped a picture to add to the four hundred he probably had in his phone. "I'm fascinated and proud of everything he does," he whispered.

His mother touched his arm and said softly, "Spoken like a true father."

"Can't say the same about my own father." Bitterness weighed down his chest like a boulder on a feather.

"No one is all bad," Wendy reminded him, patting her shoulder-length bob. "I see my children as the best of both of us."

His lips quirked. "Mom, you're the queen of optimism."

"Well, sometimes life gives you a second chance and you have to learn to take it when it comes."

Nash cocked his head. Something about her tone made him feel like she wasn't just talking about him. "Anything you need to tell me? You've been real chipper lately."

Wendy played with her shirt collar but didn't meet his eyes. "I'm just happy for my children, that's all." Then she quickly changed topics. "I think it's great Imani is back in your life."

"Okay, Mom. But you know this is just temporary, right? She's staying with me at the guesthouse for a little bit. So this reunion is very much about Colt." A picture of him and Imani reminiscing earlier about their ice-cream dates as a couple hit his mind. He hadn't had that much fun on an actual date since they parted ways.

"If that's what you believe, I won't argue," Wendy said in a singsong voice, her green eyes sparkling. Imani stirred and his mom gestured toward the door. They crept outside the room, making sure to dim the lights. "You have to get the guesthouse ready."

His brow furrowed. "What do you mean? I just had it cleaned from top to bottom a couple weeks ago. It's move-in ready."

"That's not what I meant." She clucked her tongue. "Colt might be tiny but he comes with serious baggage." She counted her fingers as she rattled off a list. "You'll need a crib, a bassinet, car seat, diapers and wipes, bottles—"

"She's breastfeeding," he interjected, rubbing his eyes. What a lengthy list, and she sounded as if she could keep going. His heart thumped. What had he gotten himself into?

Wendy rolled her eyes. "If that baby is anything like you, she'll need to supplement with bottles. Or she'll be a zombie trying to feed him." She chuckled and tipped back her head. "You sure had a hearty appetite." She sighed, caught up in her memories. "I can still remember the day I brought you and Jade home. I held you both in my arms against my chest, with you wiggling against me. You looked at me like I was your favorite person in the whole world." Her eyes popped open, slightly misted. "Now, look at you. Over six feet tall."

Nash smiled despite himself. His mother had a way of making him feel like he could do anything. Like be a father to his son. "Mom, you're gushing over something I couldn't control. My height is based on genetics."

"Doesn't make me any less proud. You'll see the same thing with Colt. The smallest thing they do is remarkable." She pinned him with a gaze. "That feeling doesn't change as they grow older, either."

"I think I know what you mean." He grinned. "Colt burped after Imani fed him. *Burped.* And I kid you not, I felt pride hit my chest."

Wendy cracked up. "Yes! And when he wraps that tiny hand around your finger, your heart will twist, and you'll know for sure there's nothing you won't do for him."

Standing there with his mother, he felt confident. Wendy had a strong will and a quiet strength that he had drawn from when he was a child. And even now, she always knew what he needed to hear and the precise moment he needed to hear it. Leaning into her words, Nash believed he could do this father thing.

Perhaps not so much over the next couple of days, when he decided to tackle things off the extensive list Wendy had texted him before leaving the hospital. Plus, his son was getting circumcised this morning and that made his gut tighten.

Nash stood in the baby section at GreatStore by the strollers and car seats, and rubbed his temples. He had been there for an hour reading the different advantages of this brand and that brand, until everything became a blur. The salesperson had been patient, but he couldn't make up his mind. Having lots of choices wasn't always good. He had immediately sent out a distress signal.

Thankfully, his two younger sisters were on their way. Nash exhaled. With the fraternal twins, Dahlia and Sabrina, coming to take charge, all he would need to do is the heavy lifting and hand over his credit card, which was perfect.

His mother was already at his guesthouse to begin decorating, as she had ordered all sorts of things using next-day delivery. Wendy had texted him to choose a theme—stripes, safari, Southwestern—but in the end, Nash had told her to go with blue and white. All she had done was sent him a thumbs-up emoji. He prayed she kept it simple, all the while knowing she wouldn't. Wendy had already knitted the baby a huge blanket with the name *Colt* embroidered on it. How she had gotten that done in two days was beyond his comprehension.

But he was grateful.

"Hey! The helping brigade is here," Dahlia called out with a wave. Goodness, she was looking more and more like Mom all day. All of his sisters, except for Jade, had inherited their blond hair and tall, willowy figures from Wendy, although Dahlia normally wore her hair long in a low ponytail while Sabrina tended to keep shoulder-length curls. Dahlia had Wendy's presence, and her resilience, while Sabrina had his mother's sense of humor.

"How you doing, Dad, Daddy, Papa, Pop," Sabrina teased, her hazel eyes twinkling. She rested a hand on her rounded stomach. She was engaged, pregnant with twins, and Nash couldn't tell when he had seen his sister look more lovely...or happy.

"Have you decided what you want to be called yet?" Dahlia asked. She pointed to a car-seat-stroller combo and Nash obliged, placing it on the flatbed.

"No, I have no idea what Colt will call me. I don't know if I'll be around when he starts talking to make a decision. Maybe I'll suck at this and Imani will cut ties with me." He busied himself by reaching above Sabrina's head to get the bassinet. He wasn't about to let either of his sisters pick up any of the heavy items.

"Nonsense," Sabrina said. "You'll get the swing of things."

"Yeah, your worries are unfounded," Dahlia added.

"Unfounded?" he asked. "Did you forget about who our father was?"

"Did you forget about our mother?" Dahlia snapped back, her piercing blue eyes ablaze.

"Can we talk about more pleasant things?" Sabrina said. "Like how adorable Colt is and how Imani looks positively radiant for someone who just delivered." She rubbed her tummy.

"I have to agree. Colt is…perfect. And, Imani, well, she's never looked more beautiful to me," Nash said proudly, pulling up his phone to share pictures of Imani and Nash. As he continued piling the flatbed with baby gear, Sabrina snagged an empty cart and began filling it with baby wipes, diapers and bottles.

"Are you two getting back together?" Dahlia blurted.

His heart twisted. "No. We're just cohabitating and co-parenting for now." How hollow that sounded.

Sabrina raised an eyebrow. "Are you good with that?"

He wasn't too sure how he felt, but the past two days had been a whirlwind and he had to settle into the idea of parenting before he could tackle the question of his relationship status with Imani. "It's what's best for now," he said instead.

Luckily, his sisters didn't press further, and Nash left them gawking over the baby clothes—never mind that he had ordered a miniature Dallas Cowboys jersey online—and headed over to the grocery aisles. GreatStore was the primary place to buy anything and everything in Chatelaine. Nash waved at Paul, the general manager, before making his way through each aisle as they picked up all of Imani's favorites. Then he added a few ingredients to make her his special vegetable lasagna.

Imani wasn't a fan of vegetables. She only liked brussels sprouts (odd) and carrots mainly, but she would eat every single vegetable he put into his dish. He gathered the Parmesan, mozzarella, provolone and ricotta cheeses that he would need. He was almost certain he had pasta sauce and noodles at home. Nash planned to have it ready by the time she was discharged. Then maybe they could curl up by the fire and snuggle like old times once the baby was asleep.

A clank against his cart made him jump. It was his sisters. With the baby goods. This was about fulfilling his *son's* needs. Not his. He'd better keep that at the forefront of his mind. Because to get back with Imani meant giving her the whole shebang—love, marriage and, well, he'd already done the baby carriage.

But he couldn't be the father Colt needed. No matter what his mother or his sisters believed, he knew the truth.

Deep down, he believed that he lacked the ability to be a

good father. He was positive that the worst thing he could do for Colt was remain in his son's life. So he would soak up these few months, and whenever Imani was ready, he would let them go. His gut twisted.

Easy to say but it was going to be hard to do.

But he would. Nash already loved Colt too much to ruin his future.

CHAPTER SIX

"Awww. Why did they have to do my son like that?" Imani sniffled and looked at her mom for answers.

Abena and Zuri had driven to Chatelaine Hills to visit with her the night before, alternating between fussing at her for running off and hugging her with relief that she was safe. That Colt was here and doing well. Then they had stayed the night at the Chatelaine Hills Hotel and Resort, the only one in town.

Her grandmother had stayed behind at the resort this morning to work out. For an octogenarian, Zuri was extremely fit. Nothing interfered with her routine. She ran two to three miles and did close to fifty squats a day, keeping her legs and abs well-toned. She had passed on her love for running to all her grandchildren, though they weren't as disciplined. Zuri had even encouraged Abena to take up the sport.

Thinking of her mom and grandmother, Imani smiled. When she was younger, she believed Zuri was actually her mom's mother because they were that close. Abena confided that their bond was cemented because of loss on both their sides. Abena had lost her mother when she was a teen and Zuri had miscarried a daughter, making Phillip an only child.

Imani wrapped her son close to her bosom and kissed his little head. His body shook from his tears. The obstetrician had returned with Colt, who was all red-faced from screaming after his circumcision, and her heart ached seeing him so distressed.

"You just have to nurse him and all will be well with his world," her mother said, seated across from her. She ran her fingers through her locs, which hung past her shoulders. "He won't remember it."

Imani had inherited Abena's high cheekbones, bronzed skin, narrow waist and wide hips. They were even the same size and height, both standing at five feet eight inches, which Imani loved once she was grown, because her mother's wardrobe was banging. Abena was always coordinated and well put together. They shared similar tastes, but her mom definitely veered toward the more refined, suitable for the daughter and wife of successful businessmen, while Imani's style could best be described as comfy chic.

She ran a hand through Colt's curls, watching his lower lip tremble. He hiccupped. "Hush, Mommy's baby. It's going to be okay." Soon, he latched on and his cries eased.

"Where's his father?" Abena asked, swinging a leg that showcased those ridiculous high heels she always wore. Her mom had on a two-piece royal blue pantsuit with a crisp white shirt and accessories that were an exact match with her color scheme.

"Nash was here early this morning, but he left to get his guesthouse ready for me and Colt, since we're getting discharged today." Which reminded her. Imani texted Nash a picture of Colt, now that he had calmed. Nash had low-key freaked out at the thought of his son getting circumcised, fleeing to go shopping for baby supplies and to set up the nursery. Not that that task didn't need to be done but he could have done it *later*.

Our little champion, Nash texted, along with a muscle-arm emoji.

Imani smiled. That he was.

Once Colt's breathing slowed and he fell into a slumber, Imani placed the baby in the bassinet and went to take a seat in one of the chairs by the window. Before she forgot, she also texted her father the same picture she had sent to Nash, although she was sure her mother had sent Phillip plenty of photos as well. The sun was out, and the skyline was filled with hues of blues that would make an amazing stock photo. Abena took out her hairbrush, oil and edge tamer and started working on Imani's curls.

"Thanks, Mama."

"Of course. You know I can't have you looking a hot mess. Do you want braids or a bun?" She gave Imani's hair a vigorous brush.

"A bun is fine. Wait… Braids." That way she wouldn't have to worry about fixing her hair for a few days and she could devote all her energy to taking care of Colt.

"Braids it is." Her mother got to work, parting her hair. "Have you spoken to Simon at all?"

"No, I blocked him after he texted me saying that we could still go through with the wedding." She bit her lip. "I really mucked things up."

Abena gave her shoulders a squeeze. "I'm sure that cat will land on his feet. Don't give him a second thought. I know you were friends since college but I never liked him. I always thought he had ulterior motives. It's going to be rocky for a while but I'm sure you'll find your way." Then she asked, "Is Nash going to take off from work to help you?"

"Yes, I think so. At least for the first few days. Then I don't know… We didn't finalize anything."

Abena tilted Imani's head and began the first braid, her hands moving fast. "I would have thought delivering his own baby would put things in perspective for him."

She didn't have to see her mother's face to know her lips were pursed. The classic sign of Abena's displeasure. Plus, that long, exaggerated sigh. "What do you expect? That he's going to ask me to marry him because I birthed his child? A child he told me didn't want? He has a real fear of messing up. His father did a number on him."

"I get it. But that will all change the more he's around his child." Her mom started on the second braid.

"And what if it doesn't? I can't be with someone who might resent me for making him take on a responsibility he didn't want."

"Nash might be a tad bit unsure, but he will come around.

The man asked you to move into his guesthouse after all. His mouth might be saying he's scared, but his actions are showing he very much wants you around..."

"I know he wants me. I've never had any doubts about that." She touched her chest. "It's Colt I'm worried about. My desire to have children is literally the reason we broke up. But since he found out, Nash has been doing all the right things—he gave Colt the Fortune name, a place to live and he's out there buying supplies to get our son all he needs." Her voice hitched. "But will he give Colt his time—*quality* time? And will he give him his whole heart? Those are the questions I have."

Abena rubbed her back. "Ah, my child. I get it. I get it. Only time will answer those."

"I mean, I'm sure he has the best intentions, but that might not be enough." She dabbed at her eyes. "Are you and Grandma planning to stay with us? I'm sure I'm going to need your help."

"Yes, we will come to help. But we'll stay at the resort so you and Nash can settle in, spend time with your son as parents. I won't be far away if you need me." Abena brushed a few knots out of her hair before starting on the second-to-last braid.

Imani's cell phone buzzed. It was Nia video-calling from Paris. "Did you get the pictures I sent? Are you calling to see your new cousin?"

"I did and I can't wait to squeeze those cheeks," her cousin said with a frown. Abena gave Nia a wave before mouthing that she would be back.

"Is everything alright?" Imani asked once her mother had left the room.

"No. I just got a call from our warehouse assistant manager. Brad didn't show up to supervise the unloading." Brad was the manager and Imani had been counting on him to be there today.

"*Say what!* I can't believe he flaked like that," she whisper-yelled, slaking a glance Colt's way. His little body rose and fell and she sighed with relief. The last thing she wanted was to jolt her baby out of his sleep.

Nia ran a hand through her curls. "It's okay. I walked his assistant, Stella, through what needed to be done. I'll wrap things up here and come home on the next flight."

Her cousin sounded exhausted. "I can handle the meetings until you return," Imani offered.

"No, you're now officially out on maternity leave. Focus on the baby and I'll figure things out." Her brow furrowed. "Hang on. I didn't check my email until just now." She started tapping the screen.

Imani waited for her cousin to share the contents.

"Oh, snap! Our plans for expanding Lullababies to host elite baby showers have been approved. We can begin construction as soon as we have secured all the permits."

"Wow." Her heart thumped.

Once again, Nia tapped away at the screen. "Don't worry yourself about this, cuz. I'll schedule discussions when I return."

Imani bit her lower lip. This baby boutique had been her dream for so long. She had used her trust fund when she came of age to chart her own path—and Nia had been the perfect business partner. Her cousin had a degree in fashion, specializing in merchandizing and textiles. With Imani's business acumen and Nia's creativity, Lullababies had blossomed, and now, they would be taking on another venture. She felt a pang that she would be missing out on negotiations, but another glance Colt's way made her decision easy. "Go ahead. Don't put it off. Just keep me posted." Her voice cracked a little.

"Alright," Nia replied, and whooped. "I'll set up talks and send you updates along the way." Imani nodded, bunching her lips, her eyes misting. Nia must have misinterpreted her reaction because she said, "Imani, I've got this. You can trust me. I know this store is your heart, your baby. I won't fail you, I promise."

Imani drew in a deep breath. "I trust you. It's not that. It's…" Her stomach knotted. She couldn't say the words she knew she wanted to say just yet. "I know Lullababies is in good hands. I'll look out for your updates." Then she ended the call.

She walked over to the bassinet to check on her baby. Needing the physical contact, she rubbed Colt's head. That very act centered her.

"What's going on?" Abena asked, coming back inside with a fruit cup for Imani and a yogurt for herself.

Imani wrapped her arms about herself. "Lullababies is about

to blow up." She filled her mother in on the expansion plans, then added, "Actually, speaking of Nia, I'm thinking of leaving her in charge and selling her my shares, once the expansion is finished."

Abena's eyes widened. "Are you sure you want to do that? You guys worked your butts off and I'm proud of you." She flailed her hands. "I'll support you either way but give it serious thought. Besides, your hormones need to settle before you make that kind of a decision." Her mother could be right. Abena often was. But when Nia called the store "her baby," Imani knew that was no longer true. Colt now filled that space.

Abena beckoned her back to the chair. "Come. Let me finish your braids. When the time comes, you'll know what to do." Imani gave a jerky nod and returned to her position. Her mother gave her a hug before finishing up her hair. Abena must have known she needed to process, because she hummed some random tune but didn't continue making conversation.

Until recently, Imani had worked sixteen-to eighteen-hour days easily. But she hadn't thought about her store at all during the past few days. Granted, she had just given birth, but once she'd held Colt in her arms, her priorities had shifted.

She knew she wanted to be there for all of Colt's firsts.

And…didn't Nash deserve the same opportunity?

Wait… What was she saying? She mentally backtracked, rubbing her eyes. Imani was getting ahead of herself. She didn't know if Nash would truly embrace fatherhood once the thrill of Colt's arrival waned.

Imani released a plume of air. She anticipated every single moment of raising their son—the highs, the lows and everything in between—and could only hope Nash would as well. But that was up to him. They would be at his guesthouse long enough for those questions to be answered. And all she could do was wait.

Wait, and pray that Nash accepted his rightful place in his son's life.

CHAPTER SEVEN

WITH THE FRIDGE stocked and the nursery complete, all Nash had left to do was move his family into his home. Yet he was petrified. He'd never shared his private space full-time with anyone. Since moving out of his mother's home, Imani had been the closest he had come to living with a woman.

Imani, he could do.

Imani and Colt, however, were an entirely different dynamic.

Still, Nash engaged in a steady stream of conversation with his baby mama as he drove them home from the hospital later that evening. He had already shared about his father's death and the family's decision to purchase the ranch. He didn't know how she didn't hear his heart galloping inside his chest as each mile brought him closer to the Fortune family compound.

"So tell me about your family ranch," Imani said, wiping at a speck of lint on her jeans. She had on a pretty, long-sleeved blouse with sunflower-shaped buttons.

"Well, it's about thirty-five hundred acres and if you ask me, it was like it was made for us."

She gasped. "Thirty-five hundred acres? Wow. I can't even picture how big it must be. You guys must have to drive everywhere."

"It's huge. We mostly used golf carts to get around the ranch.

There's a main house, and then there are six log cabins that each of us occupy."

He drove through the iron gates and the huge awning at the entrance that boasted their new ranch sign. Imani straightened and looked outside the window, her mouth agape. It was dusk, so the oranges and purples of the vibrant autumn Texas landscape made for a majestic sight as he made his way down the half-mile strip leading to the ranch itself. He took in the fields on each of their sides, his chest puffing at its resplendence.

When he came to the fork in the road, Nash decided to go left to give her a driving tour, pointing out the stables, the barns, the cattle and horses grazing.

"How many people do you employ for upkeep?"

"We have about fifteen new employees and a plethora of day hires—people just passing through who want temporary work." He stopped to show Imani the main house, which had been constructed using weathered light-colored stone, a sloped metal roof and wood finishes. The covered porch extended from either side of the front door and had six posts and a white railing.

"There's a dirt back road directly from the ranch to my house, but I drive this way home sometimes."

"Yeah, so now that I'm not swimming through an abundance of hormones, why don't you bring me up to speed on this name change and how you all ended up here."

Nash pulled away from where he'd parked. "My mom's the best person to tell this story because it's quite fascinating, but I'll do my best." He cleared his throat. "Wendell Fortune—that's the grandfather my mother was named after—had a secret illegitimate daughter, Ariella McQueen. Ariella was in love with a poor miner, which Wendell didn't approve of, and she ended up getting pregnant—a pregnancy she hid from everyone. With her mother deceased, Ariella really wanted to please Wendell and have him acknowledge her existence, which he refused."

Imani's eyes went wide. "Goodness. This is like a storyline from my mother's soaps. Too bad I don't have any ice cream."

Nash chuckled. "When the baby was a month old, Ariella decided to choose love over a relationship with Wendell and went to the mine to get her lover, so that they could elope. She left her baby girl with a sitter named Gertie Wilson. Gertie was the only person who knew of the baby's existence. But Ariella did write a letter to Wendell telling him of her plans and confessing that she had given birth to a daughter—his grandchild. But Wendell never actually read that letter. He kept it but said he was afraid to open it and read what was inside."

"Wow. I wonder how Ariella hid the pregnancy?" Imani asked, before waving him on to continue.

"Unfortunately, we will never know because Ariella was one of fifty-one people who lost their lives in a mining disaster that very same day."

"Oh, my." Imani wrapped her arms about her. "I'm sorry to hear that. Ariella was your grandmother, correct?"

"Yes, but it's okay. I didn't know her."

"Wait, rewind. So what happened to the baby back then?" Imani rubbed her chin. "I mean, I realized the baby is Wendy, but I guess my real question is, how did Wendy find out she's Wendell's granddaughter?"

"Good question." He squared his shoulders, his fingers drumming on the steering wheel. "Right...so when Ariella didn't return, Gertie believed the baby was abandoned. Since no one knew of the baby's existence, Gertie moved hours away and raised my mother as her own, as Wendy Wilson. It wasn't until she died six months ago that my mother learned the truth. Gertie had left her a letter confessing everything."

Imani released a long breath. "Whew. Wow. That's something. Two letters bearing some tough truths."

"Yes, which is why I hate secrets." He shook his head. "No one thinks of the damage they bring to the next generation. Imagine learning that your grandma isn't really your grandma."

She gave his hand a squeeze. "I wish I had been there for you."

"Me, too." He exhaled. "But, when my mother contacted Wendell with her discovery, he confirmed its veracity by sharing the letter from Ariella." He dabbed at his eyes. "That was one massive family reunion, let me tell you."

"I'm so glad this story led to a happy ending for you, your siblings and your mom."

"Yes, and in addition to gaining family, my mother inherited Fortune's Castle in Chatelaine."

Imani's mouth dropped. "You guys have a real-life castle? That's some whole other level of wealth right there."

"I guess." He could feel his face heat.

"My mother had the number fifty-one etched into the cement to honor my grandmother and the others who died in the mining disaster and is currently in the process of transforming the castle into a luxury hotel, suite of offices and venue for events. Then she purchased this place for all of us and we took on the Fortune name, which you already know about."

"Yes, and this ranch is *enormous*. What a place to come home to," she breathed out, then he mentioned that the lake separated Chatelaine Hills from the town of Chatelaine.

His heart filled. "I love that me and my siblings all live together, but with enough space between us so we're not in each other's way." Nash returned to the entrance and this time took a right turn by the lake.

He passed Jade's home first, then turned toward his own entrance. He drove through the metal gate and the stone pillars. His house was recessed farther than the others, hidden from the main path. There was also a wall of privacy trees surrounding the property.

Imani's breath caught. "This is what you call a *cabin*? It's more like a waterfront mansion with log exteriors." She placed a hand to her chest. "When you said you lived on a ranch, I didn't envision anything this fancy."

"I guess. I have four bedrooms in mine, but some of the others have six." He pulled next to his golf cart and parked, intending to give her a tour of his home. He couldn't wait to show her the 1980 Jaguar that he had had restored. When they dated, Nash had told Imani how much he wanted to own one. They had brainstormed everything from the dark green color and gold trimming as a must-have, to the places where they would go in it. The sports car now sat in his garage, though he had only driven it once. Maybe he had been waiting for Imani and he didn't realize it. Excitement flowed as he envisioned seeing her face when she sat on the plush leather seat for the very first time.

Just then, Colt started fussing in the back seat. He swallowed his disappointment and gave her an apologetic smile. "Rain check? We can tour my home another time. I imagine you want to get settled in and Little Man needs your attention." She raised an eyebrow and he slapped his forehead. "I meant *our* attention." He peeked behind him and saw Colt still had his eyes closed. "He's not fully awake yet," Nash whispered.

The baby whined.

"Yes, he's probably hungry and needs a diaper change." He could hear the worry in her tone.

Nash felt a surge of protectiveness and patted her leg. "He's okay." He hoped. What did he know?

"Yes, you're right," she said, obviously trying to sound brave. "Crying is how they communicate. You can change Colt and I will search for something to munch on while I'm nursing."

"That will work," he squeaked out, wiping his palm on his leg. Nash started up the Range Rover and backed out—the only sound now was the gravel of the packed earth beneath his tires. Then he drove around to the guesthouse, this time, taking the only other spot next to her Jeep.

They heard a small whimper.

"Perfect timing," she said, opening her door—before he could do it for her.

Nash lifted a hand and went to lift the car seat. Taking Imani's hand, he led her up the small path and opened the door. Colt was now crying at a louder volume. Nash gripped the car seat and took him inside.

Colt bunched his fists and stiffened before he wailed.

A full-fledged red-in-the-face wail. Dang, this child went from calm to storm in under sixty seconds. Nash rested him on the couch and stepped back.

"Somebody's impatient," Imani cooed, reaching down to unbuckle her son. Then she held up the bundle in Nash's direction.

His heart thundered and he gave Imani a look. "I don't know what to do."

"Can you change his diaper?" she asked. "I've got to use the bathroom."

"Sure. The bathroom's down the hallway on your right." He held the baby close and Colt calmed a little, his little mouth searching. "Um, I don't have what you're looking for." It was like Colt understood him because he started to cry. Nash realized that he hadn't grabbed any of the baby's things from his car, including the diaper bag. What should he do?

Maybe he was holding him wrong. He placed the crying bundle back into the car seat and clenched his jaw. Imani sure was taking a long time in the bathroom. Did she leave him alone with Colt on purpose? His brow furrowed. *"Imani!"* he yelled, panic pumping through his veins.

"I'm coming," she yelled back. He could hear the toilet flush and the water running.

"I'm out of my league here." Nash wiped his brow. Colt had now squirmed so much that he had ended up in an awkward position. "I left the diaper bag in the car."

Imani rushed over and gathered the newborn in her arms. She sounded out of breath and cross with him. "I'm sure there are diapers in the nursery. Why didn't you just rock him or something, then? I was gone less than a minute."

Though she asked that question, what Nash heard was, *Why do you suck at this already?*

He jutted his jaw and stormed outside to get the baby's possessions, furious at her and himself. His chest heaved. He told Imani months ago that fatherhood wasn't for him and what did she do? Sprang a baby on him and expected him to be a contender for father of the year. He didn't know a daggone thing about babies. Nash placed both hands on the rear of the Range Rover and drew deep breaths. He hated the surly thoughts flowing through his mind and needed to redirect before he said something he regretted.

Inhale. Imani hadn't gotten pregnant by herself.

Exhale. Colt didn't ask to be here.

Inhale. Imani was here because he had invited her.

Exhale. Colt was a baby and, what did Imani say? He was crying to communicate.

His panic ebbed. Knowing he couldn't stall any longer, Nash opened the trunk and filled his arms with as much stuff as he could take in one trip and headed back into the house. Colt was contentedly nursing while Imani sang to him. "He couldn't wait to eat. I'll change him after."

Envy slapped him in the gut. Imani was born for motherhood. While he was just woefully inadequate. Nash placed the baby bag next to her, unable to look her in the eyes.

His cell phone pinged. There was a text from Ridge. His brother was on his way to his house. *Lifesaver.* "I've got to head out but I'll be back to check up on you." Or maybe he would just call instead. Yeah. That was a much better plan.

"Alright," Imani said, giving him a beatific smile. "We'll be here."

Nash went to the fridge to get her cheese sticks, apple slices and yogurt. The delight on her face proved he could do right when it came to Imani. His son, not so much.

Helplessness and guilt made his steps heavy as he walked to his house, taking the stairs to his multilevel deck and entering through the sliding door and into the kitchen. Placing his hands on the granite countertop, Nash pictured the seven-pounder in his guesthouse who made him quake and fumble. If his mother had been here, he would be bending her ear right now.

He heard a rap on the door and shook his head, his curls cascading in his face. "Come in," he hollered, knowing it was Ridge. Nash ran a hand through his unruly hair. He needed a trim.

"Hey, bro, how's fatherhood treating you?" Tall and lanky, Ridge was the youngest of the six siblings. He held a small package in his hand—which Nash assumed was another gift for Colt.

"I'm a wreck right now," he confessed, dipping his head to his chest. "It hasn't even been five minutes and I'm already screwing up. Just like Dad." Nash then told his younger brother what had transpired moments before in the guesthouse.

"Aww. You'll get the hang of it, bro, but you've got to leave Dad out of this."

Nash's head popped up. Ridge spoke with certainty, his brown eyes earnest. The certainty of *current* experience. The past few months, Ridge had been helping to take care of baby Evie while Hope waited for the return of her memories.

After placing the package on the countertop, his brother strutted over to give his shoulder a squeeze.

Ridge thumped his chest. "Evie isn't even my child and I feel so much for her—a natural protectiveness, a surge of love. Fatherhood is a combination of instinct and hands-on learning. I've had a huge learning curve, but I made a conscious choice to be the kind of father figure Evie needs right now during this strange time that Hope is in my life," his said, his voice full of steel, "for as long as she needs me. And Casper Windham doesn't dictate what I do from the grave."

To hear the family heartbreaker, who ran from any form of commitment, speak with such conviction really moved Nash. His brother had matured in character since acquiring a ready-made family and Nash felt nothing but pride about that.

"That's great, bro. I just wish it were that simple for me... that I could will myself to be a good father to Colt. To be honest, I'm all discombobulated over this. Nothing I'm experiencing so far with fatherhood feels instinctual." He jabbed a finger to his chest. "Yes, I felt a bond the moment I held Colt in my arms. But all I feel about parenthood in the long years to come is fear and dread."

"I, too, am experiencing moments of fear and dread," Ridge admitted. "But it's at the thought of losing Hope and Evie when her memory fully returns." He chuckled. "I've kinda gotten used to having them around."

Whoa. It was evident that Ridge had strong feelings for Hope and Evie. Nash's heart squeezed. "Have there been any new developments with her regaining her memory?" he asked gently.

Ridge shifted and rubbed his chin. "She has flashes of memory and it's clear she's running from something," he said, his voice filled with unease, "but what she's running from, I have no idea."

That had to be tough. "Yet you're still putting yourself out there with Evie...?"

"Yeah, and though I have no idea what lies ahead, I'd do it again."

Nash drummed the countertop with his fingers. "That's remarkable." He pinned his brother with a gaze. *"You're* remarkable."

Ridge shrugged, his skin reddening. "Yeah, well, this might be the dumbest and bravest thing I've ever done in my life. But at least I'll have no regrets."

"Good for you." Nash hugged him close. "Just know that the entire family, especially me, is rooting for you. You have my support."

"I appreciate that." Ending the embrace, Ridge cocked his head. "You have my support as well. Love on that baby," he said, his voice cracking a little, "especially since you know for sure he's yours."

In other words, unlike Ridge, Nash didn't have to worry about another daddy popping up and taking his family from him. "Hang in there," he told him. His brother left after that and Nash mulled over Ridge's passionately spoken words about having no regrets. Nash needed to be able to say the same when it came to Colt.

He bunched his fists—ready or not, he had to at least try. For Colt's sake as well as his own. But he wasn't about to show up empty-handed.

CHAPTER EIGHT

HER BABY COULD die if she closed her eyes. If only the nurse hadn't mentioned SIDS when she was in the hospital, then maybe Imani wouldn't have done some research and now she wouldn't be all paranoid that her child could become a horrible statistic. Especially since it was more common in boys than girls.

Ugh, she should have avoided the internet search. Why didn't anybody tell her not to do that? Not that she would have listened.

Fear cloaked her heart, and she couldn't shake it off no matter how much she tried. Now, her heart clamored in her chest and her eyelids burned. Because she couldn't get to sleep!

Imani had placed Colt next to her on the king-size bed so she could watch him breathe. He was holding his breath for about two seconds and then expelling the air out of his body in one whoosh. Was that normal? She didn't know and she didn't want to look it up because that's how she'd ended up here.

It was close to 11:00 p.m. and she had been up since 5:00 a.m. that morning and Nash hadn't returned yet, like he'd promised. *Yet?* She was kidding herself to think he would. Nash had dashed out of the guesthouse within minutes of their arrival, leaving her alone to figure things out with their newborn. Imani hadn't dared call her mother because, well, she didn't want Abena thinking badly of Nash. She sniffled and wiped her face.

Colt released shallow, staccato breaths.

Oh, goodness, her body shuddered. He wasn't breathing properly. Something might be wrong with his lungs.

Maybe she could call the pediatrician to find out.

Her cell phone chimed with a text from Nash. You up?

Yes. Are you com— She deleted. Don't want to pressure him. With a sigh, she just texted, Yes.

Okay. I'm on my way.

It's about time, she typed. *Delete. Delete. Delete.* Instead, she texted, Let yourself in, then placed the baby in the bassinet, which she had moved into her bedroom. Then, after grabbing the baby monitor, she went into the living area to wait for him. Nash had installed cameras around the circumference of the property and in the nursery, but Colt was too young to be in that big old space by himself, no matter how lovely it was.

She heard a whimper and skedaddled back into the bedroom, slightly out of breath.

To her relief, she saw Colt's little chest was rising and falling with those little fists in the air. Aww. *My sweet baby.* Imani took what had to be picture number five hundred and eighty-seven and settled back on the bed to continue her vigil. As soon as Nash entered the room, holding a huge bouquet of flowers, she released a long exhale.

"I'm so glad you're here," she choked out, suddenly overcome at being able to voice her fears aloud. "I'm so scared."

Nash rested the floral arrangement on the nightstand, then came to sit on the bed and took her hand. "What's wrong?"

"C-Colt c-could die a-any minute." She flung herself into Nash's arms. His hands rubbed her back and she breathed in his masculine scent. Being in his arms soothed her. "K-keep an eye on h-him," she hiccupped. "I j-just need a minute." Then she sobbed, the fears oozing out of her shaking body as his arms grounded her.

She felt a kiss on the top of her head. "What's going on?"

Imani pulled out of his embrace, squared her shoulders and shared what she had found out about SIDS. His eyes went wide and his brow furrowed. But then he shook his head. "My mother had six children and we all turned out fine. I know it's a reality, but I choose to believe that Colt will thrive. You did. I did." He pointed at Colt. "And, he will, too."

She rubbed her eyes, dried out from all that crying. "You sound really sure. But there are no guarantees."

"Do you want me to call my mom?" Nash asked, looking at his watch. "Or get you some ice cream?"

"No. No. She might be asleep. That's why I didn't bother my family. And if I eat ice cream feeling this way, my tummy might get upset. I—I'd rather stay up until daybreak, or we take turns watching him."

"Alright, if that's what you want, then that's what we'll do," Nash said. "If it's okay with you, I'll stay here and I'll take the first shift. You get some sleep."

Grateful, Imani gave a jerky nod and snuggled in his arms. "Wake me up if he needs to feed."

He lifted a hand. "I can feed him. I saw the bottles you put in the fridge with the date and time labeled on them."

Imani had pumped for the first time that morning at the hospital, and while that task had been no easy feat, she wanted Nash to be able to feed Colt if he desired. When she had opened the fridge earlier to store the bottles, that's when she saw that Nash had purchased a lot of her favorites. She had gotten all mushy inside that he remembered what she liked. "Are you sure you're okay with feeding him tonight?" When he nodded, she asked, "You know how to use the bottle warmer?" Another nod. "You won't fall asleep?"

"No. I will be up. Get some rest. I won't let anything happen to our son."

Our son. Her heart warmed at him taking ownership. "You're going to be a great father."

"If you say so. The jury is still out on that one," he scoffed.

"Just give it a chance. By the way, that nursery is beyond my expectations. You didn't spare any expense." She yawned.

He preened. "Yeah, it turned out pretty good. Colt is worth every penny."

"Yes, but I'll speak for him until he can speak for himself.

Colt would much prefer your time, your heart, over your money any day. All this—" she splayed her hands toward the baby paraphernalia in the bedroom "—is just…stuff." Her lips quirked. "Great stuff. Expensive stuff. But stuff, nonetheless. Material goods will never replace the security of having a father's unconditional love."

"I get that." She could tell from his tone that he was thinking of his own strained relationship with his father. Her heart squeezed. She couldn't bear her son growing up feeling the same about Nash the way that Nash felt about Casper Windham.

"You're a good man, Nash Fortune, or I wouldn't have come this close—" she brought her index finger and thumb close to each other "—to falling in love with you. I'm sure that goodness will transfer over to our baby boy."

Nash patted Cole's bum. "Okay, I'll do my best. I want to be there to meet all of his needs."

"I hope you feel that way when you have to get up in the middle of the night." Her eyelids fluttered closed.

EVERYTHING WAS GOING WELL. Until…it wasn't.

Imani lay snoring, her arm slung across her face. Nash quirked his lips. He had spent just as much time watching her as he had watching Colt. And he couldn't decide who was the cuter of the two.

It was the wee hours of the morning and Colt had awakened. Nash had been sitting up against the headboard on the other end of the bed, alternating between scrolling through his cell phone, reviewing his strategic plans with Arlo's comments and watching random baby videos—including one on learning CPR, because you never knew—when Colt stirred awake. Nash had looked over to see a pair of hazel eyes staring back at him. At least they looked hazel—he couldn't be sure.

That's when he sprang into action, going through his mental checklist so he got everything perfect.

He used the bottle warmer to warm the milk. Check. Not too cold. Not too hot. Just right.

He fed Colt. Check. Tummy nice and full.

He burped the baby. Check. Nice, strong burp.

Then after several YouTube video tutorials, Nash changed his son's diaper, even managed to get the diaper snug across his bottom, with no accidental whizzing. At this point, a solid hour had passed. Yet, here it was 5:28 a.m. and he couldn't get Colt to go back to sleep.

Sitting on one of the two rocking chairs in the nursery, Nash experienced none of the calm vibe the decor in the room was meant to solicit. Wendy had embraced a nautical theme—right in line with his choice of blue and white. Everything from the area rug, the lamps, the bedding, the matching accessories and the artwork, which he had hung, made Colt's room classy and organized. There was even a nook that held baby's first books and teddy bears, along with a sound system with the option of water waves or white noise—neither of which were working at the moment in settling his newborn.

Nash rocked. And patted. And rocked some more. Yet Colt was very much awake. And now, that cute face appeared scrunched and his stomach felt tight to the touch. Nash had a fussy baby on his hands.

With no clue what to do.

In an instant, Colt was screeching at the top of his lungs, and he had the wriggling tyke on his chest, his shirt getting wetter and wetter with tears. Nash decided to walk him, pacing back and forth before venturing into the living area.

"What's going on?" Imani said groggily.

He whipped around to see her standing there in just her black boy shorts and she had traded the blouse for a cotton maternity top. Dang, she looked good. Her hair was all messy and sexy, like she'd just rolled out of his bed. *Whoosh.* Nash licked his lips. He wanted to—

Colt must have heard Imani's voice because he stiffened and cried even louder.

"Let me hold him," Imani said, coming to his side. She took the baby from Nash, then cooed and snuggled Colt in her arms. "Is he hungry?"

"No. And I just changed him a few minutes ago." Nash's shoulders sagged. "I told you I'm no good at this." If he closed his eyes, he would fall right asleep.

"You're fine. He's just fussing, that's all." It took her a few minutes but Colt settled and went to sleep.

"No, I just don't have what it takes. This just proved it." Feelings of inadequacy overshadowed his earlier ones of competence. Or at least of surviving.

"Not from my perspective." Imani placed a finger over those enticing lips of hers and gestured for him to wait. Then she tiptoed into the bedroom to put Colt into the bassinet, and came back into the room a few minutes later with the baby monitor in hand.

Her face shone and she did a light jig, almost skipping over to him. His eyebrows knitted. Why was she so chipper? He hoped she wasn't about to brag on her parenting skills. "Guess what?" she asked, resting the baby monitor on the nightstand.

"Yeah. I know he's sleeping. I was right here when Colt's head lolled back and I could see the drool running down the side of his face." He glanced at the small screen. Gosh, Colt looked so cute.

"No, silly." Imani did some silent claps before gyrating her hips, then waving her hands in the air, going in beat to the water waves. Alright, she had his attention now.

Nash stood and stretched before joining her, spooning her from behind. He closed his eyes and allowed the beat of the water and the sounds of the waves to fill his senses. Their bodies took on a familiar rhythm, moving in sync, stirring emotions and heightening senses that had been in stasis. For six long months. He ground his hips against that firm butt and groaned.

Her arms circled his neck as his hands traveled the path from her abdomen under her shirt to give her full breasts a gentle squeeze, their larger size a perk of pregnancy.

He whispered in her ear. "Not that I mind, but what exactly are we celebrating?" His voice deepened with desire, electrical sparks igniting wherever they made contact.

"We survived Colt's first night home alone as parents and, most importantly, so did he. Colt's alive and breathing and my heart is doing somersaults right now." She spun to face him. "Three down and one hundred and fifty-seven to go."

"I don't get it."

"The risk of SIDS is higher between one and four months. We're on a countdown." She spun to face him. "And day three is in the bag, all thanks to you. You got me through the scariest night of my life."

Her breath was minty—but how? She must have brushed her teeth when she put Colt down to bed. He had brushed his with a spare toothbrush that he'd left for guests, and then helped himself to a small glass of orange juice, while he waited for Colt's bottle to warm.

He used an index finger to dip her chin toward him. "You can't do that, Imani. You can't count days, afraid of mortality. That's not living. You want to allow yourself to thrive in all the wonderful aspects of motherhood. I understand your anxiety. I feel it, too, but it can't consume you. It can't overshadow the good moments."

"You're right. I'll try." Imani relaxed her shoulders and molded her body into his, then tilted her head to look into his eyes. "You should do the same."

Pleasure infused his heart and his lower region. Nash's hands cupped her bottom, loving how they fit well into his palms. Aching need thrummed through every area of his body where they connected. If this had been many months back, he would be ridding them of their clothes to sink deeply into her soft, welcoming folds. But Imani had just given birth. His eyes dropped to her mouth. Judging by the invitation in her eyes, Imani was as caught up as he was and in agreement.

He caressed her face before gripping the back of her head. His hands caressed her soft curls, loving the scent of jasmine. Her lips parted.

What kind of man would he be if he didn't oblige?

Nash pressed his mouth to hers, desperate for another taste after so, so long. And, oh, she tasted so good. He feasted on those decadent, luscious lips. Passion ignited within him, his body remembering her achy sweetness, yearning for more.

He moved to end the kiss but she grabbed on, her tongue dueling with his, an unspoken challenge that he was determined to win. But then, she reached up to massage his earlobes. Goodness, she remembered his Achilles' heel. His toes curled in his boots and he stifled his moan. Nash knew he had to put an end to this sensual madness before he lost complete control.

After tearing his lips from hers, they faced off, chest heaving, panting, gasping for breath.

"Whoa, that was… I don't even have the words," he said, his mind scattered with his swirling thoughts.

She smirked. "That was long overdue." She passed by him and swatted him on the butt. "Now, go get you some sleep."

Nash yawned. "I probably should head down to the ranch. Arlo said he would cover for me, but I think I should at least show my face." He had been so caught up in Imani and Colt that he hadn't even checked on Stanley since the other man left the hospital. Plus, he had another new hire, Roger Pitts, that he needed to check on.

"You're the boss. You are entitled to take some kind of family leave," Imani said. "Plus, you'll be of no use to anyone if you're too exhausted."

By this time, sleep fanned at his eyes. "Alright. I'll be back in a few. I'll get a nap and I'll be back over early afternoon. What do you want for lunch?"

"Sounds like a plan. And hmm…well, I've been craving a nice, juicy burger and a big plate of fries." She licked her lips.

"I'll pick some up on my way back."

"Awesome." She blew him a kiss and headed back into the room. "I'll put Colt's laundry on to wash and then I'm going right back to bed myself. The rule is, I should sleep when the baby sleeps and I'm going to try to follow that."

With a wave, Nash departed, walking out into the early sunrise, enjoying the autumn breeze and the breathtaking beauty of the fall season. The oak, cypress and maple trees produced vibrant hues of orange, yellow and red, a majestic view of transition. He stopped a moment to take in the chirr of the American robins and the peacefulness of the lake. Like his siblings, he had his boat tethered to the docking station. By now, Nash could barely keep his eyes open.

Instead of entering through the back, Nash walked around to the front of his home to get the morning paper. There was a young teen who delivered *The Chatelaine Daily News* before going to school. Nash hadn't heard the signature hum of the teen's doctored Mustang that morning. After bending over to pick up the paper, he used his phone to unlock the front door.

As soon as he closed the door behind him, Nash texted his brother for an update. Arlo replied immediately.

I've got it handled. Stanley called about coming back to work today. Dahlia convinced him to take leave. Everything is as it should be.

Alright. Reach out if you need me.

Will do… Do you need me to move the family meeting to the 15th?

Okay. That's not a bad idea.

I'm on it. Enjoy your family.

Family. Wow. In a matter of days, Nash had been given a family of his own. He stewed on that realization as he made his way up the stairs. Thanksgiving was a few weeks away and it would be nice to have Imani and Colt with him.

Nash sauntered down the hallway to his bedroom, done in beige and deep browns, with a couple of his ranch hats on the walls. But now, where there used to be a blank space, there was a picture of Colt. Beside it was a small picture of the baby's tiny feet on the left, and another smaller picture of Colt on the right. Funny. He didn't recall taking that picture. He moved close to investigate, then gasped.

That was him as a baby.

Colt was what Wendy would call his spitting image, the only difference being his son's olive-toned skin.

He staggered backward, until he touched the edge of the bed. Nash sank down on the mattress, gripping the comforter, and sat there in awe for a beat.

Imani's words came back to him. *Colt would much prefer your time, your heart, over your money any day.*

How many times had he felt those sentiments regarding his own father? Nash didn't want Colt to feel that pain of rejection, of not being good enough. He curled his lips inward, vowing to be there for his son. To be the role model Colt would need so that years from now, he wouldn't be in a similar position, questioning his ability to father his child.

Yes. He would do everything in his power to be the father for Colt that he wished Casper had been.

Nash eyed his son's picture as determination strengthened his will. Then he uttered, "I promise to do my best, son. I won't let you down. You're going to know you're loved by me, every single day." And he would start today.

Taking a chance, he called Imani's cell phone. "Everything okay?" she whispered. "Colt is still asleep."

"Yes, can you take a video call?"

"Sure, the laundry cycle just started. I thought you'd be knocked out by now."

A few seconds later, he was staring into Imani's sweet face, her eyes inquisitive. "Would you mind taking me to see Colt for a second?"

"He's still asleep."

"I know. I won't wake him." She did as he asked. As soon as Nash saw the infant, his heart expanded. In a hoarse whisper, Nash said, "I love you, son. Daddy loves you." When Imani turned the camera back to her, she had tears in her eyes. All she could do was nod, and he figured she was too emotional for words, which was alright, because so was he.

CHAPTER NINE

WHY ON EARTH couldn't Hammond Porter keep things simple?

Her grandfather had called to say that he was coming to visit and Imani had prepared lunch for two. Okay, so it was a bagged salad and premade grilled chicken strips, but in her defense, she was a new mom nursing a baby who needed to be fed every two hours. She honestly didn't think she had enough milk to sustain Colt's appetite and that made her heart ache. Made her feel like less than. But she planted a smile on her face and pushed all that aside since her grandfather was coming to visit.

She was looking forward to their lunch date, but hadn't expected to see three black Escalades pull in front of the guesthouse carrying her mother and grandmother, her two aunties, Mazie and Yemana, and five of her six cousins—Zaire, the twins, Kamara and Ashanti, Xavion and Omari. So much for an intimate family gathering. However, since each person carried a platter of some heavenly comfort food, she had forgiven him.

Besides, she hadn't had to change or feed her son once he had awakened from his nap. Her family, who assured her they were well and up-to-date on shots, had taken care of all of Colt's needs, giving her a much-needed respite. Though she still had her qualms about so many people being around her newborn, at least they were family. Nash had helped himself to a plate then dashed off to the ranch, using the excuse of giving her private time with her peeps. And, yes, he had used the word *peeps*.

Exclaiming about the picturesque foliage lining the bank of the lake, Imani's cousins decided to venture out to explore the hiking trails on the ranch. Her mother and grandmother caught up on the latest episode of their favorite soap opera, and Auntie Mazie napped on the recliner. It was Auntie Yemana's turn to tend to Colt.

Since everyone was occupied, Grandpa beckoned to her to join him for a walk. They took the path down to the dock. He clasped his hands behind him. He was a stately man and looked more like sixty than the eighty-eight years he was. Hammond bench-pressed two-ninety and could still drop and give you twenty push-ups on command. What could she say—her grandparents personified her fitness goals.

Grandpa cleared his throat and stroked his pepper-gray beard. "I got a chance to talk with the board about my retirement next year and your taking the helm to continue my legacy."

"Oh?" Her eyebrows raised. "I don't imagine that went over well." The group of six men and one woman could best be described as archaic and stuffy.

Hammond cleared his throat. "Well, their exact words were 'Imani isn't qualified enough to take the reins of such an illustrious company.'"

"I can't say I disagree with them." They stopped by the lake to admire the calm waters. A couple wood ducks hovered close with about five ducklings behind them.

She shoved her hand in the pockets of her black-and-cream striped button-down dress, which she wore with slip-on shoes. Thank goodness, she still had the weekender, and shopping bags in her trunk. Plus, her mother had also brought a suitcase with more clothes for her extended stay. Imani touched her belly, feeling her luxury tummy shaper designed to feed her love for sexy underwear and get back her pre-pregnancy bod. It wouldn't take long, since she had run every morning up until seven months.

"Don't listen to those old fuddy-duddies. They are not going to tell me what to do with my company and I do think some of their concerns are plain old gender bias."

Imani turned to rest a hand on her grandpa's palm. "Even if they feel their opinion is based on my being a woman, you do need to see if their objections are valid." She squared her shoulders. "I don't think I'm the person for the job."

"Nonsense." Hammond gave a dismissive wave. "You are more than qualified. But I'm retiring, not dead. I'll be on hand to guide if you need. Though I doubt you will."

The one stubborn, and at times useful, quality about her grandfather was that he didn't quit. A necessary trait if you were going to maintain billionaire status. When he wanted something, he had tunnel vision. And she had no doubt Hammond was going to use his gift of gab to sweet-talk her into seeing things his way.

Before Colt, she would have caved.

But her priorities had shifted and she told her grandfather as much. "I don't want my business life to consume my personal one. I want to be present in my son's life to see every single milestone. Porters eat, sleep and play oil, and that's not me."

Hammond nodded with understanding but he wasn't easily thwarted. "How about we do this instead? Let me scout around for a suitable replacement over the next few months. Once I'm gone that person can oversee the everyday operations, but then you would have the final vote. How does that sound?"

"What about Jonathan? He would be perfect for the job."

"Your brother has a serious case of wanderlust. I don't think he's ever going to ease up on his jet-setting ways. Jonathan is just like his father. Although, I never thought Phillip would marry and yet he gave me two amazing grandchildren."

Imani raised her shoulders. "Jonathan already travels back and forth between here and Dubai. He can attend meetings here using videoconferencing. It's not like it was in your day. And maybe one day, he'll settle down, maybe start a family, like Dad."

Her grandfather made one last attempt to plead his case. "To run my business, you need the right balance of heart and cunning. Both of which you already possess, my darling granddaughter. I just had to nurture it, and with you at the helm, I know our business will last for generations." He grimaced. "I can't have all that I took my lifetime building squandered or divvied up and sold to the highest bidders. Or, worse, I don't want your mother or grandmother to ever have to worry about finances. Only family will make sure of that."

The concern in his tone almost made her rethink her position. "Okay. Talk to Jonathan. See if he will run the day-to-day after you retire and I can have the final vote. I believe that is a fair compromise."

"Alright, that's doable." He took her hand in his and they resumed their walk. "I've set up a trust for Colt so he will never have to worry about his future."

"Thank you, Grandpa. Nash did as well. My child is already a millionaire, and he isn't even seven days old." She didn't add that Colt would be the chief beneficiary of Lullababies, if she kept her company.

"Yep. Colt Porter Fortune is one blessed child." Grandpa kissed her cheek. "In more ways than one." He cocked his head. "Having both parents in his life will be an even bigger blessing." That was a not-so-subtle way of inquiring about the status of her relationship with Nash.

"I know I didn't go about this the traditional way, Grandpa, but Nash and I are both committed to co-parenting."

His eyebrows rose. "I guess that's the in thing now with you young people. Back in my day, we would have been Mr. and Mrs. before the baby's birth."

"And back in your day, people stayed married through misery. Thirty, forty years spent despising each other all for the children's sake." She pursed her lips. "Won't be me. The person I marry will want to be with me for always. Or, I'll remain single. I won't subject my son to a toxic environment."

"That's a good point," he said. "I never looked at it like that. Lucky for me, Zuri and I are in love. Every day I get up happy to see her face."

"Aww." Imani touched her chest. "I hope to get the same."

His cell phone vibrated with a message that made him look down. She was willing to bet it was her grandmother, judging by that huge smile across his face. After typing a response, Hammond said, "Nash seemed smitten with you when I met him."

"Well, I'll rely on your verdict about Nash's level of smitten-ness when you see him again today." She looked at her watch and hurried her steps. "It's time for me to nurse and Nash should be back from the ranch by now."

Her grandmother strolled toward them. She had on a sweat-suit and sneakers. "There you are. I was wondering where you both got off to." Then, eyes peeled on her hubby, Zuri made her way over to Hammond.

"We'll be back in a few," Hammond called out, snatching his wife close. "We're going to catch the sunset on Nash's boat."

"Uh-huh. So that's what we're calling it these days." Both gave her unapologetic shrugs before heading to the dock arm in arm.

Imani swallowed the bit of hopeful envy. Man, she really hoped to have something enduring like her grandparents had. Speaking of endurance, her mind kept straying toward that kiss she and Nash had shared. It had been sensual torture, be-cause she had a few weeks before she could engage in inter-course. But she had no regrets. Her lips tingled as she replayed that encounter in her mind—the heat in his eyes, the shock waves going through her body, the feel of his hands and that low growl in her ear.

It had been too much and not enough at the same time.

And, oh, she needed more.

Maybe tonight, they could steal a few minutes to themselves for part two. In the meantime, Imani would think about all the wicked things that firm mouth and demanding tongue would do to her. But when she entered the guesthouse, all those thoughts flew out of her head.

Nash was there.

Holding her wedding veil in one hand.

The unspoken question was evident in the knit of his eye-brows.

Everyone around him was silent. Her mother held Colt, panic in her eyes. "Nash was just asking about this gown, and who it belonged to…" her mother squeaked out. Abena's flustered tone increased Imani's discomfort. Why hadn't she tossed the jumpsuit in the trash? He must have seen it inside the shopping bag that she must have left in the nursery.

Well, sometimes the best response was no response. Or a clean exit while she gathered her frazzled thoughts. Breaking eye contact with the father of her child, and ignoring her hammering heart, Imani marched over to her mother and held out her hands. "I'm sure Colt is hungry. I've got to feed him."

As soon as her mother placed Colt in her arms, Imani took off for the bedroom. How on earth did that jumpsuit end up in the nursery? She vaguely remembered her mother and grandmother clearing her trunk, but then… Wait. She had been changing Colt and had told her mother to leave it by the closet, and she would get it later.

But, of course, she had forgotten.

And now, she had Nash almost breathing down her neck, striding after her. She ducked inside the room but before she could close the door, he stood by the doorjamb holding up the veil. "Care to explain?"

He had a frown on his face, but his tone was gentle.

That was the only reason she stepped aside to let him enter. After undoing her buttons, she got Colt situated to feed and then faced the only man she should have ever thought about marrying.

"It was for convenience," she admitted. Good grief. That wasn't the thing to say. Colt began to fuss so she latched him on again.

Nash's eyes narrowed. "What do you mean?"

"You told me you didn't want children and I didn't want Colt to grow up without a father's love."

"So you decided to get a substitute?" He sounded butt-hurt.

She rushed to explain. "I wouldn't call it that. I wasn't looking for a substitute dad for Colt, more like a…"

"Replacement?" he growled out.

Dang, that didn't sound good, either. It would be misleading for her to blame it on pregnancy hormones. Imani had capably run her company the entire term of her pregnancy.

"These past six months I lived like a hermit. I tried not to think about you. I spent hours listening to Taylor Swift to try to get you out of my system, all the while you were looking for someone to fill my shoes."

"Wait. You listen to *Taylor Swift*?"

"Uh, what does it matter?" he countered. "My life is the equivalent of a sad song."

"B-but I didn't go through with it. I c-couldn't marry a man I d-didn't love," she stammered, burping Colt and then changing his position to her other breast. "That's what counts in the long run."

"Fair enough." He bunched the delicate material in his fists. She really wanted to save the veil, as it had been handmade and cost more than it should, but she knew this wasn't the time to point that out. "So who is the mystery man?"

Of course, he would want to know. "It was Simon. My friend from graduate school. Well, former friend."

"Si—" He paced the room. "*I knew* it. I told you when I met him that he had the hots for you. And why wouldn't he? You're attractive, way out of his league, obviously. But what man can resist your charms?"

"Excuse me?" Colt startled in her arms. "Sorry, little one." She rubbed his back to comfort him. Lowering her voice, she spoke through her teeth. "It was a business arrangement with a friend. Nothing more." The memory of the look of heated attraction in Simon's eyes made her squirm. Well, it was just friendship on her part. She blew out a breath of frustration. "But either way, it doesn't matter because I didn't marry the man. I ran out of the courthouse before we could finish saying the vows."

Nash's mouth dropped. "You did what?"

"Yes, I hid in the bathroom and then as soon as the coast was clear, I was out of there."

Nash covered his mouth but a snort escaped. "I actually pity the man." The snort led to a full-on laughing fest. He bent over, clutching his stomach.

"Stop!" she said, feeling the giggles rising within. "It's not funny."

"It's like a scene out of a rom-com or one of those movies you used to make me watch."

Colt disengaged and she placed him on her shoulder to burp

him again. To her surprise, Nash came over and took over the task. Within minutes, Colt released a healthy belch. Nash then offered to change his diaper. Her heart warmed. He was really trying.

"I love you, little man," he said, bending over to kiss Colt's forehead. Their son drifted off to sleep and Nash swaddled him, then placed him on his back in the bassinet. Imani bit on her lower lip to keep from commending him, but also, she didn't think he would want her watching his every single move. Even if she was.

Nash placed a hand on his hip and asked gruffly, "So were you going to tell me?"

Her stomach clenched. "Tell you what?"

"About Colt? Simon?" He flailed his hands. "All of it."

She bit her lower lip again and shook her head. "I..." Imani trailed off. Her eyes misted. "I was going to tell you about Simon."

"Good."

"But if I hadn't gone into labor and you weren't my rescuer, I honestly don't know when I would have told you about Colt."

Nash nodded and then stalked out of the room. Imani grabbed the baby monitor and dashed after him as he uttered a curt goodbye to her family and raced out of the guesthouse. After begging her mother to keep an eye on Colt, Imani knew she couldn't let the night end this way. "Nash," she called out. He kept moving, cutting across the lawn to get into his house. "Wait! I need you to—" In her haste, she twisted her foot on a pebble and screeched, her butt hitting the soft earth beneath her.

In a flash, he was by her side, helping her to stand. When she cried out, he swung her up in his powerful arms. Nash turned to return her to the guesthouse, but she insisted they go to his place instead. After a moment's hesitation, he changed direction.

When he turned on the interior lights, Imani gasped at the cathedral ceiling, the wide-open space and the wall of windows that faced the deck. "This place is gorgeous."

He grunted what sounded like a thank-you before setting her back down on her feet, but she couldn't be sure. Time to get back to the topic on hand. She placed the baby monitor on the foyer entrance table, right beside a white envelope with what appeared to be a wedding invitation on top. The baby monitor fell, causing the invite to fall onto the floor.

"Sorry about that," she said and stooped to pick it up.

Nash rushed over to take it out of her hand. "Oh, I forgot about that. It's a wedding invitation for the end of January..." He trailed off. "But get this, I don't even know who the bride and groom will be. It's all pretty weird. My brothers and sisters received the same one, and maybe that's the only reason I haven't thrown it away." He shook his head before dropping the envelope on the table.

"Oh..." Imani wasn't sure what else to say so she backtracked to the previous, pressing conversation. Twisting her fingers, she shuffled from one foot to the next and continued. "I'm sorry you're mad at me but this isn't all on me," she said in a gentle tone.

"I'm not mad at you," he groaned, jabbing a finger in his chest. "I'm mad at *me*. None of this would have happened if I weren't such a...coward." He deflated. "I pushed away the best thing to happen to me because I was afraid."

Her heart squeezed. "What you're feeling is understandable. And if we dwell on the what-ifs and should-haves, we won't move forward." Her shoulders sagged. "And that's what I want to do, Nash. Move past all this."

"I'm not good at that. I keep allowing my past to dictate my actions in the present. Like my relationship with my father." He rubbed his head. "But I know I must." His voice cracked. "Because now that I have you back in my life, I know I can't let you go. And now that I have a son, I can never *not* be his father. No matter where I go in the world, I can't run from that. And though I'm not gonna lie, I'm scared as all get-out, I don't want to.

Imani folded her arms and arched an eyebrow. "So don't."

She didn't know who made the first move, but the next thing she knew they were hugging, kissing and touching. Trying to assuage a six-month hunger from which there could only be one relief.

With a savage growl, he crushed his lips to hers. She moaned, long and loud, welcoming his hands exploring the top half of her body, appreciating his mindfulness that she had just had a baby.

The friction, the fire, threatened to consume her. Nash's tongue explored where his hands had been, an enticing substitute. Her knees buckled, and he came down with her, his arms a steady brace. It was the feel of the cool marble on her back that made her senses return.

"Nash, I can't..." His lips found the base of her neck.

"There's many things I can do," he said, his voice a rumble, his teeth grazing her earlobes. He wasn't playing fair.

"I want to, but we've got to get back. Colt won't sleep for more than twenty minutes max. Plus, I have a house full of family waiting on me, clamoring to see how this all plays out. I can't have them barging up here to—" she made air quotes "'—help resolve our dispute.'" After pressing her hands against his shoulders, she stood and rebuttoned the top of her dress.

"I understand." Nash got to his feet, too, then whispered, "I miss you. I've missed you and I will be missing you even more tonight."

"Same." She picked up the baby monitor. Colt was still asleep. Good. She splayed her hands on his chest. "How about you give me a quick tour before we return to my welcome party?"

"Alright. There's one place in particular I'd like to show you." He waggled his brows.

Imani rolled her eyes. "Let me get the clearance from the doctor first and then we can revisit that possibility."

"Okay, it's a date."

She teased, "But it will be hard for you to top the private plane ride to New York City so we could see a Broadway show, especially with a baby in tow."

"I'll think of something." Nash led the way to the spacious kitchen. As expected, he had top-of-the-line appliances and the decor was a mix of modern and rustic. She drooled over the glass-door refrigerator, which appeared to be stocked with the bare minimum. Not that she commented. She had a similar situation at her home in Cactus Grove.

His master suite was on the same floor and there were three other bedrooms on the second floor, each with their own bathrooms. From his bedroom, there was a walkout that provided an impressive scenic view.

Her new-mother eye detected his place would need serious toddler-proofing when that time came. *Hold up.* Just because Nash still desired her and had voluntarily changed a diaper, it didn't mean he was in it for a lifetime. Because as her mother told her, parenting was a never-ending commitment and it wouldn't get easier with age. The older they got, the bigger the problems. Imani touched her abdomen. She didn't even know if *she* was ready for what was to come. But at least she knew she wanted motherhood.

She sauntered outside, enjoying the gentle night breeze, the night sounds and the tranquility. The fresh fall air cleared her mind.

Nash was still quite a few steps behind her in embracing parenthood. She had to allow him time to catch up, so she couldn't complicate that process by allowing him into her bed. No matter how much she wanted to.

He came to stand behind her, wrapping his arms about her waist. The scent of his cologne served as an aphrodisiac. "Guess what I have in my garage?"

She paused before turning in his arms. "You didn't?" There was only one vehicle she knew of that would put that sparkle in his eyes and excitement in his voice. "You *did*?" she squealed, and did a little jig.

"I sure did." He grinned, hand extended. "Care for a five-minute ride?"

"Five minutes?"

His voice dropped. "There's a lot we can do in five minutes."

Well, okay then. She sure was game to find out.

CHAPTER TEN

FIFTEEN MINUTES. THAT'S how long they had been gone from the guesthouse.

Nash had kept a close eye on the time. Now, he turned on the light in the garage, appreciating Imani's harsh intake of breath. The dark green color of the Jaguar sparkled under the showcase lights he had had specially installed.

"She is a beauty," she said, and whistled, running her free hand on the hood. The other clutched the baby monitor. He made a mental note to install the app on her phone, as he had done with his. "What do you call her?"

"I haven't named her."

Imani placed a hand on her hips. "She is a horse on wheels. She needs to have a name."

"Good point. Okay, I'll think of one." Nash opened the car door for her and waited until she was settled before jogging around to the driver's side and starting up the Jaguar. Then he pressed the garage-door opener and crept outside, taking in the night sounds. Once he had backed out, he put on the old Rascal Flatts hit "Life Is a Highway."

"When this song ends that's our cue to end this joyride. Deal?" he said.

They bumped fists. "Deal." Nash hit the gas, loving the perks of living on a private compound. Imani squealed, raising her hands in the air. "Whoa. Go, baby, go!"

And go, he did. In a matter of seconds, they were at 100 miles per hour. It felt smooth, like butter...like velvet, eating up the gravel, flying past the fields, the fall colors a satisfying blur. He glanced at the beautiful woman next to him and smiled. This was what he had been waiting on. Imani by his side in his restored ride. With the window down, her hair blew in the wind. He dipped the curve, enjoying her whoop of delight, and headed toward the entrance. He'd stop beneath the awning.

He snapped to attention and hit the steering wheel. "That's it!"

"That's what?" she asked.

"I'm calling her Velvet."

"Ooh." Imani gyrated her hips. "I like it." She rubbed the plush leather. "Velvet, you're giving me quite a ride tonight."

"This is just like old times," Nash murmured, expecting her to laugh in return. But she sobered, sinking back into her seat. He slowed and turned down the music. "What's wrong?"

"You know we can never go back, don't you?" she asked, her hands folded in her lap.

He shook his head in confusion. "Go back to what?"

"Our lives are forever changed because of Colt and I'm not looking to relive—" she did her second air quotes for the night ""—old times.'" She gestured her hands between them. "We have a son to think of."

Nash cringed. "Listen, I meant we were having fun like we always do. I have been in a funk these past few months and this is the first time in a long time, I am enjoying the company of a fine woman—a woman I have strong feelings for—and it feels good to feel that way again. I'm not going to apologize for that and I'm not going to regret it, either." He executed a U-turn, the air tense between them.

After a few beats, she mumbled, "I'm sorry if I ruined the vibe or misjudged you."

"Thank you for apologizing. Your assumption ruined this vibe and you did misjudge me. I still plan on having loads of fun with you…and Colt. Just being around you is fun for me. That's not going to change because we're parents."

They finished the rest of the way in silence and he entered the garage in a way different mood from when he had left. The song ended. Neither moved.

"I'm sorry, again. I propose a do-over." She sniffled. "I'm just worried about you forgetting about Colt. It's easy to get caught up and…" She trailed off and murmured, "Never mind, it's hard to explain and I'm feeling like the big, bad monster who shackled you with a baby you didn't want." She opened the door and made a move to get out.

Nash held her arm. "Baby, you really think I would forget, or rather, *want* to forget my son?" The fact that he had to ask this question crushed him.

"Not on purpose," she whispered, her head dipped to her chest.

"Yes, Colt has changed my life, and yes, I am processing and dealing with that right along with my fears. But you didn't shackle me with anything, to use your words, and I'm glad that he's here." His words jarred him into realizing he had spoken nothing but the truth.

"You are?" she said, her voice quavering with relief.

His chest tightened. Goodness, Imani really believed that he resented Colt's presence, that he saw his son as an intrusion in his life. No wonder she had reacted the way she had a couple of minutes ago. "Yes, I'm glad that Colt is here. I'm glad he has all his fingers and toes. I'm glad at everything he does. I love him. I'm not just saying that, Imani. I love my child."

Imani gave him a bright smile, and her eyes welled up. "I'm glad…and relieved."

"Good." Nash opened the door and once again reached for her hand. He craved any kind of physical contact with her. "Now, let's go check on our son." When they made their way back, he went out of his way to follow up his words with actions. He remained glued to Colt's side for the rest of the night, making sure to tell Colt he loved him.

Before her family left, they gave him kisses and hugs, praising him for a job well done. But if he was being completely honest, he was exhausted.

AND THAT EXHAUSTION grew throughout the next week and a half. Being a daddy was the hardest and most demanding job he had ever had. He barely slept, helping with diaper changes, feedings, baths and bedtime. Repeat, repeat, repeat. But Nash was not about to voice that aloud.

Nope.

His mother and siblings had called to offer help but Nash had declined.

He wasn't going to chance Imani thinking he wasn't committed, or was foisting his responsibility on to someone else. Because he was committed. He just wasn't able to think coherently and he had a meeting coming up that he needed to prepare for, but any free moment was spent taking power naps because Nash had given up on ever catching up on sleep.

Sleep? Who needed it?

If he stopped moving, he would pass out and he wouldn't wake up for days. Imani was just as tired as he was, yet she kept at it. And so would he.

So they stayed on the grind, in an unspoken face-off, like Energizer Bunnies, making Colt their only priority, providing round-the-clock care. The same thing, day in, day out. Imani even took a step back from being involved with the expansion of Lullababies. He knew for a fact that most of the time when Nia called, Imani would find an excuse to end the conversation.

But then, Ridge called early that morning to inform Nash about an emergency on the ranch. Nash insisted on going in to the office to investigate. Not even to himself would he admit that it was because he sought a much-needed break. And if he avoided meeting Imani's eyes when he told her he had to head into work, and thus, potentially miss Colt's first doctor's appointment, though his mother was on her way to assist, it had nothing to do with guilt. Nothing at all. At least that's what he told himself as he got dressed and headed out of the house, his steps light. Was it him? Or did the air feel sharper and the sun seem brighter this morning? He marched toward the Range Rover loving the crunch of the autumn leaves under his boots. Jumping into his Range Rover, Nash took off, leaving nothing but dust in his wake.

Since he hadn't eaten breakfast, he decided to stop by the Daily Grind to get a cup of coffee. The coffee shop was once a one-story modest home that had been converted to a restaurant in the 1930s. Situated across the road from the feed store made it an ideal location for ranchers to stop in for coffee and sweet treats.

After parking out front, Nash traipsed across the wide front porch and opened the door. The bell chimed when he entered and he greeted the workers. The place wasn't fancy but it was cute and bright, with red gingham curtains. There were about a dozen small wooden tables, as well as a counter along the back with stools. The Daily Grind was a hang out spot for the locals to engage in local gossip, and Nash always felt right at home.

While he waited for his order, Nash noticed a queue at one of the tables and beelined over to investigate. To his surprise, Beau Weatherly sat there with his Free Life Advice plaque posted. Beau was a retired ranch investor who had lost his wife about five years ago. The man was a big contributor and had brought in many initiatives to Chatelaine. He was loved and respected by the community. Nash had heard about Beau giving out advice every morning from 7:00 to 8:30 a.m. from his siblings, but this was the first time he had seen Beau "open for business."

Nash's order came up. After tipping the waitstaff, Nash took a hearty sip of his Americano and then decided to join Beau's line.

Once it was his turn, he slipped into the seat and got right to it. "If a man had a terrible role model for being a father, can he still be a good father to his own child if he works at it?" His face heated at his question. Maybe it was too deep for the kind of advice the distinguished gentleman usually doled out.

Beau took Nash's hand in both of his and looked straight at him. "Absolutely. You determine who you are—no one and nothing else." Nash thanked the older man, then stood. He hadn't expected Beau to say otherwise but his spirits lifted at those words.

A few minutes later, Nash pulled up to his designated parking spot at the ranch offices near the main house, with the gusto of a bear coming out of hibernation. There was a whole other world going on while he had been sequestered in the guesthouse with Imani and Colt.

There were a few other parking spaces in front of the building for guests and more in the back of the ranch for employees. Nash pulled open the door of the building, then wiped his boots on the welcome mat and entered the small reception area. He tipped his hat at Maria, the part-time receptionist who helped with basic clerical duties such as filing, handling emailing and other duties as assigned.

"Arlo is waiting for you in your office," Maria offered, once he had shared the perfunctory baby pictures. He passed Sabrina's and Jade's offices before rapping on the last door at the end of the hallway.

"Come in," Arlo said. Ridge was also inside and seated on one of two chairs on the other side of the desk.

Nash squelched his surprise at how comfortable Ridge looked behind his desk. He paused. "Am I about to lose my job?" he asked, only half-joking. His heart thumped in his chest.

Ridge gestured him inside, his tone solemn. "Hey, bro. Come sit down. You need to see this." A sense of dread lined Nash's stomach. Both men had grave looks on their faces.

That's when Nash zoned in on the photos spread across the desk. He gasped and shot his brothers a glance. "This can't be real."

"It is."

Nash dropped into the chair. A chill ran up his body. If what he was seeing is true, that meant someone was purposely sabotaging their business, and unless they found the perpetrator, the Fortune family plans for the ranch would come to a screeching halt. He could almost hear Casper laughing from beyond the grave.

CHAPTER ELEVEN

ALL THE PHOTOS that she'd seen of happy mothers, pushing their happy infants in the strollers, were nothing but lies. For her, motherhood was like a Jenga game and it only needed one small error for everything to fall apart. Imani stood in her driveway with the passenger door ajar, her mouth open in shock.

After Nash had bolted out the door early that morning, Imani had swallowed her resentment. It must be really nice to be able to drive away without a backward glance, but she wasn't about to call him and get on his case about it. If he didn't want to be there, she wasn't going to force him. And, no, she hadn't bought his thin excuse that he was needed at the ranch, when she had heard his brother tell him that they could meet virtually.

Frankly, Imani was too tired to argue.

Her bones ached from trying to survive on roughly three hours sleep. Colt needed to be fed every hour, sometimes less. She fretted that he wasn't getting enough but she wasn't sure.

Her pride gave her the wind she needed to get Colt ready for his doctor's appointment but she had run out of time to tame her unkempt hair. Honestly, she didn't have the energy to care. Stifling a moan, she had donned a wrinkled long-sleeved T-shirt and a pair of stained black jeans.

But just as she placed Colt into his car seat, she noticed he had soiled his clothes, the refuse seeping out, while he just stared at her.

"Why couldn't you have done this five minutes ago?" She grunted, dropping the baby bag at her feet. Imani hated being late and this mishap was going to set her back by at least twenty minutes. Colt's response was to burst into a full-fledged wail.

Her shoulders shook as she began to weep right along with her baby boy. "H-hang on. I'm going to h-help you. Just as s-soon as I g-get my-myself together." This was ridiculous. She had experience running a million-dollar company and she couldn't handle a week-old baby?

A hand on her shoulder made her jump. "How can I help?" Wendy asked, slipping an arm around her shoulders. Those soft-spoken words were her undoing. She had been too distraught to register the other woman pulling up in the golf cart. Leaning into the embrace, Imani fell apart. Wendy rocked her while she cried. Eventually, with gentle prodding, Imani was able to explain the problem. "There now, I'm pretty sure the pediatrician will understand if you're running behind schedule. You're a new mom and these things happen. Now, why don't you call the office and let them know what's going on and I will get Colt cleaned up?"

Imani exhaled and nodded.

In a flash, Wendy was heading back into the house with the crying infant, with Imani trailing behind. The guesthouse was a mess—there were diapers, baby clothes, empty food cartons littered throughout the living room and kitchen—but she was too exhausted to be embarrassed.

Imani plopped into the couch and called the doctor. The receptionist pushed the time back to later that afternoon. Imani set her alarm in her phone so she wouldn't forget. She could hear Wendy singing and talking to Colt while the bathwater ran. Dropping her phone in her purse, she sunk farther into the cushions and closed her eyes.

The next thing she knew, Wendy was giving her a gentle shake. "I'm sorry to wake you, but Colt's hungry and I didn't see any milk in the fridge."

"I didn't get a chance to pump this morning. Honestly, I've

been breastfeeding more than I've given him bottles." Not that she was able to produce more than an ounce or two. Imani thought her milk would be gushing like the videos she had seen on pumping. She made a move to stand.

Tucking the baby under her arm, Wendy waved for her to sit. "You can pump later. Right now, let's get him fed and then we will be on our way."

"They gave me an afternoon appointment instead." Dang, she could barely keep her eyes open. That mininap was a tease.

"Awesome. So after you've nursed, you're going to go into your bedroom and get some more rest. I'll take care of Colt." She looked around the space, taking in the disarray. Imani opened her mouth to apologize but Wendy lifted a hand. "I'm going to start cleaning up while you feed your son. No need to explain. I have been there."

Grateful tears slid down Imani's face. She choked out a thank-you and fed Colt. Within minutes, he was asleep. Poor little guy. Colt hadn't slept well the night before. To Imani, he seemed hungry all the time and she didn't know what to do to help him. Oh, goodness. What if she wasn't able to provide milk for her child?

Imani rubbed his little cheek and gave him a kiss before placing him in his bassinet. She did a quick pump, praying for a heavier flow, ending up with a couple ounces this time. Whew. Imani put the two bottles of milk in the refrigerator. Wendy was in the laundry room adjacent to the kitchen, humming some tune.

She shuffled into the bedroom to get some shut-eye. When she awakened three hours later at 1:00 p.m., she popped out of bed. She couldn't believe she had slept that long. Imani headed into the living room, eager to see her son. Then she stopped.

The guesthouse was immaculate. Everything shone. And the smell of lemons filled her nostrils.

Wendy and Jade sat on the couch and both women gave her a smile. Colt was awake on his aunt's lap, pumping his legs.

"Oh, my goodness," Imani said, dabbing at her eyes. "Thank you so much for cleaning and for watching Colt." She lowered her eyes, wishing they hadn't had to tidy up for her, but she was doing the best she could considering the circumstances. Imani changed the subject. "I feel refreshed after that nap."

"It was our pleasure," Wendy said, coming to give her a hug. "We were glad to help. Colt's laundry is finished and folded and his tummy is full."

"Plus, I had fun playing with my nephew," Jade said, taking in Imani's getup. Her sister-in-law wore jeans, boots and a colorful blouse, and she looked lovely. And clean.

"Nash texted that he should be back in time to take you to Colt's appointment," Wendy offered, breaking into her thoughts.

Imani folded her lips into her mouth to keep from uttering something surly about him. Instead, she planted a smile on her face and muttered, "That's fine." Her phone alarm went off and she went to retrieve it out of her purse, which Wendy must have moved to the coffee table.

She gave her curls a futile pat and looked at her watch. Maybe she could squeeze in a shower and wash her hair... "If you don't mind hanging around a little longer, I'll freshen up a bit. Get some me time before our appointment at three thirty." As soon as she said those words, she chided herself. She should be all about her son. Right now, she sounded selfish.

"Take all the time you need," Jade said. "We ordered pizza and Nash is picking it up on his way back."

"And don't you dare feel guilty about taking time for yourself." Wendy wagged a finger. "Self-care is important for your mental health and overall well-being."

"Duly noted," Imani said, before excusing herself. How her life had changed in such a short time! She had underestimated just how much but it would be good to feel like herself again.

"I CAN'T BELIEVE he grew an inch already," Nash said when they left the pediatrician's office later that afternoon. Wendy had ventured with them to the doctor's office while Jade had left right after Nash came. Nash was now on his way back home, but he was dropping off his mother first.

"And I can't believe he's only gained a couple of ounces," Imani replied, disheartened, her tone tinged with frost. She cupped her abdomen. Disappointment in herself as a mom weighed her down. Plus, she was still low-key ticked off at Nash for his brash exit that morning but since his mother was around, she held her tongue. Imani didn't want Wendy viewing her as churlish, especially since Nash's mom had been lovely and supportive during the appointment. Watching Colt get his first shots had been traumatic for her and so it was good that Wendy had been there to keep her calm.

She had gritted her teeth, when Nash cooed, "Come on, little man, be a tough guy" over and over. It had taken an enormous amount of restraint to keep from snapping that Colt was just a baby.

Wendy reached over from the passenger seat to pat her shoulder. "He'll put on some weight soon." Imani gave her a slight smile before turning her head to look out the window.

When the doctor said that Colt needed to gain a few pounds, she had held her breath to keep from breaking down. All the long hours and sleepless nights had been for naught. She was failing at motherhood. And she couldn't blame Nash for this because she was Colt's sole nutrition supply. The doctor had suggested she consult with a lactation specialist and supplement with formula, because she might not be making enough milk.

She, Imani, who had been high-school salutatorian, maintained a 4.0 in college and had launched a successful retail chain, couldn't produce enough milk, a couple of ounces actually, to sustain a newborn.

This was beyond mortifying.

"Yeah, that doctor doesn't know what he's talking about," Nash added, giving her hand a squeeze.

Imani rolled her eyes. She knew he was trying to be encouraging but she just wasn't in the mood.

Nash pulled up to the main house. Wendy asked if they wanted to come inside and offered to give Imani a tour. Plus, she had made a hearty bowl of chili and corn bread. Imani's stomach growled. But Nash was already shaking his head.

"Can we take a rain check?" he asked. "There's a lot going on at the ranch and I've got to get to the bottom of it."

"Okay, call me later and let me know what's going on," Wendy said.

"I will. If I figure it out."

Ugh. That meant Nash was going to be busy tonight, leaving her to deal with Colt on her own. The fact that he didn't have to because his brothers would handle whatever it was irked her to another level.

Throwing them a kiss, Wendy exited and strutted inside her home.

Imani turned to check on Colt, avoiding meeting Nash's eyes.

She sure was cross with Nash. Maybe her grumpy disposition was because he had the nerve to look fine and rested while she felt worn-out and drained. Even though she had washed her hair and donned a cute brown ribbed dress, she could see her face looked gaunt and her eyes had dark circles under them, plus her nails were cracked and her feet sore. But she needed to take care of Colt and make sure he gained weight by the next appointment.

And if it meant she was going to lose more sleep to make it happen, well, that's what she would do.

CHAPTER TWELVE

HE WAS GETTING the silent treatment. And he deserved every bit of it. Imani hadn't fussed or argued, but her displeasure hit him like a tsunami. She hadn't even asked what was going on at the ranch. And she hadn't allowed him to do anything for Colt since he had gotten home.

Sitting on the rocker in the nursery with his laptop on his lap, Nash regretted leaving her in the lurch that morning. But he hadn't anticipated that he would be facing such a big crisis at work, or that he would really want to talk to Imani about it.

Only, she wouldn't even look him in the eyes.

Just then, the door creaked and Imani sauntered in, holding a laundry basket. Colt must be asleep in the next room. She opened the drawers and began placing the clothes inside. She was dressed in her pajamas, which said, *Colt's Mom*. He figured it was a specialty item from her store. Colt was one of the most well-dressed babies he had ever seen. He had a plethora of coordinated monogrammed onesies, blankets and bibs.

"Do you need any help?" he asked, placing his laptop aside, already knowing what the answer would be.

"Nope."

He exhaled. "Ugh. This is ridiculous."

She swung around, eyes blazing, and placed a hand on her

hip. "*Ridiculous?* Really? Is that what we're calling your juvenile actions?"

Nash stood and walked over to her. "I'm the foreman. If something is wrong, I have to—"

She wagged a finger, interrupting him. "Don't even utter the rest of that exaggeration. You didn't have to do anything this morning. You chose to go because you didn't want to be here with me and Colt." Her voice hitched. "You would rather be anywhere than here. So all that talk about wanting to be a father to Colt was just talk."

Nash could hear the hurt in her voice and his shoulders sagged. "I want to be here helping you and I want to give Colt my best, but I just need…balance. It doesn't mean that I don't care."

Tears streaked down her face. "Well, you could have fooled me. I don't get to pick up and run off when things get tough. That's not what you do when you love someone. You don't… leave."

Her words pierced his chest. Is that how she saw him?

Their breakup was on him but he didn't see it as running away. He saw it as being upfront about how he felt at the time. Colt's arrival changed all that, but Nash refused to feel guilty about trying to insert normalcy into his life. She needed to do the same.

"You're behaving like parenting has shackles. You stay cooped up in here twenty-four hours a day. The only reason why you left the house was because Colt had a doctor's appointment. This isn't healthy."

To his surprise, Imani sunk into the rocker and wept. "You're right. I—I'm sorry for coming at you like that." She looked up at him and the fear in her eyes made his stomach clench. "I'm scared of going outside and Colt getting sick. I'm scared to leave him alone too long." She flailed her hands. "I'm just scared of everything. But most of all, I'm scared Colt is going to starve because I'm not feeding him enough." She broke into a heavy sob.

Nash got to his feet and hugged her close, allowing her to get a good cry in. He kissed the top of her head. "Oh, baby, you're doing way more than enough. In fact, you're going overboard.

We are here acting like zombies when the solution is right in the kitchen cabinet."

She wiped her face and furrowed her brow. "What do you mean?"

"Come with me." He took her hand, led her into the kitchen and turned on the light. She slipped into the chair at the kitchen table. Then he opened the cupboard and took out a metal can.

Her reddened eyes went wide. "You took out a can of formula?"

"Yes. We need to use it."

She cocked her head. "Every book I've read on raising babies says breast is best."

"And where's that getting you? Neither you nor Colt has gotten a good night's sleep in days."

"I'm not doing it." She lifted her chin. "I'm not about to score a one on the motherhood scale."

"Motherhood scale?" He shook his head. "What on earth are you talking about? You're in competition with yourself. You know that, right? You're already the most amazing person in the world as far as Colt is concerned. You are the number-one voice he wants to hear, the number-one face he wants to see."

On cue, Colt began to wail.

She looked upward and groaned. "I just fed him twenty minutes ago. Why is he up?" Her lower lip trembled. She made a move to stand, but he placed a hand on her shoulder. "Sit."

Colt's cries got a little louder.

"Let me just go get him," Imani said, her butt half out of the chair.

"No, you need to rest," he said gently. "Colt will be alright for a few minutes while we talk. Besides, his lungs could use the workout and it's not like there are neighbors close by to hear him." Nash lifted her chin with his index finger. "It's wise to accept assistance when it's needed. Please quit punishing yourself for not producing enough breast milk. Love means doing what's best for him, not for you. What's important is that Colt is getting what he needs."

Her eyes misted as he continued. "I'm giving you permission to be human. You don't have to be a superwoman. You don't have to be perfect at everything. And, it's alright to take a break. Let me help you and our son."

"Okay." She took her seat.

A small win. Whew. "Great." He massaged his neck. "So, how about we try him with the formula? What do you say?" For several heart pounding seconds, he watched the varying expressions play across her face.

Then she tucked her lips into her mouth and nodded.

Nash pulled the tab on the metal container. It made a satisfying rip in the otherwise quiet of the night. He took out the baby-formula mixer, plugged it in and then poured the right amount of water and formula as directed. He turned on the mixer, loving the whirr. Secretly, Nash had been waiting to use this gadget that many parents had said was a must-have.

He peered over to Imani. She gripped the chair, her knuckles white. He knew the decision wasn't easy and prayed the benefits would outweigh any guilt she might feel.

Nash quickened his movements before she caved. Judging by those escalated cries, their son was impatient, a characteristic he shared with both his parents. He hurriedly got one of the baby bottles that his mother had sterilized and stored. Setting the dial on the mixer to two ounces, he placed the bottle under the spout and pressed the switch, appreciating the gurgle as warm formula poured out.

"Okay, I'm ready," he said.

Imani bolted out of the chair and scuttled into the room, coming back with Colt in her arms. Nash gestured for her to hand him over and then slipped the bottle inside that tiny mouth. Colt's mouth opened and closed as he tried to assimilate to the new bottle.

Poor little guy was frustrated that he couldn't latch on, his mouth seeking. Imani hovered close. "Let me try."

Nash did as she asked and wiped his brow. "That wasn't as easy as I imagined."

"It never is."

They shared a laugh at her dry response. Their first laugh in days. His chest lightened. Returning to her seat, Imani plopped the bottle in Colt's mouth and he began to feed, guzzling down the contents with speed.

"Wow. How did you do that?"

"I have no idea." She eyed the bundle in her hands. "Look at him go." She gave Nash a beaming smile, her lashes thickening with unshed tears. Her curls rested on her shoulders, framing her face just so, and his heart skipped a beat. She looked beautiful. "I have to admit he's pretty impressive."

"I agree. He had to have had an ounce already." Nash's chest puffed. "He's a champion."

Imani pulled out the bottle to burp Colt, who immediately started to fuss. "Hang on. I'll give you back your bottle in a minute." Of course, then he burped, so she gave him the rest. Soon Colt was fast asleep, leaving a small remnant of milk at the bottom of the bottle.

Gratitude flooded through Nash at his son's satisfied expression. A small niggle of doubt at his own incompetence teased his mind but he was too happy at the progress they had made tonight to dwell on it.

"If that snore is any indication, I think he'll be out for a while," Imani said, relief etched on her face.

"I'm counting on it." He gave her a pointed look. "You need a break."

"You're right."

"And admitting that doesn't make you a bad mother. It makes you a wise one. You don't want to burn out and become impatient and overwhelmed." He knew that admission had been difficult for her. "I'll make sure you get a break. How about a spa day soon?"

She closed her eyes briefly. "That sounds heavenly."

"I'm on it."

"I'm going to put the baby down and then you can tell me all about what's going on at the ranch," Imani whispered and walked toward the nursery. "Let's see how he does in here tonight." Nash rushed to get the bassinet out of the master bedroom and hauled it into the nursery, setting it next to the changing table. He made sure to turn on the baby monitor, then he grabbed his laptop.

Side by side, Nash and Imani rested the infant inside. Colt didn't even budge. Nash couldn't resist taking a picture.

They made their way to the living room. "You did good, Daddy," Imani said, sitting and tucking her legs beneath her. She had no idea how those words served as a balm for his unease.

"Let's see if he sleeps for an extended time."

Imani rubbed her eyes. "I hope so. He needs it."

"So do you." Nash went behind her on the couch and massaged her shoulders. He kneaded her back muscles, making sure to work out the knots in her neck. His baby was tense.

Tilting her head back, she groaned. "That feels so good."

Lowering his head, Nash cradled her head between his palms and placed a tender kiss on her lips. "I can't wait until I can use my lips. I'm going to kiss every delectable inch of your body."

He heard a sharp intake of breath. "I'm going to hold you to that." Imani patted the space next to her and he went by her side. "Now, get to talking…"

Nash opened up his laptop. "I met with Ridge and Arlo. Someone cut a few of our metal fences and opened some of our livestock cages."

Imani gasped. "Say what?"

"We were able to find and rescue most of the animals, and fortunately, none were hurt." He tapped the screen. "That's why I have been reviewing the recordings over the past couple days to see if we can find the person or persons responsible."

"Oh, no. It sounds like someone is trying to sabotage the ranch." She scooted forward, her brow furrowed. "Did you call the cops?"

"Yes, two deputies came by and questioned our workers. They said they plan to launch an investigation. But they didn't have faith that the culprits would be caught. They speculate it could have been day-labor workers, who would now be long gone. None of the other ranches have reported any strange incidents. Frankly, the cops were shocked to hear about this happening on this side of town." He scoffed. "According to them, nothing generally happens in Chatelaine."

"Honestly, I'm floored," Imani said. "This is a small town

where everyone seems to know everyone. Are you sure these local cops are trained to conduct a wide-range investigation?"

"Honestly? I don't know. But I convinced them to allow us to do our own investigation as well, make the guilty party think they've gotten away with it. I want to catch them in the act. So I'm not just reviewing past footage, but daily footage as well."

Her eyes were filled with empathy. "I'm just glad no harm came to the animals. Is there something I can do?"

"No, I've been going through hours and hours of recordings from our security system for the past couple days or so. Our holdings are large, and luckily, we had just installed security cameras at different angles. But that's another reason why it's taking a while to go through." He rubbed his eyes. The work was tedious and, yes, they could more than afford to hire their own investigators, but Nash needed to help. He was foreman and responsible for the safety of the people and animals on the ranch. "I'll take my time and go through the footage, and you've got your own business to run," he reminded her.

"Yes, well, I'm toying with the idea of selling my shares of the company to Nia." She pulled on her pajama top and didn't meet his eyes.

His mouth dropped. "Why would you do that?"

"I don't want to miss out on anything with Colt. I can't. My father is wonderful, but he was and is a part-time father. Now, when he's here, he is the absolute best. But he isn't always here." She ticked off her points with her index finger. "Dad missed recitals, and tennis matches and school performances." She dabbed at her eyes. "I can't do the same to Colt. I want to be in his life full-time. That's also the reason why I couldn't assume full responsibility for my grandfather's company when he retires. I'm hoping Jonathan will agree to take over the helm stateside when that time comes, though I offered to be the final vote when needed."

"I understand where you're coming from, but you can make a conscious choice not to make the same mistake your father did." She raised her eyebrows at him. He lifted a hand. "I know. I know. Pot. Kettle. I need to take my own advice. But look at your mother. Though she married into one of the wealthiest families in Texas, she kept working as a guidance counselor. Even now, your mom is involved in charities and all sorts of hobbies. And my mom raised six children and still did her own thing."

He ran a hand through his hair. "You're not looking at this from the right angle. You're the boss, Imani. You don't have to miss anything. It's called scheduling. And Colt won't be young all the time. The older he gets, the less he'll need you. Heck, as soon as I hit the fourth grade, I didn't want to be seen around my mother until I graduated high school. And the main reason I hung out with her on graduation day was because Jade had let it slip that Mom was getting us both cars as gifts."

"Oh, snap. I get it. I didn't want my mother around much, either." She appeared pensive, then admitted, "You're right."

"Of course, I'm right. Now, how about tomorrow morning, we get out of this house and get lattes at the Daily Grind? It's not as fancy as the LC Club, but they have the best caramel macchiato I've ever had."

She arched an eyebrow. "Hmm…you remembered my favorite coffee." Then she shrugged. "Alright, let's go. But it's cold outside. Colt might get sick."

He wasn't about to let her back out now. "We'll bundle him really good and we'll take him some formula in case he gets hungry." He watched her face fall at those words, but Imani didn't say anything, and he figured she was still grappling with her inability to nurse. In time, he hoped she would accept she didn't have to be perfect to be a great Mom.

"We'll go after the morning rush," she said.

"Deal. It's a date."

SITTING NEXT TO him on the couch, Imani expelled a long breath. Nash sounded so excited about their excursion that she didn't have the heart to turn him down. She was pretty sure he recalled that visiting coffee houses had been one of their many dates as a couple. Coffee and cupcakes. They typically spent hours talking and people-watching in the coffee shop. Nash gave her an expectant look. "Remember, I'm waiting on you to tell me when you want to do the spa visit."

"Yes. I'll reach out to Nia and see if she wants to come with me." Imani pulled out her phone. After a couple of texts back and forth, she asked Nash, "How about the fifteenth?"

"That could work. I have a meeting with my family in the morning, but the rest of the afternoon is wide open."

"Are you sure?" Nash sounded confident but he had never been alone with Colt before. Imani didn't know how she felt about that.

"Yes, I'll be okay." He didn't come off as sure this time, but she decided to take him at his word.

"Okay, but I'll be calling to check on you guys."

Nash slapped his jeans with his hands. "Now that all that's settled, if you were serious about helping me, I have hours of recording and I could use an extra eye."

"Okay, let me get my laptop. Let's meet up in the kitchen." Imani scuttled into the bedroom, making sure to also grab the charger. She peeped in on Colt and he was still asleep. Putting on the Keurig, Imani made two cups of coffee, while Nash got them situated.

Then they watched reels and reels of recordings, even getting a few laughs in between. Who knew it could be fun watching silent videos, especially since they sped them up? It was even more hilarious when they made up possible conversations. But anything she did with Nash was fun, because it was Nash.

When she finally went to sleep that night, Nash Fortune filled her mind, her dreams. Imani thrashed about in bed, wanting and hoping he would join her. They couldn't have sex, but she craved the warmth of his hard body, how she used to snuggle against him and how he would draw her close to cuddle while they slept. Things a real couple did together that went beyond physical attraction. Things that bound one heart to another.

Pillow talk...

Playing footsies...

Intimacy.

But after the way things ended between them, Imani knew she couldn't put herself out there again. When she got the all clear, she would content herself with assuaging the physical need. Yes, she loved him, but she wouldn't become consumed with him. She would keep a small part of her heart in reserve. It was the only way she would be able to move on when their time here came to an end.

CHAPTER THIRTEEN

COLT REFUSED TO latch on. He scrunched his face and screamed before seeking… Seeking nourishment she didn't have. A bonding she couldn't provide.

Imani squeezed her eyes shut to keep from breaking into tears. When she had awakened that morning, her breasts had felt full and she'd taken that as a sign that her body was ready to continue doing what should be natural. Not to mention that the lactation specialist had called to ask how everything was going. When she conveyed her continued struggles with breastfeeding, the specialist had encouraged her not to give up, but also reassured her that she was doing the right thing by ensuring the baby got the proper nutrition through supplementing as needed.

Nevertheless, Imani had tried again. And again. Now, both her and her baby were frustrated. He stiffened, bunched his fists and wailed, his face red and puffy.

Ugh. Why had she gotten her hopes up?

After placing Colt into his bassinet, she stomped into the kitchen, his cries slashing at her heart. She sniffled while she prepared the formula, resisting the urge to bang and slam the cupboards. When the bottle was ready, Imani wiped the tears with the back of her hand and took a moment to gather herself before returning to feed her son. She didn't want him picking up on her distress.

As soon as she placed the bottle in his mouth, Colt began to gulp, swallowing hard. Poor thing was so hungry. It wasn't his fault his mother was...broken.

Ineffective.

Tears ran down her face. She consoled herself by repeating what Nash said, hoping to drown out the despondence. What was important was that Colt was getting what he needed. Hopefully, the more she repeated that, she would eventually be able to forgive herself.

Just as she finished burping the baby, there was a rap on the door.

Imani knew it wasn't Nash since he had a key, and it was only a little after 8:30 a.m. Tucking Colt close under her arm, she went to open the door. When she saw who stood there, she choked out, "How did you know?" Imani stepped aside to let her cousin inside. Nia had a gift in one hand and a take-out bag in the other. She placed the gift on the couch and the food on the coffee table. Imani's tummy rumbled. Whatever was inside smelled good. Imani scurried to put Colt down in his bassinet, then grabbed the baby monitor. Nia was right behind her.

Once her arms were free, Imani and Nia hugged and hugged, then hugged some more.

"You don't know how glad I am to see you, right now," Imani said once they had broken apart. Her cousin had brushed her hair in a bun and was dressed in a tapered pantsuit with patches of gold. "How was Paris?" she asked.

"Paris was dreamy and—" she patted her tummy "—I ate way too many beignets but I have no regrets."

Acutely aware of her disheveled state, Imani gathered her hair at her nape and used the scrunchie on her wrist to secure it. She was still dressed in her jammies but at least she had brushed her teeth.

Nia's eyes narrowed. "Have you been crying?"

"I..." No point in denying it. Nia wasn't going to accept anything less than the truth. "A little bit." Imani plopped onto the couch and her cousin joined her. Clasping her hands in her lap, Imani said, "My milk is drying up and I can't provide for my child. I have to give Colt formula instead."

Nia shook her head. "Is something wrong with formula? Isn't that still providing?"

"I guess, but..." Imani lifted her shoulders. "A part of me knows it doesn't make sense but I feel like I failed Colt. I wanted to be good at motherhood. Check off all the must-dos from all the baby books I've read. Plus, I own a business that caters to babies but I can't do the same for my son. I feel guilty."

"How can you even begin to equate the two? You're approaching this wrong," Nia said, drawing closer. "You beat so many other statistics. Did you know that Black women are the least likely to survive delivery? You, my dear, are a walking miracle. Colt's being here is a miracle." She waved a hand. "The rest is just gravy. You'll figure it out."

Imani's mouth dropped. "I did know that. But, you read up on all that?"

"Yes, girl. You know I believe in research. But research has its limitations. There's also functioning. People beat statistics every day. Don't forget that."

"See, that's why we make such great business partners and cousins." The women shared another brief hug. "It is just gravy. I just wish I could get rid of this wedge of guilt in my heart."

"It will ease. You have to accept what you cannot control. If I know you, I know you tried. But for whatever reason, your body refused to cooperate and now you have to refocus on the benefits of using formula." Nia counted off her fingers, "Flexibility. You can get more help. Both you and baby can get more sleep."

"Wow. You really have been reading up on motherhood." She gave Nia a pensive look. "Anything I need to know?"

Nia held up both hands. "No—no children in the horizon for me. You know after Derek I don't do long-term. I speed date. Get what I need and get out. The books were just a great airplane read and I wanted to be prepared to help because I thought you were going to be a single parent and I was ready to be your sidekick." She changed topics. "But your life has been a whirlwind of late. Almost marrying one man and now getting back with your baby's father."

Imani felt her face warm. "I couldn't marry Simon knowing

I wasn't in love with him especially when you and Mom and Grandma had bad vibes about his motivation."

"I'm so glad you didn't go through it because that would have been an absolute disaster. And being married to someone else would have been a major stumbling block in your and Nash's reunion." Nia's voice got dreamy. "You don't know how glad I am to hear the news. You both are my couple goals... Well, if I wanted a relationship."

"Nash and I aren't back together," Imani said stiffly.

Nia made a point of looking around the space. "Come again? Then why are you here? I know it's not because of financial reasons because the Porters make the Fortunes wealth seem like chump change. And you've always been Miss Independent, so I can't think of any reason you'd be here if it wasn't a matter of the heart."

"It *is* a matter of the heart. Colt's heart. Colt deserves to know both his parents. Nash and I agreed that I would stay here for a few months while we get acclimated with parenthood. We haven't discussed anything beyond that point." Imani gestured toward the food bag.

"Help yourself. I bought us some breakfast burritos," Nia said with a wave. "You forget you're talking to someone who knows you. We slept in the same bed together at many sleepovers. I know all your secrets and you know mine. Your being here is a matter of your heart. Not just Colt's. I could understand if you stayed here a few days to recover, but if this was anybody but Nash, you would be long gone."

"But I—"

Her cousin held up a hand, determined to say her piece. "Now, don't get me wrong. This property is gorgeous and I'm hankering for a tour of the ranch, but if not for this man, you would be back at home. Nash Fortune has your heart and you're wishing and hoping for more, but you don't want to admit it."

Her words slammed Imani in the gut. "Am I that obvious?"

"Only to me. And probably Auntie and Grandma." Nia grabbed one of the sandwiches and took a big bite.

"The *more* I'm hoping for is all physical, though." She exhaled. "My body remembers oh-too well. I'm looking forward to resuming certain extracurricular activities with Nash once I get the all clear." That's all she could own up to.

Nia raised an eyebrow. "I'm calling your bluff. It's not just your body. Keep telling yourself that, though, but this *ayaba* ain't buying it." She peered into the baby monitor. "Hey! The little guy is awake. Can I go get him?"

"Sure."

Nia was gone and back with him in mere seconds. "It's beautiful out. Do you feel like going somewhere?"

Imani shrunk into the chair. She had to go out tomorrow with the baby and that would be traumatic enough. She wanted to chill inside today. That's one less day she would have to worry about Colt's lack of a great immune system. "How about we try out the swing instead?" Imani took Colt from his bassinet and buckled him into the swing. Then she put it on the lowest setting. Soft music played.

"Now, let's have you open your gift," Nia said.

Nia picked up the small rectangular package and handed it to her. It was a onesie that said, My Favorite Cousin Gave Me This, which made Imani smile, especially since Nia also had a matching shirt for her. She showered and then dressed in the shirt and a pair of jeans while Nia changed Colt. Watching her adept cousin struggle to get the article of clothing over his head was worth recording, much to Nia's chagrin. But once they were both ready, Nia had a mini photo session with all three of them. Imani had been delighted to see Nia's shirt under her jacket read, Their Favorite Cousin.

She sent Nash a couple of the photos when they were finished. Nia was now settled into the couch and was watching reality TV.

What a cute way to start my day, he texted. I'm on my way over in a few.

Her heart jumped. Avoiding her cousin's keen eye, she texted back: Nia wants a tour of the ranch.

That can be arranged. I know the owners, LOL. XOXO.

Whoa. She hoped Nash didn't think she planned on going. Just her cousin. And she told him as much.

You sure? It could be fun for Colt.

Yep.

He sent the thumbs-up emoji, followed with: I'll ask Jade. Grateful that Nash hadn't insisted she go on the tour, she addressed Nia to let her cousin know about it.

"Oh, that's exciting!" Nia said, clapping her hands.

"His sister Jade will probably be the one taking you around the property," Imani replied. Before Nia could ask why she wasn't going, Imani brought up the perfect distraction. "You can catch me up on what's going on with the additions at Lulla-babies while we wait for Nash."

Her cousin's eyes flashed. "Did you get my emails?" she squealed. "I sent you over three potential designs."

"I glanced at them but I've been helping Nash with a project so I didn't study them too much." She hid a smile. Nia loved talking shop.

"Me and the designer butt heads a bit but I think you'll be happy with the plans. I've got them in my car. Be right back." Nia rushed outside to get her laptop and the printouts.

Colt seemed to be enjoying the swing, so she could pay attention to what her cousin wanted to share. She cleared the coffee table so Nia would have room for the blueprints. For the next twenty minutes, Nia went through the designs. Imani selected the second one that was spacious and had light decor and a warm color scheme.

"How did I know you would choose this?" Her cousin pumped her fists. "I've already ordered the supplies. By the time you're ready to come back to work, I think the expansion should be ready. I'll send you our publicity plans."

"I'm sure you can handle that without me." Imani rested a hand on Nia's arm. "I wanted to talk to you about something, actually."

Nia's enthusiasm waned. "What's going on?"

"I wanted to make you company head. I don't know yet if I want to come back to work full-time anytime soon."

"Is this about Nash? Don't think I didn't catch it when you said you were helping him with a project." Nia eyed her with suspicion. "You're getting all wrapped up in him again and I don't mind for the most part, unless it is interfering with our bottom line. And, to be clear, this feels like the bottom line."

"No, this is about me. How I'm feeling. I was actually thinking about selling you my shares to Lullababies." Nia gasped at her confession. "But Mom and Nash talked me out of it."

Nia's shoulders sagged. "Good, I'm glad because this is *both* of our dreams and I need you with me." She released a breath. "Then what is this about?"

"Since giving birth to Colt, my anxiety has been off-the-charts. I've never been so scared of everything in all my life. I've also never been more certain that I want to be there for every milestone of his development."

"So bring him to work. We own a baby business," Nia said. "If we can't accommodate real-life infants then we need to be doing something else."

"I just need...time." Her voice broke. "And I need you to be okay with my decision."

Nia hugged her close. "Alright, *ayaba*. Take all the time you need. I'm sorry if I overloaded you with all this shop talk."

"You didn't. It invigorated me," Imani said. "I just can't be involved one hundred percent in the day-to-day like before."

"Understood. Just promise me you'll talk to a professional if you get too overwhelmed."

Imani nodded. "I will."

CHAPTER FOURTEEN

IT WAS JUST after 10:00 a.m. the morning of the fourteenth when Nash drove past Longhorn Feed, a quiver of excitement in his stomach. It had been a two-hour production getting themselves and Colt ready, along with all the just-in-case paraphernalia packed in his trunk, but they were out of the house and heading to the Daily Grind.

Imani kept peering behind her to check on Colt. Nash bit the inside of his cheek to keep from telling her that their son was alright. The only other place she felt comfortable going to with him was the doctor's office. Nash then distracted her by pointing out the orange and browns of the leaves and the different kinds of trees, and they discussed a possible venture to the pumpkin farm.

He pulled into the only empty space in the lot before opening the passenger door for Imani. Tilting his head up toward the sun and spreading his arms, Nash inhaled, his lungs expanding. "What a beautiful fall day for an outing with a beautiful woman. This is my favorite time of year."

"Thank you. It's mine, too, actually." Imani had dressed in a long-sleeved purple dress and paired it with boots the same color. She gave a jerky nod, shuffling from one foot to the other. If he didn't move now, she might change her mind.

Nash opened the rear door to lift the carrier, smiling at his son, who looked at him with curious eyes. Imani had provided both Colt and Nash with matching checkered shirts that they had paired with dark blue jeans. "Hey, there, little fella." He had a preview of them spending Thanksgiving with his family and Christmas with hers, the three of them sporting coordinated outfits and found he liked that visual.

Imani grabbed the baby bag and stalled. "I don't know about this…"

"Imani, Colt has been around my entire family and yours. He'll be alright."

"But that's different. That's family. I don't know how I feel about Colt being exposed to a bunch of strangers. Not to mention how some people feel it's okay to be all up in a baby's face with their germs and hot breath." She gritted her teeth. "And they had better not use their dirty hands to squeeze his cheeks."

Oh, boy. Nash shifted the carrier to his other hand. "No one's going to do anything because we're here. And how are people we don't know going to get close to him unless we allow it?"

She snorted and visibly relaxed. "I know I sound ridiculous but I was reading up what to avoid when you take your newborn out in public places and you can't believe some of the stuff that goes on."

Oh, he could believe it. "Please stay off Google," Nash warned. "Yes, we need to be careful, but Colt needs to build up his immune system."

"I'd feel better if we came after he was past the two-month mark and had more of his immunization shots."

Nash opened the rear door and placed the carrier on the seat. Then he cupped Imani's cheeks. "Sweetheart, prepare yourself. He's going to eat paper, bugs and dirt. He's going to drink his bathwater, eat the pet's food, if we, er, either of us get one, and he's going to share his friend's lunches at school. And you know what? He will be just fine."

She wrinkled her nose. "How do you know all this?"

"Because I did it. My brothers and sisters did it, too, and we turned out just fine."

"Did you?"

He chuckled. "What I'm trying to say is that we can't keep

Colt in a bubble. He's going to fall and scrape his knee. He might even break his front tooth and need to have it capped at ten years old. But that is a long way off and whatever happens, we will deal with it, and we will survive. Now, can we go inside and enjoy our lattes?"

She gave a jerky nod before grabbing his arm. "Wait. Did all that happen to you?"

"No comment." Nash picked up the carrier and closed the rear passenger door. Colt appeared to be falling asleep. His little head was tucked all the way in his chest. Then they headed inside the coffee shop. He loved the bustle around him. Right now, there were a few patrons bunched in the corner, waiting on their orders.

He waved at the workers and trailed after Imani, who had chosen a table the farthest away from the door. He placed Colt's carrier on the end of the table near the wall, and Imani sat facing him. Once they were settled, Nash joined the queue to place their orders—the caramel macchiato for her and an Americano for himself. He added a couple of scones and an everything bagel with cream cheese that they could split, then stifled a yawn. They had stayed up for a good two hours the night before sorting through more video recordings, distracting themselves by cracking jokes. He only had a few more videos to go through but he was sure he'd find the perpetrator. The culprit had been smart, avoiding the cameras, but Nash was counting on that person getting cocky and messing up.

And the good news was that Colt had slept for five hours. Five amazingly long, perfect hours. Nash had made sure to give their son more formula that morning and Imani hadn't had any objections.

Small steps with glorious, giant differences.

Their orders came up and he made his way back to the table, scooting his chair next to her. He loved the feel of her legs and arms brushing against his. It was sweet, electric...and *torture*. While they enjoyed their meal, they talked about their upcoming appointments the next day.

"My meeting with my family starts at nine, but we should be finished by ten thirty at the latest."

Imani took a sip of her latte, licking her lips. "You're right. This is delicious."

Nash put down his Americano and leaned over to give those luscious lips a taste. "You're so right. It is."

Her cheeks reddened but she strove for normalcy, her voice breathy. "I have a checkup with my ob-gyn and then Nia and I will have lunch and then our spa appointment at one o'clock."

"Yes, the owners have you down for massages, manicures and pedicures."

"Are you sure you'll be okay with Colt on your own?"

"Yep." He drummed his fingers on the tabletop. *There she goes tugging on those lips again.* He had to get another taste. But the perfume she wore distracted him, so he nuzzled her ear before getting another sample. Ooh, it was just as good as before.

"Nash, we're attracting attention," she whispered, running a finger down his cheek, her chest heaving.

He turned his head to see an older gentleman frowning at them. The man sat near the entrance, holding the town paper in his hand, and he wasn't even trying to pretend not to stare. Nash didn't know if the older gentleman had a problem with them being an interracial couple or with their making out in public.

"Let's give him something to look at then." Nash had never had a problem with PDA, especially when it came to Imani. He wrapped an arm about her waist and kissed her like he hadn't had a drink in days. Oh, how he had missed this.

Forgetting about their audience, Nash explored her mouth thoroughly and she responded in kind with a low, throaty groan. It was only because Colt made a sound that they pulled apart. He was pleased to see they were now the only ones in the shop, the only other sounds the chatter of the workers and the grinding of the espresso machine. He placed a hand on Imani's thigh and gave it a squeeze. "I hope all goes well at the gynecologist's tomorrow." He waggled his eyebrows.

She slapped his hand and giggled. "It's only been two weeks and it should be a quick appointment. It'll be at least four more weeks before we can make love. Well, if we were, um, inter-

ested in that. Now, let's finish these delicious coffees before
Colt gets up."

"How about we go for a stroll on the ranch when we're done
here?" Nash suggested. "We can take a walk around the lake?"

"I'd like that," she said, lowering her lashes.

Nash couldn't hide his enthusiasm that they would be using
one of Colt's two strollers for the first time later that day. Sabrina had chosen a designer stroller and car seat that was "all
the rage" now because it was super-secure, lightweight and even
had a privacy drape. Nash liked that it had foam and side-im-
pact protection. Dahlia had urged him to get a jogging stroller
as well since she knew Imani was a runner. Nash had placed
that stroller in Imani's Jeep.

There was a light breeze that made the seventy-five-degree
weather feel even more glorious. Before they left for their walk,
Nash rushed into his house to get his hat and sunglasses. It was
in the mid-70s and with these mild temperatures, it was hard to
believe that Thanksgiving was so close. While he was at it, he
decided to retrieve his mail. It had been a couple of days since
he checked it. Among the usual junk mail, there was another
envelope sealed with an emblem, just like the wedding invitation he had received.

Curious, he slid his finger under the seal to open it. His eyebrows rose. There were instructions enclosed:

Please choose a quote or passage from a book or movie or
a loved one that captures how you feel about love and family. Maybe you'll even give a toast with it at the wedding...

After placing the card back into the envelope, Nash dropped
it next to the invite. This mystery bride and groom seemed confident that he would attend, and now, it appeared as if he they
were asking him to give a toast. He had to admit he was in-
trigued and he was already mulling over the request... Just in
case. As he walked back to the guesthouse, Nash recalled something his mother always recited to him and his siblings before
bed: *Good day, bad day, you are loved and love is everything.*
With a demanding father like Casper, Nash had clung to those

words like they were a lifeline. He wasn't too sure about love being everything, though.

Like he knew he loved Colt, but his devotion toward his son wasn't enough. He had to be a good father, a good provider, a good caretaker. And in that, Nash knew he was sorely lacking. Seeing Imani waiting for him, Nash gave her a wave and jogged to her side.

"Ready to go?" she asked.

He took the handlebars and slapped on his ball cap and sunglasses. "Let's do this." They trekked down to the lake, stopping by the edge of the water, taking in the serenity. He slipped an arm around Imani's shoulder, bringing her close to him. She snuggled her head on his chest. Nash peered over her shoulder to see Colt was still asleep. "He sure does sleep a lot."

"I know, but he won't be like that for long. Soon, we'll be running after him and wishing for these days." Imani chuckled. That comment gave the impression that she had permanent intentions of sticking around, which made Nash hopeful.

"I can't wait until Colt is old enough for me to take him fishing."

His cell buzzed. It was Ridge. He sounded flustered when Nash answered. "We have a problem. I've got Arlo here with me."

He put the phone on Speaker and they turned back toward the guesthouse. "What's going on?"

Arlo jumped in. "Someone messed with the cattle feed. We found ground up metal shavings in the silage chopper. One of the farmhands heard noises in the machinery and stopped to investigate. That's when he found the ground-up pieces."

Imani's eyes went wide. They sped back to his place.

Nash expelled a breath, his strides long. "Wow. I can't believe someone is intentionally trying to destroy our cattle." His body chilled at that realization. Imani pushed the stroller even faster then.

"I know. This could have caused serious internal damage to the cows if they had ingested it," Ridge said.

"Or, it could have killed them," Arlo muttered. "We lost a couple hundred acres of silage."

He whistled. "I... Wow. I can't even wrap my mind around this. How did they do it?"

"They tied metal around the corn stalks."

"But how could we have missed this?" Nash asked.

"I think they did it over time. This was obviously planned. The deputies are on their way back. Turns out this kind of mischief happened a few months ago on another ranch a few hours away. That was never solved, either, so they really want to get their hands on the recordings."

He dashed into the guesthouse, welcoming the blast of air. "I don't have much video footage left to go. I'll finish going through them since I don't think the deputies will be back until late. In the meantime, keep me posted." Nash ended the call.

Imani smoothed her dress with her hands. "I'll order lunch and we can finish going through the videos together." Without waiting for an answer, she said, "Let me go get my laptop."

We.

Together.

Those words were a balm to his heart, flaring hope and weaving an even stronger bond than he and Imani had shared before, a sense of belonging. Of family.

And he was there for it. All of it.

CHAPTER FIFTEEN

"It's about time you called to check out your nephew," she said. Sitting against the headboard, Imani smiled at the familiar face on her screen. "Even Dad beat you to it." Phillip had called for a few minutes to check on her, but she had been too exhausted to talk much.

Her eyes felt gritty from lack of sleep but she was too caffeinated and excited to fall asleep just yet. It was now 2:00 a.m. and Nash had laid down on the couch, tuckered out but relieved. They had found the perpetrator and he would be sharing that news with his family at their business meeting later that morning.

But since it was only 11:00 a.m. in Dubai, Imani had texted Jonathan a picture of Colt dressed in a two-piece sweater set that had a little fluffy lamb on the chest. With their living in different time zones, they communicated most of the time through text messages. But every now and again, Imani craved to hear her brother's voice.

"I know, but between you and Mom, I have tons of pictures to keep me up to speed." His eyes sparkled. She took in the familiar brown eyes, chiseled jaw and a perfect smile created by the top dentist in Texas. No one could tell he had been born with oversize front teeth, something Imani never made him forget.

Like a good sister, she had called him Chipmunk during his middle-school years.

"You actually caught me at a good time. I'm in between meetings." He glanced at his watch. "I've got about ten minutes before I have to go."

"My heart is happy to see your beautiful face," she said, angling her iPad so Jonathan could get a good view of Colt.

"Likewise. Oh, look at the baby. He's all bundled up," Jonathan said, in a higher pitch than his normal bass voice. She had swaddled him and rested him on a baby blanket on the other side of the king-size bed. Her son was awake, and looking her way. She rubbed his tummy. Colt gave a sweet reflexive grin, a tiny dimple in his right cheek on display. She couldn't wait until he started smiling for real in a few weeks.

Jonathan addressed her. "So what's this I hear about you selling Lullababies? Are you finally about to grant Grandpa his wish and take over the family business stateside? It would be good to partner with you. *Finally*. Like we planned."

Hearing his desire for them to join forces made her gut twist with nostalgia. Since they were eighteen months apart, they had been reared like twins, making them closer as siblings. But she knew her brother would support her decision.

"Um…one of the reasons why I was thinking about selling my portion of the business to Nia was because we're branching out to offer exclusive baby-shower experiences, which means more hours and more work. But there's no way I would put down a molehill and pick up a gargantuan mountain that's Porter Oil."

"Whoa. I always figured you would do both—keep your company and lead Porter Oil in the US. You can scout for the right staff to assist you as needed with both. Grandpa has been preparing you to lead Porter Oil from the moment you could walk and talk." Hmm… Grandpa must not have approached Jonathan yet about taking over in her stead. Imani decided not to mention it. She would leave that for her grandfather to do when he was ready.

"That was my intention…before Colt."

"Wow, sis. Becoming a parent seems like a huge paradigm shift."

"Yes, but it's one I find myself eager to do. I welcome the changes. I have a child to raise, and I don't want to be an absentee parent."

"Yeah... I wouldn't want to be that kind of parent, either."

"Both Nash and I had that in common—though our dad wasn't anything like his—but regardless, we want to be involved in Colt's life. I need to be there for each precious moment."

"Whew. Parenting sounds like it requires major sacrifices, which is why I don't plan on having any children," he scoffed.

Her eyebrows rose. "Not at all?"

"Nope."

"Be careful, bro. Life has a way of making you eat your words," she joked, thinking of how committed she had been to her business. A commitment now surpassed by the infant mere inches away from her.

"Not the life I have planned," he countered. Jonathan sounded so sure, Imani had to remind him of her experience.

"Neither Nash nor I knew when we broke up that we would be welcoming a baby six months later."

His brow furrowed and he cocked his head. "So what's up with all the me-and-Nash comments? Did I miss the memo? Are you two back together?"

"Well, I don't know exactly... I'd say we're co-parenting."

He arched an eyebrow. "And cohabitating?"

"I'm staying in the guesthouse," she said, her voice firm. "Nash stays here on the couch at times to help me with Colt." How could she define their current relationship status when she needed clarity herself? Yes, they had shared tender moments, touches and steamy kisses, but that was all physical. Imani knew she wouldn't take their attraction to mean more than that. She wouldn't make any assumptions. The last time she had, it had led to her and Nash's breakup.

"Ha! Okay, just be careful. I don't want this dude hurting you again," he said, his voice holding an edge.

"Stand down. Might I remind you that I'm the older sibling? I've got this. I don't interfere in your personal life, so you need to take your foot out of mine."

He exhaled and ran a hand across his beard. "Okay, sis. I'll leave it alone. *For now.* I know that Nash is good people but I'll never forget that he wasn't there throughout your entire pregnancy."

"Jonathan, for the umpteenth time, he didn't know I was expecting," she groaned.

"But he would have, if he hadn't run you off."

"Ugh." She ran a hand through her curls and drew in deep breaths. "It's pointless arguing with you." She appreciated her brother being her champion but she was more than capable of handling her own messy affairs.

"I agree," he teased. "Well, I've got to go but don't allow that man back in your bed until you are sure of his intentions." He disconnected before she could respond. Imani released a long plume of air. Typical Jonathan. Goodness, that man liked to have the last word.

Right as she ended the call, Imani noticed Nash lounging against the doorjamb. He had changed into a pair of pajamas that hung off his waist, but because he was shirtless, those abs were in full view. She swallowed. Was it her or was he looking extra ripped? Her insides ached to get a touch. Dragging her eyes upward, she noticed he had a self-satisfied smirk on his face. The man knew he was beyond fine.

He strutted into the room and came over to kiss her on the cheek. Tease. "I heard voices and came to investigate." His breath smelled minty and fresh, making Imani all too aware of the tuna-fish sandwich she had had earlier.

"I was talking to my brother," she said. "It's late morning there." She stood, pointing to the baby, and placed a finger over her lips.

"He's up?" Nash whispered, his eyes filled with delight. This man had better not start playing with the baby. Imani needed Colt to get used to sleeping at night.

With a nod, she gestured for Nash to keep an eye on their son and went to brush her teeth and take care of her nightly rituals. When she returned, he was alternating between playing with the baby's feet and rubbing his nose in Colt's tummy. The baby was bright-eyed, his little fists bunched, and watching his daddy. She wondered what Colt was thinking. Did newborns even have thoughts? She needed to look that up.

"Quit messing with him," she chided gently. "Unless you want to pull another all-nighter?"

Nash stopped immediately. "Does he need a diaper change?"

Imani hid a smile. He had become quite the expert. She could tell he was proud of that. "No, I just changed him and fed him. He should be good. The only thing left for him to do is get back to sleep."

Colt emitted a sigh before yawning. "Aww, somebody's ready for a nap," Nash said, picking him up and cuddling him against his chest. "Daddy will rock you to sleep." He began to hum some lullaby off-key, then whispered, "I love you." Imani's chest expanded at the sight. She reached for her iPad and snapped a picture. The scene was so sweet and authentic that her eyes misted.

That's something Colt would miss out on once they were back home in Cactus Grove. His father's touch. Imani pulled up her phone and typed *How important is a father's touch?* in the internet search bar. She read the first thing that popped up and it basically said that a father's touch was equally important as a mother's. Physical contact is a crucial part of a child's development between parents and their child.

Huh. Wasn't that something? As an adult, she craved Nash's touch, but she was ready to put on her proverbial big-girl boxers when the time came and let that go. But Colt was just a baby. He couldn't advocate or express for himself how the absence of his father affected him.

However, she could.

And so could Nash.

They both knew what that felt like and those feelings didn't disappear. They intensified. They dictated their actions even as grown-ups. Now, she had a father who was devoted to her when he was around, so there was that. But look at Nash. He had been petrified, was still petrified, with embracing fatherhood because of the kind of father he had had. Because he had lacked a father's touch.

She wiped away the impending tears. She couldn't have Colt feeling the same lack of affection. Not when she had the means to do otherwise. Maybe she could look at a place in town or something… She would figure it out. A light snore made her refocus on Nash and Colt.

They were both asleep. Another picture worth taking.

But if she settled nearby, it wouldn't be the last.

CHAPTER SIXTEEN

FROM WHERE HE stood on the veranda at the LC Club, which overlooked Lake Chatelaine, Nash could hear the water trickling and the birds chirping on this sunny mid-November morning, though it was a bit muggy for this time of year. But a beautiful day nevertheless for good news. Nash had arranged for a large spread of varied breakfast items, as well as fruit with an omelet stand.

He scanned each of the tables on the veranda where his family—his mom, Dahlia and Rawlston, Sabrina and Zane, Heath and Jade, Ridge and his mystery woman, Hope, as well as Arlo—had gathered for their strategic meeting. Everyone except Imani, whom he had advised to sleep in with Colt after their long night.

"Before we officially begin this meeting," Nash said, "I wanted you to know that after reviewing countless hours of footage, Imani and I found the perpetrator early this morning. I've handed over the footage and the police are arresting Roger Pitts as we speak."

Collective gasps could be heard around the veranda, followed by collective applause.

"We need a more rigorous application and screening process," Arlo called out. "We'll work on that.

"Agreed." Nash hated that it was someone he had employed

who did this but the deputies assured him that Roger had conned many other ranch owners as well. The man's next step would have been to approach Nash to "investigate" and pin the deed on someone else while pocketing a good chunk of money.

"Way to go, bro," Ridge said, coming over to slap him on the back. He was holding six-month-old Evie in the crook of his arm. "Tell Imani 'thank you' for us."

"I will, but why don't you tell her yourself? How about you and Hope come over later so we can catch up. I'm sure she and Hope would hit it off."

"Alright. I'll let Hope know and get back with you." Ridge looked so comfortable holding the little girl and everyone in the family could see he was crazy about his houseguest and baby Evie.

Nash slapped his forehead. "Wait. Let's plan for another day instead. I forgot that I'm on baby duty later so Imani can go to lunch and a spa appointment with her cousin."

"Okay, talk it over with her and I'll wait to hear from you." Just then Evie grabbed Ridge's nose. Nash and Ridge cracked up trying to free it.

"That's some grip," Nash joked.

"Yeah, there's nothing stronger or faster. You'll see."

Nash's stomach clenched. *Would he?* Imani had promised him four months. And, of that time, fourteen days had whipped by already.

"Hey, Nash, quit your lollygagging and get on with the rest of the meeting," Jade called out. "Some of us have places to go and people to see." She was the only of his sisters to have dark hair and hazel eyes.

"You just saying that because you want to get back to your petting zoo and the kids." He smirked. "You can hang with us bigger humans for a little bit."

She tossed a Danish toward him. Nash ducked and it landed somewhere over the fence. From his peripheral view, he saw one of the servers scamper to pick it up and gave them a wave. He would leave an even more generous tip.

"Quit it, you two," Wendy called out from the other end. "But I agree with Jade, let's get this meeting going. It's starting to get muggy out here. And we didn't even talk about Thanksgiving yet."

"It will be at your house," Sabrina announced. "We'll show up in time to eat. Planning over."

Dahlia snickered right along with the rest of the fam. Wendy rolled her eyes, but Nash knew his mother was secretly pleased. She enjoyed preparing and overseeing the family feast each year.

"I'll delegate who's bringing what in the group chat," Wendy said.

"Snap, snap," Jade said. Heath placed an index finger over her lips. Just like that, they only had eyes for each other. He reached in to give her a kiss.

"Ugh. Get a room," Arlo called out. He was the only person unattached at the moment—well, besides Mom—and he apparently intended to remain that way.

At his comment, the other couples began to smooch just to tease Arlo. Nash loved seeing his sisters really happy and in healthy relationships.

"I don't get why whenever you all get together, you're back to acting like children again," Wendy chided, fanning her face.

Of course, that made Nash think of Imani. He missed her. And he hadn't kissed her that morning. He planned to rectify that as soon as he got home. Clearing his throat, Nash asked everyone to pull up the plans he had emailed the night before on their devices.

"Our first order of business now that our ranch is no longer under attack is to discuss our plans for supplying local business and restaurants with our Black Angus cows. Since we aren't the only ranch in the area, I say we target five-star restaurants."

"Good idea. We can start with this very club," Ridge said.

"Yes, I say we prepare a proposal to pitch them in five months or so. We should have doubled our Angus cows by then. How does that sound?" Arlo asked.

"That will work." He tilted his head toward Jade. "How are your educational programs with the petting zoo going?"

"They are going well," his twin said, giving him a thumbs-up. "I'll email you an update."

"Fair enough." Nash swiped his iPad to his next bullet point.

"I was also thinking that one of the things we could do is breed racehorses. We certainly have enough land space for this. What do you think?" All heads turned to Dahlia since she used to be a Texas junior champion barrel racer as a teen. She'd also worked as a groom at the racetracks.

"While I think racehorses would be a good investment, breeding quarter horses is a much better choice, since they are versatile and trainable."

"That a great suggestion, Dahlia." Nash jotted some notes on his plan.

"Quarter horses?" Wendy asked.

"Yes, they are a mix of Arabian and mustang," Dahlia further explained. "You can't go wrong with that investment. I'll scout around and purchase our first set of horses."

"And I'll review what we have so far and prepare our budget and potential profit-and-loss," Sabrina added, ever the numbers woman. Of all the siblings, she'd inherited her father's money skills the most. And, as such, she took her role as ranch accountant very seriously. When they first moved, Nash had squabbled with her over the brand of paper clips to purchase at the GreatStore. *Paper clips.*

Sabrina then shared their projected earnings and expenses for the remainder of the year and they recorded potential future ventures. Nash decided to plug in a couple dates on their calendars for them to meet again.

Everyone agreed, although he could see their general vibe was "we have more money than we could ever spend in this lifetime or the next." But still, as the ranch foreman, he felt these meetings were important in establishing good working practices.

With the meeting adjourned, Nash hugged all the members of his family, which took some time. But he made it back to the guesthouse in time to help with Colt, so Imani could get dressed for her doctor's appointment and spa date with Nia. Nash used that time to fill her in on the meeting and also on Ridge's intention to visit. Imani told him to confirm for the following day. She told him she had washed the baby bottles for when Colt awakened.

Before she left, she asked once again if he was okay being on his own with Colt.

"I'll be alright."

"Okay, well, Wendy said to call or text if you need anything."

Ignoring his pounding heart, Nash repeated, "I'll be alright."

Imani lifted her index finger. "One more thing…" She fretted with her bottom lip. "I think I want to stay here in Chatelaine Hills indefinitely."

Wow. His heart sang. "I would love that."

"Yeah, I'm going to go house hunting in the upcoming weeks."

His stomach dropped. "Oh, I thought…" Nash ran his hands through his hair. "I mean, you could stay here…" Things between them were going well and he hoped in time Imani would love him again. That they could be a family unit.

She bit on her bottom lip "I don't know if that's a good idea, especially since we're not *together* together."

Nash stood and got into her space. "I'm not kissing anybody else." He snatched her close to him, appreciating her sharp intake of breath. Rocking his hips into hers, he slipped his hand under her shirt and mumbled in her ear. "I'm not trying to get close with anyone else."

"Me, either. We can be co-parents with benefits… No lasting commitments. No expectations," she breathed out, her hands going around his neck.

"If that's what you want." That was so not what he desired but he wasn't about to reject such an enticing offer. Knowing she was right next door had kept him awake for more hours than he could ever admit. The scent of jasmine teasing his nostrils, his hands found their way into those lustrous curls, and he kissed her neck.

She moaned and tilted her head back, her hands gripping his shoulders and that desirable mouth open. Waiting. Nash crushed his lips to hers, their tongues engaging in a hot tango. They heard a honk.

Nia had arrived. They broke apart, his mouth already hungering for more. Imani wobbled her way to the door. His chest puffed at her disorientation.

"Hurry back," he teased.

Once she was gone, Nate grew serious. He rubbed his chin. Oh, he would go along with this scheme of hers. For now. But he intended to turn the heat way up. For if things went according to *his* plan, at the end of the four months, Imani would be a permanent fixture in his bed...and in his life.

CHAPTER SEVENTEEN

"How was the tour yesterday?" Imani asked as soon as she strapped in her seat belt in Nia's Porsche. She struggled to sound normal and not like someone who had been kissed thoroughly mere minutes ago.

"Why are you all flushed?" Nia asked. "Were you and Nash sucking face in there?"

"Gosh, nothing gets by you. If you had any decency, you would pretend not to see."

"And miss out of the fun of seeing your cheeks red with embarrassment? No way." Her cousin put the car in gear. On the way to her doctor's appointment, Nia filled her in on the tour. "The grounds are spectacular and Jade is so passionate about her petting zoo. I had a lot of fun feeding the animals. But the horses were my favorite. Man, it's been a minute since I've gotten on the saddle, but I might have to before I leave for Cactus Grove tomorrow morning." She released a breath. "I was still tired and jet-lagged last night, but Jade said I could come back this evening. Mom is preparing a welcome-home luncheon for me even though I told her I was only gone for a couple of weeks, so I've got to hit the road by nine. You want to come with?"

"I'll pass this time," Imani said, missing Colt already. "I don't want to leave Nash too long with the baby. This is his first time watching him on his own and my first time leaving Colt and

I'm a bit nervous." She glanced at her watch. They had only been gone for five minutes. Good grief, she didn't know if was going to make it. "Maybe I should cancel the spa appointment. I feel like I'm abandoning my son." She slid a glance Nia's way. "Do you mind?"

Nia pursed her lips. "I mind for *your* sake. You need this more than you know. I understand your concern and I respect it, Imani, but you're using words like *abandoned* when Colt is with his father." She patted the steering wheel. "Nash will call for help if he needs it."

"I—I supposed you're right." She turned to look out the window, admiring the passing scenery. "By the way, I'm going to connect with a Realtor to look for something more permanent here in Chatelaine Hills."

Nia stomped on the brakes, then pulled over near the entrance of the ranch. "Girl, I can't keep up with you! You're giving me a mental whiplash. You want to *move* here? Won't that make things harder for you emotionally when Nash decides he's done with fatherhood?"

Imani winced. "First, Nash intends to be a full-time father. Second, I want Colt to have the benefits of both parents if that's possible. I was doing some research online and—"

Nia slumped. "Oh, spare me the research right now. I like living in the penthouse next door to you." She continued, "I recognize that I'm being extremely selfish right now when you're only doing what's best for you and Colt. And you don't need me throwing a tantrum. You need me in your corner rooting for you." She sighed. Imani opened her mouth but Nia was still caught up in her meltdown. Her cousin clasped her hands and looked up. "I just hope this man treats you right." Nia reached over and patted Imani's hand then exhaled. "Pretty soon, you'll both declare your undying love for each other and all will be well in your world again. Okay, good talk. Good talk." She put the Porsche in Drive and they continued on their way.

After a routine visit with the gynecologist, the women made their way over to the spa. On their way, Imani texted Nash to check on Colt. She had pulled up the app but Colt wasn't in his crib.

How is he?

He's fine. Nash sent a photo of Colt in his arms.

Her heart melted. I miss him. I'm having an extreme case of separation anxiety.

That's normal. Take a deep breath. Have fun.

I'll try.

Don't try. Do.

"Girl, put your phone away," Nia advised. "If it makes you feel better, Colt doesn't even remember you to miss you. He's a newborn. He won't have object permanence until about four months or so. How's that for a fun fact?"

"No, it doesn't make me feel better and there's nothing fun about that tidbit you just shared." She dropped her phone in her purse and clutched it close. "To use your words, spare me the research right now."

Nia chuckled. "Touché. Okay, I'll use a different approach. If you're planning to get intimate with Nash soon, it's a good idea to get your lawn mowed, and your trees trimmed. You don't want the man lost in a forest, if you get my drift."

"Ugh." She covered her face. "Can we talk about something else...please?" The ob-gyn had reported that she was healing nicely and had even declared her good for intercourse at the four-week mark instead of six. Plus, her abdomen had shrunk and Imani was nearly back to her prebaby weight.

"You know I've got no filter when I'm hanging with you," Nia said, unapologetic. "All throughout my day, whether I'm at work or traveling, I've got to have my friendly face on. I've got to watch the way I act, the way I speak, or people might see me as the proverbial angry Black woman. It's refreshing to not have to worry about any of that with you. I can just be me."

"I get it."

"I know you do. Add all that to being a woman in business where you have your every move questioned. It's *exhausting*."

Imani knew Nia had been frustrated with the designer coun-
teracting her ideas, but she hadn't seen how that impacted her.
"Do you want me to fire the contractor?" she asked. "He gets
paid to meet your asks, not to question your choices."

"No. I can handle him. I just don't want to operate on the of-
fensive all the time." She turned into the spa entrance. "That's
why I'm looking forward to this massage and being pampered.
Plus, I have this cute design I want when we get our mani-pedis.
I hope the technician has the skills to pull it off."

Imani vowed not to ruin Nia's good time. They gathered their
purses and headed inside.

"I'm getting a burnt orange color, and beige since Thanksgiving is coming up," Imani said, inhaling the scents of vanilla
and mint. Now that she was here, Imani found she was looking
forward to some girl time.

"That sounds cute."

They placed their belongings in lockers and changed into
the fluffiest robes she had ever worn. Then they headed to
get their massages. Nia had chosen the stone massage while
Imani had gone with aromatherapy. Midway through, her cousin
started groaning and moaning so much that Imani knew she
was blushing.

"Girl, will you quit with all that noise. You're getting a massage, not having sex."

"Ooh, this feels way better," Nia said, while the masseuse
kneaded her back muscles. "Not that I haven't gotten sex. I've
had plenty for your information. While I was in France, I met
this Swedish dude—"

Imani's head popped up. "Wait, *Swedish*? I thought you were
only all about the brothers." Her masseuse gently pressed her
shoulders, a cue for her to lie back down.

"Well, as you said, don't knock it 'til you try it." Nia giggled.
"And tried it I did. I must have sampled that about four or five
times and if I had to rate it, I'd give it five stars."

"You are a hot mess." Imani chuckled. "I'm glad you're getting back out there after Derek, even if you're—" she put up
air quotes "—just sampling." Derek had been Nia's first love

and he had hurt her cousin so bad that Imani wasn't sure that Nia would ever fully recover.

"Derek who?" Nia scoffed. "It's all about Magnus now."

Imani's mouth dropped. "Magnus? Really? That's his name?"

"Girl, blame his mama. I didn't do that."

"I forgot how much fun you are. I'm glad I did this."

The women shared a laugh. While they had their mani-pedis, they each had smoothies and even added a facial and waxing to their spa plan. When they walked out of the spa salon, Imani lifted her hands. "That was an amazing experience. I feel like a whole new woman."

"Great because I booked you several appointments for the next four months when I was leaving my tip."

The cousins engaged in small talk all the way back to the guesthouse. She noticed that Nash's Range Rover was missing. She pushed the door open to the guesthouse and was greeted with quiet. Where was he? Nia rushed into the bedrooms, calling out for Nash.

Imani's heart galloped like a racehorse. She dug into her purse and pulled out her phone but there was no message from him. She placed a hand over her mouth. "What if something happened to my baby?" Her knees buckled and her chest tightened. "Please. No. Not that. My baby. My baby." Her shoulders shook and her body trembled.

Nia rushed over to take her hand. "Nash would have called or texted if anything was wrong." Then she made her take long breaths. "He's okay. Colt is okay," she soothed.

At that moment, she heard a car door slam. Nia helped her stand. The lock turned and Nash entered, holding Colt in his carrier. "Oh, good. You're back. How was your visit?" He gave them a wary glance.

"We had…a great time," Nia said, trailing off, giving Imani's arm a quick squeeze.

Imani blinked rapidly. How dare he sound so calm when he had disappeared without telling her his whereabouts! Anger pulsed through her veins. "Where were you?" she demanded.

Nash's eyes widened. "Twenty minutes after you left, I started feeling nervous so I took Colt to my mother's house."

Wow. He hadn't lasted past twenty minutes on his own. "On my drive back, Colt became fussy and I figured a longer ride would help him fall asleep and it worked."

"That was a great idea," Nia said, looking between them. It was obvious her cousin was trying to signal at her to remain calm, but forget that. She was furious and he was going to know it.

Imani bunched her fists. "So you left the house with my child without leaving a note? Or texting me?"

"*Your* child?" he asked, his voice like steel.

"Yes. My son."

Nash placed Colt on the couch. She could see the fury emanating off him in waves, but she wasn't about to apologize. Nia picked up Colt and whispered to Nash, "She's just worried," then scampered into the nursery with the baby.

Nash faced her, eyes flashing. "Don't you ever say something like that to me again. My name is on his birth certificate right next to yours. I would never put our son in harm's way." Imani opened her mouth to snap back, but he spoke first. "Think long and hard before you say something you'll regret. You're spiraling right now because you're in mama-bear mode, but I'm going to need you to bring it down. Way down."

They faced off. Her temper was at a whirlwind but her breathing normalized and rational thought returned.

Whoa. He was right.

But shoot, so was she. "I apologize. I went too far just now. I panicked when I didn't know where Colt was." Imani massaged her temples. "However, in the future, it would be extremely helpful if you communicated when you're leaving with Colt. It helps with my anxiety. I'm just afraid of something happening to him."

"That's fair. I'm sorry I didn't think to leave a note. That's a good idea. I promise to do that next time." Nash came over and pulled her into him. She molded her body into his. "I've never seen you lose your temper before, and I don't think I want to see that anytime soon."

Imani melted into him, welcoming his strength and then pulled out of his arms. Reluctantly. "I'm usually more even-keeled. Frankly, I'm surprised at my reaction." She dipped her head to her chest. "Now I feel silly for overreacting but I genuinely felt like something catastrophic had happened to Colt. It's hard to explain the sensation."

"Don't." Nash gathered her close once more, then kissed the top of her head before trailing kisses across her neck. "Hmm... You smell amazing...and your skin feels like butter." Imani smirked. It was obvious he was ready to forget the past few minutes, but she couldn't. Nash was being very understanding but this freak-out was a wake-up call. Imani needed balance in navigating the new feelings that came with motherhood. She was going to schedule an appointment with a therapist tomorrow morning. Feeling better already now that she'd made that decision, she lowered her hands to cup his firm butt.

"I guess that means you all have settled your dispute," Nia said wryly.

Nash and Imani sprang apart.

"Oh, snap, I forgot that you were here," Imani said. "Did you want to stay for dinner?"

"Naw. I'm not about to be a third wheel," Nia joked. "Actually, Jade texted that she was ready to meet up at the stables. We're going to get dinner after that." She walked over with her arms spread wide. "So let's say our goodbyes from tonight." She gave Nash a hug and he gave her a friendly salute before going into the nursery. Then Nia strutted over to Imani. The women embraced and rocked and hugged some more.

"Thanks for today," Imani said, rubbing her cousin's back. "I needed it."

"You are so welcome."

Imani's took her cousin's hand and whispered, "I'm going to make an appointment to talk to someone."

Her cousin rested her forehead against hers. "I'm so glad to hear that."

Would you know her cousin refused to leave, but stood there with her arms folded until Imani had scheduled her first session? Nia just warmed her heart.

CHAPTER EIGHTEEN

IT WASN'T POSTPARTUM DEPRESSION. At least he didn't think so.

Not that he was any kind of expert. Nash sat outside on his porch doing research while Imani and Colt went for a walk. Imani's rage the night before had stemmed from genuine fear and all he wanted to do was comfort her. Help her. Based on her symptoms, she appeared to be struggling with maternal separation anxiety.

Common for new mothers.

That was a relief to know. He massaged the back of his neck and exhaled. He just needed to be patient and encourage her to verbalize her feelings. Then he would do his best to put her at ease.

Feeling satisfied that he had a game plan, Nash texted Imani to let her know he was going by the ranch for a bit. They had purchased a new feeder and he wanted to see for himself that everything was working as it should.

She texted back: I ordered salmon, whipped potatoes and salad from the LC Club for dinner. Are your brother and Hope still coming by tonight?

Okay. Yes.

Can you pick up the order on your way back?

Happy to.

When he arrived at the ranch, he was pleased to see his mother hanging about. She had stopped by to post a catered Thanksgiving menu for the ranch hands and their families. They planned to set up tents, tables and chairs and decorate the day before. Then the set-up crew would break everything down the next day. This was something Wendy intended to do every year as a means of appreciation for their workers right along with giving them a bonus. That was in addition to the bonus the workers would receive during the Christmas holiday season.

"This is such a thoughtful idea, Mom," Nash said, taking the signs and taping them in the break room.

"Thank you, son. Luckily, I was able to find caterers willing to come out and set up on Thursday afternoon."

"I think the ranch hands will be gratified by your efforts." Nash rubbed his chin. "I wonder if we can get a little band out, make it a bigger celebration."

Wendy's eyes lit up. "I like the idea of having a band. I'll check on that. If I can't arrange it this year, then definitely next year."

"Well, I can contribute as well. Or, we can check with Sabrina to see if we can cover this using our petty funds?"

Wendy waved a hand. "I'll just take care of it since this is last-minute planning. We can consult with Sabrina to set it up that way next year."

"Did you need me to do anything for our own Thanksgiving meal?"

"I think between me and the girls, we're good. But if you want to bring some pies or something that would be great." Wendy cocked her head. "How's my grandbaby doing?"

Nash's chest puffed. "He's getting bigger every day."

"Yes, he'll be walking around before you know it." Her eyes had a faraway look in them, like she was reminiscing.

"I can't imagine what it must have been like running after six of us."

She smiled. "Oh, it was wild and crazy and fun all at the same time. The years go by in a flash." Then she pinned him with a gaze. "Treasure every moment. Because years down the road, that's all you've have—fond memories and photos."

"I hope my son will have fond memories of me," he said, then snorted. "I still have this lingering fear that I'm not doing a good enough job with him and for him."

"You're here and you're loving Colt. That's what matters."

Nash's heart squeezed. He had been so busy with Colt that he hadn't visited with his mother in a while. Wendy shook her head like she was shaking off the memories and planted a kiss on his cheek. "I've got to run, but tell Imani I'll be stopping by soon. Thanks for the pictures and videos that you've sent me. They have been such a delight." Then with a two-finger wave, she said, "We'll catch up soon."

Nash walked his mother out. Was it him or did she have an added dose of enthusiasm and energy these days? She seemed to have an extra bounce in her step. Maybe it was because she was a grandmother now. It appeared that the move out here to Chatelaine had been a good choice. His heart lifted. His mother had spent so many years unhappy that he was glad to see her excited about this Thanksgiving feast. There was nothing his mother enjoyed more than having all her children around her.

After checking on the feeder, Nash was pleased to see all was as it should be. He also took the time to visit with Stanley, who had returned to the stables from his leave that morning.

"I'm right as rain," Stanley said, while giving Onyx a brush-down. "Truth be told, I could have come back to work the next day because I was worried about not getting a paycheck. But Miss Dahlia told me to take the full two weeks off to recuperate. With pay." He touched his chest. "I'm so glad to be working for such a caring family."

"We are happy to have you," Nash said, giving him a pat on the back. "How are Penelope and Valentina getting along?"

"You remembered their names?" Stanley eyes were wide as saucers. "They are both doing good. Penelope is about ready to crawl."

"Good to hear. Give them my regards."

"Yes, sir. I'll let them know you asked about them." Stanley cocked his head toward the stables. "Midnight and Leviathan could use a stretch. Those horses are such beauties. Miss Jade and her guest took them out yesterday."

He must be talking about Imani's cousin, Nia. Nash smiled. "Go ahead and take them out, but be careful. I'll be back for a longer visit soon. Don't stay too late." Hopefully, Imani would be down to go horseback riding with him. He looked at his watch. She would probably be done with her walk, and he wanted to be there when she returned.

As he was about to climb into his vehicle, a car pulled up and parked in the visitor parking. It looked to be a newer-model silver station wagon. Nash peeped at the Audi logo. A middle-aged couple exited the wagon and gave him a friendly wave. They were both dressed in blue jeans and tweed shirts although he had on a cowboy hat.

"I'm sorry but if you're here for the tour, our last one has already ended."

"We would love that. On the drive up, we were talking about how your property is beautiful and well-tended," the man said, splaying his hands. Nash surveyed the fall foliage, the deep oranges and yellows and browns, adding to the picturesque view.

"I saw your face on the billboard in town," the woman added. "That picture doesn't do you justice."

"Thank you, I guess."

"Do you get a lot of visitors?"

That was an odd question. Nash raised an eye brow. "It depends on the day. We have a vast property and a lot going on throughout the day."

The couple looked at each other before the man stepped forward. He shoved his vein-filled hands into his pockets. "I wonder if you know if a woman and a baby might have stopped here a few months ago. She has long auburn hair and blue eyes."

"Her baby looks just like her. Can't be more than about six months old or so," the woman said, wiping her brow. Her hand shook a little.

Their question seemed innocent enough, but their tone held an undercurrent of desperation that didn't sit well with him. "Sorry, I don't think I've seen anyone fitting that description.

And even if that were the case, we get so many visitors, it would be hard for me to comment."

Both faces dropped. The older gentleman used the tip of his boot to scuff the packed earth, then asked, "You sure about that?"

A knot formed in his stomach, but Nash shrugged. "I don't recall."

The couple thanked him and drove off. Nash watched their departure until they were out of sight. He exhaled. The truth was, he *did* know someone who fit that description. A mystery woman in a barn with a baby bearing a strong resemblance. He texted Ridge.

Have I got something to tell you!

AFTER THEY HAD eaten and Imani opened the gift from Hope— a pair of infant rattle socks—the two couples settled in the living-room area. Hope and Imani had hit it off upon meeting, bonding over motherhood, with Hope sharing more of what to expect. He had overhead Imani whispering to the other woman about her inability to breastfeed. Nash hadn't heard Hope's response, but whatever she said boosted Imani's spirits. Evie and Colt were now asleep in the nursery, with Colt in the bassinet and Evie in the crib.

"So what's going on?" Ridge asked, seated next to Hope. Nash joined Imani on the love seat.

"An older couple stopped by the ranch earlier this evening." Nash jutted his chin toward Hope. "I think they were asking about you."

Hope stilled. "Me?" She glanced at Ridge, twisting her fingers in her lap. Ever since Nash's brother had found her unconscious with her baby in his barn, Hope had been on a quest to learn her true identity.

"What did they say?" Ridge asked, immediately on alert.

"They asked if I've seen a woman with long auburn hair, blue eyes and a baby who looks just like her."

"That could be anyone," Ridge said, his eyes darting between Hope and Nash. "Plus, they didn't mention Hope and Evie's matching birthmarks."

"That's right... But if it weren't for the fact that something seemed off about them, I would have told them about Hope."

"But what if they aren't? What if they hold the answers to my identity?" Hope asked, running her hands through her hair. "What did they look like?"

"They were both average height and looked to be in their late fifties, early sixties. The gentleman was clean-shaven with pepper-gray hair and the woman, whom I assume is his wife, had blond, shoulder-length hair. They were both neatly dressed and drove a station wagon."

Hope closed her eyes and rubbed her temples. "I have flashes of memory with a middle-aged couple. I can see them holding out their arms, and at first, they seem kind, but then their faces and voices turn angry..." She shook her head and slumped. "That's all I've got."

"It's okay," Ridge soothed, reaching to take her hand.

Goose bumps popped up on Nash's arms. He had a sinking feeling that the couple he had met earlier was the same couple from Hope's flashes. Nash wished he had thought to ask them their names. However, if he had done that, the couple would have persisted and he couldn't be sure they meant Hope well.

"Do you think it could be your parents or the paternal grandparents?" Imani asked, her tone empathetic. She moved to Hope's side.

Hope lifted her shoulders, then sighed. "I have no idea."

"I could see if the cameras picked up on their license plates and we could investigate," Nash offered.

"Ooh, that's a good idea!" Imani chimed in, scooting to the edge of the love seat.

But Ridge lifted a hand and shook his head. "I think the best recourse is for us to wait. We need Hope's memories to return before we do anything."

Nash could see how much Ridge cared for Hope and he wondered if his younger brother was afraid of Hope finding out the truth about who she was, then possibly leaving him. After all, for all they knew, Hope could be a married woman.

Jumping to his feet, Nash went to get some water. From where he stood in the kitchen, he studied Imani chatting with Hope and his brother looking at Hope with such devotion. Such certainty. His gut twisted.

Months ago, he had let Imani go without too much of a fight because she wanted to be a parent. Meanwhile, he was pretty sure that Ridge would trade places with him faster than he could snap his fingers. His brother had taken to fatherhood like a horse to carrots and he would love to have a real relationship with Hope.

His brother's plight strengthened Nash's resolve. He needed to up his game. Be the best father he could for Colt. Imani's eyes met his. She gave him a shy smile. And he needed to hold on to Imani with all his might.

Evie cried out. "I'll go check on her," Hope said, getting to her feet. Ridge was right behind her.

Returning to where Imani sat, Nash held out a hand and pulled her to stand. He gave her a quick, passionate kiss. Tenderly, he ran his hands through her curls, before touching her cheek.

Her eyes narrowed. "Are you alright?"

"Never better. I'd love to take you out on a real date."

"A *real* date?" Imani repeated, her brown eyes warm and inviting.

Gosh, she was beautiful. She took his breath away. Nash nodded. "Yes, and before you ask, I can think of the perfect pint-size chaperone."

CHAPTER NINETEEN

THE NEXT EVENING around six thirty, Imani left the guesthouse to meet Nash on his boat down by the water, or more accurately, on his cabin cruiser. He had already gone ahead with Colt to get everything prepared. She had strict orders to wait twenty-five minutes before venturing down to the dock.

Imani fretted with her hair, which she had pinned in a messy bun, while she made her way down the path. Nash had said to dress casually so she had chosen a cardigan set and white jeans. She walked down the ramp and gave him a wave.

Colt was in his swing under the awning. Imani hadn't noticed Nash leaving the house with it but that was a good idea.

As he helped her onto his cruiser, she asked, "Are we going out on the water?"

"No, we're on this vessel strictly for the ambience." Nash gave her a wide smile and tipped his cowboy hat. He had on a sweater and a pair of white shorts along with loafers.

She placed a hand on her chest, unable to hide her relief. It was a warm night out and Colt was dressed in a sweater set, under his blanket, but she feared him catching a draft. Imani didn't want to deal with a sick infant anytime soon. She would say not at all, but she knew that wish would be unrealistic.

Underneath the awning was a built-in table and seating. On the table, Nash had laid out what appeared to be sandwiches, fruit and—she sniffed—chicken noodle soup, if her nose was to be believed. There was sparkling cider cooling in an ice bucket with three wineglasses she assumed were plastic. The good thing was everything was disposable, so there wouldn't be any lengthy cleanup needed. Next to Colt's swing, there were three sets of canvases on easels and paint supplies.

"What's this about?" She snorted. "I know Colt isn't about to pick up that paintbrush."

"You'll see." He winked at her before extending a hand toward the food. "Are you ready to eat?"

"For sure." She rubbed her tummy.

Ever the perfect gentleman, he took her hand in his and gestured for her to take a seat. Then he slipped in beside her. Everywhere their bodies touched, she felt electric impulses. Her body hummed because of their proximity. While they ate, Nash leaned over to kiss her cheeks and played with the tendrils of her hair at the base of her neck.

"Hello?" a voice called out just as they finished eating.

"We're over here." Nash popped up to greet the newest arrival. Imani tossed their refuse in the trash.

A young woman dressed in all black appeared, her apron covered with pictures of paintbrushes. Nash made quick introductions. "Tonight, we are going to sip sparkling cider and paint, following Alana's directions."

Alana sported an afro with supersize earrings that swayed with the tiniest of movement. "We are going to paint the sunset over the water. I will guide you each step of the way."

Imani's eyebrows rose and she addressed Nash. "I'm impressed."

He bowed. "I aim to please."

Alana began with the blue paint and by starting the outline in the middle of the canvas. Imani and Nash did the same. The gentle sway of the boat and the dipping sun became the perfect backdrop for their scene. With each stroke of the brush, step by step, they created similar images, then they each added personalized details with Alana's guidance. Nash also used every free opportunity to touch her, kiss her, play with her hair. Not to be outdone, Imani's hands had been busy, too. Their playfulness left them with paint in their hair, on their noses and their clothes.

Colt slept the entire ninety minutes of their date. Talk about perfect planning. That and the fact that he drank close to two ounces of formula.

Once their painting session was over and Alana had departed, Imani wrapped the baby about her and took the small bag of trash, while Nash took the swing and the paintings.

"This was a marvelous date," she breathed out, as they traipsed back to the guesthouse. "From start to end, I can't tell when I've had a more enjoyable time. Thank you, Nash."

"You're welcome." His chest puffed. "I have Google to thank, though. I believe my search words were *dates for parents with a newborn*."

"Oh?" Her brow arched. "What else did they suggest?"

"Walks, board games, visiting a farm, the beach…stuff like that."

"I like that." She smiled. Her heart warmed at his thoughtfulness. And she appreciated that he had researched things they could do with the baby around. They arrived outside the guesthouse and the sensor lights came on. After putting down the swing, Nash opened the door.

She tilted her head back and took in the glorious feel of the crisp fall wind in her hair and the back of her neck. "What a beautiful night."

"What a beautiful woman," he murmured. His eyes glinted in the moonlight. She shivered and it had nothing to do with the temperature and everything to do with the man slaking his eyes down the length of her body.

"Soon," she whispered.

He pinned her with his fiery gaze. "I'll hold you to that."

Stepping past the threshold ahead of him, she could feel his eyes on her butt. Once inside, Imani handed Nash the trash and rested Colt in his bassinet in her bedroom. He didn't even stir. It was a little after 8:00 p.m. She ran her hands through her hair. Ugh. She needed to throw these clothes in the wash and take a long, hot shower.

She said as much to Nash when he entered the room. There

was a streak of blue paint across his cheekbone. "Why don't I join you?" he suggested.

"The shower can fit the both of us but it will be a tight squeeze."

"That'll work for me," he said, his voice husky.

"Alright. Just don't drop the soap," she teased.

He smirked. "Oh, please do…"

Imani slipped her shirt off her head and wiggled out of her jeans with Nash eyeing her every move. She tossed them in the hamper and sauntered into the bathroom, making sure to grab the baby monitor. The bathroom was done in white with chrome trimmings. Meanwhile the floor, counter space and tiles were all marble. Though each had variations of the design. The mats and towels were a deep chocolate-brown. Turning on the spigot of the walk-in shower, she tested the water. Ahh. Nice and hot. She walked under the spray, running her hands through her hair. Nash entered behind her, his gaze lustful and wanting.

It had been a minute since she had seen him naked. She took her time reacquainting herself with those wide shoulders, that broad chest, his taut, tight stomach muscles and his engorged member. *Oh, my.* The space in the shower suddenly felt smaller. She was so aware of this man—he sucked up all her space.

Nash was also checking her out.

"I have stretch marks," she pointed out, when she saw his eyes on her tummy.

"They humble me," he said quietly, reaching out to touch her abdomen. "Thank you for my son."

Imani busied herself with lathering her body before pumping a handful of shampoo to massage her hair. Nash did the same. Then he washed her back and she washed his, their bodies touching this way and that. A bump here, a graze there, made for a sensual experience that left them both wanting, hungry for more than food.

They used their lips and hands to provide pleasure, stoking the fire within her that he did his best to quench. Imani took care of Nash, though. His satisfying grunt signaled the end of their shower.

Engulfed in a warm, fluffy towel, she dried her hair. "Thank you for an amazing time from beginning to end," she murmured, her heart light.

"The night's not done yet," Nash said, snuggling close to her, his towel wrapped around his waist.

Colt's wail came through the monitor. On cue. "You're right." She laughed. "It sure isn't."

He gave her a quick kiss and squeezed her shoulder. "Finish up here. I'll go get him." Watching his departure, Imani concluded that his confident swagger as he left to care for their son was by far the sexiest thing she had seen all night.

CHAPTER TWENTY

COLT HAD GAINED two pounds and he had even grown an inch. Nash whooped when he heard that. Imani practically skipped out of the doctor's office.

She was winning at motherhood.

And she was also winning at rebuilding her relationship with Nash.

The past few days with Nash had been nothing short of marvelous. He had been a model parent...and partner. Their dates consisted of walks around the lake with long talks, while eating corn dogs or ice cream. All of which continued to draw her closer to him. Her heart rate accelerated when she was in his presence and Imani was enjoying the rush.

After waving off Nash, who had started his morning very early at the ranch, she buckled Colt into his car seat and began her trek back to the guesthouse.

Imani also credited her sessions with a mental-health professional who specialized in working with new mothers for her renewed optimism. Her therapist had suggested she purchase a journal, and who knew? Journaling helped.

That's why this evening, she was surprising Nash by taking him up on his offer of visiting his beloved horses. She couldn't ride until she was about six to eight weeks postpartum, but she figured this was the next best thing. Besides, she knew this would make Nash happy. A lot of his talks with her revolved around ranching.

But she was going without Colt.

Her stomach knotted a wee bit at that, but she was determined to push through. Her mother and grandmother were back at the resort, and would be coming over to babysit. Abena had been overjoyed when she heard her intentions.

Imani had also extended an invite to Wendy, who was more than happy to reconnect with Imani's family and see her grandson.

She had used a personal stylist, and settled on a faux suede fringe jacket, a button-down top, denim leggings and Italian cowgirl boots for this excursion. As soon as her mother and grandma arrived, Imani rushed to get dressed. She completed her look with a little bronzer, eyeliner and ruby-red lipstick. Nash was due to arrive home in about ten minutes.

"You look stunning," Abena said, eyeing her from head to toe.

"Yes, have you been exercising?" Zuri asked.

"Nash and I have been walking the expanse of the lake, but it's only been a few days," Imani said. "I think Colt's going to love the outdoors. Just like his daddy."

Her mom arched an eyebrow. "So I take it Nash has finally embraced fatherhood?"

"I think so. Although, I feel like he is still wary of staying with Colt on his own for an extended period of time. The day Nia and I went to the spa, he told me he went by his mother's house not too long after I left." She didn't mention her panic attack when she discovered Nash wasn't there. "I don't think Nash trusts himself around a newborn so I suspect he just wanted someone else around—just in case."

"I get that, but a part of bonding is spending that one-on-one quality time with your child," Zuri chimed in. "I did that with Phillip and I made Hammond do the same." She chuckled. "His first time alone with Phillip was pretty memorable."

"What happened?" Abena asked, her face alight with fascination.

Imani smiled. She loved when her grandma shared stories of her dad. "Yes, do tell. Inquiring minds want to know!"

Zuri's skin tinted crimson. "Well, when Hammond fell asleep, Phillip had a bowel movement in his crib. I don't know what Hammond fed him. I still don't know. I'll be delicate and say, we spent the next three hours cleaning the baby, the blanket and the crib." Her shoulders shook with mirth.

Imani's eyes went wide before she and Abena dissolved into laughter.

"Whoa. That was hilarious. I'll never look at Dad the same." She glanced at her mother. "Do you have stories like that of me?"

"No, dear. You were my little angel," Abena said, then shook her head. "Jonathan, however, was a different story. I couldn't take my eyes off him. He was a climber. Whenever he went missing, I would always have to look up because that little stinker would be in the cupboard, at the top of the curtains. Problem was, he didn't know how to come back down."

"Yes, that boy was a handful. I'll never forget when your father called to tell me they caught Jonathan sitting in the fish tank grabbing after them," Zuri added. "The only reason they found him is because you were standing there crying and begging him not to kill the fishies."

Another round of laughter followed.

Her grandmother scrunched her nose. "I'm pretty sure I have a picture of it somewhere. I've got to search my albums."

"I'd love to see those." Imani dabbed at her eyes. "I look forward to Nash and I having stories like these to reminisce of Colt one day."

"Well, they weren't funny at the time," Abena said. "But they do make for heartwarming memories."

Imani ran her index finger down the bridge of her nose. "Maybe all us women need to go out to give Nash alone time with Colt. It might boost his confidence once he gets through it."

"How about tomorrow morning?" Zuri suggested. "We can go for an early morning walk and then head over to the LC Club."

Abena's eyes flashed. "I like that idea."

Imani placed a hand across her tummy. She hadn't expected

to put their plan in action the very next day. But there wasn't any reason not to...

The lock clicked.

"Let us know before we leave," Abena whispered. "I'm in."

Wendy came in, followed by Nash. They must have arrived at the same time. "Look who's paying us a visit," Nash said.

A round of greetings and hugs ensued. Nash's eyes slaked her body with barely banked passion, flaring her own. "You look nice." He emphasized the word *nice* in a way that made Imani blush. He had on a cowboy hat, and a checkered shirt tucked into a pair of jeans that appeared to be tailor-made. "Going somewhere?"

She lowered her lashes. "Yes, I'm going out to dinner with you," she said breathily. "It's my turn to plan a special date."

He leaned in. "Out, as in leaving this house?"

"Mmm-hmm." She nodded as she smiled, even as her heart rate escalated. "Our mothers agreed to babysit."

His lips widened into a slow, sexy smile. "Where do you have planned?"

Those cognac eyes of his made her tummy dance like a jitterbug. "I figure I could meet Onyx or Leviathan today, and then we grab a quick bite afterward at the diner."

"Really? You want to go to the ranch?" He gave her a quick hug. "I didn't think you could ride again yet."

"I can't, but I can watch you do your thing so I can scratch *date with a hot rancher* off my bucket list," she teased, giving him a once-over and fanning herself.

Her grandmother snickered. "Watch yourself, now. That's how you ended up pregnant the first time."

"Yeah, you both made a cute baby together," her mother said. "But still..."

"Ah, you two need to get going," Wendy chimed in. "The diner won't be open much longer. Small town." She shooed them toward the door.

"Alright. We'd better go," Imani agreed, before rushing into the nursery to give Colt a kiss on his forehead. "Mommy will be back soon," she whispered. After slinging her backpack over her shoulder, she joined hands with Nash before she stepped outside. As soon as the door closed behind them, Nash whipped her around and kissed her with urgency. Imani moaned, grabbing the back of his head as their tongues engaged in a tug-of-war.

"I've been thinking about doing this all day," Nash said, his chest heaving.

"Less thinking and more doing." Imani brought him in for another searing kiss.

Needless to say, during the short car ride to the ranch, raw tension crackled between them along with...frustration. Oh, how she wished she could cool down this heat with some no-holds-barred lovemaking.

Whew. November 28th couldn't come fast enough. Thanksgiving. And oh, how she planned on giving thanks that day.

SHE COULD FEEL Nash's eyes on her rear. Like lasers. Swinging her hips, Imani decided to give him a show, smiling with satisfaction at his groan. She entered the stables first. Since the workers were finished for the day, the two of them were the sole human occupants inside.

Perfect.

It was time to check off another bucket-list item.

Nash took her to the first stall, standing on the left. Holding her hand, he introduced her to Onyx first, then Leviathan and Midnight. Imani marveled at the strength and beauty of each horse. All three horses were gorgeous black thoroughbreds. Nash was so patient, stroking their manes and talking to them, and it was evident how much he loved these animals. They followed him with their eyes. The affection between man and beast was mutual. Her heart warmed.

Next, Nash got on the saddle and showed off some of his riding skills with Midnight. Which meant she had to take her camera out because, talk about hot. He sure looked good with that cowboy hat.

"I'm so glad you're doing what you love," she said, linking her arm through his once he was finished. "For many, that's a luxury."

"I know I'm blessed I have the means to make my passion my work."

She got on her tiptoes to give him a peck on the cheek. "But I would love to see your other riding skills."

Her low, throaty spoken words caused his eyebrows to raise. "Now you know you wrong for trying to be flirty right now when there's nothing I can do about it."

"I know, but as you see when we showered, we can be creative..." She let the suggestion hang between them, hiding her smile.

Nash stepped back. "Easy now... I'll be back in a minute. Let me go to wash up a little before we go to dinner." He strutted out of the barn like he knew she had her eyes on him. Which she did.

As soon as he was out of sight, she dug into her backpack and took out the cowgirl lingerie featuring a long-sleeved fringe bodysuit with garter straps. She shimmied into the mesh stockings before slipping into thigh-high black boots. They couldn't sleep together but she could give him an appetizer, something to look forward to. Gosh, her hands were shaking and her palms were sweaty but she got everything on without ripping the scraps of material. It was a good thing it was warm in the barn.

Once she was dressed, she jumped on top of the bale of hay and settled into a seductive pose.

She hoped Nash appreciated her efforts. Because her butt itched, and hay was all in her hair. She gritted her teeth to keep from scratching. Dang. Why hadn't she brought a blanket?

She heard a whistle before Nash rounded the corner. He dashed toward where she was and looked down at her. "Whoa." The look of hunger on his face was worth every discomfort. His mouth opened and closed, then opened and closed again.

It wasn't often she saw Nash Fortune speechless.

She licked her lips and recited the line she had practiced in her head countless times. "Do you prefer your cowgirls naughty or nice?"

He dropped to his knees and responded with an intriguing question of his own. "How about a little of both?"

CHAPTER TWENTY-ONE

HE LOVED HIS MOTHER. Dearly. But Nash wished she would leave and take Imani's folks right along with her. He was ready to continue what he and Imani had started in the barn. It was like only having one scoop of ice cream.

But the women were watching a movie about a book club and they were only halfway through. He loved how both his and Imani's families blended well together. At one point, his mom and Abena had been huddled in the corner, conspiring together about something.

Nash sat in the armchair with his hat over his eyes so he could trail Imani's every move. He was aware of every step and every breath she took. That's how tuned into her he was. She held Colt, rocking him back and forth. But all Nash could think about was the fact that she was still wearing that scrap of lingerie underneath.

He still couldn't believe Imani had been daring enough to pull that stunt in the barn. She had done things to him that were so naughty, but oh, so nice. Seared in his memory for life was when she flipped onto her tummy, then asked the most enticing question he had ever heard: *Why don't you get your camera out?*

Nash had gone along with her cheeky suggestion, snapping a few pictures, but he had every intention of deleting them all after their fun time. However, Imani urged him to store them in a photo-lock app. And, of course, she had taken a few pictures of him. *For later,* she had said with a mischievous giggle.

He had indulged her whimsy, while warning her they were for her eyes only. It was the twinkle in her eyes he was low-key worried about. Nash didn't need her boasting of his assets to anyone. As soon as they were able to make love, Nash planned to clear the photos out of both their phones. She didn't need a still when she had access to the real thing.

Though he had to admit that Imani had fulfilled one of his teenage fantasies. And then some. He would never be able to enter that barn without thinking of her again. It had taken every ounce of willpower he possessed not to sink into her while she was on that bale with her leg propped up. But he wasn't about to cause her harm because he couldn't wait.

Besides, as Imani said, they had gotten creative. *Real creative.*

Colt's cries made him focus on the present. Imani's curls looked wild, bouncing as she rocked the baby—patience had been needed to remove the hay from her hair. But to Nash, she had never looked more beautiful. She had showered and changed when they returned from their date before getting Colt out of his bassinet.

He jumped to his feet and went over to take his son from her. "I've got this," he said, his stomach rumbling. They had been so caught up in each other that they hadn't eaten dinner.

Her lips quirked. "Let's get Colt fed first and we can eat after."

"Yes, because you were wrong, you know?" he said under his breath.

"Wrong about what?"

"We can't live off love," he rasped, repeating the words Imani had voiced when Nash reminded her that the diner was about to close while they were fooling around in the barn. "A man's got to eat."

She winked. "I've ordered special delivery from the LC Club. It should arrive shortly."

They high-fived. "Now, that's what I'm talking about." Colt squirmed against him then opened his mouth like he was trying to eat Nash's shirt. Oh, no. He should have gotten a receiving blanket. Holding Colt a few inches from him, he went to get one and slung it across his chest.

Imani returned with Colt's bottle and Nash returned to the armchair to feed his son. Colt's hair looked even more curly and his lashes touched his cheeks. He could see the dimple on display every time Colt sucked his cheeks in. "I love you," he whispered. Less than five minutes later, Colt had finished his bottle. His son had a healthy appetite.

Nash sat the baby up and patted his back. Colt burped soon after. Nash felt adept at feeding him, though he still hadn't mastered changing his son's diaper. The day he was watching him by himself, Nash had tried three times and each time, there was a gap big enough so that the diaper had slipped off Colt's legs. That's why he had gone to his mother's house.

Imani came over with the baby wrap sling for him to use. She kissed the top of Colt's head and then did the same to Nash.

His heart somersaulted.

This woman was the whole package.

That's why he loved her.

Yes, he loved her. Acknowledging the feeling blossoming within his chest was that easy, like crossing home plate after hitting a home run. He didn't have any angst or need to agonize over how he felt about Imani.

Nash stood surrounded by noise—the mothers laughing at the screen, Imani talking with the delivery guy at the door, Zuri lightly snoring—and all he could hear was the quiet certainty of his heart.

He knew he would spend the rest of his days with this woman. If she would have him. He loved her and he had a hunch that he would continually fall into that abyss with a smile on his face.

Imani sauntered over, holding up the paper bag bearing the LC Club logo. "Dinner is served." *She was a provider.* He fell a little more.

Abena paused the television. "I hope you ordered enough for all of us. I know I ate earlier but I could eat."

"I sure did," Imani said.

She was thoughtful. He fell even deeper.

Washing her hands, Imani addressed Wendy. "Oh, before I forget, remind me to give you the monogrammed onesies. I also had a special set made for Dahlia's twins."

"Oh, wow. Thank you. How sweet."

She was kind. And there he was falling for her all over again.

Wendy came over to assist Imani with laying out the spread. He must have an incredulous look on his face or something because she tilted her head. "Are you okay?"

"Oh, yes. I've never been better."

"Just checking because you spilled some of the gravy all over the baby bag." Nash looked down to see the liquid seeping down the sides and soiling the contents inside. Mortified, he took out the clothes and diapers to inspect them.

"Don't worry about it," Imani said. "I'll wash the clothes and repack the bag later. Go eat." She quickly wiped out the bag with bleached wipes and chucked the diapers in the trash.

"If you're sure…"

"Positive." After their meal, Imani joined the women to finish the last half hour of the film.

Nash wandered over to the kitchen counter, where Imani had placed the real-estate agent's contact information along with several listings. She was in the investigation stage but as soon as Colt was two months, Imani would start house hunting in earnest. Her ideal home would have at least six bedrooms, a large office area, a spacious nursery and enough acreage for her to have a playground, a pool, a tennis court, a trail and, of course, a privacy fence. Imani's intention was to close on a property in time to move in at the four-month mark.

Hopefully, his love and offer of a more permanent living situation would change her mind. And what better day to express how thankful he was that she had returned into his life and captured his heart, than on Thanksgiving?

A FAINT CRY awakened him.

Stretched across the bed in Imani's room the Monday of Thanksgiving week, it took a moment for Nash to register where he was and that he was hearing Colt crying from the baby monitor. He propped himself up on his elbows before zeroing on a note on the side of the bed.

Left early to go with our mothers on a walk. Be back soon.

He tensed. That meant he was alone with Colt. On one hand, Nash was glad Imani was overcoming her separation anxiety. But on the other...he was alone with his son. The cries became more persistent. It was six in the morning, which meant Colt had slept for a good six hours. The baby wasn't going back to bed. It was feeding time. Nash swung his legs off the side of the bed and rushed into the nursery. Colt was now in full wail, his fists bunched and his face scrunched. Nash picked up his child and held him close to rock him.

"Okay, okay, Daddy's here." Colt hiccupped, his chin trembling. Swaying from side to side, Nash felt a little heat radiating from the infant's back. He frowned. Actually, Colt felt *really* warm. Maybe he had overheated from his crying bout. Placing him in the bassinet, Nash reached for a diaper. Colt started fussing again. What should he do? Change him or pick him up? Nash wiped his forehead with the back of his hand and attempted to ignore the panic rising within. Colt stiffened and his face reddened. Uh-oh. He knew what was coming.

Colt bellowed.

Maybe he was hungry. Man, this felt easier to navigate when Imani was around. Nash bolted into the kitchen and grabbed a bottle out of the bottle sanitizer. Thank goodness, Imani had made him wash them all the night before. Colt was now having a major meltdown.

Snatching the baby in his arms, Nash tried to give him a bottle, but Colt refused. In fact, he seemed to be really congested and was grunting, and now his hiccups had gotten worse.

Nash's chest heaved. He hated seeing his baby boy so upset. Helplessness threatened to engulf him, but he gave himself a pep talk. "Okay, Nash, you can do this. You've been doing it for the past three weeks. This is nothing new." Then he tried again. This time, Colt latched on and began sucking away. The whizzing sound of the milk made Nash heave a sigh of relief. "Alright, little guy. Fill your tummy."

Then Colt hiccupped while feeding. Nash took the bottle out of Colt's mouth and scrambled to set him upright. Colt began to heave, spitting up all the milk he had consumed. Nash grabbed some napkins and wiped the baby's face, then patted his back, but he just got fussier.

Nash paused. He hadn't changed Colt's diaper yet, which could be the cause of his unease. Poor little guy couldn't talk about what was bothering him. Nash rested him on his back and took off his diaper. He gasped. Was it him or did Colt's skin seem flushed? Nash moved with speed to wipe his son down and apply some ointment, the way he had seen Imani do. Then he put him in a fresh diaper, tightly securing the sides. Lifting the baby up, Nash exhaled when it stayed on.

Colt was silent for a blessed three seconds. Then he arched his back and screamed.

Nash stilled.

This was *not* normal.

He had to get Colt to the pediatrician's office. He put his boy back into the bassinet before speeding into action. First, he dialed the doctor's office, yelling above the infant's screams, and almost cried when they told him he could bring Colt in. Nash's heart pounded as he grabbed the baby bag. Then, he tossed some diapers inside and checked to see if there were wipes inside, then raced outside the house.

Colt's screams pierced Nash's ears and his heart.

On the way to the doctor, he called Imani to let her know he was on the way to the pediatrician.

"Does he have a fever?" Imani asked, her tone frantic.

"I—I don't know…"

"You didn't check?" Maybe he was being sensitive but her tone sounded accusatory. That put him on the defensive.

"N-no. I was busy trying to feed him and change him and he's crying and throwing up. I—I just don't know…"

"There's a thermometer in Colt's bathroom. All you had to do was check." Nash slumped. He could hear their mothers trying to calm Imani down. Nash understood her fears, but she wasn't the only one scared. In the back seat of his Range Rover, Colt was inconsolable. Nash groaned.

"I didn't think. I'm sorry. Colt is screaming and I panicked. I told you I wasn't good at this, and you left me to look after him by myself," he said, lashing out.

"I'm just asking you what anybody would know... I shouldn't have left him behind to go walking." *Wow. So Imani really didn't actually trust him alone with their son.* That gutted his heart. Yes, he had his doubts about his capabilities, but he did his best to be helpful and to assist with Colt however he could. As Nash tried to process her words, she grunted out, "I'll see you at the doctor's office." Then the line went dead.

CHAPTER TWENTY-TWO

"KEEP CALM," ABENA SAID, patting Imani's hand. "Don't get yourself worked up until you know what's going on." They had met up by the lake at five that morning and had just finished one lap around the circumference when Nash called.

How was she to stay cool with Colt screaming like he was in pain? This idea of theirs to leave Nash alone with the baby had backfired big-time. Instead of helping him gain confidence in his parenting skills, it only made Imani acutely aware of what she was lacking in hers. Regret filled her gut, twisted it tighter than a Bantu knot. Fighting back tears, Imani prayed her baby was okay.

She shouldn't have relaxed her routine and left Nash to take care of Colt. She could have strapped her baby boy into the stroller and taken him on her walk. A cloak of guilt wrapped around her. No. No. She couldn't think like that. What was happening to Colt would happen if she'd been there or not and it had nothing to do with her negligence. She had left him with his father.

The very father who now blamed her for Colt getting sick.

Her stomach churned with that knowledge.

The women hurried toward Imani's car. Imani handed her mother the keys. She was too shaky to get behind the wheel.

"Take deep breaths. All will be fine," Wendy said, with the

cool manner of one who had reared six children. She didn't sound alarmed and Imani drew from that and tried to quell her body quivers. All she could hear were Colt's screams. All she could feel was her self-reproach.

"How was Colt last night?" Wendy asked.

Imani narrowed her eyes, picturing Colt the night before. "He seemed okay. Slept well. Got up about eleven and stayed up until about one in the morning. I didn't notice anything wrong." Or had she missed something?

"It might be colic," Zuri added, tapping her chin. "If I remember right, of my three girls, Abena used to get colic all the time. You don't know how many nights I stayed up massaging her tummy and trying to get her settled."

Just as they pulled into the parking lot of the medical building, Nash texted. I am here. They are taking Colt back now.

Tossing her phone in her purse, Imani jumped out of the vehicle and rushed inside the building. "Keep us posted," her mother called out.

She caught up with Nash as they were being led into Exam Room 2. Colt wasn't screaming but he was sniffling. Seeing his puffy face made her heart ache. She stood back while the nurse's assistant took Colt's temperature and his weight. He didn't have a fever, thank goodness. And he hadn't lost any weight.

Without meeting Nash's gaze, Imani held out her hands. He handed Colt over to her and though she could feel Nash's eyes on her, she didn't acknowledge him. She was too upset at him for blaming her for leaving Colt with him. As if he was a stranger. Colt snuggled into her and yawned. Poor baby wanted to sleep. Sitting in one of two free chairs, she massaged the baby's tummy. Colt began passing wind.

"Are you upset with me?" Nash asked.

"Yes." She spoke through clenched teeth.

"I'm sorry I didn't think to check his temperature."

"I'm not upset about that."

He furrowed his brow in confusion. "Then what did I do?"

The door creaked. "We'll talk later." The pediatrician entered with his assistant. Within minutes of his examination, he diagnosed Colt was colic, suggesting that they change the formula.

"What brand does he use?" the physician asked.

"Let me show you a sample," Imani said, opening the diaper bag. "We've used two different kinds." She rummaged around the interior but all she saw were diapers and baby wipes. There wasn't even a change of clothes.

"Ugh. I—I must have forgotten to pack the formula," Nash slapped his forehead.

The doctor must have sensed the tension between them because he jumped in before Imani could speak. "That's okay. I have a couple of samples for a gentler formula that you can try. Your baby's digestive tract isn't fully mature yet and so he could be getting used to the shift."

By then Colt had finally fallen asleep. The pediatrician gave them at least six small bottles and promised to call them in a few days to check on Colt. Placing Colt on her shoulder, Imani thanked the doctor, then left the building ahead of Nash. She had every intention of taking the baby into her vehicle, but her Jeep was gone. So she had to ride back to the guesthouse with Nash.

Imani surmised their mothers had driven off to give the two of them space to talk, which now that she thought about it, was a good thing. She wasn't going to walk around with her chest tight from all these emotions.

Once they had Colt secured and Nash was on his way, she cleared her throat. "I didn't appreciate you coming at me for going on a walk with our mothers this morning. In these past twenty-one days, I have barely left my son's side. In fact, the only time I did was because you suggested it. I'm not a neglectful mother so for you to imply that was below the belt, especially since I was gone for about an hour."

Nash's mouth popped open. "When did I say that? I think you are an amazing mother and I'm glad when you take time for yourself. I was the one who talked about balance, remember?"

"Yes, but you blamed me for leaving Colt with you." She folded her arms.

He shook his head. "You misunderstood what I meant. You have a natural instinct when it comes to Colt and this morning proved that. I'm woefully unequipped to deal with a newborn on my own. I'm just like my father."

"You are nothing like the man you described," Imani replied vehemently. "Every day you tell Colt how much you love him and you have been there. Why are you letting a couple mistakes interfere with the overall picture?"

He tossed a meaningful glance her way. She shifted in her seat. "I get that I'm doing the same thing but the difference between you and me is that I am trying to work through my doubts. I'm not going to let anxiety get in the way of my giving Colt what he needs."

"Our son doesn't need a father who doesn't think to check his temperature, or one who leaves the house without thinking about how he is going to eat."

She placed a hand on Nash's arm. "We're going to make mistakes. The main thing is that we love Colt."

"Yes, but some are forgivable. And I do love Colt. That's why I know I need to stay away from him if he's ever going to turn out right."

"I can't believe you would even say something like that. If you cut him out of your life, you're causing the same trauma you experienced as a child."

His eyes widened. "Negative. I'm sparing him from similar trauma." He parked in front of the guesthouse. "My being in his life could bring him more harm than good. It's in my blood."

"Some of your siblings became parents and they are coping well. You will, too, in time."

"That's them." He pointed to his chest. "This is me."

She sighed. "I can see that no matter what I say, you've made up your mind." Tears welled. "How am I to explain to Colt when he asks why he doesn't have his father in his life?"

"When he's older, I'll explain it to him."

She lifted her chin. "And what if he doesn't want to hear a word you have to say?"

Nash looked her square in the eyes. "I'm willing to take that chance."

Her shoulders slumped. "I see." She placed her hand on the door handle. "Then I guess there's nothing left to say."

I'M WILLING TO take that chance.

Three hours after he had spoken those words, Imani and Colt were gone. She must have called a moving company and hired a cleaning crew to remove all signs of their occupancy. Everything was the way it had been before. Immaculate. Pristine… Quiet.

He hated it.

After their talk, Nash had gone to the ranch to work and to give Imani some space. But he had missed them and had returned home, scrambling immediately toward the guesthouse. Walking through the empty space, his footsteps echoed throughout, a cloud of loneliness shrouding his every move. The nursery had been completely dismantled, like she had been trying to erase any evidence of Colt's existence.

Imani hadn't even left a note or a forwarding address so he had no idea if she had returned to Cactus Grove or if she was still in Chatelaine Hills.

He fired off a rapid text to Imani. I can't believe you left like that.

Her response was quick. I can't believe you would think I would stay.

Despondent at her comeback, Nash walked the path back to his home. Flipping on the switch, he thought about taking his Jaguar out on the road. But when he went into the garage, the vivid image of Imani relaxing against the seat, her curls flying in the wind, made him retreat.

He ran his hand across the hood. "Sorry, Velvet. Maybe another time."

Puttering around his house, Nash wiped the already clean counters and dusted the fans, but there wasn't much to do. Not even Taylor Swift helped. Talking to his mother about it hadn't helped, either. When the silence became overbearing, he drove back to the ranch. He would visit with his horses and fill their stalls with fresh hay. He doubted they would need it but it would fill the void left by Imani and Colt's sudden departure. The tents were already laid out on the field for the Thanksgiving feast Wendy had arranged for the workers. And the party supplier would lay out the tables and chairs soon. Their staff had been delighted at Wendy's gesture.

Going into the barn, memories of his visit there with Imani filled him with melancholy. At dusk, he took Leviathan for a ride when he thought he saw his mother in the distance. Nash was about to trot her way when he saw a man approach. They were far enough away that he couldn't make out any features but they seemed to be deep in conversation.

"Whoa." He cued the horse to stop. Leaning forward in the saddle, he squinted. Wait. Was his mom dating someone? That was…interesting.

Nash straightened, then smiled. He hoped so. Mom had been lonely for a long time, even before his father's death a year ago. It would be good if she had found a new partner, a second chance at love. Especially since she had been encouraging all of her children to do the same. The two people strolled away from him, arm in arm.

Leviathan whinnied, lifting his legs, restless. "Steady. Steady," he commanded gently. His horse snorted. Nash used his left leg to give the horse a squeeze and tilted his head and shoulders to the right. The horse turned and they trotted back to the stable. After placing Leviathan in his stall, he went outside to take in the glow of the full moon. Seeing his mother with someone magnified Nash's sudden solitude.

The next seventy-two hours were excruciating. Nash awakened at odd hours, thinking he had heard Colt's cry. He sent Imani text messages and called a few times but she didn't respond. Battling insomnia, he did some work inside his house, his heart aching for Imani's company. Her voice. Her touch. Nash bunched his fists. This was what he wanted, so why was he feeling so…on edge? Especially when he knew he had made the right decision. Colt would be better off without him.

But he hadn't been without his father. Yet, he was hoping for a different outcome with his son when he was doing the same thing to Colt that Casper had done to him.

Nash didn't feel good about that.

CHAPTER TWENTY-THREE

THANKSGIVING DAY, NASH started his day early, having spent most of the night tossing and turning in bed. He went over to the ranch to help with last-minute setup and to thank the workers for all their hard work. He also promoted Stanley to full-time status. Seeing Stanley's wife and daughter cheer for his accomplishment made Nash think of Imani and Colt.

When Imani and Nash parted ways before, it had been difficult to move on, but it had been doable. However, this time, his heart felt ripped to shreds, the pain doubly intensified. He couldn't sleep, his appetite deserted him and regret ate at him. He missed Imani's voice, her laugh, her touch. The feel of his son in his arms, the look of trust on Colt's face. And, more than anything, he missed telling his son he loved him every day.

His dour mood was in direct contrast to the festive music, and though he had planted a smile on his face, his heart was heavy. Being here without Imani and Colt was a struggle.

Wendy came over to where he stood by the side of the tent. She handed him a cup of apple cider. "How are things with Imani?"

"I haven't spoken to her in days," he croaked out. "The silence is interminable."

"Oh, son. I'm sorry to see you like this. But have you learned anything?"

"Yes, I know I'm miserable without them. I want Imani and Colt in my life. For always. I want to be there to celebrate Colt's first Christmas. When we were children, I remember how we would gather in the kitchen and bake pies together. I want to continue that tradition with my child."

Wendy chuckled. "I can't believe you remember that. A lot more of the apple slices made it in your mouth than in the pie."

"Yeah, I didn't know you caught that. I figured you would think it was Ridge." His chin dipped to his chest. "I wonder if Colt will like granny apples like I do?"

Instead of answering his question, his mother patted his back. "I really hate to see you suffer, but there is an upside here."

"And what could that possibly be?" Nash grumbled.

"You now see the value of family. Which means you know what to do to fix this."

"You're right… I do. I just hope Imani takes my call this time. I've already tried a few times before, all with no response."

"Only one way to find out." She tilted her head and studied him for a beat before she gave his hand a squeeze. Then with a hum, she wandered off.

Nash took out his phone and called Imani. He needed to hear her voice. But once again, his call went directly to voicemail. His shoulders slumped. If it wasn't for the fact that he knew his siblings would drag him out of the house before they let him spend Thanksgiving alone, Nash would have just gone home to hibernate with his despair. Besides, he had been tasked to bring the pies and he didn't want to shirk that responsibility.

After showering and changing into an orange shirt, black jeans and his black sneakers, Nash arrived at his mother's house after 5:00 p.m. with a couple pies in hand. He parked next to one of the numerous vehicles out front. When he stepped inside his mother's home into the living-room area, Nash greeted Arlo, Ridge and Jade. He did his best to shuck off the blues and gave them each a hug.

"It's about time you got here," Arlo said. "Everybody else is outside."

"Who's everyone?" Nash asked.

"Heath's sisters and ours."

"Mom insisted we wait for you," Ridge added, coming over to grab the pies from Nash. "Let me take these off your hands."

Swerving out of Ridge's reach, Nash chuckled. "Nice try, bro, but Mom would have my head and you know it. That's why she made you bring the juices and water because she knows you would hog the pies." Ridge would eat half of the pies on his own if allowed to. He had such a sweet tooth.

"Whatever. I'll buy my own." Ridge gave him a playful shove. "See you out there."

"Hurry up," Arlo said. "All I had was a PBJ for breakfast, so I'm ready to eat."

Nash gasped when he saw Colt's picture had been added to the family photos on the brandy-colored mantel over the marble fireplace. He went to over to stare at his son's first picture, where he had been swaddled in the hospital blanket. Nash touched his chest. He missed the little guy.

Jade sidled up next to him. "He looks just like you did when you were a baby."

His twin's words made his chest tighten. "Yes, he does."

"If he's anything like you, he'll be remarkable." She gave him a kiss on the cheek.

"I hope he has Imani's spunk, because his father is a coward."

"Ouch. Don't talk about my twin brother like that." Jade's eyes filled with sympathy. "He might be a little pigheaded but he's loyal and he loves hard." She squeezed his arm. "Things will work out as they should."

She sounded so certain, he just had to ask… "How can you be so sure?"

"Look at Heath," Jade said, referring to her fiancé. "What are the odds that after thirty years he would discover then find his long-lost sisters? They grew up apart but now look at them." She pointed to the siblings sitting under the tent with their significant others, along with Charlie, Jade's beloved basset hound. "You would never know they only just met. They are so close."

Nash eyed how they were talking and laughing, and just so… happy. "Their reunion was something, wasn't it?"

"It sure was."

For a little town, Chatelaine had some big secrets and Heath's backstory was just one example. When Heath arrived in Chatelaine, he came with the intention of finding his siblings, the Perry triplets—Tabitha, Lily and Haley—who had each found true love with a Fortune man. With the help of Doris Edwards, an elderly GreatStore employee, who insisted there had been four of them, the Perry sisters and Heath had finally pieced everything together. Heath was born two months before his sisters and they were actually half siblings, as Heath had a different mother. But in addition to finding his sisters, Heath had found Jade.

He had never seen his sister so content. "I'm glad you've found your match."

"Heath's wonderful, thoughtful and he has my back." She had a dreamy look on her face.

"Yes, he was alright with me when he rescued you from that bully, Nina, and agreed to be your fake fiancé." Nash had hated how Nina had picked on his sister when they were in high school. But Jade had held her own and had snagged a good man in the process.

She flashed her ring finger and giggled. "Fake fiancé no more." She held Nash's hand in hers. "You have a chance at the real thing, too."

"I think I blew it with Imani. For good this time." Nash gave her a quick rundown of what had happened.

"You can fix it. Just let your heart lead you." How he wished he had his twin's confidence. Her cell phone chimed. "Heath needs barbecue sauce."

"Go on. I'll be out in a second."

Strolling into the kitchen, Nash placed the pies on the island. The entire expanse of the white marble counter was covered with covered foiled containers. He inhaled, the scents of turkey and roast beef filling his nostrils. Wendy had set up burners under the tent in the back of the house, which overlooked the lake and multileveled deck and patio.

Peering outside, Nash could see Heath was by the grill, tending to the chicken. Jade was right next to him, basting while he turned. Nash loved how they did things together. He grabbed a bottle of water and made his way outside.

To his left, Ridge, Arlo and the Perry triplets' significant others—West, Asa and Camden—were playing football. Ridge cupped his hands and called out. "Get over here! We need a third person."

Shrugging off the doldrums, Nash jogged over to them. "What am I playing?"

"You're on defense," Arlo said.

"We're three-two," Ridge added. "So bring your A game."

West gripped the football and stepped forward. After swinging the ball in an arc high above his head, he released it. Arlo jumped and snatched the ball midair before he sprinted down the field with Nash on his heels. Seeing his cousins run toward him, he braced for impact. That's when his eyes met those of the person standing by the sidelines. He froze for a beat before lifting his hand in a wave.

The next thing he felt was a *whoosh* and he was falling to the earth with a thud.

CHAPTER TWENTY-FOUR

Earlier that day

"HONEY, AS MUCH as I've loved having you here, you've got to get back to your life," Abena said, rocking Colt in her arms. He had been fussy the past few days, crying nonstop. After Nash's brash words, Imani had given the movers her parents' address since her penthouse was occupied—and she had needed her mother's comfort. "This little guy misses his daddy," her mother continued. She raised an eyebrow and settled farther into the couch of her living room. "And I'd bet all the shoes in my closet, he's not the only one."

It was a little past eight thirty in the morning and Abena had been up from dawn preparing her annual Thanksgiving breakfast feast. Because Jonathan and her father lived in a different time zone, Abena had started celebrating Thanksgiving at nine o'clock, which would be 6:00 p.m. in Dubai. Her grandparents, aunts and cousins were due to arrive in a few minutes and then the family would have a video conference while they shared their meals.

"I'm just giving Nash what he said he wanted." She jutted her chin and folded her arms.

"Yes, but at your heart's expense."

Imani snorted. "My heart is just fine." She looked away from her mother's knowing stare and dabbed at her eyes. "Or it will be." Once she had arrived on her mother's doorstep and had had a good cry, Imani had set up in her old bedroom of her parents' six-bedroom home, using the connecting room for Colt's nursery. Most of her possessions were still in boxes. "I got over Nash before, I will again."

"I'll believe that when you stop checking your cell-phone notifications."

"Oh...you caught that?" Imani's cheeks warmed.

Her mother chuckled. "Yes. You've checked your phone at least ten times already this morning." She smoothed a hand down her burnt orange slacks, which she had paired with a cream sweater and nude pumps.

"I read online to avoid communication with your partner for at least seventy-two hours when you're upset about something. That way both parties have time to calm down and reflect on what they have done."

"Oh? How's that working out for you?" Her mother stood to place Colt in his bassinet. Imani was relieved to see he had finally fallen asleep. She followed her mother into the kitchen, and they began to place the food on the well-dressed table. Her mother had outdone herself with a spread of chicken, waffles, eggs, turkey bacon, a fruit-and-charcuterie board, cinnamon rolls and various Danishes and croissants. Everything was covered or wrapped in cellophane for when the rest of the family arrived.

"It's been tough," Imani admitted and exhaled. "He's texted and called but what else is there to say?" She shrugged. "He doesn't want to be a father to Colt."

"Doesn't *want* to be? Or doesn't think he can be?" Her mother wagged a finger. "Because there's a difference." Her gentle words pierced Imani's resolve.

She outstretched her hands. "I've tried to reassure him, but it's like Nash doesn't get that there is no perfect parent. He doesn't understand that we just want him in our lives."

"And you're conveying that want by being away from him?" Abena pulled out a chair and sat, tapping the space next to her.

"Ah, er…" Imani twisted her lips and slid into the adjacent chair. "He believes Colt will be better off without him."

"And you believe differently, correct?"

"Yes, of course, I do. I know with all my heart that Nash will be the best father. The father that Colt needs. I've seen him in action and don't doubt it one bit."

"So why aren't you acting on that belief?"

Imani shook her head. "I don't get what you're asking."

"Nash is acting on his belief that he's no good for Colt by pushing you both out of his life. If you don't agree, why aren't you pushing back?"

"You expect me to chase after someone who told me that he was willing to take the chance that his son might want to have nothing to do with him if he's out of his life?" Her voice held an edge. Ooh, every time she thought about those words, ire curdled in her chest.

"I expect you to fight for what you believe and want. Fight for the man you love. And fighting isn't running back home to me, though I love having you."

Is that what she was doing? *Running?*

"My dear daughter, I love you, but you need staying power. When things get rough or you feel cornered, you run. How do you think I've stayed married to your father this long? Though we live thousands of miles apart, our bond is tight. That's because I refused to let distance interfere with our love and our commitment to each other."

"I didn't run…" A visual image of her racing off in her wedding gown from the courthouse and yet another of the moving truck and her SUV packed with her belongings as she evacuated Nash's guesthouse hit her mind. She drew in a breath. "Do I?"

"You do." Abena patted her hand. "You want a man who is honest with you. One who will tell you his deepest fears, knowing you will still be there, that you will have his back." Her mother cleared her throat. "When your father first left for Dubai, I was furious."

Imani gasped. "You were?"

"*Ab-sol-ute-ly* livid." Abena nodded. "He left me here with a brand-new baby so he could expand the family oil business.

Can you imagine? I didn't speak to him for two weeks. But then one day, I heard about some explosion or something near where he worked and lived in Dubai and I was sick to my stomach. For days, I waited for word. But nothing. I couldn't take it no more. Though I'm not fond of flying, I left you with your grandparents and headed to Dubai."

"You did?" Imani's eyes were wide.

"You were too young to remember." Abena waved a hand. "When I got there, I headed straight to the hospital, my heart in my throat. All I could think of was, was Phillip gone? Did he die before I got to tell him how much I loved him?"

"Oh, my goodness." Imani's eyes misted. "Was he hurt?"

"No. He was helping. When I got there, I saw him covered in dirt and refuse but he had been helping to pull others to safety." Her mom shook her head. "I wanted to rage and hurl, but at that moment when our eyes connected, I knew what he needed. What *I* needed." She spread her arms wide. "I opened my arms and welcomed him."

Imani sniffled. "Wow…"

"I learned that day that love is more powerful than anger." Abena's voice wobbled but she winked. "I'm pretty sure your brother was conceived that night."

"It's no wonder Jonathan loves Dubai." Imani laughed.

Abena joined in before she gave her daughter's hand a squeeze. "You have to decide for yourself if your love is more powerful than your anger at Nash. 'Cause I know this isn't about waiting seventy-two hours to communicate. You are mad at him for not choosing right, but how long do you plan on making him pay?"

That question stayed with Imani throughout their breakfast. While she enjoyed herself, she knew it was time to go back to her own family. It was time to return to Nash.

"NASH! NASH! ARE you okay?"

Imani broke into a run toward the figure prostrate on the ground. She had dressed in a green blouse, dark blue jeans and brown cowboy boots, which was not exactly the best outfit for running. His family surrounded him while he lay still. Imani stood close behind them, her heart pounding in her chest. Her mother's story from that morning about almost losing her father echoed in her head. *This is different. He's okay.*

Ridge and Arlo pulled Nash to his feet. Holding his head, Nash grunted and rubbed his scalp. "I'm alright. I lost focus. For a second, I thought I saw Imani and..."

She stepped up, fiddling with one of the turkey earrings in her ear. "I'm right here."

His eyes went wide. "Imani? I thought you were back in Cactus Grove." His family dispersed, giving him pats on the back, along with some good ribbing blended with relief.

"I was. Your mom had invited me earlier in the week." She pointed at Wendy, who was holding Colt. Nash reached for her hand. The instant electricity flowed between them. "I had Thanksgiving breakfast with family and then I drove out here to be with *my* family." She gave him a pointed stare while her words sunk in.

Nash touched his chest. "I'm glad you came." His eyes welled. "I've missed you and Colt more than I imagined I could."

Her chest tightened. "We've missed you, too." Wendy called out that it was time for them to gather at the table to eat. There was quite a spread—turkey, roast beef, barbecue chicken, corn, mashed potatoes, mac and cheese, green bean casserole, grilled asparagus, cheesecake and pies. Everything looked and smelled delicious. Since she hadn't eaten since breakfast, Imani was more than ready to enjoy their meal.

"We'll talk later?" Nash asked, linking his fingers with hers. She nodded and then he touched her face, as if reassuring himself that she was there. They took the last two chairs near the edge of the tent. Wendy came over with Colt in her arms.

Nash's face lit up. Imani could see the love reflected there and she silently thanked her mother for urging her to return. Nash held his son close to his chest and closed his eyes. "I love you, son. Daddy loves you." Then he kissed the top of Colt's head, not caring that they had an audience.

Imani would have fallen apart if Wendy hadn't cracked a joke—not that Imani heard what she said—but she laughed along with everyone, her heart suddenly joyous. Throughout the meal, Nash couldn't keep his hands off her. At one point, he drew her onto his lap, having handed off Cole to one of his cousins. Then he kissed her neck, her ears, her chin and, finally, her lips.

"Come up for air, man," Arlo called out. "You're ruining our appetites."

"Dang, you two need to give us a break with all the PDA," Ridge said.

Imani knew her face had to be beet red, but she didn't care. She was right where she needed to be. In Nash's arms. But she did have to answer nature's call. She gave him a peck on the lips. "I've got to use the bathroom. I'll be back in a jiffy."

Cupping her face with his hands, Nash pinned her with a fiery glance. "I love you and I am never letting you out of my sight again."

"I love you, too, but I won't be but a minute or two," Imani said, sliding off his lap.

"I'll come with you." Nash stood. "We'll be right back." He led her into the main house, ignoring the catcalls behind them. He showed her to the bathroom, waiting outside the door. As soon as she was finished, Nash snatched her into one of the empty bedrooms and closed the door.

"You know your family thinks we are up to no good in here," she giggled. Her heart was so happy for her to care too much.

"And they would be right." Nash plopped onto the bed, drawing her close. Resting his head against her abdomen, he exhaled. "I'm so glad you're back. I thought I had lost you and Colt for good."

"No. We just needed some thinking time." Imani tucked her index finger under his chin and prodded him to meet her eyes. "Our time apart showed me that there's nowhere else I'd rather be than here with you."

Nash pulled her down on the bed next to him. "I wish I could show how much I've missed you," he growled in her ear, then tugged on her earlobe with his teeth.

"We will have years for you to show me how much, but you can start later tonight," she said, caressing his cheek.

"Tonight?" he breathed out.

"Yes, the doctor said I'm good to go on the four week mark."
He grinned. "Well, Happy Thanksgiving to me."

"Happy Thanksgiving," she chuckled, fussing with his hair.
"Did I tell you how much I love you?"

"Yes, but you can tell me again because I'll never tire of
hearing it. And I'll never tire of telling you and Colt how much
you mean to me."

"I love you, Nash Fortune. One lifetime will never be enough
for me to show you how much." She drew his head down for
a kiss.

Several minutes later, Imani and Nash rejoined the festivi-
ties outside. He beelined for his son, strapping the carrier to his
chest. Everywhere he went, Colt was with him. Imani's heart
rejoiced. Everything was finally as it should be.

It was late that night when Imani returned with Nash to his
home. She trailed behind him up the stairs and followed him to
the nursery. She gasped. It was the exact replica of the nursery
in the guesthouse. She scanned the space. Her eyes met Nash's.
"When did you do this?"

"While you were gone, I had time on my hands." He gave
her a sheepish smile. "I was afraid to hope but I had to prepare
for the possibility."

Fighting back tears, Imani said, "You do want Colt. You
wouldn't have done this if you didn't."

"I do. I really do. I'm sorry it took you leaving for me to really see how much I want him in my life."

She wiped her face. "Colt is lucky to have you."

"And I'm blessed to have you both in my life. I'll never forget just how much."

They tiptoed inside the room, and rested Colt inside his crib.
The baby squirmed then settled, his bottom in the air. Both
parents released sighs of relief. Taking the baby monitor, Nash
clasped her hand with his and led her down the hall to his master suite.

Another gasp escaped.

Done in whites and browns with huge windows providing
a view of the lake, Imani lost her breath at the luxury of the
furnishings and the pictures of her and Colt on the wall space.

His painting from their night together was also on display. But, um, that bed was huge.

"You're the only woman to enter this space," Nash declared. "Well, except for my mother, when I just moved."

"Am I really?"

"Yes." Nash swung her in his arms. "You don't know how many nights I wish you were here with me." He placed her in the center of the bed. "No other woman has been in this bed, either."

"Good, because I plan to be the *only* one." She slipped out of her clothes, giving him a view of the lingerie she had worn underneath.

"Whoa. I'm so glad you got the all clear because there's no way I could lay beside you and not touch you when you're dressed like that," he groaned. "I'm going to make love to you all night so I hope you're up to the task."

"Well, I'm not one to back down from a challenge," she teased, her voice husky.

Nash went over to the chest on the other side of the room and took out a small box. Imani propped herself up on her arms, her mouth agape. "Is that what I think it is?" she squeaked out. Her heart started to pound in her chest.

His response was to slip to his knees. He wrapped his arms around her ankles and pulled her down to the edge of the bed. She sat up. When he opened the box, her breath caught at the solitaire sparkling in the moonlight. *Ohmygoodness. Ohmygoodness.* Her chest rose and fell. Was he about to do what she thought he was about to do?

He looked into his eyes. "Imani Porter, you have given me my son, the best gift of my life. Being without you these past days showed me I never want to wake up another morning without you at my side. I want to spend each sunset with you. I want to—"

She grabbed his head and kissed him to stop him from delivering the long speech. "Nash Fortune, can you skip ahead to the part where you ask me to marry you?" she asked. "We have love and the baby carriage, so let's get to it, shall we?"

He chuckled. "Alright. Imani Porter, will you agree to a name change and be mine for life?"

"Yes. Yes. A thousand yeses!" she exclaimed, holding out her hand, squirming with excitement.

Nash slid the ring on her finger. "A perfect fit."

She gave him a knowing grin. "Exactly." Nash stood her and drew her into his arms to seal their engagement with a searing kiss.

And now, everything was as it should be.

Finally.

* * * * *

Don't miss the stories in this mini series!

THE FORTUNES OF TEXAS: FORTUNE'S SECRET CHILDREN

Follow the lives and loves of a complex family with a rich history and deep ties in the Lone Star State.

A Fortune Thanksgiving
MICHELLE LINDO-RICE
October 2024

Fortune's Holiday Surprise
JENNIFER WILCK
November 2024

Fortune's Mystery Woman
ALLISON LEIGH
December 2024

MILLS & BOON

The Rodeo Star's Reunion
Melinda Curtis

MILLS & BOON

Award-winning *USA TODAY* bestselling author **Melinda Curtis**, when not writing romance, can be found working on a fixer-upper she and her husband purchased in Oregon's Willamette Valley. Although this is the third home they've lived in and renovated (in three different states), it's not a job for the faint of heart. But it's been a good metaphor for book writing, as sometimes you have to tear things down to the bare bones to find the core beauty and potential. In between—and during—renovations, Melinda has written over forty books for Harlequin, including her Heartwarming book *Dandelion Wishes*, which is now a TV movie, *Love in Harmony Valley*, starring Amber Marshall.

Brenda Novak says *Season of Change* "found a place on my keeper shelf."

Books by Melinda Curtis

Harlequin Heartwarming

The Cowboy Academy

A Cowboy Worth Waiting For
A Cowboy's Fourth of July
A Cowboy Christmas Carol
A Cowboy for the Twins

The Blackwell Belles

A Cowboy Never Forgets

Visit the Author Profile page
at millsandboon.com.au for more titles.

Dear Reader,

Many of my stories begin with a question: *What if...?*

I've had a lot of fun writing Griff as a supporting cast member in The Cowboy Academy miniseries. Early on, I established something had happened between Bess and Griff on the night of their high school prom. Turns out, Griff was a no-show. And he refused to explain himself to Bess. Since then, Bess has harbored a grudge. But what if...they had to work together over a dozen years later? What would it take for Bess to finally forgive Griff? And since it's high-energy, jokester Griff, would he get in his own way of earning her forgiveness and a second chance? You'll have to read along to find out.

I hope you come to love and root for the cowboys and cowgirls of The Cowboy Academy series as much as I do. Happy reading!

Melinda

To my family, who always nod their heads when
I talk about my book characters as if they are real.

PROLOGUE

February

ON THE MORNING of her best friend's wedding, Elizabeth "Bess" Glover had the strangest inkling—that at thirty-one, she'd always be a bridesmaid, never a bride. And her chances of becoming one suddenly felt slim-to-none.

Me, an old maid? How had it come to this?

Bess had an active social life. She went to honky-tonks, danced with handsome cowboys and accepted dates. She had a widespread network of friends and sisters who fixed her up, especially when she was a bridesmaid, which had increased in frequency over the past year. Her cowboy prince had yet to arrive. The only thing she hadn't tried was paying her best friend—Ronnie Pickett, today's bride and a professional matchmaker—to fix her up.

Bess had her pride, after all. Perhaps more than her share.

She always followed her mama's advice about looking her best because you never knew when Prince Charming would ride up on a fine piece of horseflesh or drive past in a sports car with hundreds of horses under the hood.

But despite the fact that Bess often dressed like a cowgirl princess and had kissed a lot of frogs...er, *cowboy* princes, she'd never come close to being a bride. Bess had no one by her side.

No partner to rely on when ranch work or bills overwhelmed her. No one to lean on when her high school teaching and coaching overwhelmed her. And lately, a lot overwhelmed her.

And so, on a Sunday morning in February, in Clementine, Oklahoma, Bess was unusually moody—downright tearful even—as she got ready for Ronnie's wedding to Wade Keller.

Later, Bess also cried in the bridal vestibule at the church. Someone gave her a shot of whiskey from a flask. And *whew*, that strong alcohol dried up her waterworks. But then she'd spilled silent tears at the altar in her position as the maid of honor while Ronnie recited her vows. And because no one offered her whiskey, Bess had stopped her weepiness by staring at her frenemy, best man Griff Malone. He smiled at her kindly, as if they were more friends than enemies.

He's single.

Bess barely stopped herself from scoffing. She wasn't that desperate. Besides, Griff didn't meet her dating criteria. Yes, he was handsome and smart. Yes, he could be charming and sweet. But he wasn't trustworthy.

Cross him off the list.

Bess reminded herself that being thirty-one meant she had lots of time to find her special someone. That and staring at the back of Ronnie's head for the rest of the ceremony had dried her tears. She even managed to make it through most of the wedding and reception without turning on more waterworks.

But now, inexplicably, Bess was feeling weepy after having caught the wedding bouquet.

I'm not a crier.

Bess was more likely to just move on.

But something had her on edge. And it wasn't her scalp-pulling updo.

Another bridesmaid handed Bess a shot of whiskey. She downed it quickly. It was Oklahoma strong. The burn of alcohol had Bess coughing so much that she missed seeing who caught the garter the groom threw.

A cheer rose in the community center and then a man in a black tuxedo and cowboy boots emerged from the crowd; his light brown hair was unruly without his cowboy hat to mash it down.

Griff.

For a short time, he'd been her dream guy in high school. She'd been drawn to his mischievous smile, his quick wit and deep laugh, his soulful brown eyes and untamable brown hair. He took her sometimes cantankerous nature in stride and smiled good-naturedly when Bess teased that her mother wanted her to marry well—a doctor or lawyer.

Predictably, according to Mama, their relationship had ended, and not at all well.

Fifteen years later, here Griff was, smiling and reaching toward Bess as if he'd just passed the Oklahoma bar exam or finished his medical residency, and had returned to Clementine to claim Bess's hand in marriage.

I always dreamed of marrying a cowboy.

"Bess?" Griff's smile didn't waver.

Bess's heart urged her to take that hand and smile right back, to pretend they'd returned to square one—flirting, kissing and trusting. Meanwhile, her head urged her to refuse the unreliable cowboy. They'd already danced once as part of the wedding party ritual, during which time Bess had pretended there was no need to be polite and make small talk. She'd stared over Griff's shoulder, very much aware of his warm hand encompassing hers, his strong arm encircling her waist, his mouth so close. She'd been torn between lifting her face to kiss him or to bicker about something.

She and Griff were good at bickering, friendly or otherwise, and did it on the regular. But it had been a good long while since Bess had been well and thoroughly kissed. Hence her hesitation.

Griff's smile morphed into a trouble-seeking grin as the DJ began to play a country song about love. Griff waggled the fingers of his extended hand. "Giddy-up, Bess. Folks are waiting for the cake to be cut."

Giddy-up?

Griff's cavalier attitude riled Bess more than nostalgia ever could.

She slapped her hand into his. "Let's get this over with." Lifting her long, fuchsia skirt with one hand, Bess tugged Griff out on the dance floor with the other. "Keep your mitts where I can see them, cowboy."

Griff chuckled.

They were joined by the bride and groom.

Just looking at Wade and Ronnie smiling so happily at each other had tears welling in Bess's eyes once more. They were living their fairy tale.

When will I get mine?

Without meaning to, Bess inched closer to Griff, imagining he was someone she could fall head over heels for, someone who understood her moods, someone Bess could be herself with through good times and bad.

Around the midpoint of the song, Griff lowered his lips to Bess's ear and whispered, "I know today has been hard on you." He eased back a smidge, smiling at her softly, tenderly, compassionately. "Don't cry."

Bess blinked back stupid tears once more. She didn't want to cry. Didn't he know that? Why didn't Griff grin...or joke... or...or bicker? Anything but show her empathy and kindness.

"We've got two more weddings to get through together this summer." Griff gathered Bess more securely into his arms. "Always a bridesmaid to my groomsman, Bess. Lean on me. What's the worst that can happen if you do? People assuming we're dating?"

People assuming...? Bess stiffened. *Of all the nerve.*

Her tears dried up. There was nothing as annoying or invigorating as sparring with Griff.

"Today hasn't been hard," she said through gritted teeth. "I'm so happy for Ronnie and Wade that I'm tearful. I'll be so happy that I'll probably cry for Abby and Nate, and Crystal and Derrick, too." The summer brides were Bess's work friends, teachers with Bess at Clementine High School.

"I've never known you to cry when you're happy, Bess." Those lips of Griff's moved closer to her ear until his warm breath wafted on her sensitive skin, eliciting a delicious, unwanted shiver. "But if that's the case and you want to cry some more, go ahead."

"Cry some more?" Bess jolted her shoulders back and lifted her gaze to his, to that handsome face and tender smile. "You think I want everyone to see me cry some more? You don't understand me at all. In fact, you make me want to…"

Kiss you.

Her eyes widened.

"What?" Griff stared down at Bess. His unmanageable brown hair begged to be touched. His tuxedo was a snug fit across broad shoulders that looked like they could carry any burden. He moved in perfect time to the music.

Just like my fairy-tale cowboy.

The man she'd once told Mama she was going to marry one day.

Of course, she'd been six. And, of course, Mama had reminded her that doctors and lawyers didn't have to muck out stalls or feed the chickens. Mama, having been Miss Teenage Oklahoma, wasn't keen on the ranch life. And that had been the last time Bess mentioned fairy-tale cowboys to her family.

"Bess?" Griff's voice was filled with concern.

Bess stared up at Griff, at the handsome man who suddenly didn't look like her frenemy. Why couldn't she turn off this confusing, conflicted attraction to him?

It's the tuxedo.

Mostly, Griff went around town in his ranch duds—worn blue jeans, worn boots, a threadbare button-down or stained T-shirt. But now… Tonight… Griff looked the way she'd imagined he'd appear on the night of the high school prom. The night he'd stood her up and lost her trust.

A tangle of emotions welled inside her—hurt, annoyance, melancholy, exasperation—bubbling like a pot about to boil over.

Bess stepped out of Griff's arms and marched off the dance floor in her fancy dress and her fancier heels, weaving her way through dinner tables until she reached the door separating the large hall from the lobby. There, she turned. Caught Griff's eye. And then pushed her way out the door, not thinking about what she was doing or what challenge she was throwing down. She just needed to fume, to move, to…to act out without an audience.

Bess crossed the lobby of the community center, running, lifting her long skirt slightly to avoid tripping in her high heels. She pushed out the door and into the cold February night, needing space, needing action, needing...

"Bess?" Surprisingly, Griff wasn't far behind her. His cowboy boots struck a quick cadence on the sidewalk as he followed her toward the building's corner.

Bess rounded that corner and pressed her back to the brick wall, breathing heavy.

What am I doing? What am I doing? What am I doing?

She had no idea. Her heart pounded and her head pounded and when Griff rounded the corner, she yanked him into her arms and kissed him.

It wasn't a young, tentative kiss, like the ones they'd shared in high school for a few weeks.

It wasn't a first-date kiss, where they were figuring things out and finding out where they fit together.

It was a kiss filled with frustration—over lost dreams, over lost opportunities, over the decreasing chance of ever finding her happily-ever-after.

"Bess," Griff murmured against her lips.

What am I doing? What am I doing?

What. Am. I. Doing?

The wrong thing.

Bess came to her senses. She thrust Griff away.

And then she ran back inside the community center and pretended for the rest of the reception that Griff Malone didn't exist.

CHAPTER ONE

July

THE RIDER WENT down in a cloud of dust.

The gray gelding that had bucked the boy off kicked up his heels with less fervor. It was morning but it was already hot enough to slow down both man and beast.

Griffin Malone was working as a pickup man at Clementine High School's rodeo camp. He rode his horse over to the dusty and defeated young cowboy while parents and other rodeo camp participants gave a smattering of applause, followed by a hesitant silence.

Because the kid wasn't moving.

"Is he all right?" Clem, Griff's foster brother, called from the opposite side of the arena where he'd released the bucking strap on the gelding. The horse trotted happily into the chute, none-the-worse for the ride. Clem signaled to the other cowhand. "Maggie, grab the med kit."

"On it," Maggie replied.

"He's breathing." Griff stared down at the inert teenager, registering blue jeans that weren't quite long enough, a faded gray T-shirt beneath a crash vest and what looked like a smashed cowboy hat under his riding helmet. Someone hadn't told the kid that cowboy hats didn't belong with safety helmets. Or perhaps he hadn't listened.

With the teen's fringe of unruly brown hair and his jaw thrust out, there was something about the boy that reminded Griff of himself twenty or so years ago, trying to roll with growth spurts, the increasingly compelling mystery of girls and the stifling set of adult expectations and their recriminations regarding his impulsive actions and naive mistakes.

Griff had been bad at being a teen. He was sympathetic to whatever this boy was going through.

Griff shifted in the saddle. "First time on a bronc, kid?" He wished he knew the teen's name, but he couldn't remember seeing him around town.

"What gave me away?" The teen looked okay. He just wasn't moving. Except maybe to sniff, like he was fighting tears. "The hat?"

"More like the post-ride freeze. The more you fall, the faster you bounce back up." Griff remembered those early days when he'd first moved to Clementine as a middle schooler and begun to rodeo, being thrown by large animals without knowing how to land and swallowing back tears so the other kids wouldn't tease him. "You need help getting up?"

No answer. But there was more sniffing.

Poor kid.

Griff dismounted, then bent his knees to squat next to the boy, intending to give him more time to collect himself by talking to him. Griff started with humor, which was pretty much his stock in trade. "Which girl are you trying to impress?"

"Ain't no girl," the boy grumbled.

Griff wasn't gullible enough to rule that out. "Hopefully, you'll be able to walk out of here under your own steam. Can you? We're all worried about you."

Griff had license to use the collective "we" since there was just a sparse rodeo crew from the Done Roamin' Ranch, of which Griff was part, and the kids vying for a spot on the Clementine High School rodeo team, of which Griff *had been* a part.

"I remember the first time I ate rodeo dust," Griff continued in a conversational tone, feeling the barest of breezes on this hot summer morning. "That gritty taste lingered in my mouth for days." Along with the embarrassment. "How 'bout we get you up and moving? I've got an unopened water bottle in my saddlebag."

The teen shifted his head beneath that mangled straw cowboy hat, revealing red-rimmed eyes and a tear-streaked face. He spit out some dirt. "I don't need your help."

Griff nodded, shifting on his haunches, hands clasped in front of him. "I can see that. But you're right in the path of the next chute to open with a bronc. So, you might want to get a move on."

"Best I get trampled." The boy spit again. He wasn't much good at spitting, even if he looked to be of legal driving age, old enough to have played football or baseball where spitting was something of a rite of passage. "Getting stomped on will put me out of my misery."

"Naw. Best you try again. Can't get much worse than this."

Except it could get worse. For Griff.

Footsteps approached, crossing the arid Oklahoma dirt with purpose.

Griff stood and turned in one fluid motion, facing Bess Glover, math teacher, high school rodeo coach and the one woman in town he couldn't charm. Not even after she'd kissed his socks off at Wade and Ronnie's wedding five months back. Since then, Bess had treated Griff like he had a contagious disease.

She made a man doubt his skill at the lip-lock.

"The boy just needs a tick of the clock to catch his breath," Griff told Bess softly.

Bess strode past Griff as if he wasn't there.

But Griff was present even if she didn't account for him. And her continued snubs made him wonder all the more: *Why did she kiss me?*

But truthfully, the more confounding question was: *Why did she kiss me and run?*

Couldn't have been his response. He'd been *gung* to her *ho*.

Griff studied Bess the way he studied the bucking bulls he took care of at his family's rodeo stock company where he worked—like she was unpredictable and should be understood so they could get along better. Where Bess was concerned, he wanted to bicker less and kiss more often than once or twice every fifteen years or so.

Bess Glover wore a mighty fine, camel-colored cowboy hat. Her fiery red hair lay over her shoulders in two thick braids secured with silver thread. Her jeans were black but her boots were the same tan color as her hat and the only thing that gave away she was a real cowgirl, not following some Western fashion trend. Those boots were faded and scuffed. She wore leather riding gloves and a long-sleeved, white shirt to protect herself from the sun. Sun being a redhead's worst enemy, a fact she'd confessed to Griff when they were teens and dancing around attraction.

Fifteen years later, Griff was still dancing.

"Dell," Bess said in a businesslike voice. "Are you hurt?"

"No, ma'am." Dell brought himself to a sitting position. Keeping his head bowed, he removed the riding helmet and then massaged his mangled cowboy hat back into shape, gingerly placing it on his head like it was worth something to him and putting those broken straws on full display for the world—and the rodeo team—to see. "I'm not hurt. I was meditating, thinking about what went wrong so I could do better next time."

Griff choked on a laugh. That was something he might have said.

He received a slashing, bright blue glare from Bess, who hadn't fully appreciated Griff's humor since he'd stood her up at prom and hadn't explained himself. How could he? He could barely face the facts of what had happened, himself. Maybe if he came clean with Bess now, there'd be more impulsive kisses in his future.

As if reading his mind, Bess smirked and said, *"Don't."*

"Yes, ma'am," Griff responded automatically, not certain what he was agreeing to.

"Dell." Bess helped the teen to his feet. "I know you want to be on the rodeo team with your friends, but maybe bronc riding isn't your event."

Dell winced. "That's what you said about bull riding."

Bess nodded.

"And breakaway roping." Dell went on, "And ribbon roping."

"What about chute dogging or goat tying?" Griff asked, taking pity on the boy.

Bess stared at Griff again. It was an unwelcome look, the likes of which he'd gotten used to over the years. "Are you the rodeo coach, Griff?" she demanded.

"No, ma'am." Griff gave Bess his stock-in-trade smile, the one that let the world know he was no trouble. And that would have been fine if he could have kept his mouth shut. "But you might recall that I work the rodeo forty weeks or so a year. And I recognize the grit in this here young fella." *You're pushing, Griff.* He ignored the little voice in his head, the one that sounded like his foster father, and continued, "I was just like him once."

"A little uncoordinated and a lot unfocused?" Dell asked, still keeping his head down. "That's what my grandfather says I am."

You lack just as much coordination as you do common sense.

The unpleasant memory from the past with his biological father filled Griff's head. The dust. The smarting ache after a fall. The impatient words of his ranch-hand father after Griff had taken a tumble while trying to ride bareback that first time.

Griff frowned, all levity draining. Family should be supportive. Emphasis on *should*. Griff's father left not long after that fateful fall from horseback. And Griff's mother had kicked him out of their home in Bartlesville when he wasn't much younger than Dell. Landing in the foster system, Griff had been very lucky to eventually be placed at the Done Roamin' Ranch, where he'd had all the love and support a boy could wish for. But this kid's words... They struck a chord.

Bess sighed and stood. "You shouldn't talk about yourself like that, Dell. If you have the will, I'll help you find a way. Today is just a fun day. The real work starts tomorrow. Go get some water and try again. Summer rodeo camp is all about the try."

The kid continued to hang his head.

"I'll help you, too, Dell," Griff said without thinking.

"I've got it covered, cowboy." Dismissing Griff, Bess walked away with Dell, speaking to the boy quietly.

"Way to shake it off, Dell," a man called from the stands, more commanding in tone than supportive.

There was a familiar note in that strong, hard voice.

Griff turned.

An older man sat on the metal bleachers opposite the cattle chute. He had his arms crossed and his straw hat brim low. And even though Griff hadn't seen Paul James in fifteen years, ever since he'd left Bartlesville, he knew with certainty that it was him.

Paul James, whose, daughter Avery, had been Griff's first love when Griff hadn't been old enough to drive. Paul James, who'd told Griff's mother she was failing at raising Griff right. Paul James, who'd refused to let Griff see his child. Not when he was born, not the day Avery died and not since.

Griff felt cold, despite the afternoon heat.

If Paul James was here in Clementine calling to Dell, that must mean...

Griff turned toward Bess and the young cowboy with his head hanging low.

Dell is my son?

"YOU DON'T HAVE to lie to me, Coach Glover," Dell told Bess as they left the arena via the cattle chute that led to the stock holding pastures. He tucked the battered riding helmet under his arm. "You're going to cut me from the team."

"It was your first try. Don't sell yourself short," Bess told Dell absent-mindedly. "Everybody starts somewhere." Whether it be with the rodeo or with love. "And nobody can predict what's ahead."

Back in high school, Bess had thought Griff was her something special. He'd been funny and sweet and was always interested in what she was thinking. They seemed to have a lot in common. When he'd asked Bess to prom it was like a fairy tale. *He* was her fairy-tale cowboy.

Until Griff didn't show up for the dance. Until Griff wouldn't tell her why. Until she'd told Griff she never wanted to speak to him again. And even though that had made Bess miserable, her mother had been thrilled. Mama wanted all her girls to marry well enough to escape ranch life.

And four of them had, leaving Bess feeling like the odd one out again.

The warm summer morning suddenly felt hotter than blazes. Despite her better judgment, Bess glanced over her shoulder at Griff.

The handsome, irresponsible cowboy was staring her way.

Butterflies reawakened in her chest, fluttering the way they had when Bess was in high school, when love was a new, blooming rose that promised to last forever.

No rose lasted forever.

"Don't." Bess faced forward and walked faster.

Don't think about Griff as anything other than a cowboy I used to know.

"Don't do what, Coach?" Beside her, Dell was still worried about being cut from the team.

Little did he know that Bess was determined not to cut anyone this year.

"Should I leave?" Dell asked in a small voice.

"No. I told you to try again."

"Okay." The gangly boy smiled at her with an enthusiasm reminiscent of Griff's exuberant grins.

Bess had never seen such emotion from the boy before.

He'd moved to town at the end of the last school year with his grandfather. Dell seemed like a good kid. But he had few friends and was still growing into his body, either of which were enough to derail a teenager's confidence. His grandfather might not have any tact, but he was right about one thing—Dell was uncoordinated, most likely because he was in the midst of a growth spurt. His feet were too large for the rest of his body.

Bess wanted to reassure Dell that this clumsy phase of his wouldn't last, that he'd grow into his body, gain confidence and hit the ground running toward whatever goal he set for himself. But she'd only been his math teacher for a few weeks, and his rodeo coach for less than a day. Having been a high school teacher for more than a decade, Bess knew that her words wouldn't be taken in the spirit they were given until they knew each other better.

Someone called for Dell up ahead, a thankful distraction to thoughts of Griff.

Dell had found his footing socially with two studious kids. His best friends, Kevin Underwood and Nancy Stafford, were waiting for him at the end of the chute. They'd be juniors this year, but it was the first time any of them had come out for the rodeo team.

Kevin swung the metal gate open for them to exit. Tall with acne, he aced all his math classes with Bess and had never given any indication he was a rodeo fan. "You okay, Dell?"

"He's fine." Nancy brushed dirt from Dell's shirt. Petite, blunt-cut black hair and with slim jeans she tucked into her cowboy boots, when Nancy didn't have her nose in a book, she was all tomboy and try. "Dell got up, didn't he?"

"Slow and steady wins the race," Dell quipped, face red. He squirmed away from Nancy.

There were cheers as another bronc rider gave it a go. Then gasps, and finally applause.

Wade, a champion bronc rider, was volunteering his time to give kids pointers this week. He motioned for Dell to come talk to him. The trio of rodeo rookies drifted toward him, their boots kicking up dust.

On the other side of the arena, Ronnie ran roping practice with orange traffic cones instead of the usual metal roping steers. Dell and his friends weren't the only newbies who'd come out for the team this year. Bess's team wouldn't be winning any awards, hence her willingness to keep everyone and rebuild. She had her fingers and toes crossed that there might just be a breakout rodeo star among them.

Bess sighed. It would be hard to help all her new recruits improve. Her assistant rodeo coach had taken a teaching job in the next county over and quit. None of her teaching colleagues had expressed interest in helping.

Grandpa Rascal tottered toward Bess with a bowlegged stride and a wobble to his walk. "Bessie, I need a word."

"Rascal." Bess hurried to his side, taking his arm as a stiff, warm breeze threatened to knock him over. "How did you get here? I thought we agreed you wouldn't drive anymore."

"*You* agreed, Bessie." Rascal put a hand on her shoulder and leaned heavily on it. "When the state of Oklahoma takes away my driver's license, then I'll agree with you."

Caring for a grandparent was about as frustrating as Bess imagined raising a teenager was. There was the same drive for independence, plus smarmy backtalk and a complete disregard for safety.

"You should be using that cane I bought you." Or the walker that was collecting dust near the mudroom door. "You could fall." Her biggest fear.

Rascal made noises of disagreement, sparing a hand to rub his white grizzled chin. "When you came to live with me ten years ago, it was me who said I'd take care of you. Not the other way around."

"I was twenty-one." Not in need of care. But when her parents moved to Oklahoma City that same year to be near Bess's older sister Camille and her kids, they'd asked Bess to watch out for Grandpa Rascal, a task that was becoming nigh on impossible. "What are you doing here, Rascal?"

"I'm making a stand." Her grandfather tipped his straw cowboy hat back and fixed Bess with a stern look. "Vickie Taveras showed up at the ranch to do a market estimate."

"I told you she was stopping by." It was bad enough that the school board was trying to build a vocational building or a new gym on the high school's rodeo grounds and cancel the rodeo program. It was worse that Griff was in a wedding with her this weekend and the next and was one of the cowboys sent to work the rodeo stock this week. But on top of all that, Bess and her grandfather could no longer run the ranch at profitable levels alone. Their stock numbers and annual income were down considerably.

"You're moving too fast, girl." Her grandfather's reedy voice had the tone of a poorly played clarinet. "We need to think this through. There's got to be a way for us to keep the ranch."

"There's not." Bess refused to feel guilty about that. "The place needs a full-time rancher, not a math-teacher-slash-rodeo-coach and a retired rancher who can no longer ride." Or do chores.

"You're gonna put six generations' worth of hard work on the market and sell to the highest bidder rather than family?" Rascal asked mournfully. "Where's this urgency coming from, Bessie?"

From everything.

"I want to keep the ranch in the family." Bess had a tight hold on her myriad of emotions—on guilt, on frustration, on a feeling of failure. But she was afraid they galloped into her words, giving her away. "And we might be able to if you'd let me do a genealogy search with DNA."

She'd spent most of her free time this summer searching online genealogy databases, trying to find her grandfather's long-lost older brother with the hopes that someone in her great-uncle's branch of the family tree would want to buy the Rolling G, since no one in Rascal's wanted it. But her searches had come to a dead end.

"Your scientific test won't give you the answers you want." Rascal scoffed. "Either way, you're not going to find my brother, Eshon. He's long gone. Don't hang your hopes on him."

"Unless you have a better idea, that's exactly what I'm doing." That and trying to whip the rodeo team into shape. Bess checked the time on her phone. She needed to keep things at camp moving and not get sidetracked by her grandfather. "Something's going to come up if we submit your DNA."

"Nothing's going to come up except the very real property taxes due this fall." Grandpa Rascal huffed like a steam engine pulling into the station—one big gusty sigh. "If you won't hire ranch help and are convinced that we've got to quit ranching, I want to sell to someone I know and approve of."

They walked past the part of the arena where Griff sat on his brown horse. Bess checked her phone again. She needed to wrap up bronc riding if she was going to stay on schedule.

"Howdy, Mr. Glover. Bess." Griff stared at them with interest, tipping his hat.

Rascal stopped. Or at least, his feet stopped. His torso swayed forward.

Bess roped her arm around Rascal's chest to keep him in place.

"That you, Griff?" Rascal squinted toward the arena.

"Yes, sir."

Griff's smile did funny things to Bess's brain. Thoughts of rodeo camp and logistics and missing relatives fled, leaving her with only one thought, one word, one man. *Griff.*

"I was wondering…" Griff said, still smiling at Bess. "If you'd accept my help."

"With what?" Rascal scratched the back of his neck.

"With everything." Griff gave a brisk nod, as if they should have known that's what he meant.

Bess couldn't breathe. What was Griff saying? He'd help her at the ranch? Instead of rejecting him outright, her mind put that kiss they'd shared months ago on repeat.

Her cheeks started to heat.

"Bess needs help coaching and you need help at the ranch, sir." Griff's smile no longer reminded Bess of kisses. It was almost…calculating.

"No, thanks," Bess said stiffly.

"Don't look a gift horse in the mouth, Bessie." Grandpa Rascal gestured toward Griff. "Come on by after dinner. We'll be waiting with ice-cold lemonade and warm cookies."

"No." Bess didn't trust a gift horse, especially when it was Griff. "You're not coming over. We'll manage at the ranch without you."

Griff nodded briskly. "I'll still help you out with the team."

Bess opened her mouth to turn him down. She didn't want Griff to think that kiss months ago meant anything. She didn't want him to think she was interested in him at all. And as for the rodeo team…

Dell and his friends erupted into laughter. They were so green. Bess wouldn't be able to coach forty kids by herself. She was lucky that Ronnie and Wade were helping out these first few weeks.

"All right," Bess relented, although not graciously. "You can help me coach."

"You won't regret it." Griff tipped his hat again and rode off.

Bess watched Griff ride away, taking in his good form and

skill on a horse. At times, he could be everything she admired and wanted in a cowboy, including the way he kissed nowadays.

Bess sucked on her lower lip.

Since she'd kissed him, he confused her more than usual. Griff hadn't mentioned her stealing that kiss at all, not even to joke about it. Was that because he was being a gentleman? Or a jerk—waiting to use it against her at the worst possible time?

A guy who stood up his girl on prom and refused to explain himself had to be a jerk.

"That was a mistake, Bessie." Grandpa Rascal sighed. "Think of the ranch. We wouldn't have to pay him."

"Just ice-cold lemonade and warm cookies," she mumbled.

She preferred to give Griff tepid tap water and sour grapes.

CHAPTER TWO

"HEY, DELL." Griff moseyed over to the teen later that afternoon, mustering a smile that he hoped covered his nerves.

Rodeo camp was essentially done. Griff had helped load most of the stock. Bess was busy talking to a group of parents. Many of the rodeo kids were milling about, chatting or packing up their gear.

Dell—*his son?*—was hanging out with a couple of teens, a boy and a girl Griff recognized from around town.

"Sir?" Dell gave Griff a nod of acknowledgment. He had Avery's blue eyes and Griff's stubborn nose. His hair was the soft brown of fall leaves and looked to have an unruly curl, same as Griff's.

He's mine.

Griff couldn't stop staring. *Why is Dell in Clementine? Does he know who I am?*

"Can I help you?" Dell shifted subtly out of reach, eyeing Griff with suspicion.

"Sorry." Griff shook his head, trying to pass his gaping off as something else. "I just remembered I need to buy bread on the way home." That was an improvisation. "I offered to help you. You know, with your rodeo skills?" He'd offered to help Bess and her grandfather, too, having overheard their argument about selling their ranch. It just so happened that Griff had been saving up for a place of his own. And saving. And saving. Dreaming of a day when he'd buy a ranch his son would be proud to call home. And now that he'd met his son, that day had come. Griff needed a home for his son to stay in, rather than a ranch bunkhouse shared with other cowhands. Because that's what good fathers did. They provided stability and a home base for their children, now and in the future.

My son. The words went zinging through Griff, making him want to give a loud hoot and a holler.

"Help me?" Dell scrunched his nose. "Why would you want to help me?"

"Because it's what folks do in Clementine? Help each other?" Griff struggled not to blurt the truth: *Because I'm your dad!* "You remind me of me when I started rodeo. And I... I had a lot of help."

The boy considered Griff in silence a moment before nodding. "I'll take your help. *We all will.*" He pointed to his companions, jutting his chin. "Me, Kevin and Nancy."

Griff nodded. "Okay." He would have agreed to anything if it meant spending time with Dell.

"Okay?" Dell seemed surprised he'd accepted.

Kevin, who was taller than Griff, chuckled. "Have you seen us try to rodeo?"

"We stink," Nancy, who was shorter than Bess, admitted.

"Gotta walk before you can run." Griff evaluated the group for physical strengths.

All of them had the pale complexion of teens who'd spent their summer so far in the library. Kevin had length, if not strength. He might make a good roper. Nancy was compact. Give her a fast, experienced horse, and she'd fly around the barrels. Dell was somewhere in between. Although he was all knees and elbows, there was a sturdiness about him that implied he could dig in his heels. Maybe steer wrestling? "And, as I admitted to Dell in the arena earlier, I started in the dirt. Spent a few years chasing the dream of bull riding. I'm a working cowboy at the Done Roamin' Ranch, which supplies roughstock to rodeos. Why don't you tell me why you want to rodeo, Dell?"

Dell smirked. "The only reason I'm out here is to...*oof.*"

Nancy elbowed Dell hard enough to stop him talking. "I ride barrels."

Griff nodded, taking note that there was another agenda here. "Is your horse any good?"

"Her horse is good at dumping her off," Kevin quipped, capping it off with a deep-throated laugh that belied his slim frame.

"My grandpa says Nancy would fall off a bike if she had one," Dell added, recovering his breath.

Nancy elbowed him again. "At least I have a horse."

"But not a bike," Dell teased in a voice that cracked. He laughed, then laughed some more when Nancy began to chase him around.

Dell laughs like I do—with his entire being.

Griff grinned, feeling lighter than air. He rocked back on his boot heels while the pair kicked up dust with their antics.

"Dell." That steely, familiar male voice had them all turning around.

Upon facing Avery's father, Griff came back down to earth.

Paul James had matured in the fifteen years since Griff had seen him last. His face had more lines, all pulling his expression downward. His hair was a peppery shade but still straight as hay. The cold disapproval in his blue eyes... That hadn't changed.

Paul frowned at Griff. "Dell, go get in the truck."

"But Kevin and I—"

"Do as you're told." The older man was still as authoritarian as he'd been with Avery. As he'd been with Griff years ago.

Not since Griff was a teen had he been struck so painfully silent. No smart-aleck comeback came to mind, even to defend his son.

My son. The child this man kept from me.

Long-buried resentment flared to life, crackling through Griff's veins. And still, his mind spun without finding the right words to say. *Be calm*, his inner voice advised.

Dell stomped off toward the parking lot, his friends following in his wake. None of them laughed.

Paul sidled closer to Griff, lowering his sharp-edged voice. "You stay away from my boy. He's disobedient enough without your reckless influence. He needs a firm hand."

From what Griff had seen, Dell wasn't reckless. And he wasn't Paul's.

"Still using the same bag of tricks?" The words flew from Griff's lips with unmistakable bitterness even if he'd learned long ago that humor, not anger, was the way to deal with bullies. "Shouting and ultimatums didn't work with Avery." Paul's dead daughter.

The older man's cheeks turned ruddy.

"And they won't work with Dell." Griff's breath was ragged, as if he hadn't filled his lungs with air since Paul's appearance had frozen him in place. He drew a calming breath and tried to choose his words more carefully, finally listening to his inner voice of reason. "We should be working together for Dell's sake, not fighting one another." That sounded exactly like something his foster father would say. "Why are you in Clementine if not for that?"

Paul's chin thrust out. "I had a chance to have my own insurance office here. These opportunities don't come up often and..." His voice cracked. His gaze clouded. And then Paul coughed hard and thick, like he was about to hack up a piece of lung. It took a bit for him to clear his throat and continue. "And we lost Tina...my wife...to complications from COVID last winter. It's been hard on both of us. We needed a change."

I'll give you change, Griff wanted to say. *If you give me my son.*

But Griff knew Paul wouldn't give up Dell now that he was alone.

"I'm sorry to hear about your wife." Griff understood how scary serious illness could be. His foster mother had just finished a round of chemo for cancer. "But Dell needs more family in his life, not less."

"No." Paul pushed his hat more firmly on his head as a warm gust of wind blew by.

Anger, the likes of which Griff hadn't felt since he was a teen, bunched and built inside him with time-bomb-ticking intensity, threatening to explode. That explosion was how things had disintegrated when Griff had last faced Paul's lack of compassion or compromise.

Griff rubbed at his chest, trying to cool things down. "You can't tell me no."

"I just did."

Walk away, son. Again, his foster father's voice spoke inside Griff's head, cutting through the anger that threatened to overwhelm him. But with that anger came the painful memories of the past. Griff wanted to reject that anger, wanted to suppress those memories.

But he couldn't. They were tumbling free, threatening his composure.

Standing his ground, Griff puffed out his chest. "You won't say no forever, Paul. You need me. *He* needs me." Griff spun on his heel and stalked away because anger was buzzing in his ears and jagged memories were coming at him hard and fast.

One memory dominated the rest.

Griff had never worn a tuxedo until the night of prom. He'd asked Bess to go with him and had rented a fancy black tux he'd thought she'd like, even though it had cost more. Her family wasn't too keen on Griff so he'd wanted to impress them, too.

His foster mother had been taking pictures of Griff with the other boys at the Done Roamin' Ranch before they left for the dance. They stood in front of the fireplace, decked out in their tuxedos and holding flowers for their dates when Dad's cell phone rang.

"Griff," his foster father said after hanging up, his expression grave.

Griff's stomach had knotted. He associated that expression of his foster father's with bad news. Deaths. Unexpected visits from the "reals," as Chandler, one of his older foster brothers, called biological parents.

"There's been a bad accident." Dad pulled Griff aside. "*That girl* is in the hospital."

That girl. Avery.

Raised by a mostly absent single mother and without a steady hand from his father, Griff had become a rebellious teenager. In junior high school, Griff had gotten Avery pregnant. That was the last straw for Griff's mother. Not having heard from her husband in years, she'd put Griff in foster care, and after bouncing around in temporary homes, he'd ended up with a passel of other boys at the Done Roamin' Ranch, run by Frank and Mary Harrison. Frank and Mary asked all their foster boys to call them Mom and Dad. Foster parents and brothers alike had channeled Griff's rebellious streak in a more positive direction. Eventually, he'd been given a horse and shown how to care for it. He'd been taught how to ride, how to rope and how important it was to show up even when life was tough.

That night of prom, Dad had added another sad detail. "Avery had the baby with her when the accident happened."

The baby. Griff's baby.

Griff's legs gave out. He fell to the floor, crushing the pink rose corsage he'd bought for Bess.

One of the reasons Griff had landed at the Done Roamin' Ranch was that it was far away from his home in Bartlesville. He'd been told that Avery was going to give the baby up.

My kid. His breath came in ragged gasps as he did a mental calculation. *My kid would be nearly two.*

"We'll drive to Bartlesville." Dad sent the rest of the boys off to the dance. He'd called Bess's parents and explained that Griff wouldn't be going to the dance but not why. And then they'd driven to the hospital, barely speaking along the way.

At the hospital doors, Griff held his foster father back. "Avery's parents took out a restraining order against me." Not because he was dangerous but to keep him away.

"They didn't." Dad shook his head. "Your caseworker told me tonight on that call."

"Avery's dad lied?"

"Avery's dad lied about a lot of things." Dad looked grim. He'd left his cowboy hat back at the ranch. His graying hair was flat. "They didn't give the baby up for adoption, either."

They spent all night at the hospital, unwelcome by Avery's parents, banned from receiving updates. They did hear that Griff's baby survived. But Avery... She didn't make it.

In their grief and anger, Avery's father had called the police to have Griff and his foster father removed from the hospital. Dad thought it best that they take a step back.

If Griff had known that step would last fifteen years, he might not have left the hospital.

But they did leave. They'd driven back to Clementine, pulling up to the ranch midday.

Dad had put his hand on Griff's shoulder when Griff would have gotten out of the truck. "I know what you're thinking."

Griff shook his head, filled with anger the likes of which he hadn't experienced since before he'd settled into life at the Done Roamin' Ranch. "I can't let those people raise my kid. I'll drop out of school. I'll work full-time. I'll get my own place and—"

"The courts won't let you raise that child. You just turned seventeen. Avery's parents must have been helping her."

"But they're liars!" Griff's voice had sounded shrill and raw, not strong the way he needed it to be for this fight. Even at seventeen, he knew that.

"Some folks lie when they feel threatened, especially when they're trying to protect someone else." Dad's tone gentled. "Someone they love."

Griff worked to swallow around the lump in his throat.

"This is your chance to get your life together. To grow up to be someone your child would be proud of. And then, when you're both ready, you can reconnect. You'll have the patience, the wisdom and the financial stability you don't have now. All the things your mother didn't have when she passed you on." Because she'd been a teen parent, too.

"Griff! We need you over here," Clem called, knocking Griff back into the present.

He breathed in rodeo dust, breathed out anger and bitterness from the past.

Patience, wisdom and financial stability.

Griff had all those things now. Plus, a good sense of humor and a way with kids, thanks to some of his foster brothers being parents.

Griff had been talked out of fighting for his child all those years ago.

But now, he was ready to take back what was his.

"THE FIRST DAY of rodeo camp is always the hardest." Ronnie gave Bess a side hug at the end of the day. "Don't you have a hot date tonight with that veterinarian from Friar's Creek? The one who's your date for Abby's wedding this weekend?"

"Hot date." Bess scoffed, trying not to look for Griff over by the Done Roamin' Ranch stock trailers. But she'd been unsuccessful keeping her eyes off him all day.

Those broad shoulders… That scruffy fringe of soft brown hair… That trademark grin… His intense kisses…

Don't. Bess shook her head. "I canceled my date with Brandon tonight. I've got a hot date with a stack of ranch bills that need paying."

"And you've got to make plans for your new assistant coach." Ronnie arched her finely shaped brows in teasing fashion. "How do you feel about Griff coming to your rescue?"

Bess rolled her eyes. "I didn't cancel my date because of Griff." The cowboy didn't fit her criteria for a man to fall in love with. Not only was he untrustworthy, but he could make her temper accelerate from zero to sixty just by smiling at her. "And he's not rescuing me."

"Let me fact-check you, my friend. I have it on good authority from *my husband*, Wade, that…" Ronnie put her hands on Bess's cowboy hat, ran her hands around the wide brim and then lowered it to a mischievous slant "…that Griff offered to help you, both with the rodeo team and at your ranch. That's a rescue, plain and simple."

"He's going to help with *the team*." Which was odd considering he'd never done so before and might have even gone out of his way not to. "And I admit that Griff offered to help at the ranch. But I turned him down."

"Ah." Ronnie smiled a winner's smile. "You're still prickly when it comes to Griff. Not that you aren't picky with men in general. You should loosen up. Griff is still sweet on you."

Bess chose to ignore that last comment. "There's nothing wrong with being prickly or picky. And if you believe Griff is still interested in me after all these years of frenemy-ship, then I've got a unicorn to sell you." Bess took her cowboy hat and straightened it the same way she wanted to straighten Ronnie's impression of Griff's feelings toward her. Bess had kissed Griff, not the other way around. "We've barely spoken since your wedding."

"Doesn't matter. I'm a believer in unicorns *and* happy endings," Ronnie gushed. "He still pines for you."

Bess scoffed, gaze once more drifting traitorously toward the stock trailers and Griff. "Don't play matchmaker, Ronnie."

"Ha!" Ronnie adjusted her own cowboy hat this time, giving it a jaunty tilt. "You don't need a match where there are already sparks."

"And you don't need a spark when you've already been burned," Bess tossed back. "I've played things cool with Griff for years. I was your maid of honor to his best man at your wedding and nothing happened." *Bess Glover, you are such a liar!* "Have you heard so much as a whisper about us being an item?"

"No." Ronnie admitted, suitably deflated. She was the sweetest thing, but if there was a rumor floating around, Ronnie's easygoing manner and roundabout way could pull out the truth easier than a penny nail to a dime store magnet. "But that doesn't mean I don't hold out hope. You guys are perfect for each other."

"Not hardly. Can we talk about something else?"

"Will you meet me at The Buckboard for drinks on Thursday?" Ronnie gave Bess another side hug. "Thursday is the new Friday." Especially when Ronnie had taken to traveling with bronc riding Wade to a rodeo every Friday this summer.

"Fine."

Ronnie gave Bess the smile that had won her the title of rodeo queen. "I'll be by tomorrow to help again."

"Thanks." Bess watched her walk away before surveying the rodeo grounds. Everyone had to be gone before she locked up.

Ramps and trailer doors banged closed as cowboys and cowgirls alike shut their transports in preparation to leave. The air was hot. The sun's rays unforgiving. Bess was in need of some shade and a shower. Anything to cool her off.

In the distance, a whistle blew, most likely from football practice over in the stadium.

Outside the stock paddocks, Griff set a chain on the back of a large trailer full of young bulls. He glanced around the parking lot, seeming to be searching for someone.

Me?

Bess couldn't look away even at the risk of being caught staring, even if he wasn't the type of man she was supposed to be dreaming of. There was a stiff set to Griff's shoulders and his grin hadn't made as much of an appearance this afternoon as it had earlier in the day. Was that because he was tense about his offer to help Bess?

Without connecting to her gaze, Griff got into the truck hitched to the bull trailer and drove off.

Bess turned, intending to leave, too, but Clementine's high school principal approached. "Hey, Eric. I was just locking up for the day."

Eric Epstein was a good high school principal. He may have worn khakis, a dress shirt and a tie—even today, in the middle of summer—but he also wore cowboy boots and a cowboy hat. He was fair to the students in his care and the teachers he managed. But Eric was caught in the middle of the fight regarding the land the high school rodeo grounds were on.

The fate of the rodeo team had hung in the balance of that fight for over a year. Bess was hoping they'd never resolve the issue. But the school board was united on one thing—reducing rodeo team funding and squeezing the life out of the program until it folded.

Bess was determined that wouldn't happen. This was rural Oklahoma, where rodeo wasn't just a rite of passage but an important part of the region's sense of community.

"I've got the latest budget figures for sports teams approved by the school board." Eric held up a sheet of paper, expression grim. "It's not good news. They cut your funds again. Drastically. One-third of what it was last year."

"Oh, come on. We just went to the state finals." With a team of barely thirty kids. Her spirits sank.

Their budget was small compared with other sports, like football. It covered shirts and a cowboy hat for every participant, plus minimal supplies for replacement ropes, protective gear and practice equipment. They had a few small sponsorships, plus Bess and parents donated their time and gas to drive kids and horses to events. Any additional needs—of which there were many—were paid for by Bess, herself.

Bess tried not to whine, but, "One-third of the budget won't buy shirts and hats for all forty kids."

"I know." Eric bent and picked up a small silver conch, the kind that kids tied onto saddles as decoration. It had been almost completely hidden in the dirt. He handed it to Bess.

She clenched the small, round conch, pressing it into her palm as if it were a lucky talisman. "Most of these kids are raised on ranches or have parents and grandparents who've rodeoed. They take great pride in being on the team." And Bess took great pride in coaching them.

"I know. I'm sorry. You have my complete support if you want to fundraise to keep the team going. But for how long..." Eric shrugged apologetically.

"They're going to keep chipping away until there is nothing and no one left." Until Bess gave in. She clenched the conch tighter. *Never.* "I appreciate you telling me in person." He could have emailed or texted.

Eric nodded. He gave the rodeo grounds one last look before turning around and heading back toward the school offices.

Bess banged the rodeo gate closed, then locked it. She stomped to her truck, frustrated because the program she'd enjoyed so much as a kid and had made her tougher as a person was at risk of being closed down altogether. It wasn't fair.

She pounded her fists on her steering wheel.

Detach.

That's what rodeo had taught her. Devote yourself to something you love with skill and passion. But, if you failed, take a moment to mourn before separating yourself from that loss and moving on with the pride that came from trying.

She'd taken that lesson to heart when Griff had stood her up on one of the most significant nights of her young life.

"I told you that boy was no good," Mama had told Bess after talking with Griff's foster father on the night of prom. "Frank Harrison isn't letting Griff go to the dance. Maybe now, you'll focus your gaze on more appropriate boys, like Daniel Erdale.

His folks say he's going to work for NASA someday. Or Jose Houston. He's committed to West Point. Bess, it's the least you deserve. You need someone capable of keeping up with you."

"Mama, stop." Wearing a pink, off-the-shoulder prom dress, Bess had dialed Griff's number on her cell phone while her mother ran through a litany of other eligible boys at school. "He's not answering." Bess had texted him, worry making her hands shake. "Did Mr. Harrison say what happened?"

"No. Now, get your things. You need to go to that dance and hold your head high." Mama had thrust Bess's shawl and clutch at her. "You don't want folks to think that someone the likes of Griff Malone can hurt you."

Still, Bess had hesitated. "Is Griff all right? Are they at the hospital? Was he in a fight?"

But Mama didn't know. And neither did the Done Roamin' Ranch boys who'd attended prom that night. If it hadn't been for Ronnie, Bess might have gone home to cry. Instead, she detached and rehearsed what to say to Griff on Monday—asking if he was okay, telling him that she'd understand no matter what had happened.

Not that she'd gotten any answer, not then or now. All he'd told her was that he couldn't talk about it.

"Water under the bridge, Bess Glover," she said to herself, a reminder that the past wasn't important. Bess gave herself a little shake and looked around the empty high school rodeo grounds. But she'd find no answers here.

It was time to drive back to the Rolling G, where she had stock to feed, bills to pay, dinner to make and a mystery to be solved.

Why had Griff offered to help?

CHAPTER THREE

"GOOD. YOU'VE GOT your town clothes on." Clem was shining his best pair of cowboy boots at the kitchen table in the bunkhouse when Griff passed him on his way to the door. "We can drive to The Buckboard together."

"I've got an appointment," Griff said vaguely, since there were several ranch hands lounging around the bunkhouse after a hard day's work, listening. He was going into town to find out where Dell lived and then intended to swing by. He didn't need witnesses for that.

Clem tsked. "So, the rumor is true. You've got a date with Bess."

I wish. Griff laughed, not that he felt at all jolly. "The day Bess Glover accepts a date with me is the day…" For the second time that day, Griff didn't have a smarmy comeback.

What's the matter with me?

The answer was simple: *I'm a father.*

But he was reluctant to tell anyone. Not until he made progress with Paul about visitation.

Griff sat on the bench in the mudroom and told Clem, "Enjoy flirting with Maggie while she bartends tonight." That was payback for the Bess comment.

"We're just friends," Clem insisted, despite the fact that everyone could tell Clem and his best friend, Maggie, were circling around something more than friendship.

Griff put on his best boots—black—and his best hat—a black Stetson—and headed out, walking across the ranch yard at the Done Roamin' Ranch toward his truck.

There was a peaceful quality to the ranch after dinner. The bulk of the work had been done for the day. Folks were more relaxed.

At the main house, a rambling modern ranch-style home, his foster father sat on the front porch playing cards with a couple of cowboys. Zane was working with his new horse in the arena while Dylan watched. Inside the large, six-bay garage, weights could be heard clanking together as cowboys got their workout in.

"Hey, Griff." Ronnie sat out on the front porch of the original white farmhouse watching eleven-year-old Ginny run through the sprinklers on the front lawn. "Headed into town? Can you pick up a gallon of milk for me?"

"Nope." Griff smiled at Ronnie's roundabout attempt to know where he was going but he didn't fault her for it.

Everyone at the D Double R watched out for each other. And if other folks called that being nosy... Well, Griff understood that staying up-to-date with family was just one way to show you cared.

Griff knew nothing about the foster system except what he'd learned by being placed in temporary homes as his caseworker tried to find him a more permanent place to live. Foster homes were clean. Foster parents and caseworkers were well-meaning. They wanted you to talk about your problems and resolve your feelings—all with good intentions. But at fourteen, Griff had needed physical activity—to run, to try something a little dangerous, to shout out his frustration at the top of his lungs.

Instead, the adults in foster care wanted all his balled-up emotions to sort themselves out, like cards played on a game of solitaire. They hadn't understood him at all. Oh, he could use his humor to make people laugh and make them angry. But that only caused those in charge to jot down notes: *Griff doesn't take his situation seriously; Griff is holding on to bitterness; Griff refuses to participate in therapy.*

Griff had gotten quite good at reading notes from across a desk.

And then, he'd been taken on a long car ride with his caseworker.

"You'll like this place," she'd told him. "It's a ranch and there's plenty of space to run free."

Griff had latched onto the word *free*, letting thoughts of running away fill the empty spaces in his head. If he wasn't wanted, then he didn't need anyone.

A cowboy appeared in the ranch yard in front of Griff, bringing him back to the present.

"Didn't you hear me call you?" It was Chandler, his older foster brother and the ranch foreman, although lately he'd taken over most of the ranch booking from Dad, too. "We sent too many ranch hands to rodeo camp today. How about you take tomorrow off? I've got you working a shift at a rodeo in Dallas this weekend."

"Can I take a couple of days off instead?" Griff had been looking forward to seeing Dell again. "I want to help coach the rodeo team."

"Okay." Chandler jotted something in his phone.

Griff waited for him to finish making notes. "As for this weekend, I've got Nate's wedding Saturday, remember?"

"Shoot. I didn't record that." Chandler grunted, tapping his phone screen some more. He was tall and too angular, having lost weight since his divorce and not in a good way. He lifted his cowboy hat and ran a hand over his short brown hair before plopping his hat back on his head. "You weren't so big on working rodeo camp last year. Why do you want to coach? What about Bess?"

"I can handle Bess." *I'd like to handle Bess.* But she was determined to keep him at arm's length for the rest of his life. "She's got a lot of green recruits, kids who could benefit from belonging to something." From being proud of competing on the rodeo team and being happy that their father helped them do well. "If they receive some training, that is."

"If you've got the heart for it, you do you." Chandler glanced toward the front porch where their foster mother was laughing. His brow clouded with worry. "Dad needs something to keep his mind off Mom's health. Maybe I'll send him into town tomorrow to help."

"You could send him to manage a couple of rodeos in your place." Chandler tried very hard to juggle his time with his young son, but this summer had been especially challenging. They had some high-profile, hard-to-ride bulls and broncs and attempting to ride good buckers could greatly increase a cowboy's score. Hence the surge in rodeo stock contracts. The Done Roamin' Ranch was booked and double-booked, making stock and personnel management something of a nightmare.

"Maybe I'll do that," Chandler said absently. "Thanks, Griff." He headed toward the main house.

Griff got into his old beat-up truck and took a long look at his home before he headed out, remembering his first night at the ranch.

He'd been gifted new clothes and assigned a bedroom with three other boys in the main house. He'd sat at a dinner table in those stiff, new blue jeans, with conversations flying so fast that he had trouble keeping up. No one asked Griff how he was feeling. That first day, they'd hardly talked to him at all. The Done Roamin' Ranch was unlike any other foster home he'd been in.

It had confounded him and eventually deflated Griff's hurt at being tossed aside.

His foster parents—Frank and Mary Harrison—had hugged Griff when wishing him good-night. They'd told him they were glad he'd come to live with them.

No one at any other foster home or facility he'd bounced around to had ever told him they were glad to have Griff. The Harrisons' sentiments had felt like a curveball, something that dropped in unexpectedly. The next morning, Griff had braced himself for the real side of foster care to emerge—group therapy, individual therapy, updates for his caseworker and notes. Many, many notes.

Instead, he'd been invited to go riding with the boys. It was summer and they were off from school. After their ride, they'd gone swimming in Lolly Creek. He'd played Wiffle ball, cards and participated in something a bit dangerous his foster brothers called musical horses. Every day that summer had been like that.

After a week, Griff's shoulders had loosened. Days were filled with activity and laughter. There were more hugs from the Harrisons. After a month, his jaw wasn't clenched all the time.

No one cared what Griff had done to have his mother wash her hands of him. No one asked why his father hadn't shown up to claim him, even though he'd been contacted. No one judged, possibly because everyone else on the ranch had rocky histories of their own.

It had been easy to blend in, to find his place, to become one of the Done Roamin' Ranch's foster boys. And from his foster brothers, Griff was given tips on how to ride, on how to get the business of mucking out stalls done quicker, on how to curl the straw brim of his cowboy hat the way he preferred it. And then came a day the other boys had been waiting for—they were taken to a rodeo. For the first time, Griff saw cowboys ride angry bulls and supercharged horses. They'd get flung or they'd bail. But they all picked themselves up and released a primal cry of triumph...or anguish.

Immediately, Griff knew what he wanted to be when he grew up.

One of them.

He neared town, thinking of Dell, wondering what challenges his son had to deal with, knowing that he was going to try to help give his kid that outlet for uncertainty and frustration, despite what Paul James had to say about it.

Because history would not repeat itself. Griff was going to be the kind of father who watched out for his kid through good times and bad. He was going to give Dell a stable home life and a ranch where he could spread his wings or retreat from stress when he needed a safe haven.

All Griff needed to do was claim his parental rights.

And buy the Rolling G, Bess's ranch, if she was willing to sell it to him.

"I CAME AS quick as I could." Bess slid into a booth at The Buckboard with Abby Beckett and her two other bridesmaids, Evie Grace and Kelly-Jo Carter.

Bess had left a stack of bills that needed to be paid when Abby texted an SOS. "What's the emergency?"

"Abby is having cold feet," Evie murmured to Bess, smoothing the skirt of her blue sundress, making Bess feel dowdy in her dusty rodeo camp duds.

I should have showered and changed, emergency or no.

"There might not be a wedding this weekend," Evie continued softly.

"I don't have cold feet." Abby's voice quavered. Her eyes were red from crying. Her long, blond hair looked like it hadn't seen a comb all day. "Nate didn't answer his phone last night. Or today."

Bess allowed that statement time to sink in, letting her gaze drift around The Buckboard.

Clementine's only honky-tonk was rumored to have been an old dance hall in the days of the Wild, Wild West. The decor certainly fit—rustic barnwood, brass spittoons and antlers. The bar itself nearly ran the length of the place, from the front to the dance floor in the back.

The crowd was sparse on this Monday night. Only a few cowboys were scattered about, drinking beer and eating burgers and sweet potato fries. Several tables had been shoved together close to the empty dance floor.

The Knitters Club had filled the table with skeins of colorful yarn in bright Christmas colors—red, white, gold, silver and green. It was never too early to start knitting for the holidays. Their gray-haired heads were bent over their work as they chattered about yarn weight. For years, Bess's paternal grandmother had been one of their group. She'd passed away last fall, an event that led to Rascal's downward spiral physically.

A wave of grief brought Bess back to the present.

The wedding is off?

Poor Abby. What a nightmare.

Already, Bess's mind charged ahead with what needed to be done—guests notified, flowers and hair appointments canceled, food, church and reception halls to be contacted. Bess would be stuck with an expensive, celery green, Grecian-style dress that she couldn't wear anywhere.

If the wedding was off.

If...

Abby was flighty, not always knowing what she wanted. She'd bought a car last fall and returned it to exchange for another after driving it for a day, and then exchanged it for a third the day after that. She tried every diet craze and fashion trend. She and her mother had consulted a psychic, a numerologist and an astrologer to choose a wedding date.

Abby's being flighty...

Bess turned back to her friends, determined to pump the brakes on canceling the wedding. "Can we think about this for a second? Wasn't Nate's bachelor party this weekend?"

"Saturday." Kelly-Jo nodded. She sat next to Abby and had her arm over Abby's shoulders. Her brown hair fell limply from a straw cowboy hat. She'd been working all day in the heat, too, and looked it, which made Bess feel better about her own appearance. "Abby hasn't heard from Nate since Saturday afternoon before the party."

"Could Nate still be hungover?" Bess hated to ask, but it was a possibility.

While Abby vehemently denied that possibility, movement at the bar caught Bess's eye.

Griff sat on a barstool next to his foster brother Clem. He had on his Saturday night clothes—dark blue jeans, a black shirt and cowboy hat. Nothing faded or dusty about him tonight. His appearance made Bess wonder who he was dressing up for.

Don't.

"On second thought, I suppose he could still be nursing a hangover," Abby allowed slowly. "He didn't show up to work today. But his truck wasn't in the driveway." Abby's lower lip trembled. "What if he fell in love with a stripper at his bachelor party? What if he realized he doesn't want to marry me and left town?"

Bess considered this a rash conclusion and said so.

"Then where is he?" Abby's lower lip trembled more noticeably. A wail escaped her throat.

The knitters took notice.

"Everybody just take a breath," Bess advised as Kelly-Jo quieted Abby.

"I have been breathing," Abby said in a stronger voice as tears spilled on her cheeks. "I called Sheriff Underwood, and he told me I can't report Nate missing until tomorrow night."

"Not that you should report him missing," Kelly-Jo added. "I saw Zane at the feed store before I came over and he said Nate was fine. But he wouldn't give me any more details."

"So, you've done some investigating." That made Bess feel better.

Abby nodded, blowing her nose into a napkin.

"And she's made her decision." Kelly-Jo gave Abby a supportive squeeze.

"She's going to beat Nate to the punch," Evie said softly. "And dump him first."

"But the wedding is in five days," Bess protested. She'd often been a bridesmaid and dealt with last-minute emergencies. But nothing to this magnitude. She rubbed her temples. "Didn't Nate take this week off?" Bess vaguely remembered someone telling her this. "Maybe he's trying to surprise you with a special wedding gift and went to pick it up." Although she couldn't think of what that might be. The logical choice would be a horse, except Abby didn't ride.

"Nice try. I told her that, too," Evie murmured to Bess.

"It's too late. I've made up my mind." Abby wiped away her tears. "I want you to help me figure out how to cancel the wedding."

"Me?" Bess sat back in the booth.

The women nodded.

"Because you're so good at this kind of thing," Kelly-Jo said earnestly. "You know, dumping guys."

"I don't... I'm not..." Ronnie's words from earlier that day returned, about Bess being prickly and picky when it came to men.

The women continued to nod.

Maybe I am good at getting rid of guys.

That wasn't something Bess aspired to be.

"What should I do, Bess?" Abby asked, unaware of Bess's inner turmoil.

Bess was of half a mind to tell Abby to calm down and wait for Nate to show up. But there was a code among bridesmaids. They didn't abandon the bride in her hour of need. So, Bess didn't bail. She fixed Abby with a firm stare, the likes of which she'd hadn't used on her friend since the time she'd wanted to buy a $3,000 geode to keep in the science cabinet at school. "You love Nate."

"I will love Nate until the day I die," Abby said staunchly. "But I won't walk down that aisle on Saturday if he's not standing there waiting for me. You know what it's like to be stood up."

A blatant reference to Griff leaving Bess hanging at prom.

Bess's gaze drifted toward Griff at the bar. His shoulders were hunched, and he looked defeated. Very un-Griff-like.

"You have to admit, Bess," Kelly-Jo said in a reasonable voice. "This looks bad."

"Some guys just aren't ready to get married," Evie added, unhelpfully.

"How about a little faith?" Bess said under her breath, still staring at Griff. He was a groomsman on Saturday. He would have been with Nate this weekend. "Can you excuse me for a second?" She slid out of the booth and walked over to join Griff at the bar.

"The usual, Bess?" Maggie was a jack-of-all-trades, working several part-time jobs in town, including as a bartender here, a wrangler for the Done Roamin' Ranch and a morning cook for the Buffalo Diner. "Light beer and a slice of lemon?"

"That'll do." Bess turned to face Griff, breathing in his tempting, woodsy cologne. "I'm here to ask about Nate's whereabouts. As one of his groomsmen, Griff, you were at his bachelor party this weekend. And now, he appears to be missing."

Both Griff and Clem avoided her gaze.

Guilty.

"Maggie." Bess glanced at the bartender as she accepted her glass of beer. "I think there's something funny going on."

Griff shook his head. "Nothing to see here."

Clem sipped his beer.

And Maggie? She laughed. "These two have the worst poker faces."

Bess agreed. She stared at Griff until he turned toward her, giving her the full effect of his handsome features. Those soulful eyes, that tempting mouth. Bess drew a breath and tried to focus. "Griff, as the newest member of my coaching staff, you probably don't know that I've fired coaches who aren't truthful to me." That statement would be true tomorrow if he lied to her tonight.

Griff's soulful brown eyes widened slightly, and he frowned. *Oh, I have his number now.*

Bess leaned in closer, bumping her hat brim against Griff's and ruining the feeling that she was intimidating because, *Oh, man. He smells good.* She switched to breathing through her mouth, trying to maintain her dignity. "Griff, tell me where Nate is or consider yourself fired." Bess glanced back toward the tearful bride and her bridesmaids, realizing she had another card to play. "Speak now or you'll be the one to tell Abby what's happened, not me."

Abby stared at them with mascara-smudged, bloodshot eyes, clutching Kelly-Jo's arm. "Look at Griff's expression. It's true. Nate found another woman."

Griff shook his head but still didn't speak.

Behind the bar, Maggie grabbed a bottle of tequila and some shot glasses, placing them on a tray. "You keep up the interrogation, Bess. I'm going to give the bride a round of shots on the house." She hurried off with a supply of liquid sunshine.

Still crowding his space, Bess tapped Griff's shoulder. "What's it going to be, Griff?"

Instead of caving, Griff grinned at her. "You sure look nice tonight."

An eye roll was required. "Don't try to butter me up, Griff. I'm covered in rodeo dust and sweat wrinkles." Not to mention she probably didn't smell as nice as he did.

"Still, you look good to me." His grin didn't fade. In fact, it grew. "Like a real cowgirl."

Something her mother had never wanted Bess to be.

GRIFF HAD ENTERED The Buckboard in a dark mood.

Because he'd driven into town and gone into the hardware store first, picking up a set of washers for the drippy bunkhouse sink. And then he'd moseyed up to the counter, plopped down a couple of bucks and greeted Nell Pickett, a woman plugged into the gossip network.

"Do you need a bag for these?" Nell asked, placing a hand on the small of her back and thrusting a prominent baby bump his way.

"No bag needed, thanks." Griff stuck the washers in his pocket. "Hey, have you met the new insurance agent in town? I'm thinking of changing carriers."

Nell was more than happy to talk about Paul James and his well-behaved teenage grandson. They were renting Marlene Albeck's house right off Jefferson Street.

"Needed all the windows resealed," Nell had told him. "Bought out our entire supply of caulking. Paul's been in several times since. Nice man. He's battling gophers in the backyard and a cough... I told him he should see Doc Nabidian about it."

Griff had witnessed that cough firsthand. It wasn't pretty.

Thanking her for the information, Griff made the slow drive past Marlene Albeck's old Craftsman home and struck gold.

The front window was open. Dell was reading a book in a chair beneath it, while Paul watched a baseball game on TV.

So close. And so frustratingly far away.

Griff needed a lawyer. But lawyers were expensive.

He'd circled back around and come in The Buckboard, wanting to wallow in peace. Instead, he'd felt compelled to sit next to Clem, who hadn't stopped talking to Maggie since Griff had taken a seat. And then Abby had started having a meltdown. He wished he were invisible.

At least, until Bess accosted him, having no qualms about getting into his face.

Oh, yeah. Griff was in a mood, all right. It had been hard not to reach for Bess and pull those sassy lips of hers to his hungry, frustrated ones. And then, she'd gone and threatened to take away the one avenue Griff had for spending time with his son—coaching. That had cooled his romantic jets. He'd had no choice but to try to throw her off, even as he wanted to tug her into his lap and have his way with that brazen mouth. Even if the only thing he'd thought of to say was to tell her how pretty she looked and why.

Pathetic.

Bess may have been tantalizingly close, but Griff knew she was out of reach, the same way Dell was.

Bess moved. Just a smidge.

Was she out of reach?

Her blue gaze flickered to Griff's mouth before skittering away toward the alcohol bottles lining the back bar.

She wants that kiss as much as I do.

Griff glanced in the mirror, catching Bess's gaze, letting her see how much he wanted her kiss. Slowly, he tipped his hat back and raised his brows. Maybe if he riled her enough, she'd launch another passionate assault on him.

Bess blushed. Looked down. Fidgeted, visibly trying to collect herself. And then she tsked. "I guess you made your choice."

They turned their barstools, knees nearly touching as they faced off. Her with that straightforward set to her camel-colored hat with threads of sparkling silver at the ends of her dark red braids. Here was the distraction that Griff needed from dead-end thoughts about Paul James, about astronomical lawyer bills and life's inequities.

But instead of facing him, Bess kept turning, swiveling around toward the bridal party. "Hey, Ab—"

Griff laid a finger on Bess's soft pink lips.

Her eyes widened, then narrowed. But she didn't lip-bomb him.

Nor did her friends notice he'd silenced her. Or that he was touching her lips. Or that he was staring deep into those bright blue eyes.

Over at the bride's table, Maggie led the women in an enthusiastic drumroll made by hands slapping the table. With one final hand slap, Maggie cried, *"Woo-wee!"*

"Woo-wee!" the women echoed and then downed their shots.

"Woo-wee," Clem muttered from behind Griff. "Some people have all the fun."

Meanwhile, Bess and Griff hadn't moved. And Griff wasn't about to budge.

Is this wise?

That was the trouble when it came to being around Bess—Griff didn't feel like being smart. That was why he purposefully poked at her. Trouble was, he didn't want to poke her into a kiss and become the talk of the town, not when Paul was around to hold that against him. And that meant, he had to play nice with Bess.

"I'll tell you where Nate is," Griff said, removing his finger from Bess's lips, resisting the urge to press his mouth there instead.

"Dude, no," Clem said from behind him, no longer muttering. "What happens at a bachelor party, stays at the bachelor party. That's part of the bachelor party bro-code."

"Not when it worries the bride." Griff didn't want to talk to Bess about Nate. He wanted to talk to her about that kiss all those months ago and hopefully her wanting another. "The bachelor party isn't over, Bess. Best man Trevor won a big purse last weekend gambling on a fight."

"Trevor." The way Bess said Trev's name spoke volumes about her opinion of him. "He makes you look like a saint."

Griff sat back as if struck, although in truth her comment amused him. "I'm offended," he said anyway, glancing over his shoulder at Clem. "Aren't you going to come to my rescue?"

"Yes, I was." Clem beamed with too much humor in his eyes. "Just had to swallow my beer, buddy." He took another sip, as if proving a point. "My pal Griff is an angel. He'd give you the shirt off his back if you needed it. Walked with me all night when my horse had colic last spring. A prince among men," Clem said as if reciting a much-rehearsed pledge, eager to play along. "You know, Bess, Griff doesn't have an arrest record. And Trevor does."

"I don't even have a speeding ticket," Griff said, beginning to enjoy himself. "Not to mention, I'm debt-free."

"Plus Griff doesn't drink to excess," Clem added, clinking his beer stein to Griff's. "Not even at bachelor parties. I can attest to that, too."

"So…" Griff cleared his throat and turned back to Bess. "I really am a saint compared to Trevor."

"Yep," Clem agreed.

"Yeah, yeah," Bess cut into their bromance, blue eyes flashing. "About this bachelor party… If it's still going on, where is it? And why aren't you two there?"

"We have jobs," Griff said, as if that explained everything.

"Responsibilities we care about," Clem added.

"And Nate?" Bess asked with decreasing patience.

Griff had to hand it to Bess. She was good at staying on task. "Nate's on vacation this week."

"Therefore, he didn't have to show up for work on Monday," Clem quipped, laying it on too thick.

"Where is Nate?" Bess said in a voice devoid of amusement.

"If you must know…" Griff said slowly as the hand drums began beating at the bride's table once more. He waited for the enthusiastic whoops and subsequent shots to be downed. "… Trevor took Nate to Las Vegas. They should be back tomorrow. Broke and exhausted."

Bess let out a slow breath. "So that's why Nate isn't answering his phone. He feels guilty." She frowned. "What a jerk. Nate doesn't deserve Abby."

"Hold up on the accusation train." Griff raised a hand, resisting lowering it to her cheek, her red braids, her soft hand. "Nate doesn't have his cell phone. At the bachelor party, we all put our phones in a box. There were two phones left when the night was over."

"Is a no-cell-phone policy at a bachelor party supposed to make me feel better?" Bess smirked. And it registered that even while smirking she looked pretty to Griff. "And his truck? Did Nate drive to Vegas?"

"They drove to the Tulsa airport," Clem confessed, apparently no longer concerned with the bachelor party bro-code.

"If I ever get married, I'm never going to let my fiancé have a bachelor party." Bess hopped off the barstool and announced loudly enough for the entire bar to hear, "Abby, the groom has been found and the wedding is on again." She hurried back to the bridal party.

"Considering Nate and Trevor aren't back from Vegas, that seems like an overly positive statement." Grinning, Clem raised his glass toward Griff's. And when Griff didn't answer, he set his glass back down. "I just fed you a line, to which you're supposed to build on the humor."

"Sorry. I was just thinking." Griff had been thinking that if he was ever lucky enough to marry Bess that he wouldn't mind not having a bachelor party. "You know, I don't want to live in the ranch's bunkhouse forever."

"Becoming a male spinster holds no appeal to me, either." Clem turned his stool around, watching Maggie clearing the bride's table of shot glasses. "That's why I'm saving for my own place."

"Me, too." Griff nodded. "I'm thinking it's time to talk to a Realtor. See what my options are when it comes to a small or large ranch."

"The real estate agents in town meet at the Buffalo Diner on Tuesday mornings," Clem said absently, still mooning over Maggie.

"How do you know this?" Griff set his beer down.

Clem shrugged. "It pays to have an agent looking for what you want to buy. Sometimes they know what's coming on the market weeks before it's listed."

Like the Glover place.

"Not that I've seen anything come up yet that I can afford." Clem heaved a sigh.

"How long has this search been going on?" Griff wondered aloud.

Maggie left the table with a loaded tray and headed back toward the bar.

"Not long." Clem sipped his beer, casually turning back to set his near-empty glass on the bar. "I reached out to Vickie Taveras last summer."

Vickie Taveras, the woman Rascal mentioned had come out to do a market assessment on the Rolling G.

Griff needed to get up early tomorrow. If he was going to gain custody of Dell, he'd need to have a proper home to live in, preferably a ranch, possibly the Rolling G.

He spared Bess another glance. She laughed at something Abby said. But it was one of her polite laughs. She wasn't truly at ease with those women. And it was possible that she'd never be at ease with him.

Especially if he made a play for the Rolling G.

"I THOUGHT YOU were another one of those delivery people." Grandpa Rascal opened the front door to greet Bess when she arrived home an hour later. "You got two more packages tonight."

Finlay heaved himself to his feet and ambled across the front porch to meet Bess. Half boxer, half bulldog, Finlay was 100 percent laid-back. He thrust his large head toward Bess's hand when she reached him.

"I hope one of those packages was a DNA kit." Bess stroked Finlay's broad brown head.

"Looks like." Rascal eased back into the foyer. "But the other is from that rodeo supply company." He touched it with his sock-covered foot. "I've been thinking about you wanting to sell the ranch. We might be able to make ends meet if you didn't buy so much tack and other supplies."

Bess grimaced. Admittedly, she did spend a lot on that stuff, but with her rodeo team budget being hacked away, she felt she couldn't disappoint the kids. But what about not disappointing her granddad and the Glover legacy at the Rolling G? "That's not why we have to sell, and you know it. I don't have time to manage a large herd." She and Finlay came through the front door. Bess sat on the bench and removed her boots. "And our acreage requires a large herd to make the ranch support itself."

"You could quit your job." Rascal and Finlay were moseying into the living room. "Ranch full-time."

Bess sighed. His arguments weren't new, and neither were her defenses. "I like teaching. I like coaching rodeo." She liked who she was when she wasn't feeling like she was letting the family down. Boots tucked beneath the bench, hat hung on a peg, Bess trailed into the living room, spotting the box with the DNA company's logo on the coffee table. "We might just as well get this testing over with. I can send our swabs back tomorrow."

Rascal sat in his recliner. The television was on. A baseball game was in the bottom of the ninth with two outs. Bess felt the same pressure that last batter must be feeling, as if some-one had coiled several ropes around her chest and pulled tight.

"I still say you should accept Griff's help," Rascal grumbled.

"No." Bess opened the box, finding and unfolding the in-structions without actually reading them. "Griff isn't the an-swer."

You sure look nice.

Griff's compliment from earlier echoed in her head, along with the flutter of excitement when their hat brims bumped to-gether. She thought of the flicker of interest in his brown eyes as his gaze had met hers in the bar mirror.

But Bess didn't want to let this resurgence of attraction to Griff linger or grow. She'd trusted him with her heart once. It was foolish to do so again.

CHAPTER FOUR

GRIFF ENTERED THE Buffalo Diner the next morning, looking for Vickie Taveras.

Vickie was a few years older than Griff. She had a reputation as a tough negotiator.

But today, she just looked like a very tired, new single mama, walking around the tables set up for the local agent meeting, a newborn baby on her shoulder. She had circles under her eyes, nearly as dark as the hair she'd clipped at the nape of her neck. The black-and-white-striped dress she wore with silver-and-black cowboy boots implied youthful energy that Vickie didn't seem to have today.

"Griff, thank heavens you're here. I have spit-up on my shoulder and I can't let my competition see a chink in my armor. Would you mind holding Justice?" Without waiting for an answer, Vickie passed Griff a baby wrapped in a blue blanket. She brushed at her dress with a napkin. "Lucky for me you stopped by."

"Luck? No, I…" Griff settled the baby into the crook of his arm. Big blue eyes blinked up at him with an unfocused stare. "I stopped by to talk to you."

"Looking for a ranch?" she guessed.

The baby whimpered. Griff automatically started jiggling the tyke, waiting to answer until Justice quieted. "Am I that transparent?"

"No. You're a cowboy." Vickie spit into the paper napkin and wiped at her shoulder some more, not doing any good.

"I'm interested in something like..." Griff glanced around, not wanting to be overheard.

Coronet was at the register ringing someone up. Another waitress was busing a table, clanking dishes into a plastic tub. Maggie was in the kitchen, working one of her many part-time jobs. Griff could swear that woman didn't sleep. A few other diners were seated up front and talking about a funeral they'd attended last weekend.

Satisfied that he had some measure of privacy, Griff started again, "I'm interested in something like the Rolling G." He jiggled and whispered, "You know...the Glover place." Guilt speared through him. It was one thing to dream of owning Bess's spread and another to say he wanted it out loud.

She'll hate me.

Not that she was far from hate now.

Griff stared down at the baby in his arms, wishing he had the charm of a newborn when it came to Bess. "Just like the Rolling G."

When he'd first come to Clementine with his caseworker, he hadn't realized he'd been to the town before under better circumstances. His father was a drifting, seasonal cowhand, and they'd taken a family trip to drop him at the ranch where he'd be working and staying the next six months. It had been a happy trip. They'd had lunch at the Buffalo Diner, then dropped Dad off at the Rolling G. There had been no hint of the abandonment to come.

Griff had mixed feelings about his father, but he'd held on to that memory and that ranch as a symbol of what family could be.

"The Rolling G." Vickie stopped trying to clean the spot from her shoulder and stared at Griff with more interest. "You know I was there yesterday doing a market assessment?"

Griff nodded. "I was wondering if... You know..." The baby started to fuss. He moved Justice to his shoulder. "If I could make an offer."

"Before it goes on the market." Vickie nodded, fussing with her son's blanket. "You could offer. But you don't have much hope of it being accepted. Rascal doesn't want to sell."

"Can I do that without…um…without Bess or Rascal knowing that I'm the one making the offer?" That sounded as if Griff was being underhanded. He quickly added, "You know, Bess isn't very fond of me."

"I know." Vickie returned her attention to the stain on her shoulder. "This could get complicated if any of my competition hears about this."

"I haven't said a word to anyone." Griff glanced around nervously.

"Good." Vickie was surprisingly cool in the face of planning what felt deceptive. "Are you financially qualified? It'll take a chunk as a down payment." She mentioned a number in the low six figures.

Griff swallowed back his shock. "I'm good with the down payment." He had fifteen years of savings from rodeo winnings and his ranch paycheck, from not splurging on clothes, trips or vehicles.

"Why the Rolling G?" Vicki asked. "You could buy a three-acre ranchette as a starter home. Lorana Ethridge is putting her place up for sale."

"My dream is to raise cattle. And that means acreage. Spreads like the Rolling G don't come up for sale often."

"True."

Justice squirmed, grunting softly.

Griff patted the baby's back firmly in case he was suffering from gas. Holding the little guy reminded Griff of Avery, of Dell and of all the moments he'd missed out on with his son. There were mixed feelings there, too.

I have a lot of time to make up for.

Blythe Chapman, another real estate agent in town, entered the diner, nose to the screen of her phone. Her short, gray hair was slicked into place, and she wore an ill-fitting, gold polyester jacket over black slacks. She stopped to greet the funeral attendees.

"We'll talk about this later," Vickie promised, grabbing her huge leather diaper bag. "I'm going to the restroom to try to get this stain out." And off she went, leaving her newborn with Griff.

Griff walked Justice up and down the diner with a bounce to his step and a jiggle to his shoulder. It wasn't lost on him that he'd missed out on his son's infancy. On Dell's awkward toddler years. His preteen drama. Griff didn't want to miss any other milestones, good or bad.

"Meet me at four o'clock at the bank," Vickie said to Griff upon her return. She'd looped a black silk scarf around her neck and draped it artfully over the stain. But instead of taking her baby back, Vickie picked up her phone and tapped on the screen. "You'll need to be preapproved for a loan and I'll need earnest money."

"Can do, Vickie." Griff shifted the newborn to the crook of his arm, staring down at Justice, still bouncing and jiggling. "Wish me luck, big fella."

"You don't need luck," Vickie said, tucking her phone into her diaper bag. "You have me."

Bess entered the diner and stopped short, staring at Griff holding the baby. She wore gray jeans today and a long-sleeved, blue denim shirt. Her red hair was pulled into a smooth ponytail below her right ear. Her hat today was a soft gray with a flat brim. She looked beautifully untouchable.

Just the way she had at Ronnie's wedding.

Griff shifted, showing Bess the baby's face. It might have been his imagination but he thought Bess's expression softened.

She approached him with a question in her eyes. "Did I tell you to meet me here this morning?"

"Nope." Griff didn't stop jiggling, although he stood still. "I can read your mind. And right now, I can tell you've fallen in love with this little guy." He handed the baby to Bess. "This is Justice. He's not feeling his best."

"That's too bad." Bess took the baby like a pro, reminding Griff that she had four siblings with kids. "What a sweetheart. Is he a hard jiggle or a gentle swing?"

"Jiggle and bounce." Griff was mesmerized by the sight of Bess holding a baby. She'd make a wonderful mother. A beautiful mother. And he knew other guys were aware of it. He started talking without really thinking about his words crossing Bess's personal boundaries. "I hear you're dating a veterinarian. How does he feel about having kids?" Was it too much to hope that the man wanted to devote his life to his patients?

"We've only been on one date." Bess didn't lift her gaze from Justice's face, looking utterly smitten. "I haven't asked him."

I want kids. Lots of kids.

Griff held his tongue.

"Bess Glover, you should know better." Blythe took a seat at Vickie's table. "Marriage and kids should be a first-date question." She waved to Coronet. "Coffee?"

"Coming," Coronet called back, reaching for a pot of the steaming black liquid.

Meanwhile, Bess's cheeks were a bright red.

Griff rushed to her defense. "Hey, Bess is as sharp as they come, dating-wise. She knows when to discuss deal-breakers like marriage and babies."

"Pay attention to what that cowboy is saying, Bess." Blythe held out a coffee cup for Coronet to fill. "Any cowboy who willingly says *marriage* and *babies* in the same breath is willing to settle down."

"Says who?" Griff put his hands on his hips and scoffed, if only to take the heat off Bess.

"Says me." Blythe chuckled as Coronet poured a cup for Vickie. "I hear *marriage* and *babies* and the next thing I know, cowboys are making offers on a spread of their own."

That statement struck too close to home. Griff refrained from comment.

"He's beautiful," Bess told Vickie, brushing her fingers over the baby's thatch of dark hair. "There's nothing like the smell of a newborn, is there? So sweet."

More real estate agents trundled in, all of them closer in age to Blythe than Vickie. Griff had what he needed. He could leave. There was still time to grab a coffee before heading over to the high school rodeo grounds for camp.

But Bess wasn't moving, not beyond the bounce and jiggle of Justice, that is. And Griff couldn't seem to walk away.

"I don't suppose one of you wants to be my nanny?" Vickie was in the midst of doctoring her coffee with a liberal dose of cream, but she spared Griff and Bess a smile. "Single mamas need all the help they can get."

"If I volunteer, would you or your colleagues support the high school rodeo team with a donation?" Bess smiled confidently. Clearly, this wasn't her first audience with potential donors. "Budget cuts at the high school have been brutal this year."

Vickie lifted her coffee mug, a shrewd look in her eyes. "Can I have a banner hung at the rodeo grounds?"

"If you can pay to have it made." Bess didn't miss a beat.

Blythe narrowed her eyes. "I'll make the donation *and* pay for my banner to be made."

"Hey! I offered first." Vickie gave her competition a dark look.

Griff was beginning to understand why Vickie was willing to help him make an offer for the Rolling G before any of her peers knew it was for sale. The Realtors in Clementine seemed cutthroat.

"Actually, I came to ask all of you," Bess said in a peace-keeping voice. "There's plenty of arena railing to cover."

Justice began to fuss.

Griff tried to take the baby and let Bess do her thing.

"I've got this." Bess stepped out of reach. "I'll see you at camp, Coach."

And just like that, Griff was dismissed.

"Is it me? Or did the rodeo team multiply since yesterday?" Griff came to stand beside Bess thirty minutes after she'd sold numerous sponsorship opportunities to real estate agents at the Buffalo Diner.

Afterward, she'd stopped at the sheriff's office to request a donation for the team, making sure to talk to Sheriff Underwood about the potential of his grandson, Kevin. Doing business was what she needed after seeing Griff holding that baby. She'd walked into the Buffalo Diner and there he was, looking like her cowboy fairy tale with that child in his arms. And he hadn't even been wearing a tux!

Bess very carefully looked at Griff squarely, needing to see him as just another cowboy.

She started with his boots. Dusty and dirt streaked. At his blue jeans. Faded and forlorn. At his dingy straw cowboy hat.

She sighed. Relieved. There was no attraction between them anymore. None whatsoever.

And then Griff shifted, and she noticed that bull riding belt buckle. Thought about the strength, determination and belief it must have taken to win it. A testament to his...character. It more than made up for that shabby blue T-shirt.

And, man, that was a shame.

Because attraction was back, fluttering in her chest.

If Bess had been the swearing type, she'd have dropped a cuss-bomb or two. She looked away and frowned. Deeply.

"What? No comment?" Griff gestured with a coffee cup from Clementine Coffee Roasters toward the bleachers where close to fifty teenage cowboys and cowgirls sat chattering. "Okay. I must be dreaming."

"You're not dreaming. There are more kids here today." And Bess had no idea why. She'd stayed up late last night doing the ranch books and gotten up early to make her pitch to the real estate agents meeting at the Buffalo Diner this morning. She hadn't had coffee, and her weary gaze was fixated on Griff's paper cup. "I'm going to need a lot more sponsors." And coaches. And supplies. A larger team would stretch already thin resources, including her own.

She couldn't even tell some of the newbies to come back another day when their paperwork was completed. All the new kids had turned in their permission forms, which was odd because the only way to get them was through the high school office. And the office had only opened an hour before.

Her favorite principal had a hand in this. Of that, she was certain. But why?

"You're awfully quiet." Griff glanced toward the bleachers and then back to Bess. He handed her his coffee cup. "Here. You're going to need this more than I am."

"Don't worry about me." But her fingers closed around the

half-empty cup as if of their own volition, brushing Griff's hand, making her yearn for more contact.

Don't.

She had a date with a handsome, successful veterinarian on Saturday. He was the man for her. Even her mother would approve.

Griff stepped back. "You're dead on your feet, Bess. Take the coffee. Do you want me to lead the drills this morning?"

"No. Yes. I haven't decided." Bess lifted the cup to her mouth, too aware that Griff's lips had just been there. She sipped his coffee. It was thick, strong and black, not at all the way she liked it. She pulled a face. "Yuck. You could have warned me you drink sludge. What is this?"

Griff grinned. "It's straight espresso. It's for sipping throughout the day. One shot at a time."

"How many shots did you order?"

"Six. I drank about two." Griff shrugged, almost sheepishly. "You think I keep up this energy level honestly? Honey, my smile runs on caffeine."

She liked his smile well enough not to argue. "I can't finish this." Bess handed it to him.

Griff stuck his hands in his jeans pockets. A refusal. "Look on the bright side. It won't take you but a slurp or two to get your morning dose of caffeine. You don't have to drink all my sludge. Go ahead. Have another. That is, *if* you can take it."

And there it was. Griff's challenging grin, the expression that made butterflies take flight in her chest.

"*If* I can take it..." Bess scoffed, steeling herself for another sip of thick, bitter sludge. She tried not to make a face this time.

"I guess you can take it," Griff murmured, still grinning like a goofy kid. A handsome goofy kid.

Bess's cheeks began to feel hot. She blamed it on the sludge.

Wade and Ronnie ambled toward them, holding hands and looking blissfully happy.

Babies, happy couples and perpetual bridesmaids. Or in Griff's case, perpetual groomsmen. Maybe Bess and Griff had more in common than she'd thought.

The happy couple drew closer.

Bess shifted her weight without moving her feet, bringing her within kissing distance to Griff.

"Oh, look, sweetie. There are lots of new recruits here, including Griff." Ronnie smiled like a cat who'd spent a day napping in a sunny window after eating the canary. "Bess must have a unicorn up her sleeve."

Darn it, Ronnie.

Why was she bringing this up?

The men looked confused.

"No unicorn." Bess handed Griff his coffee, smiling hard at her supposed best friend. "No magic. Unless you count how we're going to coach all these kids in the basics and field a competitive team." Finally, a revised plan for the day formed in her head. The sludge had done its trick. "Ronnie, will you take a group of kids that brought their horses and help them with their riding technique? Wade, can you take the experienced ropers and work with them? I'll take a group of newbies and give them the basics of roping. While Griff takes the remaining kids and times them as runners for ribbon roping. By lunchtime, I want a list of the fastest kids, the best riders and the most accurate ropers."

"Yes, ma'am." Griff sipped that sludge, his lips touching where hers had recently been.

Hoo-boy.

Grounding those fickle butterflies, Bess led her coaches closer to the bleachers and welcomed the kids to another day at camp. In no time, they were divided into groups and busy with their drills.

Bess had her group of beginners twirling lariats when the football coach called to her as he approached the training ground. Even from a distance, she could see the man's round face was beet red. Bess hurried to meet him.

Coach Jisecki was a barrel-chested man with blond hair and a booming voice. He didn't wait until she was close before laying into her. "You're stealing my players now?"

"No." Bess slowed her steps, wondering where his anger was coming from.

"You are." The football coach jabbed his finger toward several kids around the rodeo grounds. "There's Martin." *Jab.* "Cloverly and Blackard." *Jab-jab.* "The Smith twins and Monmouth." *Jab-jab-jab.* Coach Jisecki turned his florid, scowling face toward Bess. "You think that if you get your numbers up that it'll save this program. Not a chance." And then he stormed off, heading toward the high school's office and the principal, no doubt.

The principal who'd just helped pave the way for those football players to switch sports.

What was Eric up to?

"You all right?" Griff appeared beside Bess. "Jisecki seemed hot."

"Apparently, our new recruits quit his program." Bess walked with Griff back toward the arena. She put her thumb and forefinger in her mouth and whistled shrilly to get the camp's attention. "I need to talk to Sean Martin, Loyd Cloverly, Bobby Monmouth, Ed Blackard and the Smith twins. Over here. Now."

"And the rodeo coach strikes fear into the hearts of her new recruits," Griff said, half under his breath.

Bess didn't laugh. She had a reputation as a no-nonsense coach. And so far, it had paid off for her with winning teams.

The teens neared, dragging their feet and looking as if they'd done something wrong.

"Don't worry, guys." Griff waved them closer. "Coach Glover just wants to welcome you to the team." He gave Bess a play-along smile. "Don't you, Coach?"

"Of course. I welcome every recruit personally by stopping camp." Bess elbowed Griff in the ribs. But his words made her tone her intensity down several notches and smile reassuringly at the boys. "Coach Griff is right. Nobody's in trouble. I just want to know why you quit football so that I can support your decision."

Silence.

Sean Martin cleared his throat. "Football has never been fun."

The others nodded.

Uh-oh.

Bess exchanged a glance with Griff. She didn't run fun practices.

"I know you're fun," Griff said softly, reading her mind.

She supposed she should be thankful for that.

"Are you kicking us out?" Sean asked.

"No. Everybody's welcome." Bess sent them back to their stations. She lowered her voice to say to Griff, "How long do you think it'll be until they realize I'm not fun?"

"Never." Griff grinned. "If you keep me around."

Bess scoffed, trying not to smile. But gosh, it was hard.

"You know this football thing isn't over," Griff told her. "Jim Jisecki believes you stole some of his players. And he isn't the forgiving type."

Bess stared at Griff, the man she hadn't forgiven for something he'd done as a teen. He wasn't smiling. In fact, he had the look of a man ready to defend his woman's honor.

And that woman could be me.

CHAPTER FIVE

"WHAT WAS MY TIME?" Dell asked Griff, panting after having run from the halfway point in the arena to a practice calf with a ribbon on its rear end to the farthest gate where Griff was waiting.

"Twelve seconds." Griff showed his son the time on his cell phone stopwatch feature. Dell was in the bottom third of runners. But Griff was happy anyway. How could he not be? They were together. His kid was a goer. He'd try anything.

Bess called for a lunch break. Kids ran to the bleachers, to coolers and backpacks and the parking lot where parents were waiting with food.

Griff may have been happy. But Dell wasn't.

"Twelve seconds? I suck, Coach." Dell snatched his hat off his head, walking next to Griff toward the nearest bleachers. "I should go out for football. I hear they need kids. I don't have to be fast to play football. I could be the kicker or something."

"You're not going to play football," Griff said with too much feeling. No way was he letting that jerk Jisecki anywhere near his kid. He wasn't letting the guy near Bess again, either. "You're going to work on your rodeo skills, Dell, and watch yourself get better. You're not a quitter."

Dell's blue eyes went wide. "Okay. Fine. Over-caffeinated, Coach?"

"Nope. But I don't believe in quitting. And you shouldn't,

either." Before Griff could second-guess himself, he placed his hand on Dell's shoulder. "You can't expect to be a superstar on day two. I wasn't."

"Nice to know." Dell smiled. "How long did it take you to get good?"

"A couple of months," Griff admitted, reluctantly removing his hand instead of pulling his kid into a hug. "Like you, I started in my teens. I was a clumsy roper. And I was a slow runner. I practically bounced out of the saddle. But there was something about riding broncs and bulls that satisfied the anger inside of me. And that's where things first started to click."

"You were angry?" Dell's blue eyes widened again. "Why?"

"Because..." Griff hesitated, wondering how much he should tell his son, knowing with aching certainty that he couldn't tell the whole truth. "Because my father left me, and my mother gave up on me. And I... I thought I wasn't wanted."

"Technically... You weren't," Dell pointed out, brow furrowing. "I'm not, either. I mean, I was wanted. By my mom. But I don't really remember her. And my dad was a no-show from the day I was born."

No!

Griff opened his mouth to argue that Dell's father had wanted him from the beginning.

Paul will be furious.

Instead of bringing that up, Griff pivoted. "I said *I thought* I wasn't wanted. My parents were teenagers when I was born. They struggled to make things work. But in the end, by giving me up, I landed in a better place. Sadly, when I was younger, I didn't see it that way."

Dell's frown deepened.

"Think about it, Dell. Would you be a good dad at your age?" Griff held his breath. Hoping.

They'd stopped walking and stood apart from the rest of the team.

"Me? A dad?" Dell scoffed. "At my age? I'd suck at that worse than rodeo."

"Point made."

"But..." Dell's face scrunched up once more. "Did your parents ever reach out later? I mean, you're old now."

"Old?" Griff clutched the placket of his shirt over his heart and staggered back.

Dell shook his head. "You know what I mean."

Griff nodded, considering his words carefully once more. "My mom sent me a card once, apologizing. But my dad... He was a proud man. Pride can keep good men from admitting they didn't always do the right thing."

"My grandpa is a proud man." Dell glanced toward the bleachers where his friends sat, taking a step closer toward them and food. "My grandpa has trouble admitting he's wrong. Like...ever. And he has this idea about how my life should go. And so, when we disagree, I'm always wrong."

Griff nodded. "I have experience with guys like him." Just like him. "You have to be the calm one. Fight with facts and logic."

Dell smiled. "It's like you know him."

"Yeah." Too well. "So maybe the next time you think about your dad, cut him some slack." *Please.*

Dell's friends called out to him.

"I better go eat. My grandpa says my food needs to digest for an hour before any activity. I told him that only applied to swimming but...you know... That's one of his things." Shrugging, Dell hurried off toward the bleachers without saying what Griff wanted to hear—that he wouldn't consider his biological father a loser.

I need to talk to my lawyer.

First, Griff needed to *get* a lawyer.

"You like Dell, don't you?" Bess appeared beside Griff, still looking as pretty as she had this morning, despite the heat, sweat and dust. "He's a good kid."

"Thanks." Too late, Griff caught himself. "I mean, yeah. He is."

Bess gave him an odd look. "Maybe you shouldn't have given me some of your morning sludge. Seems like you could use a slurp or two about now."

"Yeah. I...uh... I need to take off a little early this afternoon.

I have a couple of appointments." At the bank, at the town law office and with his Realtor.

"Sure. Thanks for your help making rodeo camp fun." She spared him a sly smile before marching off and cautioning the football boys not to roughhouse.

"Vickie, what a surprise." Bess deposited her keys in a bowl on a table near the door that night. She took note that a box of lariats she'd ordered for the team had arrived, and entered the living room smiling, hoping to receive a sponsor check from the Realtor.

Finlay padded over to meet Bess. She gave the big dog a quick pat and an ear rub.

"Oh, you'll be surprised, all right," Grandpa Rascal said from his recliner, sounding riled. "Tell her, Vickie."

The real estate agent sat on the couch, leaning over to rock her baby in his car seat. She no longer wore a scarf and had what looked like spit-up stains on both shoulders. "Good news, Bess. I've got an offer on the ranch."

"Yippee," Rascal deadpanned.

Bess sank onto the arm of the couch, not trusting her knees to keep her upright. "We haven't listed the ranch for sale."

The weight of generations of Glovers bent Bess's shoulders. She hadn't really thought it would come to this. In fact, she'd been hoping it wouldn't ever come to this, that they'd find other Glovers interested in keeping the family ranching legacy alive.

"You know how small towns are. If you talked about it, chances are that someone heard about your interest in selling and decided to make you an offer." Vickie dug into her brown leather diaper bag and then laid a check on the coffee table. "Here's the money for the rodeo team banner and sponsorship."

Like that was supposed to be a peace offering? Bess longed to make a statement and rip it up. But common sense prevailed.

"Who?" Bess's mouth was dry, but somehow, she managed to string words together. "Who wants to buy our home? We're querying family to see who'll take over the ranch and buy Rascal out. That was the only reason we requested—"

"*You* requested," Rascal inserted, full of ire.

"—a market assessment," Bess continued. "Which you haven't given to us."

Finlay disliked raised voices. The large brown dog made himself as small as he could and crawled beneath the coffee table. Bess was of half a mind to join him. Her stomach felt queasy, and her mind couldn't seem to grasp what was happening. Other than her close friends, Bess didn't usually let folks know what was going on in her personal life. But this... She'd told no one.

"Your market assessment and the offer are in here." Vickie placed a large yellow envelope on the coffee table. "It's a gem of a property."

"We didn't need you to know that," Rascal said in a sour voice. "That's why we don't want to sell. Bess will have kids someday and..." He stared up at her, voice trailing off.

Even my grandfather doubts I'll ever find the right man.

Her heart sank.

"Who made this offer?" Bess demanded, frustration shoving hurt aside. "I'd like to turn them down face-to-face."

Vickie stiffened. "I'm not at liberty to say." Nor did she look happy to be put on the spot.

Too bad.

"I won't sell to nobody who won't reveal himself to me." Rascal's voice rose. "I'd rather the tax man repossess the ranch."

Bess reached over to pat his shoulder. Although she was mad, she didn't want to go that far.

Vickie stood, gathering her fancy diaper bag and then her baby in his carrier. "I'm going to leave your market assessment—which no one has seen, not even your potential buyer—and the offer for you to review. It's a good one. No inspections or contingencies. It should be a quick close."

"And where would we go if we sold?" Rascal got to his feet, swaying a little before grabbing onto Bess like a rock in rough waters. "Forget it. I'm not looking at that envelope. Not now. Not ever." He tottered down the hall and slammed the door to his bedroom.

The baby startled, then cried out once before settling back into a snooze.

"It's my job to bring you information, Bess." Vickie rose.

"The offer expires in two weeks. That gives you plenty of time to think about it."

Bess wanted to tell Vickie where to take that offer but Rascal was right. If Bess hadn't involved Vickie, they wouldn't have an unwelcome buyer.

She and Finlay walked Vickie to the door, pretending to take her news in stride.

And then, Bess went into the office and opened her laptop, trying once more to find mention of Eshon Glover.

"WHERE'VE YOU BEEN, GRIFF? You look like someone stole your best pair of boots." Clem met Griff in the yard of the Done Roamin' Ranch after he'd been to all his afternoon appointments. "And here's more bad news. You missed dinner. Dad made his meatballs."

"Never you mind." Griff lowered his hat brim and continued heading for the barn. "I'm going for a ride." He needed to clear his head about what he'd just heard and authorized.

"I'll come, too."

Griff gave his foster brother a dark look.

Clem shook his head. "You don't look like you should be alone."

"And yet, that's exactly what I want."

"Hey." Clem held out an arm in front of Griff, bringing him to a stop. "This isn't like you. What happened? Did you ask Bess for a date, and she turned you down? You know she prefers to date professional men."

"I *am* a professional. A career cowboy," Griff said sharply, not wanting to dwell on Bess's preferences when it came to men. He faced Clem. "Don't you have somewhere to be?"

"Yep. By your side." Clem grinned.

Griff took a deep breath, silently counting to ten. "Thank you. Now I know how frustrating my humor can be to others when they're upset."

When he tried to stomp away, Clem caught his arm. "This is serious? Like more than a flat tire or a nagging mosquito bite serious?"

Griff nodded.

Clem released him and took long strides toward the barn. He half turned, looking back at Griff. "What are you waiting for? Saddle up. The best conversations are held out on the range. Unless you need Dad's ear, in which case, he gives his best advice in the ranch yard or around the horse stalls." Clem resumed his march to the barn.

With a sigh, Griff followed. Talking out the hard stuff on horseback was the cowboy way. It was just that Griff didn't like to talk about the hard stuff. When he did, it was often with Wade. But now that Wade had Ronnie...

A few minutes later, Griff and Clem were riding across a pasture, letting their horses pick their way along in an unhurried walk.

"Anytime you want to talk, I'm ready to listen." Clem was trying hard to be serious but that was a stretch for him. "I should admit that there's a blackberry pie cooling in Mom's kitchen. And you know I have a weakness for blackberry pie."

"In other words, get to it? Is that it?" Griff reached over and gave Clem's shoulder a playful push, not hard enough to knock him out of the saddle, but forceful enough to let him know his impatience was Clem's problem, not Griff's.

A chorus of male laughter drifted to them from the ranch proper behind them. Just a few days ago, Griff's voice would have been among them. But now that Dell was real and here, he didn't feel lighthearted enough to laugh. There was work to be done.

"I made an offer on a ranch today," Griff admitted. "It had to be done but, man, the numbers are scary."

Clem leaned over his saddle horn and turned his head toward Griff, presumably to get a better look at Griff's face.

"What are you doing?" Griff eased away from him in the saddle.

Clem sat upright. "I'm checking to make sure an alien hasn't possessed Griffin Malone's body. Tell me what my name is. My *real* name."

"Albert Coogan, although a better name for you might be annoying." Griff felt his mood lighten. Trust his foster brother to know how to break the tension.

"I'll take that label and give you one." Clem guided his horse around a bush, startling a rabbit that made a run for the nearby tree line. "Impulsive. You're jumping the gun. You were just speculating last night about buying your own place and now you've made an offer, and you have buyer's remorse."

"I don't."

Clem tsked. "If you were comfortable with your decision, you'd be smiling, not bemoaning the finances. I think you should back out on the deal."

"I won't."

Clem frowned. "What property has gotten you all tangled in knots?"

"It's the Rolling G." Griff told Clem about overhearing Bess's need to sell and making the offer anonymously. "Whatever truce was made between me and Bess at rodeo camp will be shattered when she learns the offer is mine."

"I thought you were in love with Bess." Gone was Clem's characteristic humor and his infectious smile. "That's an odd way of showing it. No. Let me edit that. That's an underhanded way of showing you love her."

"Love?" Griff scoffed weakly, trying to deny it. "You can't be in love with someone who can barely tolerate your presence." Although the percentage of time Bess occupied his thoughts said otherwise. Griff frowned.

Clem wasn't to be swayed. "And yet, you are in love with her."

"Yes," Griff conceded miserably. "It's not completely under-handed. I'm doing this because of love."

"I'm so confused," Clem moaned. "Is there something else you're not telling me?"

"I'm going to sue for custody of my son." Griff explained how he'd met Dell and what Paul's reaction to him having a relation-ship with Dell was. "I can't do that while living in a bunkhouse."

"A home can be anywhere," Clem pointed out. "Have you considered a little house in town?"

"No," Griff said stiffly. "I want my son to have a ranch ex-perience."

Clem didn't say anything for some time. The sun was still

hours from setting. The air was hot and thick. Cattle clustered beneath trees on the far end of the pasture, occasionally lowing as they rode past.

It was just another day at the ranch. Except it wasn't. Griff had finally taken the first step toward parenthood.

"Well," Clem began. Stopped. Tipped his straw cowboy hat up higher on his head. "I forgot you're a dad."

"I forgot for a long time, too." He'd had his nose down, making money, hoping that something might change between him and Bess, hoping that his kid would come looking for him. "I went to see a lawyer today. He said I'd have a better chance of gaining custody if I was settled. A homeowner."

Russell London had told Griff to hold off taking legal action until he moved out of the bunkhouse. In the meantime, he'd encouraged Griff to try to work things out with Paul. Of course, Russ didn't know how intractable Paul was.

"So instead of renting a house or buying a little ranchette, you went all in for Bess's place." Clem shook his head. "Do you hear yourself? Bess's place. You'll lose Bess for good."

"Maybe it's time I realized Bess is just a pipe dream." Griff caught Clem's eye, tempted to say that maybe it was time Clem realized Maggie was just a pipe dream, too. "We both know that Bess wants someone…who isn't me. I've spent the last decade or so dreaming about owning my own ranch, imagining my kid coming to live with me and pining over Bess Glover. Making two out of three dreams a reality isn't bad. I'd be foolish to think I could have it all."

Clem tsked. "I'd rather be a fool than to outright sabotage a dream. That's called quitting. And Done Roamin' Ranch boys don't quit."

CHAPTER SIX

"I BROUGHT YOU COFFEE." Griff handed Bess a cup from Clementine Coffee Roasters the morning after Vickie had delivered the anonymous sales offer. "Two creams and one sugar, right?"

Bess took a careful sip, just to make sure two creams and one sugar were, in fact, in the cup, not undiluted espresso. Griff hadn't lied. The coffee was exactly the way she liked it. She decided to tease him anyway. "What? No sludge?"

"I won't judge your coffee choice if you don't judge mine." His brown-eyed gaze was as soft as his reply.

"Fair enough." Bess wondered about Griff's toned-down smile. But only briefly. She had too much on her mind—Rascal's decreasing mobility, the future of the rodeo team, the looming financial situation at home.

She frowned at a cluster of school board members standing with the football coach across the street, near the Clementine High School sign, before forcing her gaze toward the kids arriving at the rodeo grounds.

"Everything okay?" Griff caught her eye, inspiring fleeting images of kisses, from the sweet ones when they were young to the spicy one that they'd shared recently.

I can't keep giving him my mental energy.

Griff shouldn't look good to her. His black-checked button-down was missing a button. The hem of one blue jean leg was frayed in the back. He came and went on a dime—whenever his fancy took him. Bess needed, and wanted, stability, somebody solid so that she could rely on him to always be there for her. Like now. She needed advice about the ranch and the rodeo team. But Griff... What insight could he bring? Just standing next to him made it apparent that they came from different places and were going in different directions. His was aimless and hers was...hopeless.

Bess took a bracing sip of coffee and spiraled into the past. She could practically hear her sisters teasing while her mother spouted one of her lectures on life and love.

"Mama, I saw one of those Done Roamin' Ranch cowboys flirting with Bess," Camille tattled before she'd even removed her boots.

"Bess, I don't want you dating those lost cowpokes." Mama stood in the kitchen, mashing cooked potatoes. "You've got to aim high for love, just like you do for your dreams, or you'll regret settling. Lassoing a regular ol' rancher will do nothing but hold you back and slow you down. You'll be stuck in Clementine forever. Then everyone will look at you and say, poor Bess."

"Poor Bess," Camille parroted.

Bess had thrown her boot at her older sister. She'd missed, but it had felt good to toss it.

"What were my childhood dreams?" Bess murmured, having forgotten them.

"You wanted to be an archeologist." Griff touched her back lightly, making her jump. "Are you okay?"

"What? Oh, I'm fine. Why wouldn't I be?" She smiled brightly, falsely. "I may not be an archeologist, but I've got the largest rodeo team the school has ever seen, a date for Abby's wedding on Saturday night and one of the most enviable ranches in the county." If Vickie's "gem" assessment was to be believed. "There's nothing wrong."

"No, ma'am," Griff said quickly. Carefully. Annoyingly. Because...

"Ma'am..." Grrr. "I should be a *miss.*" Although what Bess really wanted was to be a Mrs.

"You can be whatever you want to be," Griff said unhelpfully. "You're old enough to have earned folks' respect in school and in the rodeo world."

"Old enough?" Her voice rose of its own volition, triggered by her recent revelation that she was getting too old to continue being a bridesmaid without having been a bride.

"I didn't say you were old." Griff quickly backpedaled. "And if you're thinking you're old or over the hill…" his gaze roamed over her, soulful, heated and igniting those sparks Ronnie had talked about the other day "…then you didn't take a long enough look in the mirror this morning."

Air went out of Bess's lungs in a *whoosh*.

No matter how often Bess disqualified him as her mister, Griff always managed to keep the embers of their attraction alive.

"You're impossible," Bess muttered, trying not to smile.

Griff's grin didn't quite reach his eyes. "Are you sure it's me that's impossible or those folks you keep on glaring at across the road?"

Bess hadn't realized she'd been so obvious.

Not wanting to admit it, she turned her attention toward teenagers leading saddled horses out of trailers or arriving on horseback to rodeo camp and the snatches of country songs blaring from truck speakers before being shut off. She listened to happy chatter, horses snorting, their hooves clopping across pavement, becoming muted when they reached the dirt of the rodeo grounds proper. She registered the clank of chains released from horse trailers and the creak of saddle leather adding to the morning chaos.

"Everybody needs somebody to confide in, Bess," Griff said, his low voice slipping beneath the noise. "As for those lookie-loos across the road… I'd have guessed they were an opposing rodeo coaching staff spying on you and your methods, except I recognize a few of those yahoos from around town. And, of course, Jim Jisecki, the louse."

"School board members." There was no evading the issue now. Bess sipped her coffee, swiveling her attention toward Griff and his powerful smile. Butterflies took flight in her chest, making her want to melt closer and gush when she talked, which was annoying. Upstanding math teachers and rodeo coaches didn't melt or gush in the presence of attractive, kissable cowboys who weren't trustworthy. "They want the rodeo team disbanded." And then she explained how they'd been slowly cutting the team off, reducing their funding. "Next year, I bet our budget will be nil."

"We should do something about it," Griff said in a tone that said emotionally he was hitching up his blue jeans, preparing for a fight. "Change the minds of the establishment."

"Have you ever tried to fight a school board?" Bess shook her head at his chivalry. "It's like being a kid and asking a parent why you can't do something and them saying, *'Because I said so.'* The board does what they think is best for a majority of the students they see attending Clementine High School *in the future*. But it's at the expense of the students here now."

"We should bring this fight out in the open," Griff said in a gritty voice, placing a hand on her shoulder.

It was a fight *not* to cover that hand with her own, not to twine her fingers with his, not to look into his eyes and say without words that she'd be open to leaning on him when she got low, especially if it came with the possibility of his kiss.

Don't.

Kisses solved nothing—not ranch problems, not rodeo team funding.

"We'll figure it out." Griff's grin broadened optimistically. "We'll get more sponsorships. Raise more money."

We. How powerful was that? Bess wanted to gush and melt all over again. Had she thought they were going in different directions? It felt as if Griff had her back.

Griff didn't remove his hand from her shoulder, which only made the urge to gush and melt stronger. "Now. What's the plan this morning, Bessie?"

"Don't call me Bessie." Bess regained her emotional footing and rolled her shoulder, easing off his touch. "That's the plan." Establish distance between them.

He smiled as if she hadn't just rebuked him. "What's the plan for this morning, *Bess*?" he repeated.

"My question exactly." Ronnie walked up, giving Bess one

of her *I-caught-you-letting-Griff-touch-you* looks. "Or rather, what's *been going on* this morning that we should know about?" She reached for Wade, drawing him to her side. "I feel as if a truce has been made between Griff Malone and Bess Glover. No one's going to believe it."

Bess frowned. *"Ronnie..."*

"No one should make a big deal about it." Griff put his hands on his hips. "We should be focusing on how to save the rodeo team."

"My hero," Ronnie teased, giving Bess that same *caught-you* look. "Bess always tries to save the world on her own."

"I'm not doing a very good job of saving anything," Bess muttered, surprised when Griff looked at her sharply. Before he could ask her what was wrong again, she gestured toward the bleachers, which seemed even fuller today than yesterday. "It looks like more football players defected."

"Hence the school board and football coach giving you dark looks." Griff sent a dark look their way.

"No sense poking a tiger until we're ready." Bess started walking toward the bleachers. "Let's get this thing rolling."

"She's good at being in charge, isn't she, Griff?" Ronnie was laying it on thick this morning.

Bess ignored her, whistling with her fingers to catch everyone's attention. "Good morning. It's time to get started. We're drilling again today."

Fifty-plus pairs of eyes stared back at her without an ounce of enthusiasm. The mood was similar to what Bess created in math class on test day.

Great.

"No one likes skill drills," Bess continued. "But—"

"That's because skill drills have a bad rap." Griff stepped next to Bess, clapping his hands a few times. "Today, there will be fun during skill drills. Fun is mandatory. That's why you're here, right? To have fun?"

Several members of the rodeo team perked up, nodding.

Bess didn't exactly feel upstaged. But she definitely was getting a good cop–bad cop vibe. Everyone always thought Coach Glover was no fun, not in math class and not in the rodeo arena.

But suddenly, Bess wanted her team to realize that she could be fun. She could be as fun as Griff.

"Thank you, Coach Griff." Bess reached over and lowered Griff's straw hat brim over his face. "In real life, Coach Griff plays the role of comic relief. But he has experience as a bull rider and he's a decent roper. So today, don't just laugh at his bad jokes. Listen to his advice." She didn't want practice to lose all focus.

Griff removed his hat and took a bow.

Several cowgirls giggled.

They probably had crushes on Griff.

The butterflies tried to take flight in her chest.

No-no-no.

"We'll be working in groups this morning rotating every hour," Bess continued, gently elbowing Griff back, which got more teens to smile. "We'll be developing good techniques for different events, and then putting your skills to the test when the stock gets here after lunch. Tomorrow will look the same. You'll be exposed to all the junior rodeo activities by the end of next week."

"And I hear we get Fridays off," Griff piped up.

Bess smirked at him over her shoulder before facing her team once more. "Everyone will drill for every event. Girls, that means you'll receive instruction on bronc riding. Boys, that means you receive instruction on barrel racing."

Several teenagers groaned.

"Keep an open mind," Ronnie added, stepping up to where Griff had been.

Give a volunteer coach an inch and the entire staff took a mile.

Ronnie shrugged off Bess's arched look and continued to address the team. "Something might scare you today that doesn't scare you tomorrow if you practice. Give every event a chance."

"Yes, boys. I heard you groan." Wade joined them on the proverbial stage. "You never know when a skill will come in handy, even the basics of barrel racing. You might be a horse trainer some day or have a daughter who wants to compete in that event." As Wade did.

Bess crossed her arms over her chest. "When did I lose control of this?" She should have known Griff would throw a wrench in her plans. He was anything but rule-abiding and her other coaches had followed his lead.

Despite her agitation, the whole group laughed.

Bess herded her volunteer coaches a few steps back before facing her rodeo recruits, all of whom seemed fully engaged now, as if skill drills were fun. She pointed to the north end of the arena where a few old saddles sat on the ground and then back to her team. "The half of you sitting nearest those saddles will start the first hour over there. Coach Wade and Coach Ronnie will be teaching technique for bull and bronc riding. The rest of you are going to be learning about steer wrestling in the first hour with me and Coach Griff." Bess pointed to the south end of the arena where she'd tied two long ropes to the middle of metal pipes that were two or three inches in diameter and about three feet long.

"My group is going to have more fun than Wade and Ronnie's." Griff trotted toward the nearest gate. "Follow me."

Boots pounded on bleachers as teens followed the cowboy pied piper.

"Nobody is more fun than me and Wade." Not to be outdone, Ronnie ran toward the other arena gate. "Come on, guys!"

Teens hightailed it after her.

Wade followed the group with more decorum and swagger. But he was grinning, obviously enjoying himself.

And Bess had to admit that this was the most fun she'd ever had at summer rodeo camp.

CHAPTER SEVEN

GRIFF SURVEYED HIS half of the team. They were a young, scraggly bunch.

But since they included Dell, Griff wasn't complaining. "Who wants to go first? I need a volunteer to help demonstrate." Because Bess was still back by the bleachers talking to some of the newer team members.

Guilt pinched his shoulder blades when he was with Bess. Guilt over writing that offer to buy the Rolling G. When he'd brought Bess coffee this morning, she'd been lost in thought. He'd assumed that he was the cause. Instead, he'd discovered the school board was trying to do away with a school institution. How long had Bess being dealing with that sketchiness in addition to her financial worries at home? And why should he be adding to her woes?

His gaze landed on Dell and guilt took a back seat to a flicker of excitement over finally being a part of his son's life. It was a privilege to be helping out with the rodeo team and...

Griff realized he had no volunteers for his steer wrestling clinic. No one had raised their hands. "What? No one wants to get dirty?"

Crickets.

"I'll be your sacrificial lamb," Dell volunteered in a tone of voice Griff might have used himself when he was young and covering his insecurities with humor.

"Sweet." Griff led his son and his crushed cowboy hat over to the pipe. "Have you ever seen a water skier?" At his nod, Griff had Dell sit down with his knees bent. "I want you to hold on to this bar the way a water skier would hold a tow rope. A bunch of us will heave this rope to tow you across the dirt while you keep your knees bent, and your butt and heels in the dirt. This trains your muscles and mind for the first position needed for steer wrestling—hard-won balance. I don't want you to stand. I don't want your butt to come off the ground. And I don't want you to face-plant."

"Me, either." Dell sat in the dirt and held the bar, as instructed, a hint of a smile on his features.

Nancy and Kevin cheered him on. Nancy was beaming with love in her eyes. Dell didn't seem to notice.

"I need half of you to find a place along this rope." Griff arranged the volunteers like a tug-of-war team, burliest at the back. "You're going to pull Dell twenty feet. Or until his behind comes off the ground."

"Thou shalt not face-plant," Dell quipped, grinning now.

"Exactly right." Griff smiled. How cool was it that his son had his sense of humor? "But if your butt leaves the ground, we'll mark that as your distance. The winner this morning will be towed the longest distance before butt-rise, and I'll buy them lunch."

The team made appreciative sounds.

Dell mashed his ratty straw hat on his head. "I'm ready."

Griff didn't waste any time. "Everybody...pull-pull-pull!"

The teens dragged Dell a good ten feet before he fell over sideways in the dirt. Everybody laughed, including Dell.

"That's it. Dust yourself off, kid, and return the bar to the starting point for the next cowpoke." Griff kept the energy high and the pace fast. "I need two new volunteers to compete against each other. The rest of you divide up between the two ropes for towing. Let's go. The faster we switch, the more turns you get."

Bess was still talking to the new recruits near the bleachers, seemingly oblivious to the group's enthusiasm. Griff wanted her to see him adding value so that she wouldn't threaten to take his volunteer role away again. He loved being with Dell. And the added time with Bess was a bonus because he was afraid the clock was ticking down where she was concerned, no matter how many pep talks Clem gave him.

The teens hustled into place. Dell took up a position on the rope in front of Griff, sparing him a happy smile over his shoulder.

Griff's heart swelled with love and pride, and it was very hard not to hug Dell and tell him what a great job he'd done. Someday, Griff would do that. He'd be a demonstrative dad.

"They're having too much fun." Bess finally joined Griff after everyone had taken a turn being dragged, bringing Griff's guilt with her presence. "Are you keeping the end goal in mind? Making note of who has good technique or the strength to succeed at this event?"

"Nope. We've been having fun just getting the hang of it." Griff assembled a sorry excuse for a smile, replaying Clem's prediction that Griff would lose Bess over that offer.

"Fun is all well and good," Bess said in her best lecture voice. "But—"

"Fun isn't everything. I get that. However, fun can motivate kids to practice harder." He gave her a gentle push toward the pipes. "Okay, kids, before we start another round, here's the match you've been waiting for. Coach Glover versus Coach Griff!"

Cheers went up in the air.

"You'll pay for this later." Bess gave Griff a dark look, one so very similar to the dark look she'd given him on the wedding reception dance floor before lip-bombing him good and proper.

Kisses are in my future.

"I'll pay the price." Griff hurried over to pick up a pipe. "Later," he told her, grinning. There was no way Bess could mistake the intent behind his words. Later, the price he'd pay would be a kiss. Later, he'd pay the price of wanting to buy her ranch. He knew which of those two "laters" he would enjoy more.

Color rose in her cheeks as Bess took her place a few feet away from him. She tugged her riding gloves down and then signaled for her rope crew to take their places. "I guess there's only one thing for it."

"One thing?" Griff's tow crew was still talking excitedly about two of their coaches competing against each other, placing friendly bets on who would win. "What's that?"

"We cheat." Bess shouted, "Pull-pull-pull!"

Griff had to hand it to Bess's tow team. They had good technique, an even pull that meant Bess was able to more easily stay seated. In their haste to catch up, Griff's crew yanked him too hard, sending him sprawling face-first into the dirt.

Bess called for a water break, which gave her a minimal amount of privacy to say to Griff, "You paid for it, all right."

"Not in the way either of us wanted," Griff groused, wiping his face on his shirtsleeves.

Bess didn't deny she'd wanted a kiss. Instead, she helped dust Griff off by gently swatting him with her cowboy hat. "Okay. After the break, we're teaching the proper grip and getting serious."

"Not so fast, Coach." Griff caught hold of her wrist, putting a halt to the hat thwacking. "If we continue with the fun, they'll be more likely to keep at it. Not just today but for the next few weeks."

Bess settled her hat back on her head. "Why do I get the feeling that the way you coach is going to be made based on what these kids love? If you were coaching the team, we'd never win anything."

"But we'd have a blast. Every day." *You and me together.* But only if he withdrew that offer for the Rolling G. That thought was sobering. *Can I have Dell and Bess if I give up on owning the Rolling G?*

"High school rodeo is super competitive, more so than when we were kids." Oblivious to his turmoil, Bess was intent upon explaining herself. "There's only so much time for fun. The season will be upon us before we know it and the kids won't be ready. Shift gears. Get focused."

"Life is competitive, if you let it be," Griff said absently, still wrestling with how much he wanted the life he'd dreamed of, even briefly in the case of owning the Rolling G. He stared into her steady blue gaze, suddenly feeling unsure about what course he wanted to chart for his life.

"There is no letting it." Bess straightened her hat brim. "Life and rodeo are competitive."

"But you have a choice. You can choose how you live and how—or if—you compete," Griff told her, unable to find the right kind of smile because he couldn't make a life-altering choice in that moment. He couldn't choose between Bess and a ranch for his son. "Life is meant to be enjoyable. And rodeo should be, too."

Instead of answering, she walked away.

I REALLY WANT to kiss Griff.

Bess had to get away from that unreliable cowboy and his ideas about fun. There was too much seriously messed up with her life right now. Too much fun and Griff's mind-numbing kisses were the last things she needed when her home and rodeo team were at risk of being taken away.

Bess walked to the parking lot, all the way to the far end. She stood beneath a tree at the corner, grateful that the school board was no longer watching. But despite logging in several hundred steps, Bess felt pent-up.

It's because Griff, Wade and Ronnie took over my team. Well...mostly Griff. And I thought he had my back.

How could he when they weren't on the same page about team management?

She walked down the sidewalk where the heat of the day was just beginning to reflect from the concrete. She felt wilted. But not because her friends had taken a more active role in coaching. She was wilted because of the things Griff had said.

Life is meant to be enjoyable.

She hadn't felt that way in a long time. Bess put her head down and kept doing what needed to be done—without looking up to see if she was on the wrong track or pausing while working to enjoy the moment.

You'll pay for this. Later.

That's what Griff had said. And then he'd given her a look the likes of which he'd never given her before. Back in high school, there were gentle teases and tender kisses. Griff had never come on strong. Back in February, she'd kissed Griff with the same intensity he seemed to have promised with that look just now.

Butterflies fluttered.

She suspected she knew how her life could get exponentially more joyful.

By kissing Griff. Again. And again. And—

Don't.

Bess moved to the side of her truck and sat on a running board in the shade of the cab. She had to sit down because those darn butterflies weren't just fluttering. They were flutter-melting—making her pulse beat faster and weakening her knees.

What am I going to do?

She didn't want to kiss Griff again... Well, she did but not if it came with other complications. She didn't like the way she lost her poise when he was around.

"I thought I told you to stay away from Griff Malone." A man's sharp voice spoke with authority and contempt.

But it wasn't a voice Bess recognized. And she had no idea why he was so scornful of Griff.

"Grandpa, he's a coach. I can't pretend he doesn't exist." That was a teen's voice. Male. "Thanks for bringing my water and lunch, but I have to get back to practice now." Boots shuffled on concrete.

"Dell, wait." The man coughed. A deep, staccato hacking.

Dell? The other voice must be that of his grandfather. Bess held her breath, feeling bad for eavesdropping.

"Grandpa, I have to get back," Dell repeated.

"You didn't take your lunch," Mr. James said in a thicker, kinder voice. Paper crinkled, as if a paper bag transferred hands. "You'd forget your feet if they weren't attached to your legs. But that's not important now. We agreed Monday that you wouldn't see Griff Malone again."

Bess's stomach dropped. What had Griff done to earn such disdain?

"I didn't know he was going to be coaching," Dell said, sounding like he was shrugging. "It's not a big deal."

"Focus on your future, Dell. It is a big deal. I don't want you talking to him without me present." Dell's grandfather must have opened a door because a latch clicked. "If you're going to be cavalier about it and give me that face, you'll get in the car, and I'll drop you at the library."

"No." Dell sounded as surprised that he'd stood up for himself as Bess was. But he rallied. "You're not going to tell me who I can and can't hang around with the way you did back in Bartlesville."

Oh, that poor boy.

Bess had a sick feeling in her stomach. She didn't like bullies or parents who subjugated their children, trying to bend them to their will. She stood and walked out from between her truck and Griff's. "Hey, Dell. Time to head back to the arena. Break is nearly over."

Dell's face flushed scarlet at her appearance. He looked horrified that she'd overheard their conversation. He turned and practically ran back toward the bleachers on coltish legs, clutching a paper bag and an insulated water jug.

Bess waited until the teen was several car lengths away before turning to face Dell's grandfather.

Mr. James looked neither horrified nor embarrassed. He slammed his car's passenger door. "I'm not fond of meddlers."

"Me, either." Bess smiled the way she had at the school board meeting in June. "Rest assured, I'm not a meddler. But I am the rodeo team coach. And our team members have gone on to succeed on many different levels—at college, in business, in ranching and, yes, in rodeo. Rodeo provides teens with structure while also allowing them to spread their wings, to learn the importance of being a team player, to—"

"I get the picture, Ms. Glover." Beneath his straw cowboy hat, Mr. James had deep frown lines and icy blue eyes. "Griff Malone is... I don't want him near my grandson."

Bess wanted to ask why but he fell into another coughing fit. She wanted to defend Griff. She wanted to tell Mr. James to go easy on Dell, that teenagers always needed to establish some measure of independence, and the freedom to find safe spaces and friendships.

Instead, she drew a deep, steadying breath and waited for

his cough to recede. "I respect your opinion, but rodeo is important enough to your grandson that he's out here trying to learn something new, expanding his horizons and his friendship group." She'd seen him joking with some of the football players. A first.

Mr. James thawed, just a smidge. "All right. He can stay. But if I hear one story from Dell about the antics of one Griff Malone, I'll pull Dell off the team." He stomped around to the driver's-side door and got in the car.

Griff, what have you done? And how can I help?

Bess hurried back to the arena and found Griff. She pulled him aside from supervising a second round of tug, this time utilizing the reverse arm grip competitors needed to hang on to a steer's horns. It didn't escape her notice that Dell was as far away from Griff as he could possibly get and still be participating.

When she'd led Griff a good distance away from the group, when they were standing toe-to-toe, she whispered, "What's going on between you and Dell's grandfather?"

The blood drained from Griff's face. "What did Paul say?" His gaze moved toward Dell. "I... Don't tell me. I can guess what he said. That I'm a bad influence. That I have to stay away from Dell."

"How did you..." Bess stopped. She didn't believe Griff could have done anything worthy of that man's disdain, but she couldn't explain it away, either. She drew Griff even farther from the rodeo team until her back was to a fence rail. "Is this battle royal between you two something I need to worry about?"

"No." Griff scowled. "Yes." He removed his hat and ran a hand through his unruly hair. "Bess, I'm so, so sorry."

Bess's fingers curled against the urge to trace the path of his hand, to smooth his hair and offer some comfort. Instead, Bess took Griff by the arms, gripping those solid biceps, offering her support. "Tell me what's going on. I can help you."

He stared down at her, seemingly frozen for a moment before saying, "It all comes back around, doesn't it?"

"Griff." She gave him a little shake, hardly moving him. "As the rodeo coach, I have to know where conflict is coming from.

If I don't, I can't fix it before it escalates to the attention of the principal. And if that happens, you'll have to leave the rodeo grounds and not return."

"I understand." Griff glanced across the arena toward Dell. Seconds ticked by. And then his soulful gaze swung around to Bess. "He's mine," he whispered. "Dell doesn't know but… He's my son."

The world around them seemed to spin.

Was this why Griff stood me up all those years ago? Did he go to the birth of his son?

Does Ronnie know? Do all the cowboys at the Done Roamin' Ranch know?

Was Griff in love with Dell's mother? Is that why he never said anything to me about his feelings back then?

"Bess? Bess, are you okay?" Griff was holding her arms now.

Bess shook her head and straightened. She brushed off Griff's hands. "I'm doing the math. Dell wasn't born on prom. He just turned seventeen." Which would have explained why Griff hadn't taken her to the dance. "He was born earlier than prom. And you… When Dell was born, you were just a baby yourself."

A teenage father?

Practically the definition of unreliable. Mama was right. I shouldn't have fallen for him.

She opened her eyes and stared at Griff. At brown eyes the color of dark roast coffee. At brown brows lowered in concern. At a mouth that wasn't smiling. At a man who'd made a serious mistake as a teenager. A disappointing mistake.

I could have ended up pregnant, too.

No. He hadn't wanted history to repeat itself.

Bess knew deep down in her bones that Griff was a good person. Sure, he wasn't anywhere near perfect. But despite that, his parents hadn't stood by him, supported him or loved him. And then, his son…

Oh, Griff.

Bess was breathing hard, painfully hard, studying Griff's handsome face as if it would reveal the answers to all her questions and insecurities. He was a father. This changed everything.

All the things Bess thought about him pre-and post-prom. And now... And yet...

And yet, I still want to kiss him.

She couldn't think about lips sparking when they touched. There were still too many unanswered questions. Still the hurdle of Mr. James for Griff to move past.

"Dell's the reason you were put in foster care," Bess said slowly, eyes filled with tears. Someone should have loved Griff enough to keep him.

If he'd been mine, I wouldn't have given up on him.

The thought was fierce and new.

"Ironic, isn't it? Given my folks were teen parents themselves." Gone was Griff's usual humor, that sarcasm he often used as a shield.

"That fact isn't ironic. It's hurtful." All these years, Bess had stared into those soulful eyes never knowing what hardships he'd suffered through. She'd suspected his smile hid emotional wounds, but she'd never guessed it was fatherhood ripped away from him or abandonment.

"At first, I was told they put Dell up for adoption." Griff produced his wallet from his back jeans pocket. A sheet of paper was folded in with his cash. He handed it to her.

It was one of those ceremonial birth certificates the hospital gave out to parents, not a legitimate birth certificate with a county seal.

Bess whispered as she read, "Baby boy, born May first. Seven pounds, five ounces. A happy blessing to mother Avery James and father Griffin Malone."

"Avery mailed it to me after I moved to the Done Roamin' Ranch." Griff's voice was as rough as the road he'd traveled as a teen. He took the paper back, folding it gingerly and carefully returning it to his wallet. "Adults told me he'd be better off adopted. And then the night of prom, Dell and Avery were in a car crash. My foster dad drove me to the hospital. Avery didn't make it. That's when I learned Dell hadn't been adopted. But Paul James still insisted I have nothing to do with my son."

"And all this time..."

Griff shook his head. "Bess, I'll answer all your questions

but for now, you need to keep rodeo camp on schedule and I…"
He glanced toward Dell, who was being teased about the condition of his broken straw cowboy hat. "I should probably leave."

Bess caught his arm. "You're not leaving. You're the one person here who can make fifty teenagers forget that it's hot and that skill drills are boring."

Griff paused but still wasn't smiling. "I know Paul. He'll cause trouble. Most likely for you and Dell."

"As much as I appreciate you watching out for me…" Bess submitted to impulse and laid her palm on Griff's stubbled cheek "…I can handle ornery parents and family members. If you haven't heard, I'm prickly."

He smiled. Just a little.

And her heart pounded faster. Just a little.

Several teens noticed her intimate gesture and began calling them out, whistling, hooting and hollering.

Bess dropped her hand, but not her resolve. "You're staying. Don't argue."

THE TRUTH IS OUT.

Past truths anyway.

Griff hadn't realized how much he'd fretted over Bess finding out he'd been a teenage dad. Given the snootiness her mother and sisters had shown toward him, he'd expected Bess to turn up her nose at the revelation. He'd expected her to say something like *I thought so.*

But he had no qualms that she'd take his offer to buy her property, as well. He went through the rest of the morning drills trying to keep things fun for the teens, feeling as if he was brittle enough to be broken by a single sharp word.

When lunch was called, he tugged out his cell phone and was about to compose a text message to Vickie, telling her to withdraw his offer, when he heard someone call his name.

"Coach Griff?" Dell approached Griff tentatively.

"Yeah?" Griff finished off his water and tossed the empty bottle back into his cooler, trying to play it casual when inside, he was doing the Dad Dance because his kid was seeking out his company.

"I was just wondering..." Dell removed his broken straw cowboy hat and scratched his thatch of unruly brown hair. "Why does my grandfather hate you?"

Oh, this wasn't going to go well. Griff glanced around, looking for a distraction, but came up empty. Bess, Ronnie, even Wade, weren't in sight. The sun caught a windshield just right, sending a blinding ray in Griff's eyes. He squinted.

Meanwhile, his son was still asking questions. "Did you beat him at cards or something? Refuse his insurance sales pitch? He's never mentioned you before and..." Dell stopped babbling and would have put that broken straw hat back on his head if Griff hadn't swiped it.

"You know, you can repair this hat." *Or I could buy you a new one.*

"Repair it?" Dell was suitably distracted, frowning in confusion. "With a needle and thread?"

"No. By weaving some new straw where the rough spots are." Griff turned the brim around, full circle, as if he was studying the damage. "It'll never be the same, though."

"Coach Glover says everyone on the rodeo team gets new straw hats." Dell held out a hand for his hat to be returned. "I'll stick with this one until then."

Griff didn't want his kid walking around with that hat for the next four weeks. He'd be an easy target to tease. He handed Dell his cowboy hat back anyway. "Do you ever watch sports? Football or soccer?"

Dell nodded, pressing his hat too firmly onto his head, as if to protect Griff taking it again.

"Have you seen the jersey swap?" Griff removed his straw cowboy hat and extended it toward Dell. "After a hard-fought game, players exchange jerseys. I'd like to do the same to you with this hat." He held his cowboy hat out farther, trying to smile reassuringly. "It's an honor to have towed rope with you."

"Why do you want my ruined hat?" Dell gave Griff a suspicious look but there was a spark of interest in his eyes.

"I was going to retire this hat at the end of summer and buy a new one," Griff lied. He'd only bought that hat in the spring and had planned on keeping it for years. "But I'm thinking if I give you my old hat—which I would have thrown away—I'll have an excuse to buy me a new one next payday."

"Why would you do that?" Dell frowned, possibly not used to being the recipient of unexpected gifts. "You hardly know me and my grandfather—"

"You should take the hat." Nancy popped up from somewhere. Wearing all black to complement her inky hair, Nancy looked like a goth cowgirl. "Your hat is done for, Dell."

Kevin joined them, towering over his two friends. "It's his mom's hat, Nancy."

Avery's hat?

More than ever, Griff wanted to repair it. "You could take both hats, Dell."

His son continued to frown at Griff. He'd crossed his arms.

"You want to know why I'm being nice to you?" Griff brought his hat back toward his chest, turning it in a circle, much the way he'd done with Dell's hat. "When I was a kid, we couldn't afford extras, like new boots if my feet grew too fast. And because of me growing up without nice things—"

"You still don't have nice things." Nancy moved to stand closer to Dell, staring at Griff warily. "We've seen your truck, not to mention that shirt and your blue jeans."

"I've been saving to buy my own ranch." Griff ran a hand over his hair, not at all relieved to confess that truth when he had so many other secrets.

"That's smart." At least Kevin was on his side.

"You didn't answer me," Dell told Griff with an edge of impatience. "Why does my grandfather hate you?"

Because he's afraid I'll take you from him.

The truth pressed at the back of Griff's throat. But the truth wouldn't serve him here. Not the whole truth anyway.

"I grew up with your mother," Griff said, tiptoeing around his emotions. "Your grandfather never liked me. I'm sure when he saw me yesterday, I was an unpleasant blast from the past."

"My mother..." Dell stared at Griff in a new light.

"Why don't we trade hats?" Griff held his out again. "You can wear mine while I fix yours. And then we'll trade back."

"Take the deal." Nancy snatched Dell's hat and traded it for Griff's. "If anyone asks you where you got it—"

"Anyone but my grandfather," Dell said.

"—if we tell them it's Coach Griff's, you're golden. Everybody loves him," Nancy finished, stretching on her tiptoes to put Griff's hat on Dell's head. "Everybody except your grandpa."

"Forget waiting for them to ask." Kevin began walking backward toward the arena gate. "We're going to tell them first. There's more street cred that way."

"You won't throw my hat away?" Dell asked Griff, ignoring Nancy's lovestruck gaze and Kevin's move to try to up their cool factor.

Griff was inspecting the hatband inside. He flipped it open to reveal Avery's name in her neat handwriting next to Dell's in a messier style. *Avery...* He'd gotten over her long before her passing but she'd forever hold a special place in his heart. "I promise to fix it and return it."

"Shake on it." Dell thrust out his hand.

Griff gave his son a firm handshake, barely resisting drawing him into his arms. "I promise to return your mother's hat."

Dell nodded.

"Hurry up, guys," Kevin called.

Dell and Nancy ran after him.

Griff hung back, studying Dell's wreck of a hat before casting his gaze to a clear blue sky. "Avery, he's keeping you alive. You'd be so proud of him."

Griff sure was.

But the question remained: Would Dell be proud of Griff?

CHAPTER EIGHT

AFTER LEARNING PART of Griff's history, Bess went through the rest of Wednesday and most of Thursday in a worse mental muddle than she'd been in after some cocky upstart had made an offer to buy the Rolling G.

Bess still hadn't looked at the offer. But she had looked at her opinions about Griff through a lens sharpened with truth. She'd been cruel to him ever since he stood her up. She wasn't proud of that behavior. In fact, she'd been doing some soul-searching and wasn't happy with what she saw.

"Rascal, am I a princess?" Bess asked after getting ready to meet Ronnie at The Buckboard on Thursday night. She smoothed her new, emerald green skirt and waited for her grandfather to answer.

He blinked awake. "Say again?"

Bess bit back her pride and repeated, "Am I a princess?"

Her grandfather looked Bess up and down, gave Finlay a pat on the head, glanced at the muted television and then gestured for Bess to take a seat on the couch.

She perched on the arm, fiddling with her skirt once more.

"Have you ever heard how I got my nickname?"

"Yes. Your mother used to call you that because you were always sneaking out to the barn and riding the horses, even before you knew how to put on a saddle or bridle."

"Well..." Rascal worked his lips together as if trying to push out the right words. "Truth is... When I was courting your grandmother, her mother told me that I wasn't the prince she wanted for her princess."

"She called you Rascal?"

"No." Her grandfather tapped his hands on the arms of his tan recliner, staring at the pink recliner next to his, the one that used to be Grandma Edie's. "I thought long and hard about your great-grandmother's words. They hurt. But the truth was that I'd dropped out of school after the eighth grade. And although I loved your grandmother, I was willing to step aside if she wanted another man than me, maybe one with more schooling or prospects."

Bess's stomach turned to think that she had more in common with her great-grandmother than her beloved Rascal. And yet, a small part of her was skeptical. "Are you making this up because of what Mama always said to us girls?" To not get stuck on a ranch, married to a rancher forever.

"Can I finish?" Rascal raised his eyebrows and waited.

Bess gestured that he should continue.

"When I asked your grandmother what she wanted in a man, she told me..." His blue eyes filled with tears and his voice became thick with emotion. "She told me...in these words... *This princess wants a man, not a prince, but preferably a rascal.*"

"Aw, that's so romantic." Not that it answered her original question.

Rascal shook his finger at her. "Now, the reason I'm telling you this is that your mama raised five princesses and told them what kind of man they *should* want, just like your great-grandmother told my Edie. So, yes. You're a princess. But that doesn't mean you need to marry a prince."

Bess stood and planted a gentle kiss on top of his nearly bald head. "It would be better for the ranch if I married a wealthy prince."

"We can cut corners, Princess Bessie," Rascal said gruffly. "We can offer room and board in exchange for ranch work, just like how I did it in the old days."

Bess moved toward the foyer where her Saturday night boots

awaited her. "If we return to the old ways, you'd marry me off to a prince for a nice dowry, King Rascal."

Her grandfather chuckled. "You've got that wrong, Bessie. You'd marry *me* off in exchange for a wealthy widow's dowry. I'm not much use to you here."

"Don't talk like that." Bess pulled on her green boots with short fringe at her ankle. "Seeing as how we need wealthy marriages, maybe you should head on down to The Buckboard with me."

"Not a chance. Edie was my one and only." His laughter followed Bess out the door, lightening her spirits.

But she hadn't even reached the main highway in her truck before her mind drifted back to Griff and the past, a past where she'd let her pride get the better of her instead of trusting her feelings for Griff.

Griff was a father. The thought was mind-blowing.

Happy-go-lucky, bachelor cowboy Griff Malone was a dad. And not just a dad but a father who hadn't been allowed to see his child and who wasn't supposed to interact with him even now. All because his son's grandfather couldn't forgive Griff.

The Griff that Bess thought she knew would have thumbed his nose at someone telling him what to do. Which raised the question: *How well do I really know Griff?*

She was afraid she knew the answer to that question: *Not well.*

Not as well as she should if every time she looked into his eyes she thought of kissing him.

Bess entered The Buckboard and breathed in the aroma of burgers, fries and beer. A DJ was setting up on the stage. Line dancing would be starting soon.

Bess loved to line dance, which didn't require a partner.

There's a reason I don't want a partner.

Bess liked to lead.

She spotted Ronnie sitting at their usual booth near the dance floor. Her best friend wore a white lace sundress with a chunky turquoise necklace. Her long dark hair tumbled to her shoulders from a turquoise cowboy hat.

"I need a drink," Bess told Ronnie when she sat down.

"I've been doing a lot of self-reflection and I'm not liking what I'm seeing."

Maggie delivered Bess a light beer with a slice of lemon. "I saw you come in with a crinkle in your brow. Thought you'd need a drink right away."

"You are heaven-sent, Maggie." Bess caught the bartender's hand before she retreated. "Nachos?"

"Already ordered by Ronnie." Maggie smiled and returned to the bar.

"I love Maggie." Bess sipped her beer. "Why isn't she married? If I was a man, I'd marry her."

"You'd have to fight Clem for the chance." Ronnie may have teased, but she didn't smile. "But Maggie is right. What's wrong with you?"

Rather than answer, Bess had a question of her own. "Do you think I'm a pain-in-the-butt princess?"

Ronnie studied her but didn't hesitate to answer. "You can be a bit princess-like but what woman isn't every once in a while?"

"I knew it." Bess held up her fingers and began ticking off her faults, "I'm prickly. I'm unforgiving. My standards for a man are impossibly high, although not nearly as high as my mother's. And... I'm no fun."

Ronnie reached across the table and took Bess's hand, gently folding down her fingers. "I think you're being too hard on yourself."

"No. I think I needed a good wake-up call. These things are exactly why I'm not married." Bess slipped her hand free. "Who could love a person like that?"

"I wouldn't go that far." Ronnie sat back, staring at Bess.

A familiar silhouette at the periphery of Bess's vision had her turning her head. "I bet I can find someone who'd agree with me."

Dressed in his best shirt and jeans, Griff took a seat next to Clem. His shoulders were pulled in. And now that she knew why his eyes had that soulful shadow, Bess felt the attraction between them, stronger than before. But this time, she was embarrassed by it.

Bess faced Ronnie and announced, "I'm dating a veterinarian."

"I know. He appeals to Her Royal Highness, Princess Bess." Ronnie smiled wryly. "But you aren't one hundred percent princess, so what brought on this bout of self-reflection?"

More people were entering The Buckboard. The volume of conversation was beginning to blend with laughter and rise, requiring Bess and Ronnie to talk louder to each other to be heard.

"I need to give Dr. Brandon Bitterman a real shot," Bess said firmly. She leaned forward to add, "Or someone like him, because the ranch finances are...*aren't* good."

Ronnie didn't look surprised to hear this. "Bess, love has nothing to do with money."

"Tell that to the bank." Bess fished her lemon from her glass and squeezed juice into her beer. "Because right now, even though I have a very low opinion of myself, I'm thinking Princess Bess could fall in love at first sight with a man who checks all my mother's boxes."

"If that were true, you'd have fallen hard after your first date with Dr. B." Ronnie sipped her beer, still watching Bess's every move and nuance.

"Can't get anything past you." Nor could Bess fault Ronnie's logic, much as it would be better for the ranch if she could.

"Maybe it's time to edit that list of yours." Ronnie snapped her fingers. "I know. You can become a professional rodeo coach."

"And this solves my romance problem...how?"

"This solves your money problem." Ronnie warmed to her topic. "You have a lot of rodeo team alumni on the rodeo circuit. I'm sure someone would hire you."

Bess set her chin on her hand. "Have you ever noticed that you're as positive as Christopher Robin and I'm more like Eeyore, who sees every dark rain cloud, not its silver lining?"

"I've noticed." Ronnie nodded, grinning. "That's part of your charm."

"And you yours," Bess allowed.

Maggie delivered their nachos and extra napkins. "Can I get you ladies anything else?"

"Prince Charming?" Bess didn't think there was any harm in asking.

"Sadly, we have no princes on the bar menu." With a jaunty wave, Maggie returned to the bar.

Bess and Ronnie dug into their nachos for a few minutes without speaking. That was the thing about salty chips, melted cheese, hearty chicken and spicy jalapeños. They demanded more action than conversation.

But finally, Bess felt bolstered enough to return to the problem at hand—money. "Name another way I can make money," Bess demanded, loading a chip with chicken and jalapeños.

"You could sell off stock."

Bess shook her head. "We've depleted our herd to the point where we won't break even if we sell off more."

Ronnie swept her chip through melted cheese and sour cream. "You can be my matchmaking assistant."

"Come on." Bess laughed. "That sounds like a volunteer assignment, not to mention I'm impatient with people. If I saw a couple that I thought was made for each other, I'd tell them in no uncertain terms to find a dark place to put their kissers to the test." That comment hit too close to what had happened between Bess and Griff. She hurried to continue. "You, on the other hand, set them up for coffee dates and wine tastings, plus give them advice on what to wear and note cards with conversation starters."

"Don't sell yourself short. Your method for helping love along might work and earn you some extra income." Ronnie's gaze roamed around The Buckboard. "There are all kinds of ways to nurture affection and help it grow into love, including not taking yourself so seriously—hint, hint. In fact, love can be found on a dance floor on a Thursday night."

"Really?" Bess scoffed. "Is that because Thursday is the new Friday?"

"Nope." Ronnie beamed.

"Hey, Bess." Griff appeared tableside without his trademark, confident grin. "The line dancing is about to start. Care to join me?"

"Is that a new dress?" Griff asked, searching for a conversation topic on the dance floor.

Smiling, Bess held out her skirt and curtsied. "It is. Do you like it?"

"I like you in your ranch duds." The words were out before Griff realized how rude they were.

"Really, cowboy?" Bess frowned, tossing her long red hair over her shoulder like she was preparing for one of their verbal skirmishes. But then she drew a deep breath and soldiered a smile. "I was fishing for a compliment and probably caught you by surprise. Let's start over." She cleared her throat, then pouted. "How do I look?"

"Bess..." Griff let slip a smile before he could erase it. He wasn't in the mood to play games, even with Bess. "I apologize. I'm just realizing I'm not in the mood to dance."

He'd made no progress with Paul today. He hadn't even seen the man pick up Dell at the end of practice. He'd talked to Vickie earlier about his offer and had been told not to get his hopes up. Griff debated whether to pull the offer or not, playing what-if games about how his life might be if he purchased a smaller spread. He'd still have to work elsewhere to make ends meet. That didn't appeal.

But Bess... He was throwing things with her away to reach for a big dream. And here she stood in front of him, flirting almost, which wasn't anything that he'd expected. It made his moral pendulum swing back toward the dream of making a life with her by his side.

Meanwhile, Bess was looking at him with a furrowed brow. "Is it because I was fishing for compliments? I wasn't... Well, I was. When a cowgirl cleans up, she appreciates a cowboy's notice."

"You look pretty, and you know it," Griff grumbled. No way was he getting sucked into an argument with her about princess pedigrees. "I was just stating a fact before. I prefer you in blue jeans and a plain shirt because..."

"Because..." she prompted.

Griff wished the music would start. He even caught the DJ's eye and made a speed-it-up motion. "I didn't say I didn't like you in a dress." That dress in particular gave him ideas about more kisses. "I said I prefer you in blue jeans because that's when you are more you and I'm more me. When you wear a dress, I feel like I'm going to trip over my own two feet and make a fool of myself."

"Are you saying I put on airs when I dress up?"

"Um... I...didn't come here to bicker." This was a sinkhole, pure and simple.

"You don't like it when we bicker?" Bess said, sounding surprised. "That's defined our relationship since..."

She didn't have to say since that fateful dance he'd missed. He caught on to the reference.

Bess smoothed that glorious red hair over her shoulder, starting to look stricken. "I'm the problem. I'll admit it."

"I didn't ask you to—"

"I owe you an apology for years of acting like my boots never touch stink." Bess bit her lower lip, probably not realizing that only made him want to kiss her. "I'm not fun. I'm hard-nosed and blunt speaking, not to mention quick-tempered. But I should have let the past go all those years back and treated you like anyone else in our friendship circle. I should have forgiven you."

Other people were filling up the dance floor, crowding them toward the stage.

Griff stared at Bess, completely flummoxed. "What brought this on?"

Bess glanced away, expression pained and cheeks flushed, bringing her freckles into full display. "I've been moving through my life without moving forward and suddenly I've found myself looking into a mirror. And... You forgive me, don't you?"

He nodded, somewhat numbly. "I've been thinking a lot about apologies lately." To her, mostly.

"You don't have to apologize to me." She smiled, small and tentative. "I mean, you said you were sorry yesterday. And now, I'm coming right back at you with my own apology." Bess rubbed his arm consolingly.

I do not deserve this woman's forgiveness.

Griff drew a deep breath, unable to stop thinking about his impetuous, anonymous offer on her ranch. "About that..."

Bess put her finger on his lips. She smelled of flowers. Nothing as simple as wildflowers. No. Bess smelled darkly floral and deeply mysterious. "You're nervous. Why?"

He was nervous. He couldn't seem to stand still. And the truth...*the awful truth*...pressed at the back of his throat like a bitter cup of coffee, demanding to be cleansed. But Griff didn't want to tell her about his ranch offer now. Here. In the midst of a crowd of their friends and neighbors.

Bess seemed aware of their audience, too. Her hand fell away.

Griff swallowed thickly and chose the other thing that had been bothering him. "Since I told you about Dell, I kept waiting for you to ask me more about... You know."

"Dell? His mother? Your parents?"

Griff nodded.

Thank the heavens above. The music started. The DJ had chosen an oldie but a goodie—"Boot Scootin' Boogie."

"I'd rather dance than talk." Bess whirled away and did just that, leaving Griff no choice but to do the steps alongside her.

This isn't like Bess.

At least, not the Bess that Griff knew. The Bess he knew would have had a list of questions written down. She'd want to know why-why-why. And then she'd want to tell him what-what-what. What to do next. What to say to Paul. What to say to Dell. And when to say and do it all.

After telling her yesterday about Dell, Griff had braced himself for her onslaught of whys and whats. Nothing. He'd brought her coffee this morning to rodeo camp. Nothing. He'd brought her lunch from a taco truck. Nothing. And all the while, at the back of his mind, that offer to buy had taken up residence in his temples. Pounding out a cadence of guilt, defensiveness and regret until Griff no longer knew if he should withdraw his offer or tell her outright what he wanted to do.

Now that she'd forgiven him... Now that she was kind of, almost, possibly flirting with him...

If he told Bess now, that would definitely push her away, back to the bickering zone.

I don't want that.

The thought made Griff miss a step, unintentionally putting distance between him and Bess.

She caught his hand, dragging him near and then letting him go. As if they were friends.

Friends?

Inwardly, Griff recoiled.

Without a word, he headed toward the bar. In his mind, he was climbing a ladder toward something more permanent. And that something was gut-cringingly either Bess or her ranch. And if Bess didn't care enough about Griff, he'd settle for her ranch and make it into a place Dell would be proud to call home.

Griff had one hand on his beer when Bess laid a hand on his arm. "Come sit with me." She angled her head toward the booth where he'd found her eating nachos with Ronnie earlier.

Ronnie was currently line dancing with Wade. They were laughing and having a good time.

"Come on." Bess tugged his arm.

"Why?" Griff leaned away from her, not a lot, but enough that Bess either had to hang on or let go.

Bess frowned, not letting go.

"If you're fishing for more compliments, I'm not interested," Griff told her, temples pounding. "You can always find some veterinarian to sing your praises."

Her eyes widened. Her fingers curled around his bicep. "Why, Griff… If I didn't know any better, I'd think you were jealous."

Darn straight.

Not that he could let her know that. She'd latch onto that nugget of information and never let go, like a burr in the folds of a saddle blanket.

"Bessie." Griff switched tactics, ignoring the way her eyes sparked blue fire when he used her grandpa's nickname for her. "Given our history together, I came here tonight to give you the opportunity to ask your questions and…" *Tell you what I've done.*

She didn't move. "And…"

And then confess that I want to make a home for Dell at the Rolling G. A home we could share.

Griff pressed his lips together, too cowardly to say that out loud to her. But he suspected he wasn't the only one standing here holding on to a secret. He fixed her with a level stare. "And maybe you can tell me what's been bothering you these past few days." Before she even got around to scoffing, Griff added, "Don't try to deny it. Ronnie, Wade and I have all been noticing. I was thinking it had to do with me but now I'm not so sure."

Bess spun around, sending that long green skirt swirling around her cowboy boots.

Griff grabbed his beer and followed her. It would be nice to know where he stood before he sent himself packing.

CHAPTER NINE

"NOTHING'S BEEN BOTHERING ME," Bess griped when she and Griff sat across from each other.

He took a chip and dug into the dregs of the nachos—*without asking!*

"You're taking your life in your own hands, you nacho thief. You know how Ronnie and I feel about nachos." They weren't community property.

Griff scoffed. "You two always let Wade have some."

"That's because he's Wade and worships his wife, Ronnie." And darn if she didn't want Griff to worship her. Not like a princess but as an equal. Bess sipped her beer, considering that last thought. Was equals what you needed to be able to fall in love?

Applause and laughter had her glancing toward the dance floor where a song had just ended.

Bess sighed. "I'd much rather be dancing." There was no self-evaluation when she danced.

"Fine. Get on out there. I'll just finish my beer, and then I'll be going." Griff took a long pull of his drink.

Bess frowned at Griff. He was so annoying. He couldn't even have a simple conversation for five minutes. "You asked me to dance. And I wanted to dance...with you," she admitted reluctantly. Because something had to be said to make him understand.

Griff set his glass down. "And then…"

Bess sipped her warm beer and said nothing.

Griff leaned forward, brown eyes watching her every move. "And then…after the dancing…"

"There's no *and then*." Bess fidgeted in her seat. Her boots were itching to dance, and her lips were itching to kiss and she wasn't happy sitting and talking. They could sit and talk any old day. Didn't Griff understand that she couldn't admit anything more about what she wanted to do with him?

"There's always another *and then*." Griff wasn't smiling, which was odd because what he was saying… It should have been delivered as a tease, a dare, something she could swat down if she was in a prickly, princess mood.

Without you.

But now he was here.

"Fine," she allowed, her heart pounding way too fast. "I come to The Buckboard. I drink. I eat nachos. I dance. *And then* I go home."

"You're dancing around my original question regarding what's bothering you." Griff leaned forward. "I know how you think, Bessie."

Bessie? "Stop calling me that." Although admittedly, there was something delicious in the way he said her nickname.

"You're thinking that if you talk about nothing long enough that I'll forget I was worried about you and let the question go." He slowly spun his beer glass. "The fact remains. What's weighing on your mind?"

"Would you believe me if I said it was you?" That didn't come out as confidently as she'd wanted it to. "You and Dell?"

"Nope."

Bess crossed her arms over her chest. "Why not?"

"Because if my challenges with Dell were top-of-mind for you, you'd be grilling me the way you did the other night when you wanted to know where Nate was." Griff popped a chip into his mouth, chewing and swallowing before telling her, "Not that I'm holding you not worrying about me and mine against you. Don't you remember the last time I bought a horse? You gave me the third degree about price and confirmation and pedigree.

And what about the last time I bought a pair of new boots? You asked me what the occasion was, what brand they were and if I'd bought them on sale. Did you even notice that I have a new straw hat?" He poked at the nacho plate with a finger, around jalapeños and bites of chicken. "And now, you know I'm a father, and other than those few questions you asked yesterday, there's been nothing." He lifted his gaze to hers and there were questions in his eyes that she didn't understand. "Have you washed your hands of me?"

So raw. So heartfelt.

"No." Impulsively, Bess reached across the table for his hand, the same way Ronnie had done with her earlier. "It's just that I'm up to my eyebrows in problems and nights like this are for beer, nachos and dancing." She'd left out the most important part—kissing.

Griff didn't answer right away. And when he did, it was more like a grunt of disbelief than an intelligible word.

Bess drew her hand back, staring at the dancers having a good time doing a quick two-step.

Griff scooped more nacho goodness from the bottom of the plate with half a chip. "Do you know why we don't work as friends?"

Because we don't kiss?

Bess bit her lip, unwilling to voice her opinion.

He picked up another chip, using it to gesture toward her, a mischievous gleam in his brown eyes. "Because we don't communicate. Because you don't trust me, and I never know what to expect from you."

Bess liked her reason better. "You make me sound like…" A pain-in-the-butt princess. She released a slow breath. Everything she should, did and shouldn't feel for Griff was tumbling together, tangling and twisting into knots, like the time Rascal had put her bras in the clothes dryer.

"Why don't you tell me what's really been bothering you?" Griff scrounged at the dregs on the nacho plate. "It helps to share."

"The doctor is in," Bess murmured.

An image of the Rolling G came to mind, or at least, how it

used to look when she was a little girl. The barn always had a fresh coat of paint. The house, too. The corrals were in good shape. All arena rails were sturdily attached. The herd was large, dotting pastures in the back forty acres. Dinner had always been served in the dining room, eaten after grace, instead of in the living room, plate balanced in her or Rascal's lap.

Bess uncrossed her arms and set her hands on the table edge. "I'm not very good at managing a ranch."

Across from her, Griff froze. A jalapeño fell off his chip as he straightened. He discarded his chip on a napkin. "Anyone who teaches and coaches full-time while still managing to have a personal life wouldn't be able to devote themselves to successfully managing a large ranch."

"My father used to do that. And before him, my grandfather." Bess gripped the table edge the way one gripped a safety bar on a fairground roller coaster. "I never saw myself running the ranch. But then my parents left, my grandmother died and Rascal had a hard time keeping up."

Griff nodded, touched his beer glass without taking a sip, stared at the near-empty nachos plate, before resting his arm on top of the booth. He always fidgeted when he was nervous.

"I'm making you uncomfortable," she realized.

"Yes." Griff nodded again, leaning forward and resting his elbows on the table. "Not that you're at ease with sharing things with me. You can let the table go. It's not going to run away."

Bess unfurled her fingers from the table and tapped the wooden top. "Good table. Stay."

Griff grinned.

And instead of that grin creating a fluttery turmoil inside Bess, she felt somehow…settled. She drew an easier breath and rubbed her clammy palms on her thighs. "In June, my grandfather fell in the barn after mucking out stalls. He was pushing the wheelbarrow and that was just too much for his equilibrium. I came home from the grocery store, and he wasn't in the house." She'd been frantic. "Luckily, he didn't break anything, but it was a wake-up call."

Griff nodded, grin fading.

"And I've been trying to find someone in the family to take the ranch on." She shrugged. "I feel like the bad guy."

"The adult in the room," Griff gently corrected. "Making the hard decisions."

That fit. She nodded. "And all of a sudden, we have an offer... *on the ranch.*" This last part came out as little more than a whisper. The music was so loud that she doubted Griff could hear.

"And how does that make you feel?" he asked, having better hearing than she gave him credit for.

Bess stared at her hands, lying helplessly in her lap. "Angry... heartsick...*relieved.*" She hadn't acknowledged that last emotion until just this moment.

"You can't care for the ranch properly, doing it justice, but you can't let it go." Griff nodded. "That's close to the way I felt when I found out Dell hadn't been put up for adoption. I... was made aware that I was really just a kid myself. I wanted Dell but I couldn't provide a roof over his head and food on the table. I felt helpless."

Bess nodded. "What did you do?"

"It felt like nothing." He tipped his hat brim up and wiped the back of his hand across his forehead. "But I've been preparing for the day when I can claim him as mine. Keeping my nose clean and..."

Griff hasn't been arrested. He doesn't even have a speeding ticket.

Griff continued talking but Bess didn't hear a word he said. She was thinking about how Griff always seemed like a good-time cowboy, someone she was loath to respect.

But he was something else entirely, something if her circumstances were different, if her family legacy wasn't at stake, she'd have a hard time living without. Handsome, smart, charming, funny. She even trusted him.

And that only served to make things worse. He deserved someone nice and easygoing. A woman who wasn't prickly, who didn't wear blinders where her family finances were concerned, who didn't attach herself to lost causes, like a rodeo team.

A sense of shame filled her.

The song ended. The DJ announced the end of line dancing for the evening. Folks began to return to their tables.

Ronnie and Wade walked right for them, arm in arm.

And Bess...

Bess slid out of the booth and said her goodbyes, unable to stop herself from giving Griff a long, soulful look before she bolted.

Because she'd done Griff wrong for years and she didn't want to do anything that would stand in the way of the happiness he deserved.

Like grabbing onto him and never letting go.

"WHAT DID YOU do to upset Bess?" Ronnie had her hands on her hips and a frown on her lips.

"I confess." Griff raised his hands in the air as if surrendering for arrest. "I ate some of your nachos."

Wade tugged Ronnie toward the side of the booth Bess had just vacated. "Go easy on him, Ronnie."

"Yes. Go easy on me, Ronnie." Griff took a chip and tunneled it into a spoonful of guacamole. "You know how Bess and I get. And bickering makes me hungry." That was a lie. Griff had no appetite. He had no idea why Bess had walked away. Had he given something away about that real estate offer? He didn't think so.

Ronnie laughed and slid into the booth across from Griff, followed by Wade.

Just looking at how happy they were made Griff miss Bess.

"True, you were getting along well with Bess until you broke nacho protocol." Ronnie considered Griff the way he imagined she considered how to pair up a bunch of her matchmaking clients.

"I don't think Bess and I will ever have a smooth relationship." Griff found a corner of a chip half-hidden under a pile of jalapeños. "The more we talk, the trickier it becomes. Sometimes, I think it'd be better if we didn't talk, period." They got along great when they were kissing.

"I think you should ask Bess out on a date," Wade said unexpectedly. He was a cowboy who minded his own business.

His statement was earth-shattering. It took a moment for Griff to recover.

"Are you matchmaking now, too?" Griff ate the chip and the pile of jalapeños, hoping the heat would put a lid on all the things he had going through his head and couldn't yet admit—his desire to be a father to Dell, his desire to buy Bess's ranch and raise cattle, his desire to have Bess in his life, his belief that he couldn't have it all. "Maybe you should stick to bronc riding advice, Wade."

"Hear me out," his foster brother said. "I've been mulling things over. You and Bess have been in limbo for more than a decade."

If you only knew that wasn't true...

"If you went on a date, you'd either fall madly in love—"

"That's my vote," Ronnie said.

"—or decide once and for all that you weren't made for each other."

"You're really good at this." Ronnie kissed Wade's cheek.

There weren't any jalapeños left. Griff sat back. "Why is this important to you?"

"Because the tension between you two is as thick as chunky peanut butter." Wade grinned, tipping his hat back and tapping his cheek once more. "That should earn me another one of your sweet kisses, honey."

Ronnie obliged.

"You can deny it," Wade said, beaming like a man still head-over-heels in love with his wife. "But we're all living in your peanut butter world. We see it."

"I don't need to ask Bess out for her to decide how she feels about me," Griff admitted. "I did something she's not going to like."

And no matter how many times Wade and Ronnie asked him what he'd done, Griff wouldn't say.

CHAPTER TEN

"HEY, EARL." Griff stuck his head out the ranch truck window as he backed up to the loading dock at Clementine Feed first thing on Friday morning. "You got the ranch's order ready?"

"It'll be ready by the time you grab yourself a cup of coffee." Earl was a smart businessman. You could find anything and everything at the feed store, from blue jeans to dog dishes to saddles and feed. But efficient, he was not. "Leave your keys in the rig."

Time in town. That was the last thing Griff wanted. Time to think and overthink about Dell, the Rolling G and Bess.

Griff cut through the loading dock to the feed store's break room, where he assumed the coffee was fresh. The coffee wasn't as strong as he'd like but if he hung around there'd probably be someone to talk to.

Griff wandered into the main store. "Hey, Izzie. How's Della-Louise?"

"Sweet as pie." Izzie manned the sales counter. She had white-blond hair and big blue eyes. She had a delicate look about her but he'd seen her heft fifty-pound bags of dog food easy as you please. She was the glue that kept Earl and the feed store from falling apart. "Are you here to pick up your order?" At his nod, she rifled through some papers to find his invoice.

"You drinking your sludge, Coach?"

Griff turned at the sound of Dell's voice, beaming at his son wearing his cowboy hat. "Miss Izzie doesn't like sludge. The only coffee at the feed store is plain old coffee."

"I'll remember that next time you mooch coffee, Griff," Izzie teased, holding out his invoice. "We're out of the iron supplements for your cattle. They'll be in tomorrow end of day."

He thanked her and turned back to Dell, only to find Paul standing next to him holding two pairs of new blue jeans. "Hey, Paul."

"Griff." The ice in the man's tone lowered the temperature in the store.

Dell stuck his hands in his pockets. "We came in to buy blue jeans."

"If you buy three, you get a discount," Griff said, noticing Dell's too-short jeans.

"We're fine with two," Paul said thickly, before succumbing to a bout of coughing.

Griff scanned the rack by the register, found a tin of cough drops and handed them to Dell. "Put these on my tab, Izzie. And give these two the ranch discount."

"Of course." Izzie nodded.

Paul continued to cough but waved his hand as if refusing Griff's kindness.

"Has he had this cough a long time?" Griff asked Dell.

"Hay...fever..." Paul choked out in between hacking.

Griff continued to look to Dell for an answer.

"A long time." For once, his son didn't look Griff in the eyes. It felt like a lie.

"Hay fever is practically year-long in Oklahoma," Izzie said kindly.

Griff sipped his coffee, nodding. But something didn't ring true. Hay fever rarely settled deep in the chest. He scrutinized Paul's face, taking in the dark circles under his eyes and the paleness of his lips.

Something wasn't right here.

FRIDAY AFTERNOON WENT by in a blur for Bess, leaving her little time to dwell on her problems or Griff.

Bess and the bridesmaids decorated the private dining room at Barnaby's Steak House for the rehearsal dinner. Then she and the others went to have their nails done. And then it was back home to change for dinner.

Bess's phone dinged with a message when she walked into the house, greeted by a low-key Finlay. "Hey, Rascal! Our DNA results are online." She'd make time to review them even if she was a little late to the rehearsal dinner.

Finlay followed her into the living room and curled up on the hearthrug.

"Oh, goodie," Grandpa Rascal said from his recliner, rubbing at his eyes as if he'd been sleeping. "My chance at being proven right has come. This was a waste of time and money, wasn't it?"

Bess sat on the arm of the couch in the living room. She opened the email attachment and scanned its contents. "Good news. I'm related to you."

"And?" Rascal sat up taller.

Bess closed her phone screen, letting her gaze drift toward a family portrait sitting on the mantel. "And no one else that has put their DNA into their database."

"Ha! I figured." Her grandfather stared up at the ceiling. "Eshon has been in heaven so long, they didn't have DNA tests for anyone but criminals."

"I had hoped..." Bess sighed, feeling the responsibilities of the ranch close around her. She could no longer hope someone else would come to their rescue. "I'd hoped Eshon had tried to find you and put his DNA on record."

"Why? I've been here all my life, including since he left." Rascal frowned. "He could have stopped by any old time if he was still one of the living."

Bess wished Ronnie or Griff were here to suggest something or find a silver lining. She couldn't find anything positive here. "Rascal, you're always so certain he's dead. Yet, I've found no death certificates. Don't you want to know what happened to him? He's your brother." And their last hope for a family member to save the family legacy.

"Eshon was never what you might call an upstanding citizen," Rascal said evenly, if coldly, indicating things might not have been happy between the siblings when they both lived here. "Eshon was always interested in shortcuts. He left Clementine to run moonshine in Louisiana. Who knows what happened to him?" Her grandfather blew out a breath as if telling her this was a weight off his shoulders. "But what I do know is that if you were looking for him to bail out the ranch, you were placing your hopes on a dead horse."

"I seem to be doing that a lot lately." Bess got to her feet. "Miracles happen." She had a date with a super-steady veterinarian tomorrow night. Maybe they'd realize they were a match made in heaven.

And maybe pigs could fly.

"I wouldn't rely on miracles, Bessie," Grandpa Rascal said gruffly.

"Then what are we going to do?" Bess whispered.

"I don't know, Bessie. I just don't know." But he was staring at the envelope Vickie left, the unopened one on the coffee table.

CHAPTER ELEVEN

ABBY AND NATE'S wedding was held at a church in Friar's Creek with the reception held at the Friar's Creek Country Club, which was swanky for this part of Oklahoma.

Bess was certain that she wouldn't be the emotional wreck she'd been for Ronnie's wedding. She'd be a calm, supportive bridesmaid, all dry-eyed smiles for the bride.

She was wrong.

Sure, Bess was fine while her hair was being styled. But then the other bridesmaids and mother of the bride began talking about babies. Other people's babies. The babies Abby and Nate were going to have soon. Kelly-Jo was just getting serious with the butcher in town, and she wanted babies right away. Evie claimed she was going to adopt or possibly even freeze her eggs if she didn't have a baby by the time she turned thirty-five. And then they all turned toward Bess.

"I have no backup plan or timeline for babies," Bess told them. Didn't mean Bess didn't vividly recall Griff holding Vickie's newborn. Didn't mean her heart didn't pang for a fairy-tale cowboy, a man who wanted a houseful of babies, knew how to run a ranch, and had the backbone and resources to do so. Didn't mean her heart didn't pang again for wishing that Griff fit that bill and she fit his. "Everything happens on its own schedule.

I'm dating." Bess continued feeling all eyes judging and upon her. "And eventually, I'll find the man I'm looking for."

Did Dr. Brandon Bitterman fit the bill? She didn't know him well enough to say.

Bess stared at her reflection in the stylist's mirror, not entirely registering the large, loose, fishtail braids that created a halo around her face. Instead, she saw Griff coming to stand by her side after the disgruntled football coach confronted her. Griff stepping in at rodeo camp to make things fun. Griff's soulful eyes when he'd told her he was a father.

Don't. He deserves better than me.

"I was active on four different dating apps before I found Nate," Abby admitted, turning her head from side to side to admire the identical hairstyle they'd given the bridesmaids. "I was on the verge of hiring Ronnie. The point is, I made finding love a priority."

"Bess's first love is her rodeo team." Evie rose from the stylist chair, shaking out the wrinkles in her yellow sundress, looking pensive. "That stands in the way of her finding a man to marry, just like my love of baking does for me."

"The rodeo team is her baby," Kelly-Jo agreed, covering her face while her stylist sprayed hairspray around her. When she was done, Kelly-Jo waved the cloud of fumes away with her hands. "Bess, didn't you just cancel a date with your veterinarian because you were too tired after running rodeo camp?"

Bess nodded. "I did cancel, but—"

"Oh, Bess. You didn't. You're ruining your chances for love and babies." Abby sounded like she was an expert at love now when just a few days ago, she'd been ready to back out of this wedding.

The bride's hairstylist placed a white flower comb at the base of her neck.

"I'd hate to see you miss out on family because you didn't make yourself a priority," Abby added.

Bess hunkered down in her stylist's chair, feeling attacked.

"I'm living proof that the longer you wait, the harder it is to find love." Evie came to stand near Bess. "If you put the rodeo team first but want to have kids of your own, you need a plan for a man, Bess. I'm taking my love obstacle—baking—and using it to my advantage. I've got it all planned out. I'm going to bake my way into someone's heart."

The stylists began whipping off plastic capes and applying more hairspray.

"I don't believe that love can be strategized," Bess said, even though her statement was at odds with her having spousal criteria. The irony wasn't lost on her. And besides, she couldn't use the rodeo team to find true love.

Could she? An image of Griff winning over her students suddenly jumped to mind.

"Poor Bess, you have to at least try to find the right man, dear, *if* that's what you really want," Abby's mother, Teddy, said in a consoling voice, probably not realizing that her words were far from consoling. "Well, ladies. It's time to get to the church and put on our dresses. My little girl is going to get married."

The stylist who was doing Bess's hair whisked the plastic cape away. Bess got to her feet, demoralized. She could see her life stretching out before her. Not only would she lose the ranch, but she'd always be a bridesmaid. Always *poor Bess, the odd one out who didn't have babies or a backup plan.*

Grrr. Pull yourself together. Detach. Move on.

Bess was fine when she walked down the aisle, focusing on Griff standing on the altar. He wore a black suit with a black Western tie. Black cowboy boots and a black cowboy hat. He looked completely comfortable while she felt like she'd been gussied up for a Greek play. She wore flat sandals and a celery-green toga, for heaven's sake. If this was her wedding...

Poor Bess. Never to be the bride.

Tears threatened to spill over again.

What's happening to me? I'm just fine the way I am. I like my life. I will find Mr. Right.

Bess reminded herself she had a hot date for this wedding. Dr. Brandon Bitterman. She gazed out over the church pews, looking for Brandon. He was handsome, successful and...

Not in the church. She'd been stood up.

I never should have canceled the date with him on Monday.

She stared at the bouquet of white flowers she held. By tomorrow, the bouquet would be wilted and tossed in the trash.

Poor Bess, the dateless one among the crowd of joyful couples.

Bess needed a distraction from her withering thoughts while the bride and groom recited their vows.

And there, standing across from her was Griff. Handsome and helpful, although she'd avoided him at the rehearsal dinner last night. There was more to him than he let others see. His humor wasn't as annoying to her as it used to be. It was uplifting. And that smile of his wasn't slick or sly. He was genuinely happy most of the time. And now she knew why his dark brown eyes often looked soulful. He was a father deprived of his child.

Even Griff had a child.

Bess's eyes threatened to tear up once more.

Something's not right.

It was as if having lost the last hope of keeping the ranch in the family, the situation was ratcheting up the stress of being perpetually single. Deep breaths were needed. Now wasn't the time for a panic attack.

Somehow, she made it through the ceremony.

At the reception, Bess didn't want to stand with the other single ladies when the bouquet was thrown. But Abby would have none of it. So, Bess found a spot to one side of the group, trying not to look like a woman who'd been stood up and had no marital prospects. She smiled for the camera. She hooted and hollered as the band played some music for Abby to wind up and throw. And then...

The large, white bouquet hit Bess in the face.

She lurched backward, clinging to the sweet-smelling bundle.

Abby raced over and hugged Bess, whispering in her ear, "I aimed right for you."

I'll be lucky not to have a black eye in the morning.

Squinting, Bess dutifully smiled for a picture with Abby while Kelly-Jo and Evie joked that Bess needed all the help she could get in the romance department. By now, they all knew she'd been stood up, although Brandon had responded to her text asking where he was with, "Medical emergency." Bess assumed the emergency was with one of his animal patients, and not himself. But how was she to know?

All Bess wanted to do was retreat to a table and drink a beer while feeling sorry for herself. She had no interest in dancing with whoever caught the garter.

That wasn't to be. Abby's mother, Teddy, shepherded Bess away from the garter toss.

"I heard your blind date was a no-show," Teddy said matter-of-factly. Her toga-style dress had a sequined belt and her sandals had a kitten heel. "Would you consider dating my son, Harold?" She pointed toward a table near the front of the reception hall. "He's nearly forty and I'd like nothing more than for him to get married and move out of my basement."

Basement? Forty?

"Oh." Despite the red flag of still living with his parents, Bess was just desperate enough to give Abby's older brother a look-see.

Harold's head was bent over his cell phone. Silver threaded his once-dark hair. He had his feet propped up on a nearby chair, revealing that he'd chosen to pair black sneakers with his suit. He had a small pair of spectacles perched on his beak-like nose that made his eyes look squinty.

Bess backed away from Abby's mother. "You know, Teddy, my date was called away for a medical emergency. He's a veterinarian and his text said he'd try to make it if he could. I need to respect that."

"That's unreliable behavior, if you ask me. How do you know he isn't off with someone else?" Teddy sniffed. "Now, Harold... Harold is reliable. Always where you left him last."

Bess choked back a laugh. Abby's mother was more desperate than Bess was.

"Harold does the books for lots of businesses in town. He doesn't go out on the weekends. He stays home and plays his video games. He won't be any trouble."

A cheer went up in the crowd. A man had caught the garter.

"You might want to contact Ronnie Keller." Bess took another step back, planning to make a run for it. "She's really good at pairing people up."

"But Harold is here, Bess," Teddy said in a tone that was too frantic for the mother of the bride. "And you want to get married before it's too late."

"When do you think it's too late?" Bess wondered aloud.

"For Bess? It's never too late." Griff appeared at Bess's side. He had a pink garter on his wrist, a fact that made Bess happier than she'd ever been to see him in her entire life. "I believe this is our dance."

"Excuse us," Bess told Teddy as Griff swept her onto the dance floor. His strong arm drew her close. "You saved me. You've been doing that a lot lately. Helping out with the rodeo team." She gazed up at Griff, not wanting to bicker the way they had the other night. "Coming to this poor sad maiden's rescue when Teddy wanted me to be her daughter-in-law."

Griff leaned around Bess, presumably looking at Harold since he was staring in that direction. "Harold isn't your type."

"My point exactly." It was Griff. He was her type. If only she didn't have a history of ignoring him.

"Are we good?" Griff asked. "We didn't exactly part on the best of terms the other night. And you avoided me at the rehearsal dinner."

"I'm stressed." She forced a laugh. "And you're forgiven because you caught the garter."

"Thanks for that." Griff twirled Bess around and out of the way of the bride and groom. "One more to go."

"One more what?"

"Wedding." He smiled upon Bess in a way that made her knees weak. "We're in one more wedding together. Next week. Crystal and Derrick. Is any of this ringing a bell?"

"No." Because increasingly, Bess wanted to kiss Griff. Who cared what went on days from now? They were both here, dancing within smooching distance. Veterinarians didn't put her first. Griff did.

"I told Nate to aim for Griff," Abby told Bess as she and her groom danced closer. "I could tell there was something between you the other night at The Buckboard."

"Oh, there's nothing between us," Griff reassured Abby. "We're just friends."

Which was exactly what Bess would have said in polite company a week ago.

We're just friends.

But this time, those three words worked their way under Bess's skin like sharp thorns on a tangled blackberry bramble during berry-picking season.

Detach, Bess.

Frustration bundled inside her, growing, until she couldn't detach. Not with Griff's arms around her. Bess needed space. And air.

"Thank you for the dance." Bess stepped free of Griff's hold and marched toward the exit, flat sandals slapping the marble floor loud enough to be heard over the buzz of conversation and the blaring of dance music.

Guests took one look at her face and scrambled out of the way.

"We're just friends," Bess muttered, walking faster.

"Am I wrong?" Griff was right behind her and once again proving that he had excellent hearing.

Bess walked faster. Anyone watching would be amazed that she could move this quickly in this dress. She barreled out the open doors and into the country club lobby, pausing to look right and left for the restrooms. Griff would never follow her into the ladies' room.

Griff didn't pause. He took Bess by the arm and swept her down the carpeted hallway, past stuffy, burgundy wingback chairs and huge paintings of cowboys displayed in gaudy gold frames. He escorted her away from the noise, away from prying, pitying eyes and away from matchmaking mamas wanting to foist their deadbeat offspring on her.

A feeling of being trapped balled inside Bess. She was desperate to kiss a man who was too good for her.

Bess, you fool.

Griff yanked open a door with a frosted window and the words *Telephone Room* stenciled on the glass. The room was hardly bigger than an old phone booth, with a small counter and one chair. Griff pulled Bess inside with him and shut the door behind them. And then he kissed her. He kissed her as if he'd been wanting to kiss her for months.

It was bruising, that kiss, perhaps payback for the time she'd kissed him at Ronnie's wedding.

Whatever the reason for its intensity, Bess didn't care. She kissed Griff back, beat for beat, measure for measure. Because she was hurt—*poor Bess*—and she was angry—*we're just friends*—and...

Griff kissed all coherent thoughts away.

And when he'd kissed his fill, Griff drew back and cradled her face in his calloused hands. "What's the matter, Bessie?"

She bristled, brushing his hands away. "Only my grandfather calls me that."

"Okay." Griff eased back against the counter. "What's the matter, Coach Glover?"

That rodeo team is her priority. It stands in the way of love.

That's what the bridal party had told her. They didn't realize that in her case what stood in the way of love was foolish pride.

Bess gasped, frustration seeking a target. "What's the matter? What's the matter?" She grabbed onto his lapels before realizing what she was doing. She released him and drew a breath, trying to calm down, trying to stop her hands from shaking, trying to blink back unwanted tears. "I told you buckets of problems at The Buckboard the other night."

"But there's more, isn't there?" Griff reached out and brushed one tear away with his thumb. "Talk to me."

And because she'd been telling herself for years that Griff's opinion didn't matter, that they were frenemies, she supposed it wouldn't matter if she did. "I've lost. I'm done. Finished. Like one of those fairy-tale characters who get their house bought out from under them by the evil troll who lives beneath the bridge. And this..." She fussed with the skirt of her dress. "I could have a career as a bridesmaid. Can you see my social media post? 'Attractive redhead who looks decent in any style bridesmaid dress, able to organize bridal showers and handle any sort of wedding emergency. Available June through September.'"

Griff smiled. "You did save the wedding. But done and finished? You can't put on that dress and believe that, Bessie."

There he goes again. Oh, that nickname!

But since he'd added it to a compliment, she let it slide. Still, his words didn't settle the frustration inside her.

"You think I'm blowing this out of proportion?" Bess knew she was sounding like a fool, but she couldn't stop. "Evidently, I'm prickly and good at disposing of men. But I shouldn't care because the rodeo team is my baby. Ask anyone. They'll tell you. But that's not even the worst part. Do you want to know what the worst part is?" She didn't wait for Griff to guess. "The worst part is that I'm the last to know."

Griff looked worried, staring at her as if Bess had just told him she planned to rope the moon and wrestle it to the ground. "What about this hot doctor everyone says you're dating?"

"He dumped me in favor of doing his duty. I can't fault the guy for saving some poor animal's life." Bess paused, replaying the words in her head. And then she laughed. "Oh, wow. Listen to me. I'm an emotional wreck because everyone is getting a dream wedding, except me." She paused again. "I'll admit, I never dreamed of Grecian bridesmaid dresses and groomsmen in Western suits, but you get the idea."

"You're feeling sorry for yourself." Griff nodded. "I've been there."

Bess was sure it wasn't the same. She shook her head. "You must think I'm a piece of work."

"I do think you're a prideful, too-honest-for-her-own-good piece of work," Griff admitted with that mischievous smile. "But we're all a work in progress."

Bess choked out a laugh, despite her cheeks heating, despite Griff not being her savior, despite her wanting to kiss him again. "Why are you being so nice to me?"

"Maybe because I'm not in the mood for talking." He rested a hand on her hip and when his touch was added to the troublemaking grin on his face, she got the message. Griff was up for a little mischief.

"Bess? Bess, where are you?" A man's voice drifted to them from the hallway.

"Kiss me in case that's Abby's brother, Harold." Bess lunged for Griff and attacked his mouth in a full panic.

"Have you seen a redhead in a bridesmaid dress?" the man asked, the familiar, deep voice ringing a bell. "She's my date. I was late. A dog was hit by a car. And now, I can't find her."

Bess eased back and whispered, *"Brandon?"*

Griff made a growling noise, deep in his throat. He wrapped his arms around Bess and kissed her fervently, the way she liked.

And then he set her aside. "You need to go find your date," he said gruffly.

Bess felt dizzy. "What?"

"Go on, Bess. You know what you want, and it isn't me."

He was wrong. He was so wrong.

But she couldn't find the words to tell him.

Because...you know...pride.

Instead, Bess bolted out the door, hurrying to save face and find her date.

Running from just one of many things that scared her lately.

Her feelings for Griff. The fate of the rodeo team. The potential loss of the only home she'd ever known.

She ran right into Brandon.

"I'm sorry, Bess." The vet's warm expression was sincere. "You must have thought I was going to stand you up."

Bess drew a deep breath and assembled a forgiving smile for her date, trying not to glance around to see if Griff was behind her. "Brandon, I understand that your patients come first."

Dr. Brandon Bitterman stood in front of her wearing a dark blue suit and a white cowboy hat. He was handsome in a refined way—black loafers instead of cowboy boots, a big, shiny watch on his wrist. His tie was silk and dotted with small yellow Labradors. He was handsome in a way that spoke of comfortable success. She shouldn't have had eyes for anyone but him.

"I'm glad to be forgiven." Brandon traced a hand down her arm, and then curled his fingers around hers with a hand lacking calluses, a touch that caused no butterflies. "When you told me the theme of the wedding was Grecian, I had this vision of white togas." Brandon's gaze was as gentle as the night air. "I didn't expect green silk. Or you looking... You look like a goddess, Bess."

"Thank you." And even though Brandon was saying and doing all the right things, Bess was unable to compare his light touches and refinement favorably to Griff's purposeful touch and cowboy casual attire.

Don't.

"We should get a drink." Bess practically dragged Brandon into the reception.

From the dance floor, Evie caught her eye and gave Bess a thumbs-up.

Behind Evie, Abby and her mother were standing next to Harold, frowning as they stared at Bess.

Although it wasn't a time to laugh, Bess couldn't help but think that if Griff were here, he'd find something to joke about.

If Griff were here...

Her gaze roamed around the banquet hall, but she couldn't find Griff.

"Would you like to dance?" Brandon waited for Bess to give her consent. A trail of kids sped by them, giggling and chattering all at once. He stepped forward and offered her his arm, which she accepted. On the dance floor, he took her into his arms with a fluid motion, holding her a proper distance apart and...

Let her lead in the two-step?

Griff would have had a field day and taken back control.

Bess smiled, but it felt more like a grimace this time. "Who taught you to dance?"

"My mother." Brandon smiled politely. No troublemaking grin for him. "My father is a cardiologist in Tulsa. She used to bring me to community fundraisers because my dad hates to dance. Plus, he always seemed to get called in to treat a patient in the midst of a hundred-dollar-a-plate dinner." Brandon chuckled.

Bess kept leading and he kept following. It was an odd feeling, unlike what she felt with Griff. That rodeo cowboy was either leading or in it with a measure equal to hers.

Don't.

Not wanting to compare Brandon with Griff anymore, Bess stopped dancing and led her date off the dance floor to the table where she'd left her clutch and cell phone. "Can I ask you a personal question?"

"Of course." Brandon may have been smiling but there was a hint of fatigue in the corners of his eyes.

Bess held her head high. "What's your plan? For me, I mean."

Brandon seemed to have trouble hanging on to his smile. "This is our second date."

"I know. But what I'm asking is…" *What am I doing?* "…do you look at me and see a future?" Bess suddenly had second thoughts. "No. Don't answer that. Let me just tell you this. I live on a ranch that needs someone to love it. That person should have been me but…" She passed her hand in the air between them. "We could date for months, fitting in time together between our busy schedules, but it's only fair that you know who I am and what I'm looking for in a man."

And then she told him.

"YOU'RE BACK EARLY." Dad came down the porch steps to greet Griff when he parked in the shadowy ranch yard.

The moon was out but the heat of the day hadn't receded.

"You've been to one wedding, you've been to them all." Griff tried to project nonchalance. But inside, he was desperate to get out of his penguin suit and burning with jealousy. *What kind of woman kissed a man breathless and then ran after her date?*

"You might just as well ask what kind of man kisses a woman who came to the wedding with another man." Dad chuckled, his words making Griff realize he'd spoken aloud. "Not that I'm judging. But I did see you flying down the driveway and skidding to a stop just now. I figured something was up." He gave Griff a keen look. "Want to talk about it?"

"No." But Griff didn't move toward the bunkhouse. His feet seemed stuck in the earth beneath his boot soles. And then he found himself giving his foster father a brief overview of the evening, leaving out how hot and heavy those kisses with Bess had been, and adding that he'd made an offer for Bess's ranch but hadn't told her he'd done it.

"Do you want my opinion?" Dad asked when Griff was through.

"Would I be standing here if I didn't?"

MELINDA CURTIS 127

"Give Bess space. It sounds like she's got some things to work out. And if you try to be more than friends—"

"More than *frenemies*."

"—before she's ready, you may end up being *enemies*, no prefix." Dad's gaze moved toward a nearby oak tree where a bird was serenading the moon, but his mind was still on Griff. "And I know you know this, but you're going to have to come clean about that offer to buy the Rolling G ranch. Sooner, rather than later."

Griff sighed. "As usual, you give good advice." It was nothing Griff hadn't heard from his own inner voice.

"As usual, you're a good listener." Dad shifted his feet. "I heard Paul James moved to town."

Griff ran his hand around the back of his neck. "He's been here for months and you're only just now asking about him?"

"Oh, I asked about him in town the first week Paul arrived, but I've been waiting for you to ask about him." Dad rested a hand on Griff's shoulder. "And your boy."

"Dell. His name is Dell." Just talking about his son soothed the hurt and confusion about Bess. "You should see him, Dad. He's going to be taller than me. He's smart, sensitive and a bit stubborn, too. He's trying to rodeo but he's in that gangly stage where his parts don't always obey what his mind wants him to do." Again, Griff smiled.

"And Paul?"

Griff's smile fell. He shook his head. "That's a work in progress and admittedly, I haven't made any progress. How do I reach out to Paul?"

"Slowly."

"That's not an answer."

"I don't always have one of those." Dad hesitated, glancing back toward the main house.

"How's Mom?" Griff's stomach fell to the gravel beneath his toes. "If you need an extra hand, you know all you have to do is ask."

Dad blinked too rapidly, gaze falling toward the ground. "She bought me some elixir to grow hair. Said I needed to rub it on my bald spots before she tried it on hers."

"Mom always says you wouldn't have lost so much hair if you hadn't taken on so many teenage boys."

"I wouldn't have had it any other way." Dad smiled a little. "But your mother… She's fretting about Christmas. Can you imagine? We're in the heat of July and she's worried *her boys* won't decorate the way she would come December."

"Like Santa's sleigh crash-landed on the ranch and decorations flew everywhere?" Griff smiled. "You know we'll do our best."

"That's exactly what I told her. But maybe you could stop by in the morning for a visit and reassure her of that."

"Will do."

Rather than let go, Dad pulled Griff into his arms for a hug. "I'm proud of the way you're dealing with fatherhood, one step at a time."

"Thanks." Griff hugged him back. "Let me know if that hair gunk works. I might be needing some of it one day." When he had a real chance to be a father.

CHAPTER TWELVE

"I DO *NOT* want to go in there."

Griff pulled into a parking space in front of Clementine Coffee Roasters after church on Sunday morning. And then he turned to face his foster mother. "You said you wanted a cup of coffee after the service."

"At *home*." Mom was sickly thin, even in her face. Her cheekbones were prominent and her eyes large and lacking eyelashes. Her blue-and-gray church dress hung off her shoulders. Her short blond wig looked like a wig. In short, she looked like a woman battling cancer.

But despite her looking like she was at death's door, Mom acted like she'd barricaded said door and tossed the key in a cow pie. Mary Harrison wasn't one to give up a fight.

Just like Bess, a woman known to come in for a coffee at Clementine Coffee Roasters on weekend afternoons.

Griff didn't want to think about Bess. Not the way she kissed. Not the way she held on to him. And not ever the way she looked walking away from him with that veterinarian last night. He hadn't been able to go back in the reception after that.

"Son." Mom fixed Griff with a hard stare. "The reason I let you drive me home instead of your father was because I thought you were taking me straight home, whereas he was going to have to whisper the details of my condition to every church member on the way out."

Griff nodded. "Dad is way more popular with the congregation than he's ever been before. But only because you won't talk to your friends yourself and let them know how you're doing."

"Your father and his medical updates... You see why I value what little privacy I have." Mom leaned back in her seat and crossed her arms over her chest. "I'll take a latte."

Griff shook his head. "It doesn't work like that. If you want a latte, you have to come inside with me."

She fixed him with another hard stare.

"The longer you dilly-dally, the more time the rest of the congregation has to get over here." Griff hopped out of the truck and went around to help his foster mother down.

"I'll remember this come Christmas." She accepted his help. "And you better tell me if my wig starts sliding off my head. Nobody had the nerve to tell me last night at dinner and this hairy thing nearly fell into my soup."

Griff chuckled, placing one arm around her waist and the other on her arm. "You can wear my hat."

"And have folks think I'm embarrassed?" Mom took mincing steps toward the door. But there was color in her face for the first time in weeks.

Once they were inside, Griff got her settled at a table before moving to order. He breathed in the smell of brewing coffee and thought about Bess drinking his sludge. There were several tables in the café, but Mom was the only person sitting at a table. She hummed to herself.

No sooner had he paid than the door opened. Griff glanced up, wanting to run to his mother's side if someone well-meaning came in.

Paul James stood just inside the door, scowling, then coughing. Dell was walking toward the cash register, a guarded expression on his young face.

Griff froze for a second, not wanting to make a scene. And then he was moving forward to meet things head-on. "Dell. Paul. I'd like you to meet my mother." His secret weapon in this fight. "Mary Harrison, this is Paul James and his grandson, Dell."

"Nice to meet you." Dell stopped to wave awkwardly, the

way teens did when they weren't prepared to meet someone, much less someone who looked seriously ill. He glanced to Griff with a question in his eyes.

"As you can see..." Griff bent his head next to Mom's "... we just came from church. You don't normally see us around town in our fancy duds."

"Griff Malone, you are incorrigible." Mom extended her hand toward Dell, who seemed to offer up his hand without thought. "I've looked better."

"Don't you believe that, Dell," Griff teased. "She could compete as Miss Senior Clementine as a blonde."

"And what would I do for the talent competition?" Mom demanded. "Power napping?"

"Speed knitting." Griff winked at Dell.

"She looks more like a trick roper to me," Dell said, doing Griff proud.

"She roped me trying to sneak off the ranch one night." Griff nodded.

"I bet she threw you down and hog-tied you." Dell laughed, long and loud.

"I like you, Dell." Mom released his hand and extended hers toward Paul, who had inched forward during their conversation. "Paul, is it? You've raised a fine boy."

"Thank you." Paul shook her hand. He was no longer scowling but he appeared to be shell-shocked, not that Griff understood why. He sent a quick glance toward Dell. "I think Mary's talent would be singing."

Was Paul telling a joke? Griff's knees nearly buckled in shock.

Mom giggled, a sound Griff hadn't heard in far too long. "Whatever makes you think I can hold a tune?"

"When we first came in, you were humming." Paul smiled, the effect ruined as he tried to stifle a cough.

Dell looked distraught, hand raised slightly toward his grandfather.

This man is seriously ill. And Dell knows it.

Griff touched Dell's shoulder, briefly. His son pursed his lips and nodded.

Paul caught the entire exchange. "It was 'Mountain Music,'" he continued when he'd caught his breath, taking a cough drop from a tin that looked like the one Griff had bought for him the other day.

"It was." Mom clapped her hands. "I think Paul wins the guess-what-my-talent-is game."

Griff would give the man a win and his good graces if he kept on smiling at Mom like that. But they needed to talk about more than Dell. They needed to talk about Paul's health and how Griff might help him.

"Two lattes for Griff," the barista called.

Griff went over to pick them up. When he turned around, Paul and Dell were saying their goodbyes, and Mom was getting to her feet.

Griff hurried to her side. "I thought we'd drink our coffee here." Especially now that Dell was present.

Mom pooh-poohed that idea. "I've got to get home and get dinner started."

Oh, boy. If that wasn't a fib, Griff didn't know what was. Mom hadn't made dinner all summer. But Griff let her get away with it. "Let me put our coffee in the truck and I'll come back to get you."

"I'll help you out, Miss Mary." Dell offered her his arm.

"Aren't you a fine young man." Mom beamed at Griff's son.

Tears pressed at the back of Griff's eyes.

"My grandpa always says I should never miss the chance to do a good deed for a beautiful woman," Dell said in a serious voice. "And I'm partial to blondes."

"Don't let Nancy hear that," Griff muttered.

"Oh, you're laying the malarkey on thick now, aren't you, Dell?" Mom teased, moving toward the door.

Griff deposited the coffees into his truck's cup holders and then helped Mom climb back in his truck. "Thanks for the help, Dell. I'm almost done fixing your straw cowboy hat."

"Thanks. See you tomorrow at rodeo camp, Coach," Dell called after him, returning to the coffee shop.

Paul stood inside, staring at Griff with an undecipherable expression. But at least he wasn't scowling.

Griff got behind the wheel.

"That was him?" Mom asked breathlessly. "He has your sense of humor. And your hair."

"Yep. That was him." Filled with pride, Griff started the truck and backed out. "And thank you."

"For what?"

"For being my secret weapon with Paul." Griff spared her a glance. "I think you cracked the glacier."

"Oh, honey." Mary reached across the center console to rub Griff's arm. Her wig slipped a bit. "That man sees you through a lens tinted with grief. I think Dell sees you for who you truly are—a good man."

"I should hire you to talk to a woman I've got my eye on. You might convince her that she needs me." For more than just the occasional heated kiss.

"Bring her by and I'll tell her the truth. You're my secret happiness *weapon*." Mom's voice started to break. She bowed her head, collecting herself before continuing. "Every damsel in distress should have a Griff Malone."

Griff pulled over.

Mom glanced around. "What's wrong? Did you leave your wallet at the coffee shop?"

"Nope." Griff righted Mom's wig. "Miss Senior Clementine shouldn't be spotted on a bad-hair day."

"You didn't have to do that." Mom patted the crown of her wig, smiling.

"I sure did." Griff gave her his most mischievous smile. "Just in case we see other Miss Senior Clementine candidates on the way home."

She cradled his face in her hands. "My hero."

"YOU EXPECTING SOMEONE, BESSIE?" Grandpa Rascal stood at the living room window on Sunday afternoon, pointing his field glasses toward the lower pasture near the ranch driveway. He shifted his weight slowly from one foot to the other. "'Cause someone's here."

"Ronnie said she'd come by." Bess sat on the couch, hunched over her laptop on the coffee table creating postings to sell various items from the ranch. She had a list of expenses coming up, including cattle inoculations, the monthly feed bill and the looming property taxes due in the fall. "And about that—"

"That ain't Ronnie's rig pulling up." Rascal hitched up his jeans. "Come on, Finlay." He tottered toward the front door. His dog padded along behind him at a more sedate and stable pace. "Best come greet our company, Bessie."

"Company?" Bess closed her laptop. "If that's Vickie, tell her we're turning down the offer." If it wasn't Ronnie, she couldn't think of who else would be visiting except the Realtor. "And take your cane, please!"

Her grandfather stepped out on the porch, his boots—and only his boots—striking wood. He'd left his cane, as usual. "Well, howdy." His effusive greeting seemed to negate the idea that Vickie was visiting.

Bess hurried to the front door, pausing to put on her boots and straw cowboy hat before opening the door and stepping over a panting Finlay on the welcome mat. It was a hot summer afternoon. The air was thick and stifling. Bess was tempted to hang out with the dog in the shade.

Rascal stood near an old red-and-white truck and their visitors.

"Bess, look who drove me out today." Ronnie made a flourish with her hands toward Griff before continuing to stride forward in her blue jeans and bright red blouse.

While Griff...

He didn't wear a tuxedo or a black cowboy hat. He didn't grin like he was here for payback over her abandoning him at the reception last night. In fact, Griff looked rather contrite standing next to Rascal in his faded blue jeans and gray T-shirt, glancing around the ranch.

Bess wondered if her handsome frenemy would see it the way she did.

The original house from the 1800s had burned down in a fire in the 1950s. Her grandfather had rebuilt it, but it hadn't seen a paintbrush in over a decade. Nor had the barn. The screen door didn't stay closed. And the walkway to the front had cracks in the concrete that were a trip hazard. In a nutshell, it must have told Griff that the Glovers didn't look after their property, either because they couldn't afford to or because they didn't care.

Bess put aside both unappealing notions and tried to offer a welcoming smile.

Ronnie trotted up the stairs to the porch and gave Bess a hug. "You wanted me to take a ride on a horse for sale and I thought it would be helpful to bring Griff for a second opinion."

"What are you up to? Bringing Griff…" Bess whispered to her bestie. *"Matchmaking?"*

"Not at all." Ronnie released Bess, scoffing. "How was the wedding last night? Or more importantly, your date with that handsome veterinarian?"

"Ugh on both counts." The only bright spot had been those cloistered kisses she'd exchanged with Griff. And she'd botched that.

"Sorry it didn't work out. Let's go look at a horse." Ronnie was in the market for a barrel racer for Wade's daughter, Ginny. She trotted back down the porch stairs and walked across the ranch yard toward the barn. "And maybe later, you'll let me do my thing and give you my professional advice."

"Matchmaking," Bess muttered under her breath, following her friend at a slower pace. "Not happening."

"Why is Ronnie looking at our horses?" Rascal demanded, crossing the yard to intercept Bess at what for him was breakneck speed. "What aren't you telling me?"

Bess's steps turned into a stiff, faster march. But she couldn't outrun her reality. "We've got to raise money for the ranch taxes, given that Eshon is a dead end, and we don't want to sell. Why don't you wait inside, Rascal?"

"Which horse are we selling?" her grandfather demanded from behind her. "We're down to just two."

Bess slowed down, turned, squirmed. "Yours. Sorry."

"Not Sparky! I need that horse to run the ranch." Rascal wobbled forward, jerking his arm free when Griff tried to steady him. "To run this ranch. *My* ranch."

Bess felt cold, despite the sun, despite the heat. "I should have had this conversation with you this morning, but it was just as painful to me as it is to you to admit that things have to change… *We* have to change and make sacrifices if we want to keep the ranch."

"We should come back another day." Ronnie curled her arm around Bess's waist.

"No. We can't afford to live in limbo any longer." Bess's voice was sharp and brittle, not because she was angry with her grandfather, but because she was disappointed in herself. "It was my job to take care of Rascal and the ranch. And I let everyone down."

"It's not your fault," her grandfather said in a gravelly voice, lowering his hat brim as if needing to hide his expression. "Your father shouldn't have left us to run things. You're busy and I'm old."

"Rascal, why don't you wait for us in the house?" Griff said consolingly.

"This concerns me just as much as it does Bessie." Rascal staggered forward on scarecrow-like limbs with Griff at his side, ready to catch him if he stumbled. "It's just as much my fault as hers."

A few minutes later, Bess had Sparky saddled and ready for Ronnie to ride.

Ronnie walked around the small brown gelding, running her hand over his chest and legs, then his haunches. "He's a compact horse, which is good for barrels. And he's not skittish, which is good for girls loving on him." She led him into the arena, which was built with wood fencing, not the metal kind, and was in need of serious repair.

Embarrassment washed over Bess. She and Griff followed Ronnie inside.

"He's an unflappable horse," Grandpa Rascal said mournfully, closing the gate, staying outside the arena. "Last time I fell off Sparky, he stood next to me, waiting for me to get back on board."

"Last time?" Bess felt her blood pressure spike. "You've never mentioned falling off him."

"Leave a man some pride." Rascal moved to a sturdy section of fencing and rested his forearms on the top board.

Bess hoped he wouldn't get splinters.

"This has got to be hard on you," Griff said quietly to Bess. "We can leave. Just say the word."

Bess felt his gaze upon her, and that familiar flutter awakened inside her chest. "I worry about Rascal more than me."

"He's more resilient than you think." Griff inched closer but said nothing more for a few minutes while they watched Ronnie warm up the gelding. "How was your date last night?"

"Who's asking?" Bess forced herself to look at him, trying not to think of the hungry look on his face when he'd reached for her last night. "My friend or…"

"Who do you want to be asking?" Griff asked, still in that low voice meant only for her.

Bess elbowed him, hard, eliciting a satisfying *oof.* "Maybe I haven't decided. Same as you, I suppose."

Griff nodded, rubbing his rib cage. "So, your date? Did it end well?"

Bess drew herself up tall to counter the feeling of failure. "Dr. Brandon Bitterman is successful, handsome, charming and *trustworthy.*"

"But…" When she didn't immediately answer, he added, "Please tell me there's a *but.*"

"But…" Bess smiled for what felt like the first time that day. "He just broke up with his girlfriend of ten years and he's not ready for a commitment…other than to his patients. Plus, there was no spark."

Griff whistled, a long, low note. "You had quite a night."

"No thanks to you." She jabbed her elbow toward him again.

This time, Griff thwarted her move with one hand. "That's enough of that. We need to talk."

Bess's heart raced with anticipation. Her mind raced with questions. "You have something you want to say to me?" About kisses?

Griff nodded, staring across Lolly Creek toward the northern pastures. "Lately, I've had a lot on my mind. And whenever I've tried to talk about any of it, the words haven't come out right."

Bess narrowed her gaze. "If you're thinking about apologizing for…*things*…" Like kisses. "You'd better think twice."

The last thing she wanted to hear was that he considered them a mistake.

Griff opened his mouth, but nothing came out. And then he pursed those lips together.

"You were going to apologize." *Grrr.*

Ronnie cued Sparky into a gallop and then sharp pivot turns, rounding imaginary barrels in the arena. A few minutes later, she dismounted and led Sparky toward Bess and Griff. "I don't think Sparky wants to be a barrel racer."

"Never say he's slow." Rascal sounded aghast.

"It's not that he's slow but that he's not a curve-making horse." Ronnie led the gelding back toward the gate, her words a bittersweet relief to Bess, at least, until Ronnie handed Griff the reins. "Do you want to try him?"

"Sure." Griff looped Sparky's reins over a rail, then began adjusting the stirrups for his longer legs.

"Hold up." Bess laid a hand on Griff's shoulder. "You don't need a horse and we don't need the charity. If we have to let Sparky go, we want him to land with a rider who needs him."

"I was thinking of Dell," Griff said, sparing Bess a glance and a small smile. "Unless you think Sparky is too headstrong for a beginning rider."

"Oh." Bess withdrew her hand. "He might be perfect. Maybe a bit small for Dell's long legs but…"

"But good-natured if Dell falls." Griff nodded, darting beneath Sparky's neck to the other side. "He won't run back to the barn."

Bess nodded, gaze moving toward her grandfather. His independence was being stripped away. But which was worse? A cowboy losing his horse? Or his ranch?

CHAPTER THIRTEEN

"DELL." GRIFF STRODE toward his son on Monday morning. He'd arrived early at rodeo camp and had been waiting anxiously for Dell to arrive. "Here's your mother's cowboy hat." It would never pass for brand-new, but the broken straws had been repaired.

"Look at this." Dell ran his fingers over the rewoven sections. "I didn't believe it could be done." He stared up at Griff, blinking rapidly, trying to stop tears from spilling over. "Thank you. Thank you so much." And then he threw himself into Griff's arms.

And Griff... Griff didn't want to let go.

However, there were teenagers present and he'd ruin the moment for Dell if he hung on, so Griff backed off. But he couldn't stop grinning as if he'd won the lottery. "I can teach you how to do it, if you like. In case that hat ever gets to looking like that again."

"I'm not going to wear it ever again." Dell couldn't stop staring at the hat. "I'm going to hang it on my wall over my bed."

Griff's heart swelled with pride, expanding his grin wider than he'd ever thought possible. "I bet your mom would like that."

"Thanks. Again." Dell was as fidgety as a puppy first thing

in the morning. "And… Can I ask you for another favor? Can we meet sometime to talk about my mom?"

"I'd like that." But Griff had to add, even if he resented doing so, "As long as it's okay with your grandfather."

"I'll ask." Dell hurried over to the bleachers to join his friends.

"That was really thoughtful, Griff." Bess came to stand beside him. She was dressed in dark blue jeans and a long-sleeved, rose-colored blouse. Her straw hat had a flat brim and a silver studded hatband. Her dark red hair was held in a low ponytail by a thin strip of leather. "Requesting Dell ask for permission from his grandfather suggests you respect the man."

"Versus playing by his rules?" Bitterness crept into Griff's voice.

Bess chewed on her lower lip, avoiding looking at Griff directly. "I know your situation is frustrating and probably has you wanting to do something drastic, rash or completely out of character."

"You have no idea," Griff said, thinking about his offer on her ranch and for her grandfather's horse, although he'd told Bess and Rascal they didn't have to sell Sparky right away.

Bess gently brushed a hand over his arm. "Have you tried doing something thoughtful for Dell's grandfather?"

"Thoughtful?" Griff resettled his new straw hat on his head. "I've bumped into him twice in town and been kind both times."

"You've got to pave the way for giving Dell a horse," Bess told him kindly, blue eyes soft as they took him in. "It's going to take more than a passing hello to win him over."

"I know. It's just that every time we see each other, Dell is with him and I can't speak plainly."

"Then you need to ask for a private meeting," Bess said softly. "If you want a problem solved, you need to do it yourself. Don't rely on someone coming to your rescue." She laughed ruefully. "Listen to me evangelizing something that I've only just recently realized."

"You're forgiven." When she would have walked away, Griff tentatively touched her arm. "So, the offer you received on the ranch…" The one he'd messaged Vickie this morning to withdraw.

"Still unopened on our coffee table. It's not an option we're considering." Bess's expression turned from annoyed to uncertain. "Hey... Is there something bothering you? You seemed distant yesterday and this morning. And after Saturday night..." When he'd practically whisked her off to claim more kisses... "We'd talk if we needed to, right?"

Wrong.

Griff needed to tell her about the offer and broach the subject of why they kept on exchanging kisses at weddings and not anywhere else. But he knew now wasn't the time for conversation. They had a teenage audience assembling, not to mention Wade and Ronnie. And once he unburdened himself of his bungling real estate error, she wouldn't want to talk to him, much less let him help with rodeo camp.

"We're good for now." Someday, he'd unburden himself and tell her everything. "As for being distant... I've just got a lot on my mind."

"Join the club." Bess tried to laugh. Failed. Forced a smile. "Come on. Let's go get camp started."

"GOAT TYING?" Griff looked shell-shocked.

"Yes." Bess stood in front of twenty-plus inexperienced team members sitting beneath a tree out of the heat. Griff stood next to her while the more experienced ropers in the group were working on roping from the saddle in the empty stock paddocks. "We talked about this, Coach Griff. Just this morning when you brought me coffee. Remember?"

"I forgot?" Griff shrugged, making the kids laugh. "Let me drink more of my coffee."

"That sludge?" Bess rolled her eyes.

Something was bothering Griff. He'd made an offer for Sparky at the Rolling G yesterday afternoon but told them to let his offer ride for a while before accepting. Was he having second thoughts about buying Sparky? Was he as confused about their passionate kisses as she was? As unwilling to broach the conversation as she was? As confused by this new turn in their relationship as she was?

"Goat tying." Griff nodded, flashing Bess a smile that was

pure mischief and classic Griff, dispelling her concerns that their relationship was in a weird place. "The instructional part of the program this hour is goat tying. I'm particularly fond of this event. Now that I'm properly caffeinated, Coach Glover, I'm ready to begin."

Without further ado, Bess launched into her spiel. "During the competition, a live goat will be staked on a ten-foot rope at one end of the arena. You'll ride lengthwise across the arena to reach it, jump off, flank the goat and tie three of its legs." Bess hefted one of the two goat practice dummies that stood at her feet. "We'll practice with these."

The "goats" had hard plastic bodies and sturdy rubber legs that were made with full rotation in order to practice gathering and tying the legs together.

"Put that down, Coach Glover." Griff took it from her and set it back on its four legs. "You're forgetting to tell them the best part." He raised his arms as if directing an orchestra. "That you gallop halfway across the arena as fast as you can. And then you swing one leg over the saddle and leap off your horse near the goat." Griff jumped forward, landing on two feet. "That's why goat tying is fun. Galloping and leaping off. You've got to have skill and swagger to pull that off."

And by the shine of his grin, Bess could completely believe that was the only reason why Griff liked the event.

"You need skill *and balance*," Bess corrected him.

The kids laughed.

Bess dragged Griff back behind the goat practice dummies. "We'll practice the so-called 'fun part' later." Bess hefted a goat practice dummy once more. The legs swayed like silent wind chimes. "This is Sweetie. We're going to use her to learn how to *flank* a goat."

Griff moved to Bess's side and gathered Sweetie's three rubber legs in one hand. "A goat has a flank but *flanking a goat* is the term we use to get the goat to the ground *and* capture three of its legs—all in one motion." His shoulder brushed Bess's.

That's all it took to remind Bess of hot kisses and heated touches.

Fantasize about Griff later, girl.

Bess set Sweetie on her four legs before moving in slow motion to demonstrate the actions that made up a flanking move. "First, body up—your knees and a bit of your thighs to touch Sweetie's side. You're going to grab hold of its body and lift with both your legs and arms before dropping to your knees." Bess came down to the dirt with Sweetie on her side in front of her knees.

Griff leaned over Bess's shoulder, reaching across her body to point at Sweetie's legs. "As you come down to the ground, you'll collect three of their legs in one hand in one of two ways." He pulled his arm back but continued to bend over Bess.

She could feel heat filling her cheeks. *Not now.*

"So many numbers," Griff quipped from just above Bess. "Good thing Coach Glover teaches math."

The kids laughed. Bess tried to.

"One way to grab Sweetie's legs is called stuffing." Bess demonstrated gathering the two hind hooves in one hand and sweeping the top, front hoof with the other. "A second way is called gathering." She scooped the three rubber legs in a hugging motion. Both techniques resulted in her holding three legs in one hand, freeing up the other to work the rope.

"You'll have a length of pigging string to tie them together." Griff handed Bess a four-foot length of rope with a frayed knot on one end and a braided finish on the other.

Grandpa Rascal had braided the lengths throughout the summer. He'd made more last week as the team's numbers swelled.

Bess held up the pigging string. "If you're right-handed, you'll thread the tassel end through the center belt loop in your jeans and through the belt loop over your left hip so the tassel hangs toward the front." Bess demonstrated. "And then the other end of the rope comes up under your right armpit and into your mouth." She bit the non-tasseled end with her teeth.

"All this keeps the rope handy for your left hand." Griff reached across Bess's body toward the loose loop under her armpit.

Yowzer.

And then he moved his hand to the tasseled end dangling near her hip.

Double yowzer.

Not that he seemed affected at all. He just kept up his humorous monologue. "And threading the tasseled end keeps the rope from getting tangled in your legs while you ride because that would be a big ouch." Griff was loving this. He straightened, allowing Bess to breathe. "Now, if you *don't* like the taste of dirt, I'd keep your pigging string clean." He passed out the lengths of rope to the team. "Because that's how you'll be riding, with the finished end of the pigging string in your mouth."

Several of the teens put the rope in their mouth and made faces at each other. Laughter rolled through the group.

When they each had a piggin' string, Bess demonstrated how to pull the rope free of belt loops and tie off the three goat legs just above the hooves.

"Everybody stand up." Griff made a grand gesture once more, raising both arms in the air. He brought so much energy to camp, which was really great for the team's enthusiasm, but only made Bess want more of his kisses. "Now, thread your pigging string in your belt loops. Then come to us to make sure you've done it properly. Only after we approve can you get in line to practice tying on the Sweeties."

"When do we get to gallop?" Dell asked Griff.

"After everyone has mastered the tie," Bess told him before Griff got too carried away. "Then we'll learn some riding and dismounting techniques."

"Then Nancy will practice falling," Kevin joked.

"I only fall when I'm circling barrels," Nancy replied good-naturedly, staring at Dell like she was interested in more than friendship.

Bess thought of herself and wondered if she looked at Griff the same way.

GRIFF WAS THE first to admit he wasn't interested in tying goats.

Hadn't been as a kid. Wasn't thrilled about it now.

But Dell seemed eager to learn no matter what the topic, even if his execution wasn't smooth or speedy.

Dell frowned as Nancy called out his time. He carefully unwound his rope from Sweetie's rubber goat legs. "I guess goat tying isn't my event."

"You're growing." Griff patted him on the shoulder. "When I was your age, I had a growth spurt that had me spilling milk every morning at the breakfast table. My brain wasn't used to how long my arms had become. There's nowhere to go from here but up."

"Spilled milk?" Dell got to his feet, hanging his pigging string over his shoulder. He shook his head. "I did that this morning." And then he mumbled, "It upset Grandpa."

"Most things upset your grandpa," Nancy said sympathetically.

Dell didn't argue but he did look unhappy about it.

"Maybe I'd be cranky, too," Griff allowed, "if I had that cough. He must not sleep well at night."

Dell shook his head. "I don't think he has since Grandma passed away."

"Riders, get your horses if you have them," Bess announced.

Nancy scurried off.

There was an uncomfortable silence between those left, which were definitely the minority of the team and all boys. Griff wished he could buy horses for all of them. They needed a distraction.

"When I started rodeo, I didn't have my own horse," Griff told the teens.

Dell glanced at him, curiosity in those blue eyes. "Did you have a girlfriend?"

Griff did a quick look-see at the boys. They all stared at him, waiting for his answer. "Uh, nope. I didn't have a girl. Back then, the opposite sex was as intimidating to me as Mr. Pacheco, who taught science."

Heads nodded around the group.

"Mr. Pacheco still teaches science," Dell said in a hushed voice, as if afraid the science teacher would somehow hear. "I suspect he has superpowers because he can stare at you *and* your lab partner at the same time."

"I think you're right." Griff gave a little chuckle. "He moved through the classroom like a ninja—"

"And slaps your lab table with his palm if you aren't paying attention." Dell laughed long and loud, in that all-too-familiar cadence. "I can't believe he did that way back when you were in school."

"Way back when I was in school," Griff mumbled. Dell would be surprised at how few years ago that was. "Do I look that old to you?"

Dell sized him up with a mischievous grin on his face. "You're not as ancient as my grandfather but yeah. You're old."

The other boys nodded.

"I'm not too old to show you how goat tying is done," Griff said without thinking.

They laughed *at* him, bruising his self-image more than the label of "old" had done.

"I need all my goat competitors in the arena!" Bess led her horse toward Griff. "Whoever doesn't have a horse here, you're going to ride Duchess." She gave the flashy-looking palomino a pat on the neck. "I'll demonstrate first."

"I can do it." Griff's hand shot up. *"Old man,"* he grumbled, then added in a louder voice, "I'll demonstrate."

Bess tipped her hat back, giving him a dubious look. *"I'll* go first."

"But will you go *fast*?" Griff strode toward her with a chip on his shoulder. "Goat tying can bring big money nowadays. But you have to ride fast, do a flying dismount and hit the ground running."

Bess frowned, addressing the team, "For safety reasons, forget what Coach Griff said. However, I think we need to see how Griff does it, because I can't remember ever seeing him compete in goat tying."

"You don't need to have competed before to be competitive time-wise." Griff let Bess see the challenge in his eyes. He had a reputation to protect—or establish—with the team.

"It's too bad we aren't timing today." Bess laughed. "Because practice and skill beat hot air every time." She gave Griff a challenging grin that walloped him with the happy.

He did so love it when Bess gave him grief.

The team enjoyed it, too. The kids were laughing and shouting the need to time, adding their choice of prospective goat-tying champion—Coach Glover or Coach Griff. Wade and Ronnie stopped their group's roping practice and moseyed over to watch.

"Are you afraid to put your time against mine?" Griff teased Bess. He had no qualms that speed on horseback could beat speed at the tying portion of the event. And as a rodeo pickup man, he was excellent at galloping in and maneuvering in the saddle. Given that, how hard could it be to jump off?

"Fine. The coaches will have timed runs today. Nancy, can you time us?" At the girl's agreement, Bess mounted up, then stared down at Griff. "Safety for these kids is just as important as speed, so don't think about the fastest time alone. Try for the fastest, *safest* time." She reached down to lower his hat brim. "For the record, I don't think you can do both."

Griff scoffed, knocking his hat brim back up with his knuckles. "Ye of little faith."

Bess rode over to the starting position, opposite the arena from the practice dummy.

Griff counted down. "Three. Two. One. *Go!*"

"Yah!" Bess loosened the reins and cued Duchess into an all-out gallop. They hit top speed halfway through the arena. Bess swung her right leg over the saddle and behind her left, found her balance on her left leg, reined in Duchess and then hopped off as the mare slowed. She ran up to Sweetie and went through the motions of tying her, then tossed up her hands. "Time!"

"Seven seconds," Nancy called out.

Griff grinned as he approached Bess. "Most of these kids can do better than that." He captured the palomino's reins.

"Maybe, but can *you*?" Bess walked with him back toward the other end of the arena. "Safely? Without falling on your dismount?"

Griff gave her a grin that said he was good enough to beat her time. By a lot.

"Best of luck," Bess told him, before turning and walking back to the midpoint of the arena.

"I don't need luck." Griff half turned in the saddle, playing to the crowd. "I have skill *and* swagger."

The rodeo team was eating his performance up. Laughing, joking, cheering him on.

Old man...

Griff backed Duchess up until her hindquarters bumped the arena railings. She lurched forward, sensing the fence was behind her. Griff held her in place. It wasn't sloppy riding. He was trying to put Duchess on edge for a speedier start.

"I won't start the clock until you've got her still," Bess called. And when he did just that, she counted down, "Three. Two. One. *Go!*"

Duchess bolted forward, faster than she had when Bess had ridden her. Griff dropped the reins when he passed Bess, trusting the mare to know what to do. He swung his right leg over the saddle, holding on to the horn and pommel so he wouldn't tumble off backward. And then, he leaped to the ground while Duchess was still galloping forward.

Griff's arms wheeled and his legs bicycled as he tried to achieve the speed of the mare. But he was only human. He couldn't run that fast. He tumbled head-over-heels. Several times.

Until he landed with his face in the dirt.

The rodeo team gave a collective gasp.

"Griff!" Bess reached him shortly after his face-plant, skidding to her knees and gently turning him onto his back.

Eyes closed, Griff spit out a mouthful of dirt, then coughed. "Did I beat your time?" His eyes eased open, Bess came into view and then he tried to smile. His face was probably the only thing that didn't hurt. But her face... It was balm to his bruised ego.

"You didn't tie the goat." Dell leaned over Griff, grinning.

Kevin leaned over Griff, also grinning. "Nancy can't stop the clock until you tie Sweetie."

"Rules are rules." Nancy found space to stick her face into the circle. She handed Griff a bottle of water, grinning, too.

"This run was a scratch." Bess got to her feet and offered Griff a helping hand to get up. "I told you goat tying requires skill *and* safety."

Griff stood but didn't let go of Bess's hand. He never wanted to let go. And not only because his back was twinging. The world felt like a better place with her hand in his. "Team, that was a demonstration on how to *fall*."

"How to *fail*, you mean." Bess gently extricated her hand. "It's still a scratch, Coach Griff. And I can't allow you to go again. We've got a schedule to keep, and the team members all need turns."

The teens moved to the starting point on the other side of the arena. Nancy walked over to Duchess and took her reins.

Bess headed toward the middle of the arena. Griff followed her, trying to stifle groans of pain.

"Aren't you going to apologize?" Bess stopped and finally gave Griff that smile he'd been looking for when he was lying in the dirt. The one that said she liked him. The one that made him want to take her into his arms and never let go. "You ate your words."

"I ate dirt."

"Exactly." Her blue eyes sparkled. "That wasn't a lesson on falling *safely* or on how to compete with skill."

"But it was fun." Griff shook his head, somewhat ashamed of himself now that the episode was over. "It served as a lesson in how *not* to compete in this event. And hopefully…" He tried to twist and arch his back, hoping to loosen up the cramping. All he succeeded in doing was releasing a groan. "No one will get hurt like me."

"You're hurt?" Bess looked him over. "Where?"

"Everywhere." He smiled, despite the pain. "Will you kiss me and make it better?"

"No." But her eyes said something completely different. "If you hurt that bad, take the rest of the day off."

"Can't do that." Griff arched his back again, wincing. "I've got to coach my…*rodeo players*."

Her expression softened, as if she knew he'd wanted to say: *I've got to coach my son.*

CHAPTER FOURTEEN

"GOOD WORK TODAY, DELL." Bess caught up to the teen as he was walking to the parking lot carrying the straw hat Griff had repaired.

"Thanks, Coach." Dell slowed, shrugged, blushed. "But I still haven't found an event I'm good at." And he'd tried them all.

"Don't worry about that. You'll have an event or two when we get closer to rodeo season. All you have to do is practice."

Dell pulled a face. "That's hard to do when I don't live on a ranch."

"You've got your pigging string. You can practice tying legs on anything. Sticks. Pancake turners. Broomstick handles." Bess tried to bolster the boy's skill and confidence with practice opportunities. "I can get you a lariat to take home. You can practice roping bushes."

"I want to ride bulls or broncs." Dell tugged his hat brim down low, hiding his features but exposing that unruly brown hair that was so like Griff's. "Bulls, really."

"You'll have to lift weights to develop your leg and arm strength. That would help you in steer wrestling, too." Bess went on to point out that the weightlifting room was in the high school gym and was available to all student athletes during business hours. "But can I ask? Why do you want to ride bulls?"

Dell blew out a breath. "Miss Glover, do you remember the

first day I came to your math class last spring? You were teaching beginning calculus, and everyone's eyes were glazed over."

"Actually, I don't remember." *But thank you for reminding me that I'm not fun.*

"I went home that night and studied the textbook. And then the next day, I had all the homework assignments for the week finished." His chest swelled with pride. "And they were all correct."

"*That*, I remember." Bess nodded. "I was impressed."

"I want to do that on the rodeo team," Dell said simply, tipping his hat brim back and looking into her eyes. "I want to do something that not many other kids do. And I want to do it well."

His determination impressed her. "We can get you there, Dell. But it's not going to be easy."

His grandfather pulled into the parking lot. He frowned when he saw Bess with Dell. But he rolled his window down as Bess approached.

"Hi, Mr. James." She bent to his level, wanting to win him over for Dell and Griff's sake. "I just wanted to let you know that Dell's working hard. We're enjoying having him on the team."

Dell got into the car.

"Thank you for letting me know, Miss Glover." Mr. James leaned forward, looking toward the grounds, and then around the parking lot.

Bess suspected he was trying to locate Griff, who was at the other end of the arena helping kids load horses into trailers.

"I don't always come across as grateful but I am thankful that you're helping Dell feel at home." He coughed deeply, adding unconvincingly, "Hay fever."

"Hot tea with honey should help. See you tomorrow, Dell." Bess straightened as they drove away.

"What's that all about?" Ronnie came to stand next to Bess. "You don't usually give a personal send-off to kids."

Bess didn't know if Ronnie knew who Dell was to Griff, so she didn't explain why she wanted Dell's grandfather to keep the teen on the rodeo team. "What do you know about Paul James?"

Ronnie watched Dell and his grandfather drive away. "I might have heard that he's having a hard time drumming up business."

"Understandable." Bess nodded. And that financial stress might be taking its toll on Paul's patience with everyone, including Dell. But she'd expected to hear something about that lingering cough. "When was the last time you changed your insurance?"

"Uh. Never."

Bess looked askance at Ronnie. "You got married in February. Didn't you combine all your policies?"

Ronnie finger-combed the dark hair over her shoulder. "Not yet. We've been busy."

"Do me a favor." Bess slung her arm over Ronnie's shoulder. "Get a quote from Paul."

Ronnie tsked. "I've been with Kyle Young since I first learned how to drive. Everyone in my family has their policies with him. I think Wade gets his insurance from him, too. And Paul James is prickly."

"That's what you said about me," Bess pointed out, still playfully mugging her friend. "And Kyle Young is older than old. How long is it going to be before he retires?"

"Are *you* going to get a quote from Paul?" Ronnie asked instead of answering her question.

Bess didn't want to and admitted as much. "But…" she said before Ronnie started to protest. "I think it would help Dell if his grandfather had an easier time of it here."

"Fine. I'll do it." Ronnie rolled her eyes. "But I'm not promising anything."

"What are we considering doing?" Wade walked up to them, Griff at his side.

Bess explained her idea about helping Dell's grandfather succeed in town.

"That's a good idea." Griff nodded slowly. "I'll swing by his place right now."

Bess watched him walk away, unaccountably proud.

GRIFF ENTERED PAUL'S insurance office a few minutes before five.

The place was immaculate. Surfaces gleamed. There were fresh wildflowers in a vase on a tiny coffee table in the small waiting area. Two orange burlap chairs flanked that table. The walls on either side of the small office had large, framed pictures of tractors working acres of hay.

Paul sat at his L-shaped desk, turned sideways while he tapped on his computer keyboard. He hit Return and swiveled around. "Can I help...you?" The smile he'd begun flatlined. He coughed a couple of times. "What do you want?"

My son.

"An insurance quote. For my truck." Griff dug into his back pocket for his wallet with one hand, pointing to the red-and-white truck sitting out in front. He handed Paul his insurance card and driver's license.

Paul stared at Griff's outstretched hand, probably totaling his utility bills—air conditioners cost a fortune to run in Oklahoma summers—and weighing that against the cost of swallowing his pride by doing business with Griff.

"Have a seat," Paul said finally, taking the small cards from Griff's hand. His hat hung from a coat hook on the wall. His straight, peppery hair was in need of a trim. "Are you looking for the same coverage?" He squinted at the card, coughing again. "Your damage amount seems high."

"I drive other cowboys to rodeos in my truck sometimes. I figured I should err on the conservative side."

Paul made a sound of reluctant approval. "Do you have any other assets to insure?"

Griff cleared his throat, feeling as if he was being interrogated. "Um...no. I have a place I'm looking to buy but for now, I'm still at the D Double R."

The older man coughed. Then coughed again. He turned and began tapping things into his keyboard.

That's when Griff noticed the framed family photos behind Paul. There was a photograph of Avery holding a baby. *My baby.* And another picture with the entire James family. Paul wasn't smiling but Avery and her mother were. Toddler Dell had the wide-eyed look of a kid suspicious of a photographer.

"You can come around and look if you like," Paul said without taking his eyes from his screen.

Griff shot out of that chair as fast and enthusiastically as a rocket into the sky on the Fourth of July.

There was a picture of Dell as a toddler, sitting in Tina's lap. Dell mugged for the camera. There was a picture of Dell standing on a school stage, looking to be about nine or ten. He held a certificate of some kind. Dell standing with a group of clean-cut boys. They all had their hands on a small trophy.

"Dell was in science club at his last school. His team won a citywide science fair." Paul was good at multitasking. He continued to tap-tap-tap his keyboard while speaking.

"He got Avery's book smarts." Griff was glad of that. Not that he'd flunked anything ever. But his grades weren't much to brag about. "Along with your family's blue eyes." Griff picked up a picture of Dell standing next to a stocky brown pony.

Paul stopped typing and glanced around to see what Griff was looking at. "That was our neighbor's pony. Dell was always trying to talk us into buying a horse."

"He's not a very good rider yet."

"I was hoping he wouldn't get distracted by that whole cowboy business. Ever." Paul gestured toward the orange burlap seat across from him, then coughed a couple of times. "Darn hay fever."

Griff put the picture back and returned to his seat. "You wear a cowboy hat. Are you saying you never had a horse or the itch to own one?"

"My father had a pasture full of horses and a desk full of bills." Paul's tone wasn't condescending. It was full of remorse. "I wanted to make sure we always had a roof over our heads and food on the table."

"Insurance." Griff nodded, finally understanding Paul a little better. The older man wanted a stable life and he'd gotten an unstable one because of Dell.

"Yes," Paul said. The printer behind him chugged and whirred. He took the sheet of paper it spit out and handed it to Griff. "If you're driving cowboys who work with you at the ranch to work for the ranch, their business insurance should cover you. You probably don't need double coverage and that will lower your monthly premium."

"That was...thoughtful of you." Griff looked over the figures. "Why?"

"Why am I being nice to you when I don't even like you?" Paul grimaced. "Coach Glover talked to me today. And then..." He pinned Griff with a blue gaze that was not as icy as it had once been. "I asked Dell who fixed his mother's cowboy hat when I picked him up from practice. He told me that the cowboy I'd asked him to stay away from had fixed it and given him his own hat so he wouldn't be teased. The same man I told him to stay away from because I didn't want him to have any connection to a man who..." Paul coughed "...made a mistake when he was young."

"Oh." Griff didn't trust himself to say anything else.

"I don't like you," Paul continued, ruining their kumbaya moment. "I'll probably never like you. But I should let my grandson make up his own mind."

Griff's heart leaped. "Does that mean—"

"No." Paul grabbed the quote he'd given Griff and tried to pull it back.

Griff held on. "You didn't even know what I was going to ask." He dug his fingers into the paper crumpling his edge.

"I'm not ready for you to come into Dell's life when he's trying to figure out what kind of man he wants to be." Paul crumpled his end of the paper.

"Because you think I'm a bad influence?" Griff's paper tore a bit beneath his fingers.

"Because the world is a bad influence!" Paul cried, ripping his half of the sheet away. He coughed uncontrollably. It took him some time to regain his composure. "You have no idea what it's like to raise a child."

Griff crumpled the scrap of a quote in his hand, holding tight to it the same way he was holding on to his hurt and the words he longed to say: *You didn't give me that chance!*

Griff stood, not trusting himself to keep the argumentative words inside if he sat across the table from Avery's obstinate father much longer. He wasn't used to walking tightropes everywhere he turned—with Paul, with Dell, with Bess. How he wanted everything out in the open.

"I accept your quote." Griff's voice didn't sound like his own. It sounded like his foster father's. Each word slowly spoken as if greatly considered.

Paul blinked in surprise.

Griff backed away slowly. "And we'll continue to have these discussions because I won't wait for my son to turn eighteen to tell him who I am."

Griff would have liked to say he walked out of Paul's office with his head held high and fully in control of his emotions.

But he banged through the door trying to get out and he popped the clutch when he pulled away from the curb.

That was the trouble with going against a man's grain. It made him rough around the edges. Griff didn't like living every day without being able to speak the truth. Soon, he was going to let the world know that he was Dell's father, no matter the cost to Paul's sense of security and pride. Soon, he was going to come clean with Bess about the offer he'd made on the ranch and how he felt about her.

Of the two dilemmas, there was one he could rectify today.

All he had to do was calm down first.

CHAPTER FIFTEEN

BESS WAS WALKING from the barn to the house after dinner when she heard a vehicle coming up the drive.

Griff drove up in that derelict truck of his and parked on the far side of the ranch yard next to her newer white truck. He hopped out and took a moment to stare at her, causing all sorts of internal flutters and frenzies.

After all these years, why do I find him irresistible?

"Were you expecting me?" he asked, walking slowly toward her.

"No." Attraction receded slightly, replaced by a bit of curiosity. "Did you tell me you were coming over?"

"No." He stared at her as if trying to figure something out, frowning slightly. "I didn't realize I was coming to you until I made the turn onto your driveway."

I didn't realize I was coming to you...

That was something a man said to a woman in the movies before he professed his undying love and affection.

Bess's heart skipped a beat. But she couldn't get carried away by fleeting impressions and a troubled cowboy. She took a few steps toward the front porch and the safety of the house, not trusting herself to be alone with him.

"Aren't you going to say something, Bessie?" Griff was baiting her. Deliberately. Ready to bicker.

Bess took a few more steps toward the porch. "Why are you here?"

His steps faltered. "Because... I'm confused and I...need to do what's right. Starting with talking to you."

Obviously, he'd come to talk about kisses—hers, his, theirs. Talking would only get things out in the open and change the status quo. But in what way?

Bess didn't like uncertainty. She turned away from uncertainty. Most days, she let fate choose its own course.

Bess felt boxed in. She planted both feet on the first porch step and let it rip. "I... I'm annoyed with you." *Because I want you to kiss me. All the time.* "I've been annoyed with you for years." *Suppressing this stupid, unwanted attraction.* "And if you don't leave right now, I just might..." *throw my arms around you* "...I just might..."

Griff's long stride ate up the distance between them as he started down the cracked front walk.

"...never speak..."

His brows were drawn low and his mouth a hard line.

"...to you again."

He stopped in front of her, one step beneath her. Their...*eyes* were on the same level.

They stared at each other in silence.

And it was just like that night back in February at Wade and Ronnie's wedding reception. Annoyance and frustration and not-knowing balled in her chest, poked and prodded by the flutters of attraction. Just like two nights ago at Abby and Nate's wedding where annoyance and frustration boiled over when Griff had called her *friend*. She felt like a horse about to compete in barrel racing, waiting for the signal to go-go-go.

"Bessie," Griff whispered. And that was it.

As one, they threw their arms around each other and kissed.

Her hat fell off, perhaps vacated by Griff's hands in her hair, loosening her ponytail until the leather strip binding it fell to the ground. Her palms scraped across the thick stubble on his cheeks and chin. And they kissed.

And kissed.

Until the cluck-cluck-cluck in the hen house made Bess aware of where she was and what she was doing. She dropped her hands to Griff's shoulders and pushed away.

Not that she let him go. There was still a bundle of divergent emotions rattling around her chest and demanding she cling to him. But now, one emotion made a stand—pride.

"I can't be kissing you," Bess told him, while realizing her hands still gripped his shoulders as if she needed him to keep her upright. "I can't," she repeated.

"And yet..." Griff twirled a lock of her loose hair around his finger. "You continue to do just that. We should talk about why."

Bess closed her eyes and wished herself miles away from debt and work and responsibility and grudges and Griff.

She opened her eyes and sighed. Wishes didn't come true. Griff still stood before her, smiling as if her kiss had just made him the happiest man on the planet. She sighed again and released her hold on his shoulders. "What are you up to, Griff?"

"Well, hello to you, too, Bess." Griff tipped his straw cowboy hat back and gave her a warm smile that made her heart beat like a fast-galloping horse.

She removed her hands from his shoulders and gripped the porch railing, wondering if the day of reckoning for those stolen wedding reception kisses was finally at hand. Although... Griff looked as if his idea of a reckoning was another kiss.

Don't.

Bess wasn't sixteen anymore, obsessing over an older boy. The increased pounding of her heart was because of the uncertainty of Griff's presence, that's all.

"And welcome to the Rolling G," Griff murmured when she didn't say anything else.

"Hello," she muttered, cheeks heating because he'd called out her lack of hospitality.

"I... Uh..." Griff cleared his throat, head hanging. "I came to talk to you and your grandfather."

Bess frowned, confused. "Why?"

"Because..." Griff's gaze traveled across the ranch yard toward the barn.

A silence fell between them, only disturbed by the rustling

of the wind through the thick foliage of a tree in the front yard and the cluck-cluck-cluck of chickens out back.

Griff's gaze returned to her, shuttered. "I haven't been entirely truthful with you."

"Which time?" The handsome cowboy had her head all turned around. "Back in school or...?"

"Now. It's...it's me," Griff blurted. He shifted his feet, removed his hat, and said again, "I'm the one who made an anonymous offer to buy the Rolling G."

Her mouth went dry. This had nothing to do with kisses, then or now. It took her a moment to collect herself enough to say, "You can't."

Griff's brows drew down.

"I don't want to sell. And if I have to, I wouldn't sell to you." Frustration welled up inside Bess, a combination of failure and resentment. *How dare he?* "Besides, you weren't man enough to make the offer to my face."

"I wanted to buy it for Dell."

Griff's words reminded Bess of Dell's complaint about not being able to practice as much as others since he didn't live on a ranch. But the anger was too new for her to forgive him.

He shifted his feet once more, boot soles scraping across the cracked concrete at the bottom of the porch stairs. "And I knew you'd never sell to me."

She refused to soften. "That's right."

Griff nodded. "So, I did something I'm not proud of. And I'm here to fess up to it because it was festering inside me."

What was festering inside Bess were the things she'd told him the other night at The Buckboard about being relieved she'd had an offer. "Well, now what you've done is festering inside of me. And just when I was beginning to trust you. Our ranch may be facing hard times but—"

"But we have to keep an open mind when it comes to offers to buy us out," Grandpa Rascal said from behind her.

Bess turned to see Rascal standing in the doorway with Finlay at his side. "Rascal..."

"You can't hang your dreams without a star to wish upon,

Bessie. Invite the man in." Rascal turned and disappeared into the house. After a moment, Finlay followed him.

Bess counted to ten before turning to face Griff. "You can't have enough money to buy this ranch and you can't kiss me anymore."

Griff gave her a curt nod. "I know you're upset, but you can't back that first claim, and as for the second... I hope you'll change your mind."

And then, he walked past her, heading inside.

THE ROLLING G needed work.

Not just the outbuildings, which Griff had seen a little of yesterday, but the house, too. There was wallpaper everywhere. Someone was fond of flowers. Poppies in the foyer. Large yellow roses in the living room. From where Griff sat on the couch, he could see tulips and bunnies in the dining room in one direction, and sunflowers in the kitchen opposite.

Griff wasn't scared of work. He wasn't scared of making a fool of himself either when it came to making things right with Bess.

Her home was a four-square farmhouse. The living and dining rooms were up front. There was cross-stitch artwork on the walls. A barrel racing trophy on a shelf in the corner next to a framed photograph of Bess as a teenager. Her red braids as bright as her smile. There was a photograph of her in an evening gown wearing a tiara and a sash that proclaimed her Rodeo Queen.

"Why do you want to buy this ranch, Griff?" Rascal asked.

"Because he's a father." Bess turned her head away from Griff, as if this was a sensitive subject. "But he can't do it, not really. Griff has no money. Did you see that beater he drove up here?"

"That old truck is as dependable as anything you've got in the ranch yard," Griff blurted, upset with himself for losing his temper. He took a calming breath. "You take care of something, and it'll take care of you." There. That sounded better. More businesslike.

Bess shook her head. "I tried that once." She bit her lip before she added ever so softly, "With you."

Griff's brain did a quick replay of Bess grabbing hold of him and having her way with his mouth. Then of him grabbing hold of her and doing the same.

He ran a hand over his cheeks and chin, trying to push memories of kissing aside.

Bess must have been replaying those moments, too. Her cheeks turned a pretty pink that highlighted the dusting of freckles across her nose.

Rascal glanced from his granddaughter to Griff and back again. "I think my ears have lost the thread of this conversation. Where were we?"

"I asked Griff why he hasn't left, considering we've told him the property isn't for sale." And then Bess gave Griff a look he was very familiar with from her. It was a sorrowful look, full of hurt and disappointment.

He'd been the recipient of that look for many years. But that didn't mean Griff could just sit in her living room and stay silent. The question became—*what to say.*

"I told Vickie this morning to withdraw the offer," Griff began. "I respect you both too much to cause you any more distress. I've been wanting to tell you for days and struggling with finding the right words."

"But you had plenty of time to. You didn't say a word to me about this today at rodeo camp," Bess pointed out. "And Vickie didn't call me."

"Vickie didn't call me, either," Rascal said. "But I do appreciate Griff telling the truth. Besides, he liked my horse."

"And that says more about his character than this underhanded thing he did?" Bess tossed her hair, looking surprised that it wasn't in a ponytail anymore. "Why on earth would you want to buy our home? Why this ranch?"

"I came here once," Griff admitted softly. "With my father. He…uh… He worked for your father, Bess. Here. At the Rolling G."

The two Glovers fell silent, staring at Griff as if waiting for more.

Griff sucked on the inside of his cheek. With a past like his, discretion was always the path of choice.

"There was a Malone who worked here for a few seasons." Rascal's brow furrowed. "Isaac Malone?"

"That's him. He was proud to work here." Griff nodded. "He pointed out everything that made this ranch a right proper spread."

Bess eyed Griff with less suspicion.

"Go on, boy," Rascal encouraged. "What made the ranch shine in your daddy's eyes?"

It went against Griff's grain to go on. He much preferred the buffer of humor to the raw vulnerability of truth. But he found himself giving it anyway. "Lolly Creek divides the property, watering both the stock and the trees that give them shelter from the cold and the heat." Despite his reservations, Griff warmed to his topic. "The southern pasture lines the road and gets sunlight all day, which is good for growing feed. The barn has a nice, level pasture attached for grazing or training horses. The bunkhouse sleeps a crew of ten. And the house..." Griff glanced around. "The house is what he called mighty fine."

"I thought you didn't know your dad," Bess said in a quiet voice, cheeks still pink.

My dad...

Griff cleared his throat, not managing to clear out the emotion completely. "I didn't hear from my biological father again after we dropped him off here for the season. That's true. But..." *Tell them* "...it was the last and best memory of my father acting like he wanted me around and..." Griff forced himself to finish "...that brief memory meant a lot more than you might think." That if the circumstances had been different, his father might have provided Griff and his mother with a happy home. "Because of that, I've always had a soft spot in my heart for this place."

"I like the way he talks, Bessie," Rascal said, voice thick with emotion now, too.

"*When* he talks," Bess grumbled. And then her expression darkened. "Is that why you dated me when we were younger? Because your father once worked here?"

"No," Griff said quickly.

"Bessie, why don't you show him around the place?" Rascal extended the footrest on his recliner. "There's a baseball game coming on soon."

Bess stood and made a show of wiping her hands together, as if washing her hands of Griff.

Her sass restored Griff's best defense—his humor. "That's mighty kind of you, Rascal. Most folks might get riled, wash their hands of me and show me the door."

"We don't treat guests like that. Do we, Bessie?" Rascal glanced over at her, seemingly cataloging her expression before saying, "If it makes you feel better, honey, I won't agree to sell to Griff if you don't approve."

Bess scoffed again. "I will never approve."

"Both points are moot since my offer is rescinded," Griff said evenly.

CHAPTER SIXTEEN

"Thanks for letting me clear my conscience, Rascal." Griff got to his feet thirty minutes later, shook the elderly man's hand and faced the woman who confused him more than any other. "Will you walk me out, Bess?"

"'Course she will," Rascal said before Bess could toss Griff out on his ear. The old man snuggled deeper into his recliner.

Griff walked out the door and down the front steps, waiting in the ranch yard for Bess to join him. She took her time. How Griff longed for the quick impatience that had led to that kiss not thirty minutes back.

"I can't believe you did this." Bess walked slowly across the porch and down the stairs like a woman who was about to give voice to strong words before kicking him off the property.

Not knowing what to say, Griff tried to smile, tried for his usual nonchalance.

Bess made a slashing motion with one hand, as if cutting that idea of kisses before he acted on it. "Why tell me now? You never had to let me know."

"Because we were getting along. Because things I have to keep hidden about Dell made me realize that I don't like myself when I'm not being truthful." Griff blew out a breath. "Because I knew you didn't want to admit the ranch had been run into the ground on your watch. Because there are things about me that attract and annoy you, and vice versa. Do you want me to go on? I can go on."

"And suddenly, he can't shut up when he's talking about important things." Bess sighed as a blackbird swooped past. "How out of character."

"It happens." Griff rolled his shoulders, trying to ease the pinching tension between them. "Walk with me." Griff ambled toward the barn. He made it halfway across the ranch yard before realizing Bess wasn't with him. He turned and looked back at her.

The sun was low on the horizon, its rays glimmering on the red notes in her hair. The soft light almost erased those freckles she worried about, the ones that dusted her nose. And the growing shadows behind her gave the impression that Bess guarded this house, her safe place.

Griff respected that. He respected her. And he loved her. He probably had since their first kiss years ago. He held out his hand to Bess. An invitation toward forgiveness and love. "I want to share something with you."

Bess frowned. "About what?"

"About me being here before. About why I wanted to try to buy this property versus another place." Griff waited for her to mosey across the yard to join him before continuing. "When I first arrived with my parents, I got out of my mom's SUV right about here." Griff looked around, excited despite the odds that were stacked against him buying this place. "I think this is the prettiest spot on your ranch." It was where he'd first seen Bess. She'd been cleaning a horse's hooves. Her long, red braids had hung down, nearly touching the ground. "But then again, there's lots to appreciate about this place."

Bess smoothed her hair over her shoulders, glancing around in spits and spurts as if embarrassed at what she saw. Finally, she said, "You can see everything but what you don't see are all the things that need fixing."

"No excuses, Bessie."

She frowned at Griff.

Griff doubled down, taking Bess by the shoulders, turning her to face the house and calling her that endearment again.

"Bessie, look at where the house sits. It welcomes you when you drive in. Those two windows upstairs look like eyes and the porch stairs to the front door give it a smile. It's a house that begs to be filled with family and love." He slowly turned her to face the barn. "I bet you've never had a hay delivery where you had to unload the hay bale by bale."

"No. The hay truck backs right up to the hayloft."

Griff nodded, breathing in the soft, sweet smell of her perfume. "That's because someone spent time thinking the layout through."

"A Glover, obviously." Bess snorted. But it was a soft snort.

"Now look at the arena." He eased Bess around to face the necessity for every horse lover, cutting off her protests. "It's on the one level spot before the bank heads down toward Lolly Creek. It should be the most active place for a family of horse lovers, full of kids practicing for rodeo. There are trees on the south and west to provide afternoon shade."

"A poor man's covered arena," Bess murmured, ignoring his reference to kids. "You forgot to point out the overgrown blackberry bushes starting to blot out the barn."

"Glass half-empty, Bessie. All easily fixed," Griff gently chastised. "Now, look to the west. Isn't that sunset going to be beautiful?" It was going to be lovely. It just wasn't as beautiful as Bess was to him.

She didn't argue. "You saw all this the one time you came here? When you were a kid?"

Griff nodded again. "I saw it all, but I saw it through my father's eyes. He's the one who explained how thoughtfully the ranch had been laid out during the drive over. And I've judged every ranch I've seen since by the Rolling G yardstick." Only the Done Roamin' Ranch was better.

"You sound like you love your father. But he abandoned you." Bess was frowning again. "How is that possible?"

"I learned a long time ago that bitterness and hate can eat you up inside. My parents had me too young. What did they know about being parents when they were kids themselves?" Because she was still frowning, Griff gave in to impulse and smoothed his thumb across the wrinkle in Bess's brow just beneath her straw hat. "I can't control how others feel about me, including you. But I can see them for who they truly are. Imperfect and beautiful and worthy of love."

I love you.

The words stuck in his throat. He cleared it and started talking before he started overthinking. "I've been driving around the county since confronting Paul earlier, going through all I've been slacking on when it comes to being truthful. Being truthful about what I dream of in life instead of waiting for it to come to me or trying to get it the easy way. I can see every mistake I've made, every moment I've wasted. And now, I just want to go for everything in my heart—Dell, a ranch of my own, and you."

"Me?"

"Yes, you," Griff reassured her with a tender smile. "Don't you see? If something doesn't change, we're destined to move one step forward and two steps back for the rest of our lives, Bessie. You don't want that, do you?"

Bess lifted her chin, not arguing over his use of her nickname, possibly taking issue with the implication that they were each making mistakes, giving no hint of how she felt about him. He'd scared her and she'd retreated.

Griff drew a deep breath. He had more to say. So much more. Things that he'd been keeping in. Things that he wanted her to understand about him. And yet, just confessing his truths was risky. He knew it just as well as anyone who'd grown up as a foster kid. "I should have told you why I missed prom. I should have trusted you'd understand and not judge. But I was afraid I'd lose you anyway."

Her chin came down a smidge, which Griff took as a good sign.

"I should have mentioned to you long ago that I've been dreaming of owning a large cattle operation. At least then when I made an offer on the Rolling G, it wouldn't have come out of the blue. Instead, I kept my dreams to myself because I was afraid people would laugh. That *you* would laugh."

"Oh, Griff." Bess shook her head, making gentle waves with her long red hair.

When she started to say something more, Griff jumped in. "Let me continue, Bessie, please." The hardest parts were yet to come. At her nod, he went on. "I should have sought out Dell when I turned eighteen. I should have insisted that I be a part of his life. But I was afraid Paul would defeat me in court. I was afraid he'd make me look like a cowboy with a history of mistakes."

"Oh, Griff." She spoke his name again, this time on a sigh.

Griff tried to imprint that sound in his head because he was afraid that whatever he said next would change everything between them, and not for the better. "I should have told you," Griff began, unexpectedly running out of air. He had to start again, speaking at a whisper. "I should have told you that I think of you all the time, Bessie. I should have told you I love you. I should have told you that years and years ago." He paused.

He'd managed to make Bess speechless. Was it a positive silence? Bess didn't interrupt him. Or frown. Or tell him that although she liked kissing him once in a blue moon that she didn't feel the same way.

That was good, right?

Griff hoped so, because he wasn't near done telling her every regret he had. "But instead of speaking my truths, I kept working and saving and waiting for something to change. And now, I have to wonder if I've waited too long, if I've spent all these years building up walls so I won't be hurt again instead of knocking them down so that I can have all the things I long for."

Bess stared at him, her expression unreadable.

"I'm done now," he told her in case there was any doubt.

Bess shoved her hands in her front jeans pockets. "Why do you always have to make things so complicated?"

He didn't know how to answer that question. They both had a habit of complicating things. "I was speaking from the heart, Bessie. What's complicated about telling you that I love you?"

"Because...because... It's complicated. *We're* complicated." Bess's gaze darted around as if seeking an escape route.

"Loving me would be complicated?" Griff glanced down, expecting his heart to be in pieces beneath Bess's boots.

"Yes." She pointed toward the house. "Not long ago, I was in that house and immensely disappointed in you. And then you started talking about love and…and love and… This is all very fast, Griff. Too fast."

"I should have followed you after you kissed me at Wade and Ronnie's wedding. I should have asked you out then instead of waiting and wondering what that kiss meant." Griff shook his head. "Are you catching on to what I'm saying here about missed opportunities that are happening because we're afraid?"

"Yes." Bess held herself very still.

And in that stillness, Griff felt the attraction between them, as strong as it had ever been. The pull had nothing to do with how lovely she was. It was her inner strength, her intelligence, her quick wit and compassion that had attracted him even as a teen. There were lots of pretty women in the world. But there was only one woman that he'd ever found it hard to stop talking to, to look away from, to walk away from. There was a slight possibility that she might feel the same way, and that gave him hope.

"Bess," he said in a thick voice, the voice of a man in desperate need of a kiss.

"What?" she whispered but her gaze dropped away, in the direction of her feet. After a moment, she took a step back, and then another.

"You think too much," he said softly. "Love isn't a thinking thing. It's trusting what's inside you. If you think it through, of course, it's going to be complicated."

"Not always." A phrase he took as a reference to those kisses they'd shared on the porch steps.

Griff gave a quick nod. "Thank you for listening, Bess. I guess I'll see you tomorrow at rodeo camp."

He half expected her to tell him his services were no longer welcome.

But she didn't say a word.

"I LIKE HIM, BESSIE," Grandpa Rascal told Bess after Griff left. *I like him, too. But do I love him?*

Bess was shaking when she sat on the arm of the couch. Her

head was spinning over everything Griff had told her. And her heart... Her heart felt shriveled.

She'd always dreamed of falling in love with a cowboy, nurturing that dream privately even when her mother and sisters had told her what she needed was entirely different. And now, a cowboy that didn't present himself like her dream had confessed his love for her and she'd felt torn.

What is wrong with me? I should be happy.

Griff had said he'd been saving, which explained his penniless look and derelict ride, not to mention his respectable offer—per Vickie—to buy the ranch. She knew that clothes did not make the man. Bess couldn't hold that against him.

In the past week, her opinion of Griff had changed but not his wardrobe. He'd proven himself trustworthy, if sometimes impetuous—kisses and anonymous contract offers proved that impulsiveness. But he was honest and good with the kids on the rodeo team. He added fun to most everything he did. He made Bess see that she didn't have to take things so seriously.

It just felt as if he'd leaped over dating and landed in the love zone. What if Bess wasn't what Griff really wanted? What if they spent more time together and they found out they didn't have what it takes to promise each other forever?

"You like him, too, don't you, Bessie?" Rascal asked, breaking into her thoughts.

"Yes." He was an A-plus kisser, a man with a moral compass, and someday she might even know with confidence that she loved him. "But I'm relieved we aren't selling to him."

"We might have to sell to someone. And I like Griff," Rascal repeated.

Before Bess could reply, someone hit a grand slam in his baseball game.

When Rascal was done griping about the hole the pitcher had put his team in, he turned to Bess and said, "We are the keepers of our legacy, Bessie. And if we decide the Glovers aren't meant to be ranchers anymore, so be it. But... I'm not ready to accept that."

Bess nodded. Truth be told, she wasn't ready, either.

GRIFF TOOK ANOTHER long drive to cool off, arriving back home as the sun was setting.

He told two women in his lifetime that he loved them—Avery and Bess. How could Bess look at him with such intensity and kiss him so passionately and tell him his love was a complication? It made Griff wonder if he told Dell he was his father if he'd receive the same cool reaction.

The lights were coming on around the ranch—in the bunkhouse from which laughter flowed, in the barn and outbuildings from which voices drifted, from the front porch of the main house where a small light illuminated Dad sitting across from Chandler shuffling cards. The sounds of home beckoned. There was comfort to be had here—among his foster brothers or coworkers, among his family or his horse.

Griff chose to seek solace with the men beneath the soft glow at the main house.

He tromped up the porch stairs.

Chandler took one look at his face and pulled out a chair at their table. "Bad day?"

"The worst." Griff sat down. "But it's better now that I'm home."

"We brought you up right," his foster father said, sounding rather somber. He continued to shuffle the cards. "Me and your older brother here."

"Mom's having a rough night," Chandler told Griff, inclining his head toward a window a few feet back. "She didn't want us around even though she was hurting. So, we gave her a cowbell and opened her bedroom window."

"We're on beck-and-call duty." Dad nodded, setting down the deck of cards. "What's on your mind, son?"

Griff recapped where he was with Dell. How his son was searching for a place on the rodeo team and his place in the world. He told them how Paul was being protective. "Overly so, in my opinion," Griff said. He included his interest in buying the Rolling G and making his son a home.

Dad clapped a hand on his shoulder. "There have been boys who came to us here on the ranch and had no idea who their father was. It's never easy when the man who sired you comes into your life. There are issues to wrestle with."

"Guilt." Griff nodded. "And this overwhelming need to make a meaningful, father-son connection." He picked a card from the deck. A joker. He tossed it to the table, resentful that people thought of him as irresponsible simply because he had a good sense of humor.

"Forget Paul for a minute and put yourself in Dell's shoes." Chandler slid the joker back into the middle of the deck. "He doesn't know who his father is, except for the negative things his grandfather may have told him. He'll want to know why you weren't around."

"It was Paul," Griff began bitterly.

Dad gave his shoulder a little shake. "It was me. I gave you advice when Avery died. I told you to wait."

Griff pressed his lips together, refusing to hold that against his foster father.

"I didn't think you'd wait until the boy dropped into your lap."

"I didn't think I should make a move until I had a home of my own." Griff glanced out across the ranch yard and the very large, very prosperous operation his foster parents had built. All the outbuildings, all the paddocks, all the ranch vehicles. It represented years of hard work and was a testament to the strength of his dad and mom. "In the back of my mind, I believed I was waiting for the pieces of my life to fall into place. A wife. A ranch of my own. A future laid out in front of me. Now, nothing is certain." He'd go wherever Dell was.

Dad went back to shuffling cards. "The hardest thing to face is the unknown. We all want to be in control of our lives and our future but sometimes there are other people who hold those reins. You have to work with Paul and Bess to get where you want to be."

"Bess?" Griff sat back in his chair, trying to scoff. Failing. "Who said anything about Bess?"

"We have eyes." Chandler tipped his hat back. "Or at least, I do. I saw you with her this afternoon at rodeo camp. You can't keep away from each other."

"And we all know that you've been stuck on her for a long, long time." Dad nodded.

"Doesn't matter." Griff reached up to mash his hat on his head in frustration, only to belatedly remember that he had no hat. "Bess doesn't want to love me. She thinks I'm a complication."

"Sometimes you have to ride down a trail to see where it leads." Voice thin and trembly, Mom stuck her head out her bedroom window. Her blond wig was askew, and she wore one of Dad's T-shirts instead of a nightgown. "Patience, Griff. Honey, I need you." She retreated back into the bedroom.

"Good night, boys." Dad got to his feet, looking weary. "Things will look better after a decent night's sleep."

Chandler and Griff bid him good-night.

Chandler glanced back up at the window, then motioned for Griff to follow him into the ranch yard. When he joined him, he said quietly, "Dad's worried about Mom. She got word today. We're going to do another round of chemo before the surgery."

We. They were family, if not by blood, then by the emotional bonds of love and acceptance. When one suffered, they all suffered.

"Patience," Griff murmured. Compared with what his foster mother was going through, he had nothing to complain about. He was spending time with his son and getting to know him. He was reaching out to Paul. He just needed to let things take their course.

The memory of him and Bess rushing toward each other earlier, so eager to kiss each other, so not patient.

"I can be patient," he told Chandler as they slowly crossed the ranch yard.

"You'll need to be because you'll have to work out a co-parenting plan with Paul." Chandler was dead serious.

"How did you figure out a plan with your ex?"

"We didn't. It's a work in progress." Chandler didn't so much as smile. "You think you have every contingency covered and then something changes."

"As my older brother, aren't you supposed to have all the answers?"

"I'm only human. And when it comes down to it, that's all

any of us are." Chandler stopped in front of the small one-story home that was the perk of being the ranch foreman. "What does Paul want? Do you know?"

Griff shook his head slowly.

"Maybe you should think on that since you need his blessing to let Dell know who you are." Chandler tipped his hat and headed for his front door. "See you in the morning."

What did Paul want?

Paul had always wanted Avery to go to college. He'd expected her to get good grades and punished her if she didn't. Paul wanted her to have a better career than he had, a bigger house, a better life. He'd never have approved of Avery ranching or competing in the rodeo.

And now, Paul expected the same from Dell.

CHAPTER SEVENTEEN

"YOU'RE STARING AT GRIFF," Ronnie said to Bess while they ate lunch sitting on the tailgate of Wade's truck. "Why not just go over and enjoy his company? You've been avoiding him all morning."

"Because..." Bess stared at Griff, unable to complete her sentence. She'd lost sleep over him last night. "His feelings are stronger for me than I'm ready for mine to be for him."

Griff sat with Wade beneath one of the few shade trees on the rodeo grounds. They were surrounded by kids who stared at both cowboys with worship in their eyes. Griff had been so good with the kids. They were excited about rodeo. *He* made them excited about rodeo. Not Bess.

Killjoy.

A warm breeze blew through at the same time that the memory of that intense kiss on the front porch last night drifted through Bess's head.

"Because why?" Ronnie tossed a potato chip at Bess. It landed in her lap. "Because talking to Griff might give him the notion that he has a chance with you again? Be honest."

"Be honest..." Bess ate the chip Ronnie had thrown. "If I'm being honest... I feel like we left things unfinished. He just...gave up in high school when he didn't show up for prom. And then..."

"You gave up on him."

"I did. I had my pride." Bess scoffed softly. "And a dream man."

"About a big-city Prince Charming?"

"More like a fairy-tale cowboy."

Without making fun of fairy-tale anything, Ronnie took another bite of sandwich. "And now, what do you want in a man?"

Someone who loves me.

But... Griff loves me.

"I'm confused." Bess sipped her water. "For the sake of argument, because I know you're dying to present it, what would happen if I asked Griff on a date? What would happen if I let these feelings I have for Griff out and—"

"I knew it!" Ronnie cried. Then when everyone turned their way, she whispered, "I knew you still had feelings for him."

Bess smirked at her friend. "What if we date a couple of times and I see it as a dead end?" After he already went on record as loving her.

"Ha!" Ronnie drew attention once more. "Meaning, you then end it with him the moment you find something that doesn't fit your vision of Mr. Right? Don't study him under a microscope looking for a flaw because you'll find one. You always do. You dump guys quicker than I rip off an old bandage."

"I don't."

Ronnie looked skeptical and almost choked on a chip. "You kind of do. Before the veterinarian, it was the mayor of Friar's Creek. You only went on one and a half dates because he didn't eat lettuce."

"Hey, salad is important to good health."

"No love is without compromise, Bess." Ronnie morphed into matchmaker mode, doling out witticisms and advice. "You have to actually talk to someone if you encounter a rough patch, not just walk away like a..."

"Sixteen-year-old cowgirl with trust issues?" Bess arched her brows.

"Exactly." Ronnie leaned closer. "What's the harm in a summer romance with Griff? You're older and wiser than you were back in high school. If you disagree on something, you know each other well enough to talk it out."

The Done Roamin' Ranch crew rolled in with roughstock for the afternoon.

"Heads up, team," Bess called. "Fifteen minutes until we start again." She began gathering her lunch trash.

"This is why I hate shopping for anything with you." Ronnie chuckled. "Bess Glover, you overthink everything."

"BUILD THE LOOP. Feed the swing." Griff walked a safe distance behind the young cowboys and cowgirls trying to twirl rope.

Bess wasn't talking to him. He'd brought it on himself, he supposed. But he couldn't regret opening up to her. He felt better about himself. Didn't change his situation where she was concerned yesterday but he held out hope for someday.

A lariat skimmed the ground, sending up a spurt of dust.

Some loops were too large. Some were swinging the rope in a windup one might see on a pitching mound, if it was in reverse. It was hard to inject humor when the worst roper of them all was his kid. Griff had to be patient. He had to be supportive. He had to allow his son to do things at his own pace, not set expectations for perfection the way Paul did.

In the arena, a chute opened, a brown horse leaped out and almost immediately a kid fell on his backside. Clark popped back up, shaking off the setback. "I know, I know. My center of gravity wasn't right." He ran around to try again.

Clem and Maggie herded the bronc toward the exit chute.

"Okay, guys. Let's stop and talk about technique." Griff waited until the kids let their loops tumble to the ground before coming closer to give some pointers. "As you start your motion, I want you to imagine that you're playing a video game where you're fighting in tight quarters." Griff pulled his shoulders in.

"Fist-fighting?" Dell's brow quirked.

"No." Griff tried again. "Imagine the fighting is with—"

"Guns?" At Griff's nod, Dell frowned. "My grandfather would never let me play a video game like that."

Several kids chortled, making Dell's face turn red.

"Tough on you, is he?" Griff asked, ignoring the laughter

and hopefully sending a message to Dell that he should ignore them, too.

"Mr. James has to be tough on Dell." Nancy piped up as she coiled her rope. "Dell's mom has passed, and his dad is a deadbeat."

Griff stiffened. But only for a moment. Dell wouldn't think of him as a deadbeat much longer. "Nancy. Kevin. Come over here." Griff positioned them on either side of Dell. "Son, you start a loop as if you're in tight quarters and don't want to hit your friends. It's not until you find the rhythm of the rope that you need elbow room. Now, everyone grab two friends and then put the roper in the middle." Griff stepped back. "Once you build the loop, your two friends are going to get out of the way of the swing."

Dell carefully used his wrist to take the loop from something small into something larger than a Hula-Hoop, twirling it next to his body.

"Good. That's it." Griff reached to pull Nancy out of the way. "Nancy, come—"

"Ow!" Nancy stumbled back into Griff. She turned, scowling. "How can Dell feed the rope with me right next to him?"

"I was just about to ask you to move." Griff smiled quickly. "Note to Dell. Wait to feed the rope until you have elbow room. Tell your bookends to move when you're ready. Now. Try again." He backed away, but not before guiding Nancy back into place next to Dell.

"How's it going?" Bess came to stand next to him, shoulder brushing his.

An electrical current seemed to jolt between them, charging Griff's smile into the lovestruck zone and rocking him back on his heels. If only he hadn't shot himself in the foot where she was concerned.

"It's going good, Coach." Griff had to work hard to keep the sarcasm from his voice.

Bess gave him a slow look before answering. "Think they'll be ready to rodeo soon? That is, if there's funding for everyone."

"Did you hear something?" Griff finally met her gaze squarely.

Bess shrugged. "My principal let me know he's got an idea to keep the program alive."

"Good." Griff eased close enough to whisper, "Because I don't like the people I love to be disappointed about things they're passionate about."

"Let's just get through rodeo camp and let the administration fight the school board." She gave Griff a brief smile. "Why do you want to run cattle?"

"There's a change of topic I wasn't expecting." Griff's smile came easier than it had all day. "I've spent more than fifteen years competing in or working rodeo every weekend. I don't want to punch a time clock or work within four walls all day. I like cattle. They don't always laugh at my jokes. But I don't fault them for that. If a cow is troublesome, I just invite him over for dinner."

Bess chuckled. "No one is like you, Griff."

"No one?" He arched a brow.

"Not to me." She flashed him the smallest of smiles, the briefest of glimpses at hope and forgiveness before shouting, *"Stop!"*

Griff already had. He'd stopped moving, stopped breathing, certainly his brain had stopped working. He couldn't think of one reason why he was being yelled at.

"We're going to make roping practice a little more fun," she said.

"We are?" Griff managed to snap out of it. Although on a one-to-five scale, it was a two.

Bess nodded, tipping her hat back. "We're going to rope Griff."

The cowpokes in training chattered excitedly.

"All right. I'm game." Griff moved to where the metal-framed steer roping targets stood. "Any cowpoke who ropes me gets ice cream after practice."

The kids talked smack to each other, jostling for position to have a first shot at roping him. Friendly bets were made. Confident claims about skill levels voiced. And behind them all, Bess stood grinning.

"I'm waiting." Griff lowered his hat brim and then rested his hands on his hips. "Less talk. More action."

The first two lariats hit his chest.

"I'm taller than those metal heifers," Griff teased.

The next ropers were successful in knocking his cowboy hat off.

"Best way to break in a straw hat is to get it dirty." Griff swatted his thigh with it before settling it back on his head.

Dell stepped up next.

You can do this, son.

"Build the rope," Dell muttered, starting his motion close to his body.

"Feed the string," Griff murmured, wishing.

Dell's loop grew bigger. And bigger. He changed his angle and...

Got his fingers tangled in the rope. It flew straight up in the air and dropped down around Dell.

The kids laughed but so did Dell.

"I think we need a demonstration." Griff pointed at Bess. "Coach?"

The kids got a little rowdy. Bess didn't seem to care.

Still grinning, she stepped up and asked Dell if she could borrow his rope. "If I rope you, you'll have to buy the entire team ice cream today."

The kids got quiet, waiting to hear what Griff had to say.

Griff would have agreed to buy the team steak dinners. That's how powerful her smile was to him.

"Lucky for me, I know someone with an ice-cream truck." Griff scuffed a boot over the dirt, like a bull pawing the ground. "I'm ready when you are." He planted his feet, pressed his cowboy hat more firmly on his head, and then made the gimme gesture. "Bring it."

Bess wasted no time. She let her roping skill speak for itself. In no time, her lariat dropped over his shoulders. She pulled it snug around his waist.

Griff was well and truly caught.

And loving it.

Another chute opened. Another horse leaped out. Another kid fell to the dirt. This was going to go down as the worst rodeo team in the history of school rodeo teams.

Griff didn't care. Bess was smiling at him. He'd have pretended to be a crash barrel in a bucking bull's path if she'd only smile at him as if he'd never let her down.

And never would.

"GRIFF."

Griff turned to face Paul, Dell's grandfather, later that afternoon. "Paul. This is a surprise."

"I brought your insurance card by." Paul handed Griff a small card. "Since my boy is determined to join up with something distracting when what he really should be doing is sticking with schoolwork."

My boy? Griff held on to his temper.

"Does he need help with school?" Griff couldn't believe it.

"No." Paul actually looked happy, for once. Maybe even proud. "He's on the honor roll. And that's why I don't want him to get distracted by rodeo or sports of any kind. He's going to go to college, if it kills me."

"He wants to go?"

"Some days. Most days." Paul looked in the direction of Dell, who was practicing throwing a rope at a short parking lot pole. He faced Griff. "I didn't know you'd be here when I came to Clementine. I knew you had a foster family in the area, but I hadn't realized you'd stayed."

"You'd hoped not," Griff surmised.

Paul nodded, struggling to contain that cough of his. "I'd prefer it if you kept your distance from Dell, but I know better. Fate has conspired against me my entire life."

It wasn't fate. It was the choices you made.

But Griff knew saying that out loud wouldn't help matters. "Look. I don't want to fight. I just want to be a part of Dell's life."

"Even if he chooses to go away to school?" Paul stared at Griff suspiciously. "Even if he aspires to a job as a doctor or a lawyer."

"Even if." Griff cleared his throat, thinking—ironically—of Bess. "Does Griff have a college fund?"

Paul frowned. "Yes, but it won't be enough. We've been hoping for a scholarship somewhere. I don't want him to drop out of college because it's too expensive."

Griff nodded, thinking about his nest egg and how that could help Dell. But all he said was, "Thanks for bringing my insurance card by. Maybe we could go out to dinner sometime... the three of us? Let's say tomorrow at the Buffalo Diner? Six o'clock?"

"If we must." Paul started coughing, gasping for breath.

"Are you all right?" Griff came to his side. "Do you need water?"

Paul shook his head, backing away. "We'll be there."

CHAPTER EIGHTEEN

"YOU WANT TO ride a bull?" Griff stared at his son, jaw dropping open toward the end of rodeo camp. He needed a drink of water for more than to wash the rodeo grit from his mouth. "Why not steer wrestling? You flew off a bronc not five minutes ago."

"Not even goat tying will do for Dell," Kevin said mournfully. "He's determined to do this, Coach Griff."

"Bad idea, right?" Nancy crossed her arms over her chest. "Can we cover him in Bubble Wrap?"

"Just because I've fallen off every time doesn't mean that I can't do it." Dell had his pointed chin thrust out. "This is what I want to do."

"Bull riding won't get you extra points, Dell," Kevin pointed out cryptically.

"Or make you any more popular with girls." Nancy was losing patience with her crush.

"I understand why they don't support me," Dell said to Griff. "But I expected different from you, Coach."

Ouch.

"I suppose you've got to try," Griff allowed, not that he didn't agree with Nancy. His boy needed Bubble Wrap.

"He'll try until he breaks something." Kevin looked legitimately worried. "I wanted him to partner with me for team roping."

Dell wasn't much good at that, either. He was uncomfortable

in the saddle and late on his rope throw. But there was something in Dell's gaze that said he would not be deterred from riding anything that bucked.

"You should only try events you think you'll have fun doing." Griff tipped Dell's straw hat back to get a better look at his face. "Do you like riding roller coasters?"

Dell's lips pursed, an expression that seemed to convey the negative.

"That's Dell speak for no," Nancy said, confirming Griff's suspicion.

"No one thinks I can ride," Dell blurted out. "I want to prove them wrong."

"Or is it your grandfather you want to prove wrong?" Griff asked delicately.

Dell crossed his arms over his skinny chest. "Same thing."

Griff rubbed the stubble on his chin. "I don't know."

"Just like you and everyone has said, we should do the events that make us happy. I'm going to do it." And then Dell turned and marched off toward Wade, who stood nearby giving instructions to other potential bull riders.

Griff faced Dell's friends. "Can't you two talk him out of it?"

Kevin and Nancy shook their heads.

Griff moved into the arena, needing to be close if his son needed him.

Twenty minutes later, it was finally Dell's turn. He settled onto a mottled gray bull's back in the chute. He wore crash gear—a helmet and a vest. He'd left his cowboy hat elsewhere. His complexion was whiter than usual. But his chin was still thrust outward.

He can do this.

Griff hoped.

Dell raised his arm and nodded to Wade. The chute opened and the bull bounded out, arching its back and bouncing around like a scared cat at Halloween. Dell kept his heels forward and only forward. He wasn't moving those heels back and forth, from neck to shoulder, which would net him greater skill points. But he wasn't falling off, either. That was something, Griff supposed.

And then, the bull started to buck.

Dell went flying over the bull's head and landed on his back.

Fear-induced adrenaline shuddered through Griff's veins, making his hands shake. But since his son wasn't screaming in pain and his chest was moving up and down, Griff moseyed over as if he hadn't just been scared to death. He leaned over Dell, resting his hands on his knees.

"Did I make the full time?" Dell wheezed.

"Nope. But there's good news. You didn't eat dirt."

Dell closed his eyes. "I really wanted to go a full ride. What did I do wrong?"

"Do you really want me to critique your ride? Or just tell you what a good job you did? And to try again." Griff's smile felt forced. How did parents allow their kids to try anything even remotely dangerous?

Dell rolled over and got to his feet. "All of the above."

"Okay." Griff hesitated. But then he laid his arm across Dell's shoulders and walked with him toward a gate. "You know how when you ride a roller coaster it slams you this way and that?"

"Yeah." Dell removed his helmet and shook the dirt out.

"If you fight those twists and turns and try to sit still, the shock of each slam hits you harder than if you rolled with the centrifugal force." Griff swayed Dell from side to side to illustrate. "If you fought my pulling you just now, you'd be more likely to stumble."

"Bend like a willow," Dell mumbled.

"That's right. A tree's roots run deep." Griff was pretty darn proud of his fatherly wisdom. "Your grip on the rigging is the root. The rest of you are the branches of the willow."

"Got it. Thanks, Griff." Dell ran off to get back in line to try again.

"He's got try." Bess came to stand next to Griff, pitching her voice low. "But Dell's not a bull rider."

"Give him a chance. Kids that age need to believe in dreams." Griff followed Dell's progress through the throng of kids practicing goat tying to the line for bronc riding. "He's tougher than he looks."

But Bess didn't answer. She'd turned to talk to someone else.

"How's the assistant rodeo coach?" Clem rode up and leaned on his saddle horn, lowering his voice. "I can't decide if I should ask you about your feelings for your boss or..." his smile spread "...how you're doing watching your son ride a bull."

"Just you wait, Clem." Griff grinned. "Someday your time will come."

Clem sat up in the saddle, gaze seeking Maggie, who was laughing at something Wade said. "I can't wait." He turned his horse around.

"Hey, can I ask you something?" At Clem's nod, Griff continued, "Do you think it's ever too late to be a good parent?"

Clem frowned. "What do you mean?"

"Well, you ran away from home because your mother couldn't protect you from an abusive stepfather. Would you give your mother a chance to be a good parent? Even after all this time?"

Clem looked baffled. "Wouldn't that depend?"

"On what?"

"On whether or not she wanted to try?"

Griff nodded. Because Clem's answer seemed to confirm what he hoped—that he could be a good father to Dell because he wanted to try. Now, if only Paul would let him.

The chute opened and a stocky black bull bucked his way into the arena with Dell clinging to his back, expression fiercely determined. At roughly six of the eight seconds required, Griff's son was thrown, landing on his shoulder and rolling sideways in the dirt, releasing a high-pitched shout of pain.

Griff rushed to his side. "Where does it hurt?"

Dell sat up, hunching. "My shoulder. Ow. It hurts so bad."

"It's dislocated." And without thinking, Griff took hold of the teen's arm and wrenched his shoulder back into its socket.

Dell cried out again and fell back into the dirt. "Ow."

"But a better ow?" Griff felt bad for hurting his son.

"Yes." Dell blinked back tears.

Griff moved behind Dell, slipping his arms beneath his armpits. "That's enough for you today. You should probably get that shoulder looked at by a doctor."

Already, Maggie and Bess were running over with first aid kits.

"My grandfather isn't going to like this," Dell predicted.

"He'll understand." Because Griff was going to make him.

"GRIFF...WAIT." Bess was terrible at making the first move.

In this case, asking Griff for a date, when she wasn't 100 percent sure if he'd forgiven her for last night.

But the more she thought about it, the more she was convinced that she needed to see this through to its conclusion. She and Griff would date a little, hold hands a little, maybe kiss a little more. And then he'd reveal a relationship deal-breaker and she'd tell him, *"We're through."*

But before she could close the chapter on the book called Griff, she had to ask him out.

Most kids had left already. Dell's grandfather had rushed over after Dell's hard landing and taken him to see Doc Nabidian. The Done Roamin' Ranch stock trucks were gone. The parking lot was nearly empty.

Griff stood at the door of his beat-up truck, with its rust and dents and dust. And despite his once-questionable actions and motives, her heart quickened when their gazes connected.

Maybe he really is my fairy-tale cowboy.

Griff removed his sunglasses as she came closer, looking handsome despite not flashing her a smile. "Are you going to ask me to get you coffee again tomorrow, boss?"

Boss. She preferred he call her Bessie.

"Yes. Coffee would be good. And nice work today. Quick thinking with Dell's shoulder." What a chicken she was, making small talk when she'd flagged him down to ask him on a date.

"I wouldn't have popped it back in, except it was Dell and I couldn't stand to see him in pain." Griff's soulful eyes conveyed an apology. "I wouldn't have done it if it wasn't my son."

"That's the exact right answer." Bess nodded. "I was wondering if you were coming to The Buckboard on Thursday." Terrible, terrible, terrible.

Griff studied her face, probably taking note of her blush. "I've been known to show up at The Buckboard on Thursday nights." There was a playful note in his voice. He was playing it cool, making her work for it.

She could tell by the way his smile grew larger.

Bess stopped a few feet in front of him and removed her leather riding gloves, clinging to what was left of her dignity. "What I meant to say was... Would you meet me at The Buckboard on Thursday for an after-dinner drink?"

"Does this drink include a slow dance?" He was no longer holding back any of his glorious smiles.

Griff made her feel powerful, beautiful, desirable. She loved it.

Bess tossed her hair over her shoulder, then rested a hand on her hip. "I've got to say, you clean up really well when you aren't working, cowboy. Makes you hard to resist."

Griff's smile faltered. "Are you saying you only find me attractive when I'm not all dusty and smelly?"

"It's a preference. Like you saying you like me in my ranch clothes more than in a dress." There. He couldn't find fault with that. "I'm asking a second time. Would you meet me at The Buckboard on Thursday for an after-dinner drink? I won't mind if you show up in your ranch duds but you might have a better time if you wore your going-out clothes."

"That's fair." His grin fairly bloomed. "Yes, Bess Glover. I will meet you on Thursday for an after-dinner drink."

"That was almost too easy. Are you giving up the negotiation for a slow dance?" That would be a shame, although Bess didn't want to make any of this a walk in the park for him.

"I never negotiate with dates for slow dances. They're always assumed to be part of the Griff Malone date package." He leaned forward, smiling conspiratorially. "Even when the lady asks me on a date."

"I've changed my mind." Bess sniffed, raising her nose in the air, in faux annoyance. "We're going Dutch."

"Whatever you want." There was a mischievous gleam in his eye that had her smiling like she was sixteen again and the future was full of bright possibilities.

How does he do that to me?

"Uh... Coach Griff..." A cracking male voice cut their flirting short. "Coach Griff... Sir... Ma'am." Dell came around the front of the truck. His blue jeans were streaked with dirt and his shirt wasn't much better. He still wore the sling Bess had put on him after Griff popped his shoulder back in place. "I just wanted to let you know that I won't be back tomorrow. Or…the next day."

"What? Why?" Griff lost his smile.

"My grandfather…" Dell glanced over his shoulder at the small, practical sedan with his grandfather at the wheel. "He thinks I might seriously hurt myself."

"Did you tell him every fall makes you stronger?" Griff inched closer to the teen.

"Griff." Bess put a hand on his arm. "You can't stop Dell from quitting if his family doesn't want him on the team."

"But his family doesn't…" Griff stopped, swallowed, started again with a fierce frown. "*I* want you to be on the team…son. Aren't you having fun?"

"Yeah." Dell scraped the heel of his boot on the concrete. "But to tell you the truth, Kevin, Nancy and me… We signed up for rodeo camp because we wanted to pad our college résumés. You know, look more rounded for college scholarships."

"You don't love rodeo?" Bess burst out. She couldn't help herself.

"Not now, Bess." Griff turned back to Dell and said in a strained voice, "You enjoyed doing the events today."

"Yeah." Dell grinned. "Even being thrown."

Mr. James honked his horn.

Dell's smile faded. He aimed a thumb over his shoulder, pointing to the car with his grandfather. "I'm awful sorry about having to quit. But…"

"You always do what your grandfather tells you." There was an edge to Griff's voice, and he almost seemed to pull himself up, the way a bull stood taller and puffed out his chest when threatened.

I've been out in the sun too long today. She shook her head.

Dell held out his hand. "Thanks for all your help."

"Not so fast." Griff stormed past his son toward Mr. James's sedan.

Bess and Dell followed in his wake.

Griff reached the sedan first and began talking before the

older man had rolled the window down. "How can you tell Dell to quit? Do you know how hard it is to be uprooted? To land somewhere and make new friends? To risk showing up to try something new when you might be ridiculed?"

Bess's heart ached. She knew that Griff had gone through all those hard experiences.

"Dell was hurt," Mr. James said as if this explained everything. "No more rodeo."

"He's tough," Griff countered. "He shrugged it off."

"I didn't even cry," Dell said quietly.

Bess put her arm around the teen.

"You're not quitting, Dell." Griff was breathing hard. "This boy isn't quitting, Paul."

"I'm his guardian." Mr. James began coughing and couldn't seem to stop.

Griff slammed the flat of his hand on the roof of the sedan, making both Bess and Dell jump. "He needs this experience, not just to round out his college résumé, but to help him grow into a man we can both be proud of."

"Intense," Dell said beside Bess.

She nodded. "Makes me glad he's on our side."

"Get in the car, Dell Bradford James!" Mr. James shouted, shaking the steering wheel in apparent frustration.

Griff took a step toward his son. "Don't get in that car, Dell."

"But...he's my grandfather," Dell said, quietly moving out from under Bess's arm.

"And I'm your father!" Griff shouted, silencing everyone.

And then Dell ran.

CHAPTER NINETEEN

"DELL…" GRIFF WATCHED his son run away, taking his heart with him.

I'm sorry. I'm so, so sorry.

Griff had done too many things wrong recently, including letting his temper get the best of him just now. Without meaning to, he'd hurt Dell.

His son ran across the street, disappearing on school grounds, his stride hampered by the sling on his arm.

"Look what you did," Paul wheezed his accusations. "You aren't fit to be that boy's father."

Griff pushed away from the sedan, needing distance from Avery's father and his toxicity. "You make me like this." Angry and bitter and impulsive.

A warm gust of air pushed against Griff, making him feel hotter while simultaneously agitating Paul's cough.

"You're both to blame." Bess came toward Griff, her blue eyes tinged with disappointment. "As adults, you should have worked this out long before now."

Paul was quick to defend himself. "I did what I thought was right." *Cough-cough.*

"What you've been doing is trying to box Dell up and package him the way you want him to be," Griff said hotly. "And you see how well that's been received. Dell ran away. He hates being fenced in. And if you don't change, he's going to hate you."

"Griff," Bess chastised softly, taking hold of his hand. "Dell didn't just run away because his grandfather is strict."

"You should listen to her," Paul managed to say, face red. "Dell ran because of *you*. He doesn't need you."

"You'd like to think that, wouldn't you?" Griff was breathing as raggedly as Paul was.

"Please," Bess cut in, staring into Griff's eyes pleadingly. "The two of you aren't saying anything that will help Dell. He's what's important right now. Not your differences."

Griff took his hat off and ran a hand through his hair, knowing he needed to set aside resentment and anger and try to find a productive path forward, one that would benefit his son. "She's right, Paul. Now more than ever, we need to present a unified front. Does Dell run away like this often?"

"When he needs his space," Paul said in a hoarse voice. "He'll come around and when he does, I'll be there for him, the way I always have."

Griff let Paul's dig pass. They all fell silent.

The late afternoon sun beat down on Griff's bare head. He ran his hand through his hair once more, mind racing, overwhelmed by helplessness and resentment, hope and fear. He was grateful for Bess's calming presence, encouraged that she'd asked him on a date, although it still hurt that she'd labeled his love a complication. He ached for Dell, and for the shock his abrupt announcement must have had on him. But mostly, Griff worried that whatever bond he'd created with his son during rodeo camp had been broken by him blurting out the truth.

But one thought kept repeating in Griff's brain. One thought that didn't concern Bess or Dell or Griff's bruised self-image.

Griff put his hat back on and fixed Paul with his complete attention. "You took Dell to see Doc Nabidian just now?"

Paul nodded. "He told Dell no rodeo for a few days."

"And you told him no rodeo ever again," Griff couldn't resist saying. "Overreacting, like always."

"Griff." Bess gave Griff's hand a squeeze as if to say, *not now*.

"Sorry," Griff mumbled. That hadn't been his intention. "I'm new at keeping my son's needs front and center."

"I suppose that's fair," Paul allowed, hand pressed to the base of his throat, making his belabored breathing more prominent.

"What did Doc Nabidian say about *your* cough?" Griff asked carefully.

"Today?" Head bent, Paul struggled to keep a cough in. "Nothing... I'm fine."

But Griff knew better. Paul's cough wasn't the dry hack caused by dust or hay fever. His cough came from deep in his lungs. Griff should have recognized it as something serious before. "What did Doc say about it on other days?"

"That's none of your business." Paul reached into a cough drop bag on his center console and unwrapped a lozenge.

"I think it is," Griff said in a mild tone of voice he'd never imagined using with Avery's dad. "Because we're going to co-parent Dell. And that means that we have to be open about communicating any changes to our health, family situation or employment." He'd learned that from his visit to a lawyer. "How sick are you?"

"I have long COVID," Paul admitted, sucking on that lozenge. "Tina and I got it from Dell last winter. He bounced right back but we... We took turns in the hospital... ICU... Tina developed pneumonia and..." He went off on another coughing fit.

"I'm so sorry for your loss," Bess said softly. She had both her hands wrapped around Griff's.

Griff couldn't spend time trying to interpret the significance of her touch. Paul so rarely opened up that Griff needed to take advantage of this opportunity. "Is that part of the reason why you moved here, Paul? In case something happened to you?"

"You make it sound so calculated." The older man coughed a few times. "So...so morbid. I'm not dying."

"Griff didn't say you were." Bess bent to peer at Paul through the open driver's window. "But every parent needs backup. Every child needs a community ready to step in when life gets rough. If that's why you're here, that's a sign of love, Mr. James, not of weakness."

"Nothing to be ashamed of," Griff muttered, trying not to process what might have happened to Dell if Paul and Tina had both passed away. But the thoughts ran through his head anyway—foster care, turned out on the streets. And even if Paul had come to Clementine on the off chance that something happened to him, he'd been holding out on letting Griff into Dell's life.

Without warning, Paul started his car. "I should go home and wait for Dell."

"Call me when he gets home safe," Griff said, but Paul didn't wait to reply. He drove off. "That man would test the patience of my foster mother." And everyone knew Mary Harrison was a saint.

Bess let Griff's hand go. "I can call Paul later and find out for you. It might come better from me than you."

"Me being the bad guy in this situation." Hurt and bitterness were worming their way back beneath Griff's skin.

"You're the one who shouted out the truth," Bess pointed out. She probably meant well, but Griff's emotions were still raw.

"I thought you were on my side." Griff turned on his heel and strode toward his truck. In his haste to argue with Paul, he'd left his door open.

"I am on your side," Bess insisted, hurrying along beside him, stubborn as always. "And more importantly, Dell's side."

"More importantly?" Griff skidded to a stop. "Is this your way of saying I need to put on my big-boy hat and stop getting hurt so easily by every little thing Paul says or does to me?"

Bess stopped, too, eyeing him warily. "In a way, yes. You're the adult here and—"

"I'm the wronged party," Griff said in a hard tone, despite the voice of reason whispering that Bess was right. "Dell and I can't get those years back that Paul stole from us. Not now. Not ever. So, maybe while you're sitting on your high and mighty horse and looking around at your loving, traditional family, maybe you should put yourself in my worn-out boots for a minute."

"Griff, I'm sorry—"

"I don't need any more apologies, Bess. I need my son." He stomped the last few feet to his truck and climbed behind the wheel. "I need someone who won't only kiss me when I'm wearing fancy duds. I need someone who understands what it's like to be shut out of a family, someone who won't spend their last penny on a rodeo team that's about to be defunct at the expense of maintaining and repairing a ranch."

He hadn't meant to go that far.

Rather than apologize, Griff slammed his door, registering the hurt look on Bess's face, knowing that she might never forgive him.

He turned the key in the ignition and instead of a familiar rumble, all he got was click-click-click. Griff tried again. Same result. He either had a dead battery or a bad alternator. In either case, he wasn't driving off in an angry, regret-it-later huff.

He got out of his truck and started walking. "I can't talk to you now, Bess."

"That makes two of us!" she shouted after him.

"BESS, DO YOU have a minute?" Eric crossed the road from the high school office as Griff stalked off. He'd probably heard every harsh word Griff said to her.

The principal's appearance stopped Bess from yelling something more at Griff's retreating backside. She'd only been trying to help and Griff had just lit into her—unfairly, in her opinion—and turned everything she said around.

Bess lowered her hat brim, not wanting her boss to see she had tears in her eyes all because of some off-limits cowboy. "Eric, if you have bad news about the rodeo, I don't want to hear it right now." But his presence reminded Bess that she needed to up her sponsorship game.

"Actually, I have good news." Eric jogged the last few feet in the heat to reach her. "We've finally found a compromise regarding the school's expansion plans."

"Really?" Bess felt her frustration and hurt quickly drain, replaced by hope. "I could use some good news right now."

"I don't know if you've heard, but Marlene Albeck passed away last week." Eric removed his cowboy hat and placed it over his heart for a moment as if paying tribute. "May she rest in peace."

Bess nodded, repeating his words. Marlene had been something of a caution, the kind of elderly woman who shouted at kids who sat on her lawn and gave out apples at Halloween instead of candy. She'd owned numerous pieces of rental property in Clementine.

Eric plopped his hat back on his head, smiling broadly and pointing down the block. "Turns out, she left the property next to the rodeo grounds to our high school in her will."

"What?" Bess followed the direction of his arm. "That little cluster of bungalows?"

"Turns out, we can expand using her land rather than the rodeo grounds. The school board has agreed to keep the rodeo team."

"That's great news." Particularly because her team was larger than ever before. "Did they increase our budget?"

Eric's smile fell. "No."

"Eric, the proper answer is *not yet*." Wanting to share her good news, Bess glanced the other way, in the direction Griff had disappeared, and then back because she couldn't see him. He must have turned a corner, which reminded her. She faced Eric. "Have you seen Dell James?"

Her principal shook his head. "Is there a problem?"

"No...at least, not yet."

"As you can see, there's lots of work still to be done."

"And you're just the one to do it," Bess reassured him. "I appreciate you, Eric. Thanks for letting me know."

While Eric walked back to the school office, Bess glanced around, but she didn't see Dell or Griff. And given the hot words being thrown around on this hot day, maybe that was a good thing.

CHAPTER TWENTY

GRIFF HAD BEEN walking more than thirty minutes in the heat when a truck pulled up alongside him.

The passenger window rolled down. "Hey, good-looking. Need a lift?"

Griff smirked at Clem, who sat behind the wheel. "What do you think?"

"I think that bucket of bolts you drive finally gave up the ghost." Clem leaned over and opened the passenger door. "Get in."

Griff hesitated, glancing back toward town. He hadn't handled himself well back there. He could have done better with Paul, Bess and Dell. There was nothing like a walk in the heat of an Oklahoma summer afternoon to bring home uncomfortable self-reflection. He'd dug himself an emotional hole and now he had to figure out what to fill it with.

"Griff? You're worrying me now," Clem said in a serious voice. He honked the horn, making Griff jump. "Don't make me get out of this truck." This last part was spoken with the cowboy's usual sense of humor, something Griff appreciated right now.

"Yes, Mom." Griff climbed in, shut the door and rolled up his window. "I'm having a day."

"Don't need to be a licensed therapist to catch on to that."

Clem drove toward the Done Roamin' Ranch. "We can saddle up and go for a ride when we get home. Then you can tell me all about it."

Griff didn't want to wait. He started talking and didn't shut up until he'd told his foster brother everything—about unrequited love, about blurted confessions of fatherhood, about Paul's health scare and stubbornness, about telling Bess in no uncertain terms what he found annoying about her.

"I'm going to start with the *A* word," Clem said when Griff was through.

"Is this a word you'd use to describe me? If so, no need to fling it at me. I've called myself worse in the past hour."

"I'm talking about *a* as in *apology*," Clem said glibly. "Holy moly, you're off your game. You need to grovel to every person you've hurt in the past twenty-four hours."

Griff stared out the window. "Right. I have to be the bigger person. Bigger than Paul."

"In fact, you're the one who lost their temper." Clem slowed and made the turn onto the ranch drive. "You don't need me to tell you this. You know the person who explodes like a volcano is always in the wrong."

"I know." Griff stared at the cattle grazing in the pasture. Just a few days ago, those cattle had represented part of his dream of home and family. Now, he was filled with regret. "But just once, I wish things would be different."

"I know what you wish," Clem said in an unusually somber voice. "You wish the woman you love would be the pursuer, for once. You wish your son would have been happy to know that you were his father. And you wish that some of that money you'd saved for a ranch didn't have to go toward your son's college education, although it's the right thing to do."

Griff made a show of looking around the truck cab before saying, "I don't get it. Where did you hide your crystal ball?"

Clem patted himself on the back. "You'll find my mind-reading device under your seat. In case of a water emergency, it can also be used as a floatation device."

"Funny." Griff sighed. "You know I don't begrudge Dell that money, even if it means I can't go all-in on a large cattle ranch.

I'm happy working rodeo for the rest of my life as long as I can be a vital part of his."

Clem nodded. They made the rest of the ride in silence.

AFTER DINNER, Griff played cards with Clem, Chandler and Dad on the front porch of the main house. It wasn't the happiest of groups considering Griff had shared his mistakes with Chandler and Dad, and Mom was starting another round of chemotherapy in the morning.

Dad paused shuffling cards. "Why do you keep checking your phone, Griff?"

"I was hoping Paul would text me when Dell came back." The sun was setting, and Griff assumed his son would be home before dark.

"You're assuming Bess would have relayed that info to you." Chandler took the deck from Dad and finished shuffling. "That's asking a lot of a woman you had an argument with."

"True." Griff removed his hat and fanned himself with it. There was no breeze this evening. "I suppose I could drive into town and stop by his house."

"I'll give you a lift. We've got to go in and pick up your truck." Clem yawned. "Assuming it'll take a jump."

"You should go, son. Apologies are best served before the hurt cools." Dad removed his hat and showed his head to Griff. "Do you see any hair up there? I'm anxious for that miracle foam to start working and get me some new growth. It'd be nice if it came in with some color, too." His hair was gradually turning white and disappearing.

"There might be a hair or two that hadn't been there before," Griff said, more to appease his father than because he saw anything.

"Just as I thought." Dad put his hat back on his head, smiling wryly. "You're a good man, Griff. But there's no hair. That sure will disappoint your mother. She's hoping her hair grows back by Christmas."

"Who's to say it won't?" Chandler asked.

"She's been looking things up on the World Wide Web."

Dad eased back in his chair, looking worn out. "Bad outcomes, mostly. She needs her best pranksters to cheer her up."

"I'll go with you for chemo tomorrow," Griff offered, although he was torn about delaying his apology to Bess.

"Only if you dish out some apologies tonight." Dad placed a hand on Griff's shoulder and gave him a little shake. "You know you should."

Griff nodded.

"I'll drive." Clem set down the cards. "I keep jumper cables under my seats."

"Along with that crystal ball?" Griff teased.

"Exactly."

"WHAT'S THAT?" Griff leaned forward, peering out Clem's windshield.

It was dark and he'd noticed something moving in the bed of his stalled truck as they neared the rodeo grounds. A head wearing a cowboy hat popped up when Clem pulled into the parking lot.

"Do me a favor and meet me at The Buckboard." Griff had his door open before Clem had come to a complete stop, leaping out with more success than he'd jumped off Bess's horse.

"Try to keep your wits about you. Good luck, brother." Clem drove away.

Griff approached his truck. "Dell? Is that you?"

"No." Of course, it was his son. He lifted his head once more and even in the shadows, Griff could tell Dell was uncertain how to act around him. "Yes."

Griff stopped at the rear bumper and rested his forearms on the tailgate. "I'm sorry."

"For what?" Dell sat up and scooted back until his back rested against the cab.

"For everything." Griff was so relieved to have found Dell that he couldn't stop staring at him. "I should have fought for custody of you a long time ago."

"Why didn't you?" Dell's voice was high-pitched and raw.

"Why didn't I?" Griff wanted to take his son into his arms and comfort him, but somehow he knew it was too soon. "Because I didn't think I could provide for you as well as your grandparents could."

"And Grandpa scared you," Dell said in that plain way of his.

"Yeah. That, too." Griff tried to smile, tried to hold the tears back, tried to act like the adult he was supposed to be. "I was there the night your mom died at the hospital. Your mom and I... We were so young when we got pregnant. And your grandfather... He was convinced that I was behind every bad choice Avery made, both before and after you were born."

Dell sounded like he scoffed.

"Yeah." Griff interpreted his son's reaction as sarcasm. "It's hard to believe that anyone could accept that malarkey. But when your father disappears and your mother gives you up, the way my father and mother did to me, it was easy to accept that your grandfather was right." Even if he'd lied and got caught doing it.

Dell didn't say anything.

Griff rubbed a hand around the back of his neck. "Oh, I blustered about not being able to raise you, mostly to myself. I said I was the one who was wronged. That it was all his fault. But the truth is that those were just excuses to stay in a place where I was comfortable, squirreling away my paychecks in the hopes that someday you'd decide I was worth a look. That's right. I'd convinced myself that you wouldn't want me, too. I didn't want to be a deadbeat dad, showing up and asking for crumbs of your affection. But instead, I was just an absentee dad."

Dell sniffed again. Griff wished his son's cowboy hat didn't keep his face in shadow. He'd like to know how his words were being received. But regardless of Dell's reaction, Griff had to press on.

"You deserve better from me, Dell. And for that, I'm sorry." Griff drew a deep breath before continuing. "And it hurts my pride to admit this, but your grandfather has done a good job raising you. I know he's strict. But he's been afraid of losing you. His decisions come from an aversion to losing anyone else in his life. You're lucky to have him."

Dell wiped his nose with his arm.

"And now... If we're going to move forward... It's not going to be easy for the three of us." Griff, Dell and Paul. "I don't say that lightly or because I plan to oppose everything your grandfather clings to in terms of rules. I say that because we're going to have to figure out how the three of us can be a family." Griff had never imagined that. In his mind, he'd always thought he'd have full possession of Dell and leave Paul out of it. "I can give you time to come to grips with the fact that I'm your father and I can give your grandfather time to come to grips with the fact that I want to be a part of your life. But that said, I can't just insert myself into your life without your permission. You're nearly a man. This choice has to be yours."

Dell was silent and unmoving. He didn't sniff. He didn't speak. He didn't give Griff any indication of what he was thinking or feeling.

Griff felt unwanted. Dell's silence was proof that he'd done a good job of ruining his life.

"Coach Griff... *Dad?*" Dell got to his feet. "My grandpa is probably worried. Can you drive me home?" His stomach growled.

"Well, I'd like to drive you, *son.* But the truth is that my truck might not start. We may have to settle for a walk."

Lucky for them both, his truck started right up. Griff drove his son home with a lighter heart, which helped him apologize to Paul and begin to rebuild his dream of family.

CHAPTER TWENTY-ONE

"WHAT DO YOU mean you haven't talked to Griff?" Bess demanded of Ronnie two days after her argument with her stubborn cowboy. "He lives on the same property as you do."

"Yes, but he went with Frank and Mary to chemotherapy yesterday. And then he went into town last night before I got back from rodeo camp." Ronnie sat across from Bess at The Buckboard on Thursday night, a plate of nachos between them. "And he wasn't home when I got back today, either. Wade said he'd heard Griff was spending time in town with Dell and his grandfather."

Although Bess was happy to hear that, it didn't solve anything between her and Griff. "He's going to stand me up tonight." She filled a chip with cheese and chicken. "And I can't believe it bothers me after the things he said to me."

"Griff was in pain. We all make mountains out of molehills when we feel threatened emotionally." Ronnie was saying all the right things. In fact, she'd been saying all the right things since she'd rushed over to the Rolling G and let Bess cry on her shoulder two nights ago.

"You look nice tonight." Bess changed the subject. She'd meant to compliment Ronnie on her outfit earlier.

Ronnie wore a red swing dress with a silver-and-turquoise belt that matched her silver-and-turquoise hat band on her black cowboy hat. Her boots were black suede with silver fringe. Her makeup was flawless, and her long dark hair draped over her shoulders in well-behaved waves.

"You look nice, too," Ronnie shot a compliment right back at Bess.

"Considering..." Bess's appearance wasn't nearly as nice as Ronnie's. She wore faded blue jeans with rips at the knees and a black, off-the-shoulder blouse. The rips had strings she should have trimmed, and her blouse had a stain near her hemline. Bess's hair had been in braids all day and when she'd brushed them out, they'd frizzed instead of looking like romantic, purposeful curls.

"Why don't you call Griff?" Ronnie continued. "You asked him out. He said yes. And yet, it looks like he had family commitments take center stage tonight instead of showing up."

"You're asking me to forgive Griff without him even apologizing." How badly Bess wanted to do that.

Ronnie set her beer to the side. "I'm *suggesting* you try to put yourself in his shoes and understand where he's coming from. Love is about giving the ones you care for grace during challenging times."

"Love... Griff criticized me for the way I responded to him telling him he loved me. Griff even criticized me for spending too much money on the school rodeo team." Just like her grandfather had.

Ronnie brushed that off. "Wade doesn't like how many clothes I have but that's mostly because I took up all his closet space." She was a model and spokesperson for Cowgirl Pearl Fashions, so she received a lot of clothes gratis. "He'd have a point if I had to buy all my clothes the way you do rodeo supplies and... That sounded cold. Sorry."

Bess tossed her misbehaving hair over her shoulder. "I admit. I could have reacted differently to Griff telling me he loved me. It's just that it came out of the blue. Aren't you supposed to date for months before the *L* word is discussed?"

"There aren't any rules in the dance of love." Ronnie chuckled. "You've known each other for years."

"But I didn't know he loved me!" Bess fell back against the booth. "We were frenemies."

"You used that label on him." Ronnie leaned forward to whisper, "Just look at Clem mooning at Maggie. He loves her and she's oblivious." She straightened, choosing a chip with jalapeños. "You've been protesting his feelings and his opinions. But you haven't said anything about your feelings and your opinions."

Sometimes it didn't pay to have a professional matchmaker as a best friend.

"There's no fooling you." Bess skipped the chip and popped a jalapeño in her mouth, letting the heat ebb and flow just like her emotions toward Griff.

"Then spill," Ronnie encouraged. "Sometimes you need to just say things out loud to sort through your feelings."

Bess sipped her beer, considering. "He's a great kisser. Like, really great. I mean, the best ever."

"Enough said." Ronnie laughed. "What else comes to mind when you think about Griff?"

"He makes me laugh. And sometimes, he makes me so frustrated, and that's because..." Bess took a moment to pinpoint her feelings. "We're just friends at the end of the day." Her mouth dropped open. "I can't grab onto him like I want to *when* I want to. Not to wake him up to something or to kiss him for any number of reasons. I can't hug him when Dell's grandfather puts him down. I can't run my hands through his hair just because. I can't call him up or text him to see what he's doing in that moment. And that's because..." Bess wiped away a tear that had unexpectedly run down her cheek "...I have to keep him at arm's length."

Ronnie's smile was gently sympathetic. "Is that to protect him from a bombardment of your love or to protect your heart from being broken again?"

"I think we both know the answer to that question," Bess said, suddenly more miserable than she'd been in days.

"I have the perfect solution." Ronnie raised her beer glass, inviting Bess to toast. Only after their glasses clinked did she say, "You're going to hire me."

"AREN'T YOU SUPPOSED to be at a rehearsal dinner tonight?" Dell asked Griff on Friday night. He still had his arm in a sling, more because of precaution of further injury than anything else.

The three of them—Dell, Paul and Griff—were coming to a good place.

"I don't need a rehearsal." Griff was cooking pasta in Dell and Paul's kitchen, while Paul snoozed in front of the TV in the living room. He'd convinced the older man to request stronger cough suppressants from Doc Nabidian, which had significantly diminished his coughing. Plus, Doc had created a plan involving other meds and respiratory therapy. "This is my third wedding this year. I file onto the altar with the groom. I stand with my hands clasped while the bridesmaids and bride enter. And I try not to fidget during the ceremony."

"And then you walk out of the church with Coach Glover?" Nancy sat at the kitchen table. She had her thumb holding her place in a book about teenagers who rode dragons.

"Where did you get that idea?" Griff dropped the spoon he'd been using to stir the pasta sauce into the pot.

Griff fished it out and rinsed it off.

"We heard Miss Ronnie tell Coach Glover about that. And that you were going to dance together," Kevin said, by way of explanation. He sat next to Nancy and had a sudoku puzzle book open.

"When are you going to come back to rodeo camp?" Nancy tucked a dried flower between the pages and closed her book. "It's not as fun without you."

"And there's only two more weeks until it ends, and school begins," Kevin said.

"He'll come back when I do," Dell predicted. "Won't you, Dad?"

As much as Griff wanted to spend time with Dell, he wasn't so sure that Bess would welcome him back. He'd said some harsh things that he regretted and hadn't apologized for, yet. He'd been setting things right with Dell and Paul. "Let's see how I get along with Coach Glover this weekend."

"My mom said Coach Glover was putting her ranch up for sale." Nancy was a fountain of information this evening. "She had a meeting with some real estate lady. Is that because Coach Glover is going to marry you and you'll both move in here?"

Griff laughed, but it was a hollow sound. "No." But it did make him wonder...

"Can Nancy and Kevin come with me out to the Done Roamin' Ranch this weekend?" Dell smiled sweetly as he stirred the sauce. "Please, Dad. You said you'd help us with rodeo skills and Doc Nabidian said I could take my sling off tomorrow."

"Oh, my gosh. That would be so sweet," Nancy gushed, staring at Dell with a lovestruck expression.

"If I can just place in one event this year, I'll be happy," Kevin said. "It's so much better than the alternative."

"Football?" Griff asked.

"Nope. Volunteering in the sheriff's office." Kevin pulled a face. "Nothing ever happens in this town."

"Someday you'll be grateful for that," Griff told him.

"WHAT ARE YOU DOING, BESSIE?"

Bess sat on the front porch steps drinking her morning cup of coffee and watching the sunrise. "Just starting my day."

Rascal tottered out of the house to join her, taking her hand to steady himself as he sat next to her. "You don't usually drink your morning joe outside in your flannel jammies with a blanket wrapped around you and my dog." He gave Finlay a pat, receiving a tail wag in return.

"I don't usually admit that I've done too little, too late." Bess set her mug on a lower step and turned to face her grandfather, taking one of his hands in hers. "I'm sorry I didn't do a better job with the ranch."

"We've been over this, Bessie," Rascal said in a gruff voice. "We're both at fault. Doesn't mean I'll agree to selling yet."

They were a lot alike. Hiding behind their pride because they were afraid. Afraid of failing. Publicly, privately, with all of their hearts and souls.

Bess gave him a soft smile. "You told me once that you'd sell the ranch if you could pick the right buyer."

Rascal's mouth worked but he said nothing.

A horse nickered in the barn. A bird chirped in a nearby tree. And still they didn't speak.

I have to find my voice.

Bess took a deep breath and asked, "Do you trust me?"

Rascal nodded.

They sat like that, holding hands, watching the sunrise and discussing the future.

They talked until they were on the same page. At which time, they hugged, told each other *I love you*, and then Bess got ready for her next appearance as a bridesmaid.

BESS APPARENTLY HAD no more wedding tears in her.

She made it through the prep and ceremony with dry eyes. Not that Crystal and Derrick's wedding wasn't beautiful and touching. Not that Bess wasn't very much aware that she was single. Not that she hadn't stared at Griff's handsome face as the vows were being said. He was devastatingly good-looking in his black tuxedo and she hoped he took notice of her in her purple bridesmaid dress.

But because she had a plan, a carefully formed matchmaking plan created in partnership with Ronnie. Step one began at the reception since Griff had "called in sick" for the rehearsal dinner Friday night.

The bride and groom had their moment on the dance floor before their attendants joined them. Bess approached Griff, who'd somehow managed to switch his position at the altar and had escorted Olivia Cantwell out of the church instead of Bess. Not that Bess was going to be deterred.

"I think this is the slow dance you robbed me of on Thursday." Bess didn't wait for his reply. She led him onto the dance floor at Clementine's community center and then swung him into her arms and began to dance.

"Are you leading?" Griff asked, staring at her suspiciously.

"Yes, I am." Bess stared up at her fairy-tale cowboy with a soft smile. "You've been avoiding me."

"Yes, ma'am." Griff grinned briefly, just a hint of what Bess had been longing for these past few days. "Sorry. I know you prefer *miss*. I've been spending time with Dell and Paul, knowing well and good that I owe you dozens of apologies. But..." he looked deep into her eyes "...I wasn't sure my apologies were welcome."

"Your apologies were missing in action, just like you've been lately, Griff." Bess danced him toward the corner of the crowded floor. "You and those apologies were both missing from my life. You even had Wade tell me you weren't able to make rodeo camp the rest of this week. I don't remember you ever avoiding me like this before."

"I'm getting my life in order," Griff told her. "Family first. Then...other things."

"Am I part of the other things?" Bess hoped so, but she still wasn't certain. "The other love in your life besides Dell?" It was a risky statement.

Griff might have grunted. The music was so loud, Bess couldn't really tell. And he didn't say anything else.

Bess sighed and drew Griff closer, still slowly dancing toward the corner of the dance floor, toward a surprise. She laid her head on his shoulder, nervous, but hopeful. Determinedly hopeful. That's what Ronnie had told her to be. "I can't believe you're going to make me do this."

"Do what?" Griff whispered in her ear.

"Do all the heavy lifting to get us back together." Bess raised her face and looked into Griff's soulful brown eyes. "You leave me no choice but to kiss you out here in front of everyone." And then she did it. She kissed him, not with heat and passion, but with love and the optimism Ronnie had instilled in her.

And all the celebrants noticed. As the reception hall was instantly filled with rising cheers and whistles. When that died down, Bess ended their kiss and took Griff's hand, leading him to a table where she'd left her clutch purse and wrap.

"Bess?" Griff watched her in confusion. "Are you leaving?"

"No. I'm not running away anymore." She withdrew a folded set of papers from her clutch. And then she faced Griff. "I've been afraid to move forward or back in my life, just like you said the day you told me you loved me. I'm afraid of having my heart broken again. Not just where love is concerned but with the ranch. I feared Rascal and I couldn't run it alone. So,

I didn't commit. I didn't repair. I found excuses not to do anything. The only place I dive in fully is with school and the rodeo team because I know those kids are moving on. I won't have them forever."

"I did that to you," Griff said softly, brushing his thumb across her cheek. "I'm sorry. I'm sorry for every bad thing I've ever said to you." He drew a deep breath as if to say more but stopped.

"You held something back just now." Bess wasn't supposed to get sidetracked. The plan was to push forward. "You were going to say *but...*"

"I was going to say that I'm even sorry that I told you I loved you, because you said it complicated things. I never wanted to hurt you again." He looked remorseful.

And she loved him for it. "Griff, you should never apologize for telling me that you love me, or for disrupting my safe, withdrawn life. You make me feel alive."

Griff's cheeks started to loosen. He was a smiler by nature, and she could tell a smile was growing inside him, just waiting for the right words to bring it forth.

"I have something to show you." Bess carefully straightened the sheets of paper, staring at the words before lifting her gaze to his dear face. "But first, I want to tell you that I love you. I've loved you since the first time you held my hand. I loved you when you stood me up for that dance and when you kept your silence about why you didn't show. I've loved you through years of back-and-forth, of bickering and laughter." She reached up and brushed a lock of soft brown hair behind his ears. "I dreamed of marrying my fairy-tale cowboy and running the Rolling G together with him ever since I was a little girl. And now, I can make it a reality." She handed him the papers.

Griff scanned the pages. "Bess... This is an offer to buy the Rolling G from your grandfather."

She nodded and drew his attention to the last page. "I had Vickie draw up the papers with our names on it. Yours and mine."

"You want to buy the Rolling G with me? But...why?"

Bess laughed self-consciously. "Well, the cowardly answer

would be that owning the ranch together is reassuring my heart that it won't be broken again."

"Insurance," Griff said, beaming.

"In a way, I suppose." Bess smiled and set the contract aside, then wound her arms around Griff's neck. "But mostly, it's my promise to you that we're in this together, like all those vows we've been listening to all year. Because I love you, so very much."

"I love you, Bess Glover." Griff was grinning for real now. She could always tell. "Have I told you that I'm a package deal? I come with a large foster family, an almost father-in-law, a teenage son and his best friends, who all seem to be joined at the hip."

"We'll be in the market for more horses, I suppose." Bess ran her fingers through Griff's hair. "In addition to all that cattle you'll be wanting."

"Can we talk about this later?" Griff pulled her close. "I've decided I really like you in a dress, although your ranch duds are still my favorite. And if I don't kiss you right now, I just might have to run outside to get some air."

"Outside..." Bess gasped, laughing and moving out of the circle of Griff's arms. "Meet me outside at the corner of the building." Where she'd kissed him months before. Bess didn't wait for an answer. She hurried toward the door.

But she wasn't fast enough. Griff ran past her, grabbing hold of her hand and taking her with him, rushing headlong into the future. Together.

EPILOGUE

"DID I MISS IT?" Nancy sat down on the bleachers next to Bess at the rodeo grounds in Tulsa, out of breath. Her inky black hair was so short, it barely peeked from beneath her straw cowboy hat. "I missed it, didn't I?"

"You didn't miss it," Paul grumbled. "Where've you been?"

"Taking my college exams." Nancy accepted the water bottle Bess handed her. She still hadn't worked up the courage to confess her feelings for Dell. "Didn't Dell tell you exams were today?"

"He's been too busy to tell me anything," Paul grumped, pulling the brim of his cowboy hat down. A year and a half after he'd let Griff into his life, Paul had gotten rid of his cough, but he hadn't gotten rid of his pessimism-first attitude, although Bess loved him despite that.

"Why you kids want to take tests over and over is beyond me." Grandpa Rascal shifted on his seat cushion on the bottom bleacher and then rested his hands on top of his cane. He'd become more wobbly over the past few months but all the activity at the Rolling G kept him mentally sharp. He spent a lot less time in his tan recliner and more time sassing teenagers.

"They want the best scores possible to submit to colleges," Bess explained gently. Nancy and Kevin weren't getting a rodeo scholarship to help pay tuition. "You know this, Rascal."

"Yeah, yeah. But I still don't understand it." Her grandfather stared out over the rodeo arena. "Where's our boy? This rodeo is at least thirty minutes late. This is like when you walked down the aisle, Bessie. You were late, too."

Bess and Griff had gotten married last July, a year after Dell joined the rodeo team. "I may have been late, Rascal, but everything else was perfect." Bess glanced at the sparkling wedding set on her left ring finger.

"A bride is allowed to be late." Mary sat a few feet away from Rascal with her husband, Frank. Her hair had grown back since her chemo treatments. No more ill-fitting blond wigs for her. The silver ends of Mary's hair nearly reached her shoulders. "You were a beautiful bride. I didn't mind waiting for you, Bessie. And neither did Griff."

It seemed like everyone special in her life called her Bessie nowadays.

Griff rode up on Sparky, tipping his hat to them and giving Bess a sweet grin that promised fairy-tale happiness and a life filled with kisses.

He was smart about how to spend and save their money, which Bess really appreciated, and he was still the man who always found humor when everyone else's spirits were low. Griff was passionate about turning the Rolling G's fortunes around. He worked the ranch most weekdays and picked up shifts for the Done Roamin' Ranch at rodeos most weekends. Griff made time to help Bess coach the rodeo team. And his lighthearted approach to coaching had spilled over to Bess's teaching style. She caught fewer people sleeping in math class.

"Where's Kevin?" Griff asked. "He's going to miss it."

"I'm here." Kevin slid into a spot next to Nancy with a bucket of popcorn and a soda.

"Kev, it's only eight seconds. You could have gotten that after." Nancy rolled her eyes. "Seriously."

"Seriously." Kevin was unfazed. "We spent four hours in that test room. Didn't you hear my stomach growling?"

Nancy chortled. "I did." She stole some of Kevin's popcorn.

The loudspeaker squawked. "Our next rider is Dell James Malone. He'll be riding Diamond Back and hoping to clinch a state title for Clementine High School. It's hard to believe that Dell was a rookie last year. Next year, he'll be competing at the college level."

Griff and Bess shared a tender smile. So much had happened in the last eighteen months. So much happiness, laughter and love. Bess could hardly believe it.

With a tip of his hat, Griff rode Sparky closer to Dell's chute. As pickup man, he'd have Dell's back if he was needed.

The chute opened and eight long seconds later, Dell was still giving Diamond Back a good ride.

The crowd cheered.

"A clean ride!" Nancy launched herself to her feet, cheering her crush.

Meanwhile, Griff had ridden alongside the bull and grabbed hold of Dell with one arm. He deftly guided Sparky and Dell away from the bull's energetic kicks. And when they were a safe distance away, Griff eased his son to the ground, then leaped out of the saddle to give Dell an enthusiastic embrace.

It wasn't just Nancy on her feet now. All of Dell's family and friends were standing and applauding.

Griff rocked his much-grown son from side to side and caught Bess's eye. *"I love you."*

Bess didn't hear the words, but she knew the shape of them when formed by her husband's lips. And she knew Griff spoke the words to more than his son. He meant it for all of them—Bess, their family and the new baby kicking Bess's ribs, raring to go.

Just like her father.

* * * * *

Don't miss the stories in this mini series!

THE COWBOY ACADEMY

The Rodeo Star's Reunion
MELINDA CURTIS
October 2024

Cowboy Santa
MELINDA CURTIS
November 2024

MILLS & BOON